I0586403

Cardinal Bonaventure

St. Bonaventure's Life of our Lord and Saviour Jesus Christ

Cardinal Bonaventure

St. Bonaventure's Life of our Lord and Saviour Jesus Christ

ISBN/EAN: 9783743345744

Manufactured in Europe, USA, Canada, Australia, Japa

Cover: Foto ©Raphael Reischuk / pixelio.de

Manufactured and distributed by brebook publishing software (www.brebook.com)

Cardinal Bonaventure

St. Bonaventure's Life of our Lord and Saviour Jesus Christ

ST. BONAVENTURE'S

LIFE OF OUR LORD AND SAVIOUR

JESUS CHRIST.

Translated from the Original Latin.

ILLUSTRATED WITH

NEARLY ONE HUNDRED ENGRAVINGS.

P. J. KENEDY & SONS

Publishers to the Holy Apostolic See

44 BARCLAY STREET, NEW YORK

ST. BONAVENTURE'S PREFACE.

AMONG the many encomiums and praises bestowed on the holy Virgin, St. Cecilie, it is recorded of her, that she kept the Gospel of Christ continually enshrined in her breast: the meaning of which seems to be, that she selected such passages from our Lord's life and actions, contained in that divine volume, as tended most to raise her devotion, and inflame her love. On these she meditated day and night, and such was the fervor of her heart, and the ardor of her affections, that she did not content herself with a single perusal, but was accustomed to read the most striking parts many times over, and carefully deposit them in the sanctuary of her heart. The like practice I recommend to you, as I look upon it to be the most material branch of spiritual study, and even the most beneficial of all devout exercises, and that which is most capable of leading you to the summit of Christian perfection. For surely the holy life of Christ, not merely free from the minutest blemish, but even divinely perfect, must be the best and only sure fountain whence we can hope to draw the perfect knowledge necessary—to arm our breast against the flattering, yet fleeting vanities of the world; to render us steady amidst tribulations and adversities; and finally, to preserve us from vice, and facilitate the possession of every virtue. Frequent and habitual meditations on that divine subject being the readiest means to introduce the soul, as it were, into such a kind of familiarity, confidence, and love of him, as will insensibly create in it a contempt and distaste of everything else, and will effectually instruct it, both in what to do, and what to avoid doing.

And first, that the contemplation of Christ's blessed life lengthens the heart against the transient pleasures and deceitful vanities of the world, sufficiently appears in the

3

life of the sacred virgin, St. Cecilie, already mentioned,
whose capacious heart was so filled with the divine sentiments gathered thence, that it had no space left for the
entrance of vain affections.   Even amidst the allurements
of magnificence, the dissipations of music and other sensual
pleasures, profusely combining to render the solemnity of
her nuptials the more inviting to the sense, her heart, un-
affected by them, and, as it were, insensible of all these
flattering appearances, remained immovably fixed on God,
to whom she often *recurred* in these words : " O Lord !
render my body and heart pure and undefiled, that I be
not *confounded.*"

Secondly, that it renders us steady amidst tribulations
and adversities.   St. Bernard thus argues : " Whence received the martyrs their unshaken resolutions amidst the
anxiety of their torments but from the sacred wounds of
Jesus, in which their hearts and affections were wholly
centered ?   Whilst they beheld and felt their bodies torn
and severed on the rack, their minds remained still cheerful and triumphant.   And where can we then suppose the
soul of each glorious sufferer to have been but in the
wounds of Christ, ready to open for its reception ?   Had it
been lodged in its own bosom, attentive to what passed
within its lacerated frame, it had been too sensible of the
torturing instrument, to remain proof against the excruciating torments inflicted ; its pains had been an overmatch
for its patience ; it must have sunk under the pressing
weight, and denied God."   From the same divine source
not only martyrs, but even confessors, virgins, and all who
lead a virtuous life, have derived their patience amidst
tribulations, and the various trials and infirmities incident
to a mortal state ; as may be instanced in the glorious St.
Francis and St. Clare, who, under the severe pressure of
afflictions, penury, and infirmities, were not only patient,
but joyful.   The same may be daily remarked in all devout
persons ; this is entirely owing to their pious meditations
on the life of Christ, which, as it were, carry their souls
out of their bodies to transplant them in Christ.

Thirdly, that it is a powerful check to vice, and greatly
disposes us to the possession of virtues, is evident from
this, that the perfection of virtues is only to be found in
the blessed life of Jesus Christ.   Where else shall we find
such moving examples, such sublime doctrines of heroic
poverty, extraordinary humility, profound wisdom, fervent
prayers, obedience, meekness, patience, and other virtues,
as in this most holy life ?

Wherefore, St. Bernard says, "that he labors in vain in the pursuit of virtue, who hopes to find it anywhere but in the Lord of virtues, whose doctrine is the school of prudence, whose mercy is the work of justice, whose life is the model of temperance, and whose death is the pledge of fortitude." Whoever, therefore, follows this divine pattern, can neither be deceived himself, nor deceive others, for the soul by frequent reflection on his virtues, is both animated and instructed in the imitation and pursuit of them, and at length becomes so habituated to virtue, that the bare light of it is sufficient to direct her judgment in discerning truth from falsehood. This is so true, that many very illiterate persons have become, by the same means, profoundly versed in the most sublime mysteries of God. By *what other means* than that of a familiar and mental conversation with his divine Lord could St. Francis of Asissium, attain to such an eminent state of perfection, so deep a knowledge of the holy scriptures, and that discernment with which he discovered the frauds of his spiritual enemies, and baffled the power of vice? Hence it was, that he grew so passionately affected with the life of Christ, as to render his own life almost a picture of it. He copied to the utmost of his power, the practice of every virtue ; and Christ, at length, crowning his affections with the accomplishment of his wishes, he became totally transformed into his Saviour, and received the impression of his sacred wounds on his person. To such an eminent state is the soul led by meditating on the life of its Saviour : and yet this is but, as it were, the foundation on which the soul rises to more sublime degrees of contemplation. For the unction therein to be found purifying by degrees, and elevates the soul, instructs it, and renders it full of all divine knowledge : but this tends not immediately to our present purpose.

Now, I propose to introduce you, gentle reader, to the meditations on the blessed life of our Saviour, though I could wish you a more learned and able guide, being myself very unequal to so great a task. However, as I conceive it to be more for your advantage that I rather say something than remain silent on so useful a subject, I shall endeavor to make the best use of my slender ability, by discoursing in a familiar, though plain and unpolished style : that you may the more easily comprehend the matter here treated, and study rather to improve your mind and heart than flatter your ears.

It is not elegance of speech, but the study of the life of

Jesus you are here to give attention to.   For as St. **Hierom** says, "Plain language reaches the heart, while florid speeches stop at the ears which they flatter."   Still I am in hopes that the mediocrity of my capacity will the better be adapted to the sincerity of your good intention.   But I hope still more, that if you are but diligent in the **exercise** of this devout study, that the Lord, whose life is here treated of, will become your master and instructor.   You are **not**, however, to imagine that we can either meditate on, or recollect every circumstance relating to our blessed Saviour.   Nevertheless, to make the more devout impression upon your mind, I shall relate those things in the same manner as if they really had happened, which either have in fact, or may reasonably be believed to have happened, according to such devout imaginations as a pious mind is capable of forming.   For it is even in the study of holy scriptures allowable to meditate, expound, and understand differently as we concieve most expedient.   In this, however, all due regard must be paid to the truth of the facts of his life, to his justice and divine doctrine, and nothing be inconsistent with faith and good works.   Whatever, therefore, I shall here lay down as acted or said by Christ Jesus which cannot be proved by scripture to be so done or said, you are to take in no other sense than as the effect of a devout meditation : that is, in other words, take it as if I said, meditate or consider, that Christ might have said or done so.   If, therefore, you are desirous of reaping fruit from this work, you must earnestly endeavor by a serious attention to be present to everything that is here written of our Lord Jesus Christ.   And that with the same fervor and devotion as if you both heard and saw them, laying aside for the time all other engagements and affairs.   In short, beloved reader, I beseech you to accept in good part, the pains I have here taken for the honor and praise of our Lord Jesus, and for your spiritual profit, as well as my own ; and endeavor, with all the alacrity, devotion, and diligence you are master of to put it in practice.

CONTENTS.

APPENDIX.

THE
LIFE OF OUR LORD AND SAVIOUR
JESUS CHRIST.

ZACHARIAH ASKS THE ANGEL FOR A SIGN OF WHAT HE HAS PROMISED.

CHAPTER I.

THE ANGELS INTERCEDE FOR MAN'S REDEMPTION.

MANKIND having for the long and tedious space of more than five thousand years continned in a miserable state of exile, not one of them being able to shake off the clog of original guilt, and soar to his native country Heaven; the blessed choir of angelic spirits, (moved to compassion, and concerned at the dreadful havoc sin had made among them, as well as solicitous to see the numbers of their own heavenly legions again completed) as soon as the fulness of time was come, resolved to renew the instances they had often before made to the Almighty. For this end, presenting themselves before the awful throne of God, with redoubled earnestness and devotion, they jointly prostrated themselves at his feet, and made the following prayer: "All-merciful Lord! Remember how you graciously vouchsafed, from the inexhaustible fund of your goodness, to create man out of nothing, and to raise him above all the works of your sublunary creation, by enriching him with the eminent gift of a rational soul, capable of knowing you; and this on purpose that he might become a partaker of our felicity, and repair the loss we sustained by the fall of our reprobate brethren. Yet behold, O gracious Sovereign, the whole species lies still involved in such woful ruin, that out of so great a number, not one has been able to escape and arrive hither in the long space of many thousand years. Our enemies thence gather new matter of triumph: when instead of seeing the vacant places of the fallen angels filled, they behold hell continually crowded with innumerable victims: to what end then are they created, O Lord? *Why are the souls, that confess to you, delivered up a prey to beasts?—Ps.* lxxiii. We are not ignorant that this severity perfectly agrees with your divine justice; yet be pleased, O Lord, to remember, that the time for showing your mercy is come. If the first progenitors of the human race

did unhappily transgress your law, let your
mercy now repair the injury in their wretched
posterity. Be mindful that you created them to
your own likeness. Extend then in pity, O God,
your hand to them, and replenish them with your
bounty. To this end, '*our eyes fixed on you, as
the eyes of servants on the hands of their masters,*'
—*Ps.* cxxii.— till you deign to have compassion
on mankind, and save them by a plentiful redemption."

The angel having concluded this address, Mercy
and Peace, supporting the petition in man's behalf, pathetically pleaded for his redemption with
the heavenly Father: while Justice and Truth
seemed to make a vigorous opposition against it:
whence (for contemplation sake) we may imagine a
kind of ineffable debate to arise between them, as
St. Bernard relates in a beautiful and ample manner. But in this I shall be as concise as the tenor
of our subject will permit. For though in this
treatise, I intend often to interweave his words with
my own, yet as our present purpose requires us to
avoid tedious prolixity, I shall differ partly in the
manner of applying them. To return then to our
subject. The sum of his discourse, in the place above
quoted, is as follows: Mercy, in the words of the
royal prophet says, " Will God reject man forever,
or hath the Lord forgotten to show mercy ?"—
Ps. lxxvi. Long and frequently importuned with
these, and such like solicitations, thus at length,
the Almighty may be supposed to have answered,
"Hold, Mercy, before I acquiesce to your petitions,
it becomes me as an equitable judge, to hear the allegations which Justice and Truth have to offer
against them." Whereupon, the two divine attributes being ready to the summons, Mercy thus re-

sumes, "Mankind, O Lord, stand in need of thy commiseration, for they are become wretched indeed, even extremely wretched; and the time for showing pity is more than come." Here Truth, interrupting the plea of Mercy, begins, "It is meet, O Lord, that you fulfil your divine word. Let Adam die, and all his race with him, since all, in him, impiously tasted the forbidden fruit." "Wherefore then, O Lord," replies Mercy, "wherefore do I subsist? if you forbear forever to commiserate, there is an end of me: this, your Truth must acknowledge." "Yes," rejoins Truth, "but yet, O Eternal Father, if prevaricating man can elude your sentence, what becomes of me? Can I, as you have promised, persist to eternity?" Thus the divine pleaders continuing to support their suit against each other, the Eternal Father, at length, remits the cause to his Son. Before whom, Mercy and Truth renewing their former pleas, Truth thus added, "I confess, O Lord, that the zeal which Mercy exerts in man's behalf is good, and worthy all praise; but does she therein act conformably to justice, in persuading you rather to spare those prevaricators than me her sister attribute?" "Ah, beloved Truth," replies Mercy, "rather consider, that your indignant rigor spares neither man nor me: by refusing to commiserate him, you involve me in his destruction, me, your sister Mercy." But Truth, unsoothed by all that Mercy could offer, still further urged: "You, O Lord, are here made a party in this cause, and therefore, it highly behooves you not to suffer the word of your Eternal Father to be made void." After this manner persisted the divine parties in opposing each other, till at length, all-uniting Peace with her heavenly voice interposing, thus addressed them: "Cease to dispute, ye heavenly offspring of God, contention ill suits such kindred virtues."—Still the debate was important, and the reasons on both sides so strong and powerful, that no means appeared of reconciling Mercy and Truth, in regard to mankind, till the divine and royal judge gave to Peace, who stood the nearest to his awful throne, the following ineffable decree to read: "Whereas, our Eternal Father's divine offspring, Truth and Mercy, have laid before us their opposite allegations concerning the salvation or perdition of our hapless creature, man: the former alleging that, if the sentence of death passed upon Adam should be reversed, Mercy herself must be involved in the destruction of Adam. Our divine wisdom suggests us a medium to preserve both inviolable and uninjured. Let Death then be made a desirable good: that the apprehensions of all may be removed and their ends obtained." No sooner was the divine decree pronounced, than all, applauding its wisdom, silently consented that Adam should die, yet Death be a means of saving mercy to him. But hence, a new difficulty arose: "How, O unsearchable wisdom, how shall Death become a desirable good to man, when the bare sound of it is sufficient to convey horror to the sense?" "Know," answers the heavenly monarch, "that though the death of the wicked be superlatively wretched, that of the righteous is inestimably precious, and the sure entrance to eternal life.

"Let one then be sought out, who, though not by nature subject to death,* will voluntarily submit to it, from a generous motive of disinterested charity. Such a one, not liable to be detained in subjection by Death, will force a passage through it, and lead

---

*Death entered by sin.

captivity after him to a blessed state of freedom."
Here all acquiesce with pleasure to the divine proposal. "Yet where," say they, "shall we be able
to find such a one;" Submissively, however, obsequious to the Eternal Word's decree, without waiting
a reply, and paying **due** adoration to the Almighty
Majesty, both depart in search of him: Truth resolving to range the earth, and Mercy the wide dominions of heaven, according to the words of the Prophet: Thy mercy, O Lord, is in heaven, **and thy**
truth even to the clouds."—*Ps.* xxxv., ":it encom-
passes the universe." Yet how vain, alas, their re-
searches! Truth travelling round the world, finds
no one free from guilt, not even the infant of a day
old. And Mercy in vain seeks, throughout heaven,
one who has charity equal to so great an undertaking.
Alas! all mankind are but inferior servants, and
the best of them must, even when they act well, say
from *St. Luke*, chap. **xvii**., "that they are but unprofitable servants." As none, therefore, could be
found so abounding in charity, as to lay down their
life for such useless servants, it was to no purpose
for Mercy and Truth to seek any longer. Hence
returning to the Almighty's presence at the appointed time, without the desired success, Peace,
with a benevolent countenance thus anticipates them:
"Ah! heavenly sisters, know you not, or have you
forgotten, that there is not one on earth who does
good: No, not even one. Or who in heaven or on
earth but **he**, whose **wisdom gave you** the ineffable
advice you are endeavoring to follow, can assist **you**
to effect it?" On hearing this, the all-wise monarch
spoke. "It repents me that I made man: Yet, as
I have made him, it becomes the immensity of my
goodness to do satisfaction for him." Wherefore,
calling to him the angel Gabriel, "Go," says he,

"and tell the daughter of Sion: Behold your king comes."—Thus far from St. Bernard. Hence you may see of how dangerous and fatal consequence sin has been and still is, and how great the difficulty of applying the remedy to it. To this purpose, however, the above mentioned attributes seem best to accord and unite in the person of God the Son. For on one side, the person of the Father, bearing in appearance a terrible and powerful aspect, might seemingly give cause of apprehension for Peace and Mercy. On the other side, the person of the Holy Ghost, all bountiful and gracious, might seemingly give no less room for apprehension to Truth and Justice. So that the person of the Son between both, was wisely accepted as mediator in the important work. This, however, must be understood, not in a strict sense, but a mystical and borrowed one. Thus, then, was at length fulfilled that prophecy of the Psalmist, "Mercy and Truth have met together, Justice and Peace have kissed."—*Ps.* lxxxiv.

This may suffice for a pious meditation on what, we may devoutly conceive, might probably pass in heaven, relating to man's redemption.

CHAPTER II.

OF THE LIFE OF THE BLESSED VIRGIN MARY, AND HER SEVEN PETITIONS TO GOD.

THE life of the Blessed Virgin, from whom the Son of God took flesh, will afford our devotion ample matter for meditation. You are then to know, Christian reader, that at the third year of her age, she was presented in the temple a sacrifice to God;

and there remained to the age of fourteen. What
was her method of life in that holy sanctuary,
during that space of time, we may learn from the
Revelations, with which she favored a devout votary
of hers ; who, as it is believed, was the glorious St.
Elizabeth, whose solemn festival the church annually celebrates. **Among the rest,** the following
particulars are contained :

"**When my** parents," says our Blessed Lady,
"had consecrated me in the temple, immediately
on their departure I resolved in my own heart to
choose God for my father : and often and devoutly
considering what I might do to please God, and
render myself agreeable in his sight, that he might
vouchsafe to enrich me with his grace ; I began, by
taking care to be instructed in the divine laws. But
of all the divine laws which I observed in my heart,
these three were **the first and** chief : Thou shalt
love the Lord thy God, **with** all thy heart, with all
thy soul, with all thy spirit, with all thy strength :
Thou shalt love thy neighbor as thyself : Thou shalt
not hate thy enemy. These I kept in my mind ;
and immediately possessed all the virtues comprised
in them ; and thus will I have you to do. But the
soul can possess **no** virtue, that has **not a** cordial
love for God. **For** it is from this **love that flows** the
plenitude of all grace, without which no virtue can
enter into, **or** remain in the soul ; but drops away
like water, unless due hatred be conceived towards
its enemies, that is, vice and evil habits. Whoever,
therefore, **is** desirous of possessing the grace **of** God,
must dispose his heart to love and hatred. I would
have you, therefore, to follow my example, and
do as I did. I rose constantly at midnight, and be-
fore the holy altar of the temple, with all the desire,
will, and affection I was capable of, I implored

the grace of the Almighty God, to observe these three great commandments chiefly, and every other precept of his law. And thus, before the sacred altar, I made the following seven petitions:

"I requested then : *First*—His grace, to fulfil the precept of charity, that is to love him with all my heart, etc.

"*Secondly* — The grace necessary to love my neighbor according to his will and pleasure, and to delight in all things that please him.

" *Thirdly*—His assistance to hate and shun everything displeasing to him.

"*Fourthly*—Humility, patience, benignity, and meekness, and every virtue that could render me agreeable in his sight.

" *Fifthly*—That he would make known to me the time in which that ever-blessed virgin should be born, who was to bring forth the Son of God ; and that he would preserve my sight, that I might behold her ; my tongue that I might praise her : my hands that I might minister to her : my feet that I might move in her service : and my knees that I might adore the Son of God in her womb.

" *Sixthly*—I implored his grace, to obey the precepts and direction of the priests of the temple.

"And, *Seventhly*—That he would vouchsafe to preserve the temple and people in his holy service."

The servant of *Christ*, when she heard this, said : " O most amiable lady, were not you full of grace and every virtue ?" "Yes," answered the Blessed Virgin : " Yet know for certain, that I thought myself as void of merit, as full of guilt, and as unworthy God's favor as you. For which reason, I continued thus praying for grace and virtue. But although you may imagine me to have possessed all the grace I was endowed with, with little or no pains, yet, be assured, that I received **no** one grace, gift, or virtue from Heaven, without immense labor, incessant prayer, fervent desires, profound devotion, many tears, and much affliction : Ever saying and thinking, to the best of my knowledge and power, what was most agreeable to him. Nor did I receive any blessings from Heaven, without all this, except the sanctifying grace, by which I was made holy in **the womb** of my mother. Know also," adds she, "that no grace descends into the soul, but by means of prayer and mortification." However, when once we pay to God all the little services in our power, though they are but few, they are of such efficacy as to attract the Almighty himself into the soul, and with him some of his choicest gifts. Insomuch, that the soul seems in a sublime measure to be carried out of itself, and forgets ever having done, or even said anything pleasing to Heaven, becoming more unworthy and contemptible in its own esteem than **ever.** Thus much may we gather from the above-mentioned Revelations.

St. Jerome, however, in the account he gives of her life, adds: "That it was the constant method of the Blessed Virgin to continue fixed in prayer, from the morning to the third hour. From the third hour to the ninth she employed herself in manual exercises. At the ninth she again returned to prayer, nor suffered anything to interrupt her devotions till called upon by the angel who attended her, to receive her usual necessary refection: And even then, from his celestial converse, she improved in the love and service of her beloved master. She was ever found the first at the sacred vigils and watches of the temple, the most versed in the knowledge of the divine laws, the most profoundly practised in true hu-

mility, the most ready and harmonious in the Royal
Psalmist's divine canticles, the most illustrious in
charity, the most innocently pure, and the most
perfect in every virtue. She was immovably constant in goodness, yet was never seen or heard to be
morose or peevish at the failings of her companions
who were less perfect. Her every word had it in such
a singular plenitude of grace, that something divine
appeared in all she said. She diligently persevered
in prayer, and the study of God's laws: and ever
watched over the conduct of her companions, that
none of them might exceed in speech, or break out
into inordinate mirth, or disgust each other by pride
or offensive behavior. She was ever intent on
praising God: and lest the greetings, which neighborly charity obliged her to use towards those of
her own station, should in the least diminish the
praise due to God, her perpetual form of salutation
was 'Thanks be to God.' Hence the laudable custom of holy men in saluting each other, to say Thanks
be to God. The food administered to her by the
hands of the angel served her for her own support:
and she bestowed on the poor the portions allotted
to her by the priests of the temple. The angel was
seen daily conversing with her, and obeying her,
as if she was his beloved sister or mother." Thus
far St. Jerome.

In the fourteenth year of her age the Blessed Virgin was espoused to St. Joseph, by divine appointment revealed to her parents, and then she returned
to Nazareth ; concerning which, you may see the
particular circumstances in the legend of her birth.
Such are the subjects proper to meditate on, which
happened before the Incarnation. Consider them
well, and take pleasure in the contemplation of
them, committing them to your memory with the

utmost affection, and practice them with all diligence, as matters of the sublimest devotion. But let us now proceed to the Incarnation.

THE ARCHANGEL GABRIEL APPEARS TO THE BLESSED VIRGIN MARY.

CHAPTER III.

THE INCARNATION OF CHRIST, AND THE ANGELICAL SALUTATION OF THE BLESSED VIRGIN.

WHEN the fulness of time was come, and the most blessed Trinity had deliberated on the means of providing for the redemption of mankind, by the incarnation of the WORD ; Christ resolved to take flesh of the Blessed Virgin, through his immense charity with which he loved mankind. His mercy moving him, and paying a particular regard to the instances of the celestial spirits ; when the Blessed Virgin was returned to Nazareth, Almighty God called to him the angel Gabriel, and said to him : " Go to our best beloved daughter, espoused to Joseph, the dearest to us of all our creatures, and tell her that my son delights in her form, and hath chosen her for his mother. Request her to receive him joyfully : for I have decreed to save mankind by her means, and to blot out of my memory the injury they have done me."

And here, gentle reader, let me once more repeat my former advice : Be mindful and take such notice of what you read, as to render yourself, as it were, present to every passage herein related. But, particularly in this place, fix God before your imagination, in the best manner a corporeal being is capable of conceiving an idea of his incorporeal substance. Conceive him, that is, as a mighty sovereign, seated on his awful throne, the paternal and benign affability of whose majestic countenance spoke in him a disposition towards reconciliation, or rather reconciliation itself : Imagine him, I say, thus disposed to utter the above-mentioned words, while Gabriel, with serene and cheerful aspect, prostrate on his knees, in a devout and reverent posture, listens attentively to the divine embassy. That received, away the angelic messenger hastens from the celestial regions, and in the borrowed dress of human likeness, quick as thought, presents himself before the holy Virgin Mary, in the inmost recess of her little habitation. Yet not so expeditious was his flight, but that the blessed Trinity, anticipating their ambassador, were in the happy mansion before him.

For this you must take along with you, that

though the person of the Son alone was made man,
yet the whole sacred Trinity was concerned in his
incarnation. The Father and the Holy Ghost co-
operating alike in this august and unutterable mystery. Here then, be specially attentive, and as if present to everything that is said and done, endeavor to
comprehend every circumstance that passes.—Oh,
what scope may not this subject afford your meditation. What reflections may you not gather from
that little mansion, where such personages are assembled, and such ineffable mysteries wrought by them.
For though the sacred Trinity be undoubtedly always everywhere present, yet, in this place, at this
juncture, it was present in a more singular and ineffable manner than usual, on account of the super-
natural and unspeakable work then and there
effected.

The angel Gabriel then arrived at the holy mansion, and entering to the Blessed Virgin, thus the
faithful proxy began his message: "Hail, full of
grace! the Lord is with thee: Blessed art thou
among women." To which, not a little disturbed,
she made no answer. Her disturbance, however,
proceeded not from any guilty disorder within her;
neither could it be occasioned by the angelical vision,
such kind of visits being, from their frequency, become familiar to her. But, to speak in the words of
the Evangelist, "She was disturbed at the angel's
speech." That is, perplexed in thought at the
novelty of this salutation, so unlike his usual manner of greeting her. Nor could the humble Virgin
be other than disturbed at the triple commendation
included in his angelical salutation. To hear herself commended, for that she was full of grace, that
the Lord was with her, that herself was blessed
above the rest of her sex, was more than one so rich

in humility could hear without a blush of concern. Her discomposure then was wholly the effect of a virtuous and becoming bashfulness; accompanied with a fear of too easily giving in to the belief of what she heard. Not that she in the least mistrusted the angel's veracity ; but, because it is ever the faculty of the truly humble to tend to perfection, by examining into and magnifying their defects, while they either remain wholly insensible of any merit in themselves, or see it through the lessening end of the perspective. Thus, as becomes a prudent, fearful, and modest Virgin, our blessed lady remained silent, returning no answer to the angelical salutation, as if not knowing what to reply. Learn from **her** example the study and practice of silence : a virtue of the greatest utility to such as are endowed with it. **The** vice contrary to which is so odious in all, but especially in women, and more in young ones and virgins, that this sacred pattern of modesty could not prevail on herself to make any answer, till she had heard the angel twice utter his mysterious message ; nor even then could she have resolved to break through her wonted silence, but that the sacred messenger, apprized of the cause of her despondency, encouraged her in the following words : " Fear not, Mary, nor be concerned at the encomiums I render you. Why should your modesty blush to receive the praises justly due to you ? You **are** not only full of grace yourself, but even born to be the means of restoring all mankind to the grace of God, which they had lost. For behold, you shall conceive, and bring forth the Son of the Most High, who has chosen you to be an instrument of the salvation, destined to all who put their trust in him." This said, the Blessed Virgin, waving the subject of her praises, was solicitous to know the manner in which this all could be done: which she could not but be anxious about, on account of her virginity, which she was resolved never to part with. Wherefore, she requested the angel to acquaint her with the manner of the conception, in the following words: "How shall this be effected upon me who have dedicated myself to God by a vow of perpetual virginity?" "It will be brought about," replied the angel, "by the singular and ineffable operation of the Holy Ghost, by whose power you will be replenished, and conceive without prejudice to your virginity: and, therefore, will your Son be called the Son of God. For nothing is to him impossible. In proof of which, know that by the same power of God, your kinswoman Elizabeth, though old and barren, is now six months gone in her pregnancy of a male child."

Here imagine yourself in the divine presence, and contemplate how the blessed Trinity, graciously waiting the answer and consent of their beloved daughter, was delighted to behold her graceful decency of behavior, and the modesty of her expressions. With what wisdom and attention does the angel employ his heavenly eloquence to persuade her, and with what sweetness, reverence, and affability he bends before her as his awful mistress, faithfully executing his embassy, and attentively observing her words, that he may reply to them in a manner becoming her dignity, his office, and the will of the Almighty. And finally, with what a becoming deportment, mixed with graceful bashfulness of countenance, she receives the sudden and surprising message, without being elated by it. She attributes wholly to the divine grace the wonderful encomiums bestowed on her, though such as were never given to any other mortal.

Consider attentively this, and learn from so great

a pattern, to behave with modesty and humility: without which, purity itself is of little signification. But to return to our subject.

The Blessed Virgin, after hearing the forementioned words of the angel, with a prudence equal to the rest of her conduct, gave her consent: and, as her revelations declare, kneeling with her hands joined in a devout posture, said : " Behold the handmaid of the Lord : Be it be done to me according to thy word." At the same instant the Son of God passed entire into the Virgin's womb, took flesh of her, and still remained entire in the essence of his Father. However, you may for piety's sake imagine, that the Son of God, undertaking this laborious embassy of obedience, reclined and recommended himself to the Father, and that in the same instant his soul was created and infused into the womb of his Mother : so that, though he afterwards grew in the womb, as naturally as other children are wont to do, yet he received not like them any increase of faculties in his soul, or diversity in limbs ; being then as perfect God and perfect man, and equally wise and powerful as he is now. But to return to the angel. Gabriel, to accompany the Blessed Virgin in her devotion, kneeled for awhile, and then rising, profoundly bent himself to her in a respectful manner to take his leave, after which he vanished immediately. The Blessed Virgin now alone all in raptures, and more than usually inflamed with the love of God, began to be sensible of her pregnancy. Wherefore, throwing herself again upon her knees, she returned God thanks for so great a favor, and with most humble and fervent supplication, besought him to vouchsafe her the instructions necessary to render her capable of acting her part towards her son, free from any defect or imperfection.

Meditate then on the greatness of this day's solemnity. Let your heart rejoice, and the day be crowned with **holy** mirth: a day hitherto unheard of since the beginning of time. A day devoted to the honor of God the Father who celebrates the nuptials of his Son, espoused to human nature, which he has inseparably united to himself. A day sacred to the wedding of the Divine Son, and to his entrance into the virginal womb, through which he has to pass into the world. A day solemn to the Holy Ghost, by whose singular and wonderful co-operation the work of **the** Incarnation was effected: and whose extraordinary benignity this day began to show itself to mankind. A day of glory to our blessed Lady, who on the same was acknowledged and assumed by the Father for **a** Daughter—by the Son for a Mother— by the Holy Ghost for a Spouse. A day of rejoicing to the whole heavenly choir, on account of the work of their reparation commencing from it; but more especially to mankind, on account of their salvation, redemption, and reconciliation; for on this day properly was the whole human nature exalted and deified.

On this day the Son submitted to the **new** command of his Father in the work of our salvation. On this day, coming forth from the highest heaven, he *exalted like a giant to run his race,* and entered into the virginal garden of his mother's womb. On this day he was made one of us, and becoming our brother, began to sojourn among us. On this day the true light descended from heaven to expel away our darkness, and disperse the clouds of our ignorance. On this day the bread of life, which enlivens the world, was truly perfected in the sacred tabernacle of the virginal womb, and the word was **made** flesh to dwell amongst us. Lastly, on this day the long continued cries of the holy **patriarchs and** prophets were heard, **and their fervent** desires fully accomplished. They **cried aloud,** with an inexpressible earnestness, saying: *Send forth, O Lord, the Lamb, the ruler of the earth.—Isa.* xvi. *Drop dew ye heavens from above, and let the clouds rain the just.—*Chap. xlv. *Would, O God, thou wouldst burst the heavens asunder and descend.—*Chap. xliv. *Lord, incline thy heavens and descend.— Ps.* cxliii. *Show us thy face and we shall be saved.—Ibid.* lxxix. These, with infinite others of like nature, to be seen in Holy Writ, were their repeated instances for the approach of the solemn day, which they so ardently expected. This day gave the first beginning to every joyful solemnity, and is the only true source of all our real happiness. For though hitherto Almighty God has been justly incensed against mankind, for the transgression of their first progenitors, yet from this time his anger against them shall cease at the sight of his only Son made man for their redemption. Hence is this day so justly styled "the fulness of time;" that is, a time of grace and redemption to man. And hence also may **we deem the** wonderful greatness of this **most solemn and** ineffable mystery, where **all is** profitable and sweet, all is gay and decent, all **is** pleasing and desirable; in a word, where all **is so** sublimely sacred, that it requires our inmost devo**tion to treat** of it, our purest transports to solemnize it, and our profoundest veneration to adore it. Let such then be the heads of your meditation—make them the scope of all your pleasure—and choose them for your frequent and favorite amusement. For who knows but the Lord may recompense your pious practice with more ample scenes of heavenly knowledge?

ST. ELIZABETH RECEIVES THE VISIT OF THE BLESSED VIRGIN MARY.

CHAPTER IV.

OUR BLESSED LADY VISITS HER COUSIN ST. ELIZABETH, IN WHOSE HOUSE THE MAGNIFICAT AND BENEDICTUS ARE COMPOSED.

OUR Blessed Lady, having conceived by the Holy Ghost, and the incarnation of the Son of God being fully accomplished in her sacred womb, recalling to mind what the angel had told her, concerning her cousin Elizabeth, she resolved to visit her; and this, not merely to congratulate her on her happy pregnancy, but rather to assist her at her approaching delivery. Wherefore, in company with her beloved spouse St. Joseph, she immediately set out on her journey, from the little city of Nazareth, towards the house of St. Elizabeth, which was near Jerusalem, and about seventy miles distant from Nazareth. Neither the length of the journey, nor the labors of the way, could deter her from her pious resolution; but without delay she went on with all speed, that she might not appear long abroad. Nor was she like other women in her condition, in the least burdened by the divine infant she bore in her womb. And now by the way accompany in mind this blessed couple. The ever-glorious Virgin, queen of heaven and earth, with her beloved spouse, proceeds on her journey; not on a pampered horse, or gilded car, not escorted by a military band of armed soldiers, not triumphant amidst a pompous crowd of nobles, not surrounded with a glittering tribe of courtly damsels. Poverty, humility, modesty, with every graceful virtue, were all their train. The Lord of Hosts, indeed, was her inseparable companion, attended by his glorious court, far outshining all the splendor of the vain and pompous sons of earth.

Come at length to her journey's end, she entered the house of Zachary, and finding there her cousin Elizabeth, saluted her, saying: Hail, my dear cousin Elizabeth. Elizabeth vehemently animated by the Holy Ghost, with transports of joy, immediately arose, and tenderly embracing her, cried aloud: *Blessed art thou amongst women, and blessed is the fruit of thy womb. And whence is this to me, that the mother of my Lord should come to visit me?* —*Luke* i. The words of the salutation were no sooner graciously uttered by our blessed Lady, than they pierced even to the bowels of St. Elizabeth, inflaming both mother and son with the divine Spirit.

Nor was the mother inflamed before her son, but he being first replenished himself, replenished also his parent; not operating anything new within her, but rather meriting that something divine should be wrought within her soul, by the operation of the Holy Ghost: Insomuch, that the grace of the Holy Paraclete was more abundantly diffused in him, and he first was sensible of its blessed effects. Thus, as she outwardly perceived the presence of the holy Virgin, he inwardly was affected by the approach of his Lord. Wherefore, he exulted for joy, and she prophesied. Consider hence of how great force and efficacy must the words of the Blessed Virgin be, that the Holy Ghost should deign to communicate himself at the bare utterance of them. For herself was so copiously filled with him, that the same divine spirit in and through her replenished others. The Virgin Mary, after hearing the salutation of Elizabeth, replied thus to her: "My soul doth magnify our Lord, and my spirit hath rejoiced in God my Saviour," with the rest of that divine canticle. Having ended, they both sat down; when a holy contention arose between them, not occasioned by ceremonious insincerity, but from an inborn humility. The sacred Virgin, greatest in that virtue, as well as in dignity, would have seated herself below Elizabeth, at her feet; and Elizabeth, conscious of the majesty of her guest, would have placed herself beneath hers. But at length both modestly yielding to each other, they seated themselves together, side by side. The pious debate was succeeded by equally pious greetings, and mutual interrogations concerning the mystery of each other's conception, which they mutually revealed, giving the glory of it to God, and crowning the day with divine praises and thanksgiving for the sover-

eign and ineffable blessings received. Our Blessed
Lady continued with Elizabeth the space of three
months, helping and assisting her as far as she was
able, with all devotion, humility, and veneration,
seeming to forget the greatness of her own dignity,
and that she was the chosen mother of God, and
the sovereign queen of the world. Oh, what a
heavenly house; what blessed chambers! What
an immaculate bed was that, which contained such
sacred parents, pregnant with such celestial infants ;
Mary and Elizabeth, Jesus and John, guarded and
attended by those truly great and venerable men,
Joseph and Zachary.

HIS FATHER WRITES THE NAME "JOHN" ON THE TABLETS.

When Elizabeth's time was expired, she was hap-
pily delivered of a son, whom our Blessed Lady
received in her arms, and carefully swathed ; per-

forming with virginal tenderness, the necessary
little offices suitable to the occasion. The infant,
as if acquaintd with the majesty of his sacred nurse,
fixed his eyes steadfastly on her, so taken with her
beauty, that when she delivered him again to his
mother, he still looked towards her as if he could
take delight in her alone ; while she, on the other
side, continned graciously playing with him, embracing him, and cherishing him with her heavenly
lips. What excess of honor was this for St. John !
What pure mortal, besides himself, was ever blessed
with such a nurse ! Yet this is not the only great
privilege he enjoyed. Many others might be named,
were they not foreign to our present purpose.

On the eighth day the child was circumcised and
called John. Then was the mouth of Zachary
opened, and he prophecied, saying, " Blessed is the
Lord God of Israel, etc." Thus were the *Magnificat*
and *Benedictus*, those two sublimely beautiful canticles, composed in this house. In the mean time,
while the latter was singing, our blessed Lady,
virgin-like, to avoid being gazed on by the men who
were present, on account of the ceremony, kept retired in a secret part of the chamber, where unseen she
could hear what passed, and there devoutly listened
to the prophesies uttered concerning her divine son:
carefully and wisely depositing the whole in her
heart. At length, taking leave of Elizabeth and
Zachary, and giving her blessing to John, she returns to her humble habitation at Nazareth. Here
again, devout reader, contemplate her poverty in
another shape. She returns home: But to what a
home ! To a home unprovided with meat or drink :
to a home destitute of every necessary of life. But
this would be a trifling circumstance, had she either
estate or money, or other means to procure her a

cheerful residence there. But, alas! that she is a stranger to. She has remained now three months with her relations, probably in no mean circumstances : and yet now, not with regret, but cheerfully of her own accord, she descends to her former state of poverty, and to gain a narrow subsistence with her own hands. Oh! Christian Soul, compassionate the Blessed Virgin in such great distress ; and learn from so great an example, the poverty of spirit you ought to have.

VIEW OF THE PRESENT CONDITION OF NAZARETH.

CHAPTER V.

ST. JOSEPH THINKS OF DISMISSING THE BLESSED VIRGIN ; AND GOD SUFFERS HIS BELOVED TO BE AFFLICTED.

WHEN our Blessed Lady and her spouse had been some time at home, and Jesus had visibly grown in his mother's womb, St. Joseph could not but perceive the pregnancy of this heavenly parent; which, with the consciousness of his own purity, stung his soul to the quick with immoderate grief.

If it should seem strange to you that Christ would have his mother espoused, notwithstanding she was to remain always a virgin; there are three very natural reasons to be assigned. First, that her pregnancy might not subject her to infamy. Secondly, that the care and company of a man might guard her from insults. Thirdly, that the veil of marriage might elude the devil's enquiry into the mystery of the incarnation.

Joseph frequently observed his spouse, but never without grief and confusion; nor could he help manifesting his concern in the disturbance of his countenance; often turning his eyes from her as from a criminal, whom he suspected of adultery. Hence, learn how God permits those whom he loves to be afflicted in this life, and how he prepares them for the crown of glory, by means of temptation.

However, amidst his concern he did not lose sight of moderation, but was contriving how to dismiss her privately, without hurt to her person or reputation. Here it may be truly said, that his praise is in the gospel: it is there said, that "he was a just man:" and great indeed does his virtue appear on this occasion. For though commonly speaking, the greatest provocation a man has to shame, grief and excess of madness, is the infidelity of his wife; yet he knew so well how to moderate his passion by virtue, that he would not so much as accuse a wife whom he thought guilty; but chose patiently to stifle the injury, and rather to conquer by goodness, than overcome by revenge: and, being too just not to desire to separate from a criminal, he was likewise too merciful not to spare the reputation of one, who was to be pitied, if frail.

Nor was our Blessed Lady without her share of tribulation; she could not but observe his disturbance; and could not but be disturbed with it herself. Nevertheless, she humbly kept peace, and concealed the gift of God, rather choosing to be reputed a sinner, than to reveal the divine secret, and say that of herself which might be discredited as an empty boast, contrived to palliate a real offence. All her recourse was to God, beseeching him to apply his healing balm of comfort to the troubled souls of herself and spouse. Hence gather what inexpressible grief and anxiety these two blessed personages were in! But the same Lord who wisely permitted them to be tried, mercifully relieved them both in time of need, sending an angel to Joseph in a dream, to inform him that his spouse had conceived by virtue of the Holy Ghost, and that he should lay aside all thoughts of leaving her; and ordering him to distrust her no more, but to remain with her in all love, peace, and alacrity. Thus their disquiet ceasing, a sovereign consolation took place in their breasts. And the same would happen to us, if we knew how to arm ourselves with patience in the day of trial: For it is a never-failing effect of the divine bounty to calm the breasts of such as behave with courage in the tempest of affliction. Nor ought we in the least to doubt it; for he is too tender of his elect to suffer them to undergo the least tribulation that does not tend to their advantage.

St. Joseph after this enquired modestly into the particulars of this miraculous conception, which the humble Virgin faithfully related to him: and he remained thenceforward with his blessed spouse with the utmost joy and content. Thus both jointly rejoiced in their common poverty; he taking the tenderest care of her, and cherishing her with chaste affection; and she honoring him with modest confidence and spotless love.

In the meantime, Jesus remained enclosed in his mother's womb, like other children, during the space of nine months, patiently and benignly waiting the due time. Reflect then, and compassionate him who, for your sake, reduced himself to such an abject state of humiliation. How carefully then ought we to study to secure to ourselves the possession of this amiable virtue, and how little does it become us to follow our ambition, and to swell with the vain desire of reputation and fame, when the Lord of Majesty condescended to stoop to so humble a state! Can we ever make a sufficient acknowledgment to him for this second proof he gives us, in this tedious imprisonment, of the excess of his love for us; at least, let us make him a cordial acknowledgment of it, and with the utmost fervor of our hearts, return him thanks for having chosen us from among the rest of Christians, to make him the slender retribution of retreating from the vanities of the world, to attend to his service.

It is true, we owe it wholly to the gift of his divine grace, not to any merit of ours; and yet he is pleased to look upon it as highly acceptable and grateful. Nor ought a Christian's retreat to be deemed a punishment, but a safeguard. For being safely placed within our pious retirement, the impoisoned darts or tempestuous waves of this profligate world, in vain attempt to reach us, unless we rashly expose ourselves to them. Let us then, with all our power, and with the greatest purity of heart, endeavor to enjoy the blessing, by looking up our thoughts, and abstracting our minds from all that is transitory. For it will little avail for the body to be separated from worldly commerce, if the mind or heart remain attached to it.

Learn likewise to compassionate our Lord Jesus for this, that from the moment of his conception to that of his death, his sufferings were continual, as he knew that his divine Father, whom he infinitely loved, was, and would be dishonored, and the meanest of his creatures preferred to him; and inasmuch as he saw those unhappy souls, who were created to his own likeness, and whom he compassionately loved, miserably and almost universally plunge themselves into their own damnation. And his affliction and torture were so much greater than his bodily sufferings, as they were the cause of them. For the latter he submitted to, purely to remove the former. What plentiful and rich provisions of spiritual food are here laid before you for contemplation! Taste them then, and, if you wish to relish perfectly their sweetness, partake of them with frequency, diligence, and devotion.

THERE IS NO ROOM FOR THEM IN THE INN.

Joseph and Mary, arriving in Bethlehem, find that there is no room for them in the inn, and are driven to seek shelter

CHAPTER VI.

OF THE NATIVITY OF JESUS CHRIST.

THE term then of nine months, from the time of the conception of our blessed Redeemer, being nearly expired, an edict was published by the Emperor, Augustus Cæsar, throughout all his dominions, whereby he ordered all his subjects to repair to the respective places of their birth, there to have their names enrolled. In conformity to which, Joseph, being a native of Bethlehem, prepared to go thither: and perceiving that the time drew near for his beloved spouse to bring forth her divine Son, he resolved upon taking her along with him. Here a second time our blessed Lady undertakes a fatiguing journey; the city of Bethlehem being but five or six miles from Jerusalem, and nearly seventy from Nazareth. All they took with them was an ox and an ass, with which they travelled on in the lowly appearance of such as deal in animals of that kind. At length arrived at the city of Bethlehem, they found there so great a multitude of people, who had resorted thither from all parts, on the same occasion, that, by reason of their extreme poverty and distress, they could find no room in the inn. Here let tenderness excite you to compassion towards the august personage of this young and delicate Virgin. Consider her at the age of fifteen, wearied with the labors of a tedious journey, confused, terrified and abashed, amidst a crowded popu-

lace : she seeks, to no purpose, a place of rest ; and
being everywhere refused admittance for herself
and spouse, is at last reduced to seek for a shelter in
a homely shed, the usual refuge of persons surprised by sudden storms of rain.   In this place, we
may suppose St. Joseph, who was by profession a
carpenter, might probably have made a kind of par-
tition, or small enclosure for themselves, in which
he fixed a rack and manger for the convenience of
their beasts.   And now let me earnestly entreat you
to be sedulously attentive to everything that passes,
concerning this subject, chiefly because what I am
now going to relate, I had from a devout and holy
man of undoubted credit, to whom I believe it was
revealed by the Blessed Virgin herself.

The expected hour of the birth of the Son of God
being come, on Sunday, towards midnight, the holy
Virgin, rising from her seat, went and decently
rested herself against a pillar she found there :
Joseph in the meantime, sat pensive and sorrowful ;
perhaps, because he could not prepare the necessary
accommodation for her.   But at length, he arose
too, and taking what hay he could find in the
manger, he diligently spread it at our Lady's feet,
and then modestly retired to another part.   Then the
eternal Son of God, coming forth from his mother's
womb, was, without pain to her, transferred in an
instant from thence to the humble bed of hay, that
was prepared for him at her feet.   His holy Mother,
hastily stooping down, took him up in her arms, and
tenderly embracing him, laid him in her lap ; then
through instinct of the Holy Ghost, she began to
wash and bathe him with her sacred milk, with
which she was most amply supplied from heaven :
this done, she took the veil off her head, and wrap-
ping him in it, carefully reposed him in the manger.

Here the ox and the ass, kneeling down, and laying their heads over the manger, gently breathed upon him, as if endowed with reason. They were sensible, that through the inclemency of the season, and his poor attire, the blessed infant stood in need of their assistance to warm and cherish him. Then the holy Virgin throwing herself on her knees, adored him, and rendering thanks to God, said: " My Lord and heavenly Father, I return thee most grateful thanks, that **thou** vouchsafest of thy bounty to give me thy only Son ; and I praise and worship thee, O eternal God, together with thee, O Son of the living God, **and** mine."

Joseph likewise paid him adoration at the same time ; after which he stripped the ass of his saddle, and separating the pillion from it, he placed it near the manger for the Blessed Virgin to sit **on : but** she seating herself with her face towards the crib, made use of **that** homely cushion only to lean on. In this posture, **the** Queen of Heaven remained some time immovable, keeping her eyes **and** affections steadily fixed on her beloved Son. **Thus far from the** above-mentioned revelations.

After our blessed Lady **had** revealed this to her devout votary, she disappeared, and there remained with him an angel of God, who spoke many great things **to her** sacred praise : and the same **were** again related to me, which **I** am neither capable of repeating nor retaining.

You have here, Christian reader, been present at the sacred birth of the Son of God, and beheld the happy delivery of the Queen of Heaven, and may have discovered in both these mysteries, the true practice of strict poverty, in the extreme penury and want of many things necessary. This most sublime virtue the Lord of heaven and earth first brought to its true lustre. This is that evangelical pearl, to obtain which, we must spare no cost, but must purchase it at the expense of all we have. This is the first and sure foundation necessary to support the whole spiritual fabric. For the soul being here clogged with the weight of temporal goods, is thereby rendered incapable of raising itself on high, and freely ascending to God. In relation to this St. Francis thus says: "You are to know, brethren, that poverty is the spiritual way that leads to salvation, as it were, the nutrimental sap of humility, and the source of all perfection: the fruit of which is concealed from and unknown to many.

"It ought then to be a subject of confusion to us, that we endeavor not with all our strength to embrace it, but on the contrary, load ourselves with the care of many superfluous and unnecessary things," when the Lord of heaven, and the Blessed Virgin his Mother, were with the greatest perfection most strict observers of it. St. Bernard also says, "The practice of this virtue is a jewel, which the facility of obtaining has rendered of little value in the esteem of mankind. The Son of God being desirous of this virtue, descended from heaven among us, that he might become capable of practising it himself, and of rendering it dear to us by the esteem he set upon it. Embellish thy heart then as a worthy sanctuary for thy heavenly spouse, with the virtues of a profound humility and a strict poverty. These are the swaddling clothes he takes the greatest delight in, and these he prefers, as the Blessed Virgin testifies, to the mantles of the richest brocades. Adorn thy soul with them, O Christian reader! and make a sacrifice to God of the vanity of pompous attire, better suiting the pride of heathens, than the humble profession of Christians." And again in his sermon on the nativity, he says: "Almighty God at length comforts his people. Would you know who are his people? Hear then the man according to God's own heart: *To thy care*, says he, *the poor is committed.—Ps.* ix. And as Christ adds in the gospel, *Woe unto you that are rich; for you have received here your consolation.—Luke* ii. And how indeed can they expect from him any comfort, who have placed their comfort elsewhere? the tender infancy of Jesus Christ is no comfort to the loquacious and evil promoters of idle discourse; his tears convey no comfortable harmony to those who are inclined to inordinate laughter and trivial mirth. They whose glory it is to shine in gay apparel, receive no comfort from the poverty and meanness of his attire, nor do his humble stall, and homely manger, contribute the least consolation to those, whose ambition is to fill the first seats, and hold the chief dignities in church or state." The joyful tidings of the eternal light, springing forth, was first carried to the poor shepherds, who were carefully watching their flocks, and it was said, "That unto them a Saviour was born; that is, unto the poor, the industrious and the laboring; not unto you, O rich, who lulled with ease, and swelled with power and plenty, have here your fill of consolation." Thus far St. Bernard.

In this same nativity of the Son of God, we may likewise contemplate a most profound humility, which is evidently remarkable, both in the Mother and her blessed Son. They disdained not a stall for their habitation, a truss of hay for their bed, dumb creatures for their companions; with everything about them that seemed lowly, mean, and contemptible. Each of them, with the greatest perfection, always practiced this virtue, and in the most minute actions of their whole lives strongly recommended it to us. Let us, then, by serious endeavors, apply ourselves to the study of it, and be earnestly solicitous of embracing it because without it there is no salvation. None of all our actions can be pleasing to God, if joined with pride: for, according to St. Augustine, pride was the occasion of that unhappy change among the angelical spirits, transforming them from angels of light into devils; whereas humility, raising mankind above their nature, transformed them unto the state of angels. Hence St. Bernard asks the following question: "What ought mankind to be, whose happy lot it is to repair the vacant seats of the reprobate angels?" Pride once invaded that heavenly kingdom, it shook its walls, and in a great measure undermined them. What then follows hence, but that a vice so pestiferous is become odious to that city, and the worst of all abominations? Be assured, brethren, that he who spared not the angels for their pride, will not fail severely to chastise mankind . for he never acts inconsistently, but is perfectly conformable in all his works.

Lastly, contemplate in this divine child and his sacred parent, but more especially in the infant Jesus, that more than ordinary anguish which piercingly affected their tender hearts. Concerning which St. Bernard again says: "The Son of God being to be born, in whose power it was to choose whatever time he pleased, made choice of that time which was most afflicting to sense and tormenting to flesh; especially to a tender infant, the son of a poor and distressed mother, who had scarcely clothes wherewith to cover him, and no better cradle than a manger to lay him in: and notwithstanding the great necessity there was for them, we find no sort of mention made of warm furs, or downy mantles ; and again, Christ. who cannot possibly be mistaken, chose that which was most disagreeable to the flesh. It is a consequence therefore unquestionable, that this in itself is most eligible, most advantageous, and infinitely preferable to all other things ; and whoever should endeavor to persuade, or teach the contrary, ought to be looked upon as no better than a public and dangerous imposter ; and as such to be shunned and avoided by every Christian who places his chief interest in his salvation." And again, "He," says the Saint, "was a long time before foretold by the prophet Isaiah to be a child, *that should know how to refuse evil and choose good.—Isa.* vii. It is therefore an evident truth, that the pleasures of the flesh are evil, and afflictions are good ; for this that the eternal wisdom, and the infant word in human flesh, made choice of the latter preferably to the former." Thus far St. Bernard. Go thou and do the same from so great an example : but with discretion, however, so as not to exceed the bounds of your own station. Much more might be said concerning these virtues, but let us now return to the little mansion of the nativity.

The Son of God being now born, the innumerable multitude of celestial spirits, which were there assisting, paid devout adoration to their God ; and forthwith hastened to the shepherds, about a mile distant from Bethlehem, and related to them the birth of our Lord Jesus, with the time and place, when and where it was effected. Thence, with joyful acclamations, singing canticles of praise and glory, they ascend with all speed the celestial regions, carrying to their fellow-citizens the same joyful news of their Lord's nativity. Wherefore the whole court of heaven, in raptures of joy at the auspi-

cious things, celebrated the sacred mystery with the
utmost solemnity : and due thanks being paid to the

**THE BLESSED MARY AND ST. JOSEPH KNEELING ADORE THE HOLY
CHILD.**

Almighty Majesty of God the Father, for the great
goodness and omnipotence he had manifested in this
work, they all successively, according to the different orders of their heavenly hierarchy, descend to
behold the lovely and gracious countenance of their
Lord, their King, and their God ; and devoutly and
reverently adoring him, and rendering all due and
profound respect to the blessed Virgin Mother ; they
filled the air with the sweet and melodious harmony
of canticles of praise and thanksgiving to the Almighty. And what one among them, having received the joyful news, could have remained in Heaven, nor descend obsequiously to visit their Lord thus

humbled, thus reduced to the lowest condition upon
earth? None of them could be capable of so great
an arrogance. And therefore the Apostle says, that
when the Father of Heaven brought his first be-
gotten Son into the world, he said, that all his
blessed angels should worship him.—Heb. i. This
to me is a most pleasing subject of meditation whether
it happened exactly as here related or not.

ANGELS APPEAR TO THE SHEPHERDS BY NIGHT.

To the angels succeeded the shepherds, who came
in their turn to pay their homely, but not less welcome homage; which done, full of joy, which the
devout practice of our known duty inspires, they departed, but not without having first related all that
the angels said to them. The blessed parent observed diligently all that was said of her divine in-

fant, and kept **a pleasing** record of it within her own
breast.   Thou too, O Christian loiterer! throw thyself **on thy knees, and in** atonement for thy past neglects, most cordially worship the Lord thy God, devoutly greet his holy **Mother,** and reverently salute
the holy and **venerable St.** Joseph.   Then in spirit
tenderly **kiss the feet** of the infant Jesus, humbly
extended on a bed of hay; and earnestly and devoutly **request him of our** blessed Lady, humbly in-
treating her to vouchsafe to premit you to take **him:**
receive him into your arms, embrace him with tender
affection, attentively contemplate the sweetness of
his sacred features, and with the most profound
respect **salute him often,** salute him tenderly, placing all **your confidence in** his goodness, and all your
delight **in his conversation.**   This you may boldly
presume **to do, though a sinner,** because he came
into the **world to sinners, to** work the salvation of
sinners; and after having **a** long time conversed
among sinners with **all** humility and meekness, he
made himself the food of sinners.   His divine bounty
therefore will **readily** grant you this favor, as often
as your devotion shall lead you to require it.
Neither will he deem it an effect **of** your presumption
but a proof of your love; let not **his** goodness, however, lessen the fear and reverence with which you
ought to approach him; but reflect that he is the
Holy **of** Holies, and awed by that consideration,
treat him with **the respect** becoming him.   **When**
you have contemplated him sufficiently, restore **him**
again to his Mother, **and** learn **from** her how **to** use
him.   See with **what** care, caution, and prudential
tenderness she executes her charge, suckles **him,**
nurses him, and performs every other little office as
occasion requires.   Be mindful often to meditate
upon these **subjects, take** a pleasure and delight in

them, and with all the devotion you are master of,
endeavor to show your desire of aiding our blessed
Lady and her divine infant Jesus; often gaze on
his amiable aspect, on that divine countenance which
the angels themselves covet to behold, but forget not
my **former** advice to you; let fear and reverence
temper your zeal and devotion, lest you meet with
a just repulse; for your **own** native poverty and
meanness ought to render **you** unworthy, in your
own eyes, the conversation of such divine and
heavenly company.

It might afford us new matter of spiritual joy,
were we to contemplate the greatness of this day's
solemnity. On this day was born Christ, that is, the
Lord's truly anointed. And therefore, this is truly
the birthday of the eternal King of Heaven, the Son
of the Almighty God. This day, *Unto us a child
is born, and unto us a Son is given—Isa.* vi.
On this day, the sun of eternal righteousness, which
before was eclipsed, spread forth the bright beams
of his mercy and grace to the world. On this day
the Holy Ghost, head of the chosen people of God's
Church, came forth from the inward recess of his
sacred bride-chamber, and the fairest in form of
the sons of men, graciously unveiled his lovely and
long-wished for and pleasing countenance.

On this day was first heard that angelical hymn,
Gloria in excelsis Deo, etc. Glory be to God
on high, etc. This day, as the church everywhere
sings, the heavens distilled honey, and the earth
echoes with angelical notes. On this day the humanity and benignity of God our Saviour first appeared among us. On this day God was worshipped
in the likeness of sinful flesh. On this day were
fulfilled those two wonderful mysteries surpassing
all understanding, and to be reached only by faith,

to wit, God is born, and a Virgin brings forth a Son.
On this day many, almost innumerable, other miracles were wrought.   In a word, it was on this day,

THE HOLY CHILD JESUS IS ADORED BY THE SHEPHERDS OF BETHLEHEM.

properly speaking, that all that has been said of the
Incarnation, shone forth in its true lustre.   For
whatever was begun before, was not completed nor
manifested till now: wherefore, it may not be improper to unite those passages which seemed different in point of time, and to make them the subject
of the same devout meditation.   Not without great
reason then, you see, is this day a day of public rejoicing, of spiritual mirth, and universal gladness.
To confirm which, God was pleased to work the following miracles in the very centre of Paganism.   At
Rome was a celebrated tavern, or house for drinking,

known by the title of the Pay-house, because thither
the Roman soldiers used to resort, to regale themselves, and to spend their pay when they received it ;
and here, on the same day on which Christ was born,
sprung forth a rich fountain of precious oil ; and at
the same time, a circle round the sun, in appeaiance
like the rainbow, was seen in the Heavens, and visible to the whole universe. And the golden statue
which Romulus, the founder of the Roman state, had
erected in his palace, and which, according to the
Pagan oracles, was not to fall till a virgin should bring
forth a son, tumbled down to the ground, and was
reduced to dust. All this came to pass on the very
day and instant that Christ was born. In which
place, in honor of the Blessed Virgin, Pope Calistus,
in process of time built a church, now called St.
Mary's Trans-Tybe

THE HOLY SIMEON TAKES THE INFANT JESUS IN HIS ARMS.

CHAPTER VII.

THE CIRCUMCISION OF OUR LORD JESUS.

UPON the eighth day after the blessed infant was born he was carried to the temple to be circumcised, according to the law of Moses. Two great mysteries were performed on this day. The first is, that the blessed name, through which only salvation is to be obtained, was this day made manifest to the world; and our blessed Lord and Saviour publicly called by the name of JESUS;

which name had been given him by his heavenly
Father from all eternity, and by the holy angel before he was conceived. And they called his name
Jesus ; that is a Saviour. *Which name*, as the
apostle says, *Phil*. ii., *is above all names. For
neither is there any other name in Heaven given
to men wherein we must be saved.—Acts* iv. The
second is, that on this day our Lord Jesus began to
shed his most precious blood for our sakes. So
earnest was he to begin early to suffer for us, that
he who knew no sin undertook this day to endure
the pain of it for us.

Here let tenderness move us to compassionate him :
let us shed at least some few tears with him, who on
this day shed so many for us. For though upon
solemn days we rejoice at our salvation purchased
by the mysteries they commemorate ; yet ought we
likewise to conceive an inward sorrow and compassion, for the anguish and pain endured by him, who
so graciously performed them. We have already
seen how many were the afflictions he suffered, together with the great poverty, penury, and distress
he underwent at the time of his sacred nativity.
But among other things was this, which hitherto
has not been related. His blessed Mother when she
had reposed him in the manger, having no pillow
with which to raise his head, made use for that purpose of a stone, which not unlikely she might cover
with hay. This I had from a devout brother who
saw it in spirit ; and the same stone being now fixed
in the wall, is a visible memorial of it. A cushion
or a pillow, we may piously imagine, would much
rather have been her choice, had she been mistress
of one ; but having nothing more proper to answer
the end, to the great affliction of her tender heart,
she was compelled to make use of that.

We have said before, that on this day he began
to shed his sacred blood for us, and that indeed in a
most severe manner ; for his tender flesh was cruelly
separated with a blunt and edgeless instrument of
stone.   What pity then ought not this move us to,
towards him and his holy Mother ? What tears then
did not the tender infant Jesus shed at the incredi-
ble pain he suffered in the incision of his sacred
flesh ; for his was truly so, and as sensible of pain
as that of any pure mortal.   And can we reasonably
imagine then, that his holy Mother, when she saw
her beloved child in tears, could contain herself from
them ?   No, we may well suppose, that like a compassionate parent, she ever accompanied him in all
his afflictions ; so that her tender heart melting now
with grief in seeing him cry, she burst forth into
tears herself, and wept bitterly.   So likewise, may
we imagine that more affected with his Mother's
grief than his own, the holy babe, as he lay extended
on her lap, waved his little hands towards her lips,
her cheeks, and her eyes, as it were to dry up those
precious drops, and to request her to forbear shedding them, struggling at the same time, to hide the
excess of his own torture to mitigate her's.   But
she, alas ! was too sensibly affected with his suffering not to shed tear for tear with him.   Yet the
divine wisdom within her, supplying the want of
speech in him, enabled her to know his pleasure,
before he had words to utter it ; hence, perceiving
that her grief added to his pain, often would she
try to suppress it, and with signs of forced tranquillity endeavor to console him ; still often would she
sigh, and with forbidden tears, ready to flow from
her eyes, and waiting as it were in a state of violence
to break forth, thus frequently would she address
him with complaints of the most tender love: "For-

bear, lovely babe! forbear those precious tears, or suffer mind to flow. How can thy loving Mother see those dear eyes bedewed and cease to weep?" Hence the blessed infant, in compassion to his holy Mother, would moderate his sobs and give over weeping, and she with a Mother's tenderness, would wipe his sacred eyes and her own, incline her face to his, closely and tenderly press his blessed cheeks, and give him **suck** ; and study meanwhile the most likely means to lull his pain and cherish **him.** In this manner, she behaved **as** often as he bewailed himself, which we may reasonably believe he often **did** after the nature of other children.—First, to show the miserable weakness, and wretchedness of man's condition, whose nature he had truly assumed. And, secondly, **to** conceal himself from the devil, that he might not as yet know him to be God: **for** this reason, the holy church alluding **to** him in part of her service, sings: "The tender infant, as he lies **in** the cold manger shakes and cries."

From this time, indeed, the circumcision of the flesh was abolished, and its obligation ceased, baptism being instituted in its place, which is a sacrament of more extensive grace, and less repugnant to nature, **as** being void of **pain.** And yet, **gentle** reader, the practice of spiritual circumcision ought still to remain in force, which consists in divesting ourselves **of** all that is superfluous, **and** embracing **true** poverty of spirit. He, and he only, is in truth spiritually circumcised, who is truly poor. This, says St. Bernard, the apostle teacheth us in few words, *Having food and raiment let us be content therewith.*—1 *Tim.* **vi.** In a word, **our** spiritual circumcision must appear in all our senses. Let us then show we are indeed spiritually circumcised, by renouncing, as much **as** our nature will admit of, the use of sight, of hearing, of taste, of touch, but above all, our speech. Much talk is a very great vice, odious to God and man, and ever attended with fatal consequences. We must, therefore, show ourselves circumcised in speech : by speaking seldom, and never but to a good purpose : to speak much is a sure sign of levity. On the contrary, silence is a noble virtue, and not without great reason, especially recommended to religious persons. Concerning this subject St. Bernard says, " He is truly qualified to speak who has first learned to be silent, for silence is the only proper nature of speech." And again in another place : " It is ever the propensity of weak judgments to be rashly forward in speaking, for the hasty conceptions of a light fancy are always as hastily delivered by an unbridled tongue." Wherefore says St. Bernard, on the same subject : " Who does not know how greatly man is defiled by the mire dropping from his own tongue : that is, by his idle discourse, by the falsehoods he advances, by slander, by flattery ; in a word, by almost all his conversation chequered with malice and vanity ? To restrain all which, he stands in great need of silence ; a virtue which is, as it were, the sentinel of religious hearts, and their chief safe-guard against irreligion and indevotion. So dangerous is too much talk, even to laymen, according to that great Saint. But much more so, if we believe him, is it to the clergy. Hear what he says elsewhere in relation to them, " Idleness," says he, " is the mother of idle jests, and consequently a barbarous stepmother to virtue. Innocent jokes are trifles in the mouths of laymen, but all ludicrous discourse is unseemly in the mouths of clergymen. Priests may sometimes take a joke, but should never indecently return it. It is unworthy their dignity to defile,

with such kind of discourse, those lips which are
dedicated to, and consecrated by the holy gospel
which they pronounce."

THE WISE MEN ON THEIR JOURNEY MEDITATE UPON THE MEANING
OF THE STAR

CHAPTER VIII.

THE EPIPHANY, OR MANIFESTATION OF OUR LORD JESUS.

ON this day, which is the twelfth after the nativity, our Lord Jesus vouchsafed to make
himself known to the Gentiles, in the person of the
three kings. Render yourself present then, pious
reader, to every circumstance herein related concerning this holy and solemn festival: for you are
to understand, that no other festival in the holy

church has such a diversity of service in its anti-phons, lessons, responsories, or whatever else belongs to its celebration as this has. Not that it is greater or more excellent than all other festivals, but only that on this day many things both great and wonderful, were wrought by our Lord Jesus, which chiefly regard the state and condition of the church itself.

First, then, the church which is gathered from the Gentiles, was on this day received by Christ Jesus in the person of the three kings. For on the day of his nativity he had manifested himself to the shepherds, as representatives of the Jews, from whom, a small number excepted, he met with no reception. But on this day he appeared again, and made himself known to the Gentiles, by whom he was immediately acknowledged and received, and from them it is that we are descended, who now form the church of God's chosen people. This day, therefore, ought specially to be kept as a most solemn feast in the church of God, and celebrated with great pomp, and with hearts full of joy, by all good and pious Christians.

Secondly, this day, nine and twenty years after his nativity, our Lord Jesus was baptized; by which mystery he spiritually wedded and truly espoused his holy church, and united it to himself. And therefore on this occasion is joyfully sung: "*Hodie cælesti sponso juncta est ecclesia,*" etc. "This day the church is wedded to her heavenly spouse." For in our baptism, which receives all its efficacy from that of Christ, our souls being cleansed from the stain of sin, and newly clothed with grace, are truly espoused and wedded to him, and the congregation of souls, thus baptized, constitute the church of God's chosen people.

Thirdly, on the same day, a year after his baptism, he wrought his first miracle at the marriage feast, converting water into wine, which by allegory, may be likewise taken for the spiritual marriage between him and his church. It is probable likewise, that on the like day, our Lord Jesus wrought that other wonderful miracle of multiplying the loaves and fishes. However, the church on this day only celebrates the three first of these mysteries.

Consider hence in what great veneration and esteem this day ought to be held, upon which our Lord Jesus chose to work so many and such ineffable mysteries. The holy church therefore mindful of the many benefits and extraordinary favors conferred upon her this day, by her divine spouse, to show her grateful sense of them, rejoices, sings, and solemnizes the same with praise, thanksgiving, and the utmost magnificence.

But as the solemn institution of this festival was chiefly to commemorate the mystery of the Epiphany, we will on that account proceed to a farther contemplation of it, and defer meditating on the others till we shall treat of them in their proper place, according to the order in which they happened. And even concerning the coming of the three kings to Christ our Saviour, my design here is not to lay before the reader any of those learned comments or moral expositions, which many holy men with great pains and industry have made on this subject ; and on this account, for the manner of their coming from the east to Jerusalem, the star which conducted them thither, what passed between them and Herod, or for the matter and meaning of their offerings, and other things of the kind, I refer the reader to the holy gospel and the expositions of learned men on these heads. As I said in the beginning of this work, my intention as well in this, as in all other incidents which occur in the life of Christ, is only to set down some few meditations, according to such devout conceptions as a pious mind is capable of forming, in relation to those things, which either happened in fact or might have happened, according to reasonable conjecture. But it was by no means my purpose to perform the office of an expositor; first, because I am unequal to the task; and secondly, it would prove too copious a subject for one man to comment upon. Be mindful then with redoubled attention, to render yourself present as it were, to every particular here treated. For in this consists the whole force and efficacy of these meditations.

The three kings, therefore, being come to Bethlehem, with a great multitude of people, and a noble retinue, stopped as the star directed them, at the little hut, in which our Lord Jesus was born. The blessed Virgin hearing the tumultuous noise of many people, snatches up her blessed Son Jesus in her arms, and in that moment the three kings entering the little mansion, as soon as they beheld the holy babe Jesus, threw themselves on their knees to adore him. Thus prostrate in a devout and reverent posture they honored him as their king, and worshipped him as their God. Reflect how great and lively their faith must be! What in reality did then appear that could excite them to believe, that a poor, tender infant, in the arms of as poor a mother, dejected, meanly clothed, in a despicable cottage without furniture, without company, without attendants, could be really a king, could be truly their God? And yet such was their faith, that they believed both, in spite of all that their senses had to offer in opposition. Such were

the guides, such the first leaders **which heaven**
thought proper to give us, and such the great
originals it behooves us to copy. After they
had devoutly paid this homage to our blessed Redeemer, and duly honored his holy mother, remaining still on their bended knees before him, we may
piously imagine that they now began to discourse
with the holy Virgin, and to ask many questions concerning **her** beloved Son, which they might do, either
by the help of an interpreter, **or** by themselves, since
they were men of great wisdom and learning, they
were probably sufficiently versed in the Hebrew
language. They therefore submissively request
her to acquaint **them with** the particular circumstances relating **to the** holy babe and herself. The
Blessed Virgin relates to them, and **they readily**
believe all that she tells them. Observe reverently,
with what awe they address and listen to her by
turns. **Mark too** with what graceful majesty, mixed
with **a becoming** modesty, the sacred Queen of
Virgins returns the necessary replies ; neither forward to talk, **nor** desirous to be seen. Yet God on
this occasion endowed her with more than usual resolution to support her **dignity** in the presence of
these princely votaries, **as** they represented the
whole church, which he **afterwards** was to establish, and **did** establish. **Here** again contemplate
our Lord **Jesus,** who not **yet** pleased to speak, with
benign **and** pleasant aspect, fixed his eyes upon
them, and with gravity becoming his full maturity
of judgment, attentively observes them, full well
understanding all that passes. And what pleasure
must not these admiring princes conceive, in beholding him, the fairest and the most beautiful
among the children of men ! And to behold him
not merely with the eyes of the body, but with **a**

kind of mental intuition, as **men** inwardly taught and enlightened by the object they gazed on. Thus replenished with joy and consolation, at length, they made their offerings to him in the following manner: Opening their coffers and spreading a carpet at the feet of our Lord Jesus, they humbly kneeled down before him, and laying their treasures at his feet, devoutly offered him the precious gifts of gold, frankincense, and myrrh in great abundance, but more especially of gold. We may reasonably suppose that the gifts of these three kings were both great and rich, and that the gold might exceed all the rest in quantity and bulk; for had their offerings been but small and of little value, it would have been a needless trouble for them to have opened their treasures, as the gospel says they did, when their servants, who were near at hand, might have helped them to what they wanted, more readily, and with less trouble.

When they had completed their offerings and laid their precious treasures before him, they reverently prostrated themselves and devoutly kissed his sacred feet. And why may not we piously imagine that the blessed infant, full of divine wisdom, the more to comfort them, and settle their affections on him, tendered them his divine little hand to kiss, and blessed them with it? After this they submissively inclined to our blessed Lady, and taking leave of her and St. Joseph, with hearts full of joy and comfort, they returned again, as the gospel says, into their native country by another way.

But what, may we imagine, did the Blessed Virgin do with those gifts, or how can we suppose she employed so great a quantity of gold and other valuable presents? Did she, think you, hoard them up for her own or her divine Son's use? Did she lay them out in the purchase of lands or houses? No, she was too much in love herself with virtuous poverty, and knew too well the will of her blessed infant, for their inward communication of souls, as well as every little outward gesture, left her no room to doubt of his contempt of riches. What use then could she make of them? What use? The best and only virtuous use that can be made of earthly riches. In a word, she distributed them in a few days to the poor: of so little estimation, nay, so burdensome and offensive in the sight of Christ and his Mother, are the treasures of this world and the pride of kings! Nay, our blessed Lady so entirely disposed of the whole, that at her entrance after into the temple, to present her child, she had not wherewith to purchase a lamb for his ransom, as the law directed, but offered a pair of turtle-doves for him, the usual offering of the poor. Thus is it consonant with reason, both to admire the magnificent devotion of the wise men in the nobleness of their offerings, and to adore the exalted charity and love of poverty of the Queen of Heaven, in her distribution of them to the indigent.

You have here, gentle reader, before your eyes, the truest and best commendation that can be given to poverty: concerning which, two things are especially worthy your observation. First, Christ our Saviour, and his holy Mother, disdained not to receive alms, like necessitous persons. Secondly, they were so far from being solicitous to attain riches, or anxious to hoard them, that they would not so much as keep what was liberally bestowed upon them, increasing daily in the love and desire of poverty.

But have you yet reflected on the profound humility that appears in them on this occasion? Surely, if you recollect, you cannot but perceive a most perfect example of it. We daily meet with many, who,

in their own eyes, are very mean, and not raised by
any opinion of merit they experience in themselves,
yet are wholly unwilling to appear such in the eyes
of others, and cannot easily bear to be contemned by
any, to have their faults disclosed, or that the meanness of their condition should be made public, lest it
might draw upon them the scorn and derision of the
world.   But this is not the example which our Lord
Jesus gives them this day, who, though the supreme
Lord and Master of all things, would have his poverty exposed to all, and his low condition appear
openly to others; and this not to a few only, or to
such as were poor and distressed like himself, but
even to numbers of rich and noble personages, to
princes, and kings, and to their numerous retinue.
Nay, and this at a time of no little danger.   For
they who came from such remote countries in search
of the King of the Jews, whom they believed to be
God and Lord of all things, finding him in so poor
and humble a condition, might thence have imagined
themselves grossly deluded, and therefore returned
home without either faith or devotion.   But this
hindered not our true lover of humility from giving
us so rare an example, that we might learn from
him never to neglect the true practice of that virtue
under the specious pretext of some fancied good,
but that we should learn to be solicitous of appearing contemptible, not only to our own, but even to
the eyes of others.

THE ADORATION OF THE MAGI ; OR, JESUS MANIFESTED TO THE GENTILES.

The wise men, or Magi, from the East, having seen the Star, of which Balaam the soothsayer had prophesied, after a long journey, during which they follow its guidance, at length arrive at Bethlehem. There they find the young Child and Mary His Mother, and offer their gifts of gold, frankincense, and myrrh, in acknowledgment of His Royalty, His Priesthood.

VIEW OF THE PRESENT CONDITION OF BETHLEHEM.

CHAPTER IX.

THE BLESSED VIRGIN REMAINS AT THE CRIB OF BETH-
LEHEM TILL THE FULL TERM OF FORTY DAYS IS
EXPIRED.

AFTER the three kings had made their offerings,
and were returning again on their way to their
own country, the Holy Virgin, with her Blessed Son
Jesus, and the Venerable St. Joseph, her beloved
spouse, remained still in the humble stall of Bethlehem, waiting with patience in that poor and little
mansion, till the full term of forty days was completed, as the law directed, for purification; as if

she had been full of sin, and defiled by her child-
bearing, as others of her sex are, and the child
Jesus only a sinful man and not God, and therefore
under an obligation of complying with the strict'ob-
servance of the law. But because they would enjoy
no special prerogatives above others, they voluntarily submitted to the law made for others. This
is not the practice of many, who conversing among
the rest of mankind, claim to themselves undue
titles to certain prerogatives above others, and seek
to be singularly distinguished from them, contrary
to the dictates of true humility.

Our blessed Lady then, like other women, remained all the while contented, expecting the before-mentioned day on which she was to enter into
the temple. During this space of time she was
studiously watchful, and diligent in the care of her
blessed Son. And oh, most gracious God, how
great indeed may we devoutly imagine was her
solicitude, and with what attention did she look
after him, lest anything should trouble or molest
him! With what caution, mixed with timorous respect, did she officiate about him whom she knew
to be her Lord and sovereign God, never taking
him from, or replacing him in the manger, but on
her bended knees?

With what unspeakable pleasure, confidence, and
motherly tenderness would she embrace him, often
kiss him, and, sweetly pressing, take inexpressible
delight in him? How often did she behold, with a
kind of innocent and pleasing curiosity, his blessed
countenance and graceful form! How discreetly was
she used to bind and swathe his tender limbs! for
as she was profoundly practised in true humility, so
was she also thoroughly instructed in true wisdom.
Wherefore she took special care to perform with the

greatest diligence every minute office or duty belonging to her charge in regard to him, not only during his infancy, but afterwards. Oh, with what a free and willing mind did she ever give him suck! And the pleasure she then conceived in suckling so divine a babe, could not but surpass that of the rest of her sex. St. Bernard says, "That it is not improbable that St. Joseph often took delight in caressing the infant Jesus, and devoutly cherishing him on his knee." Let us now accompany in spirit the Blessed Virgin at the manger, and take a pleasure in the pious meditation of our Lord, the infant Jesus, from whom there ever flows a plenitude of divine grace. For every devout and pious soul from Christmas to the Purification, ought with profound respect and joyful transports, at least once a day, mentally to visit our blessed Lady, and to adore her divine Son Jesus on her knee, piously and affectionately meditating on the poverty, humility, and ineffable goodness of both.

CHAPTER X

THE PURIFICATION OF OUR BLESSED LADY, OR CANDLEMAS-DAY.

NOW when the fortieth day was come, which was prescribed by the law for purification, the Blessed Virgin with her Son Jesus, and St. Joseph, set out from Bethlehem on their journey to Jerusalem, which was about six miles distant, there to present her blessed child in the temple, as it is written in the law. Let us here accompany the holy travellers on their journey, in devout contemplation, and help the sacred Virgin to bear her lovely charge, the infant Jesus ; and with redoubled earnestness and attention, be inwardly intent, and as it were present, at everything that is said or done, being real subjects of the sublimest devotion.

Thus then do they bring the Lord of the temple to the temple of the Lord. At the entrance thereof, they bought a pair of turtle-doves, or two young pigeons, to offer to God for him, as was the custom of other poor people. But as their circumstances were low, we may rather suppose that their offerings consisted only of two pigeons, which were of a less price than the doves ; and for that reason are mentioned the last in the law. And the holy Evangelist takes no notice here of a lamb, which was the usual offering of the rich. At this time the holy Simeon, who was a man both just and devout, being led by the divine spirit, came into the temple to see Christ the Son of God, whom he had long before desired to behold, and whom the Holy Ghost had promised he should see before his death. Wherefore, coming with speed to the temple, he no sooner beheld the divine babe than he prophetically knew him, and with bended knees adored him in his mother's arms. The holy infant blessed him ; and looking earnestly upon his mother, bent himself forward, making signs to go to him.

The Holy Virgin, full of pleasing surprise, understood his blessed will, gave him immediately to Simeon, who with ecstatic joy and reverence, received him in his arms, arose and blessing God said : *Now thou dost dismiss thy servant, O Lord, according to thy word in peace, because mine eyes have seen thy salvation, etc.,—Luke* ii. Prophesying many things concerning his sacred passion. And holy Ann, the prophetess, at that instant, likewise coming into the temple, gave thanks to God, adored the child Jesus, and spoke many things relating to him, and the redemption that should be wrought by him to all mankind. These things raising great admiration in the mind of the holy Virgin, she made a sacred record of them, and safely deposited them in her heart. At length, the holy infant stretching forth his arms towards his mother, was again delivered to her. After this they proceed forward towards the altar, in the manner of a procession, which is annually represented on Candlemas-day, throughout the whole church, by the blessing of candles. First went the two venerable old men, Joseph and Simeon, hand in hand, with transports of joy and spiritual mirth, repeating and singing: *Give thanks unto the Lord, for he is good, and his mercy endureth for ever, etc.,—Ps.* xvii. *The Lord is faithful in all his works, etc.,—Ibid.* cxlvii. *For this God is our God, without end, he shall be our guide forever.—Ibid.* xlvii. *We have received, O Lord, thy mercy in the midst of thy temple.— Ibid.* These were followed by the sacred Virgin herself, bearing her Blessed Son in her arms, accompanied by the holy widow Ann, the prophetess; who, full of unspeakable joy, walketh with profound reverence and devotion, close by her side, rendering all praise and thanksgiving to God. These, then, were all that formed this procession, which, though consisting of few persons, represented notwithstanding most great and wonderful mysteries. There were present of every sex and every state, youth, celibacy marriage, and widowhood. Being come to the altar the holy Virgin kneeling down, with profound reverence and devotion, offered her dearest Son to his heavenly Father, saying: "Vouchsafe, O most sovereign Lord, to receive your beloved Son, whom according to the appoinment of your divine will, and to fulfil the precepts of your holy law, I here, prostrate, offer unto you as the first-born of his mother. But I beseech your mercy, most gracious Father, to vouchsafe again to restore him to me;'' and then rising, she laid him upon the altar. Oh, great God, and most merciful Lord, what a precious and most acceptable offering was this! It was surely such as had never before been made from the beginning of time, nor ever shall again.

Behold here, and attentively consider how the blessed infant Jesus quietly remains upon the altar, like any other infant, and with serene and pleasing aspect beholding his mother, and the rest who stand about him, humbly waits with patience to see what is farther to be done. Then came forth the priest of the temple, and the sovereign Lord of all things was again redeemed with the low price of five-pence, or five small pieces of coin called shecles, the same sum as it was the custom to pay for poor children. After Joseph had paid them to the priest, the Blessed Virgin joyfully received him again into her arms. Then taking from Joseph the above-mentioned pair of turtles, she kneeled down, and lifting up her eyes devoutly to heaven, offered them, saying: "Oh! eternal Lord, and most gracious Father of Heaven, vouchsafe I beseech you to accept this offering, the first small gift which your beloved Son of his extreme poverty presents unto you !" Then he, stretching forth his hands towards the doves, and lifting up his eyes to heaven, though he said nothing, yet with pleasing countenance gave most expressive signs of offering them together with his mother. And thus she left the birds upon the altar.

Consider here, reader, and diligently contemplate the great dignity and majesty of those who make this offering: that is, the Blessed Virgin mother, and her divine Son, Jesus: and let us imagine whether this little offering, made by such persons, could possibly be rejected by God? No? rather may we devoutly suppose it to have been carried up to heaven by the hands of angels, and there presented by them, to have been most gratefully accepted by God Almighty, with the loud and earnest jubilees of the whole celestial court.

After the offering was ended, the holy Virgin, with her Son Jesus, and Joseph, departed from the city of Jerusalem, in order to return home again to the little city of Nazareth, their native place of abode. But the sacred Virgin, being desirous once more of seeing St. John before she left those parts, on her way home visited a second time her cousin St. Elizabeth. Go thou with her whithersoever she goes, and in devout meditation assist her in carrying her lovely babe. When our blessed Lady and St. Elizabeth met, they were extremely overjoyed at the sight of each other, but more especially in beholding their blessed Sons, Jesus and John, who, with no less tokens of joy, lovingly congratulated together; and St. John, as though conscious of the dignity of his sacred guest, behaved towards Jesus with the utmost submission and respect. When they had rested there some few days, they again prepared for their journey; and departed thence for Nazareth. And here, devout reader, if from what has already been said, you wish to learn the poverty and humility they practised, you need only consider the poverty of their offering, the humility in his ransom, and the strict compliance in both with the precepts of God's holy law.

ST. JOSEPH ESCAPES WITH THE HOLY CHILD AND HIS MOTHER.

CHAPTER XI.

CHRIST'S FLIGHT INTO EGYPT.

NOW as the parents of the holy Jesus were proceeding on their journey to Nazareth, unap-
prised of the designs of heaven, and of the treacherous machinations of Herod against the life of the
divine infant, the angel of God appeared in a dream
to Joseph, warning him to retire with the babe and
its mother into Egypt ; because that merciless tyrant

was bent upon the destruction of the child. Upon this, Joseph immediately rising, ran to awake the blessed Virgin, and informed her of the angel's warn ing. Shocked to the very soul by this alarm, she suddenly arose, and without a moment's delay, prepared to escape ; resolving to neglect nothing that might contribute to the safety of her beloved Son. They set out with him that very night, by a private way towards Egypt. Here follow them in meditation : behold how they snatch up the sleeping infant : compassionate their distress ; and reap the benefit of the many pious remarks, that may here be made.

And first, consider the many changes our Saviour experienced of prosperity and adversity. And when the like changes shall happen to you, learn to bear them with the manly patience becoming his followers. Whenever you see before you a steep ascent, be not dismayed, for know that the labor of climbing will but enhance the sweets of that repose you are afterwards to enjoy. Thus Christ was no sooner born than he was glorified by the pastors as God ; and yet, how soon after was he circumcised, as if a sinner? Thus was he honored with the homage, visit, and presents of the eastern monarchs, yet humbled to the association of beasts in a miserable stable, with no other comfort than that of tears, which the meanest child had in common with him. Thus, too, was he solemnly presented in the temple, and extolled by the prophetical predictions of Simeon and Ann, who is now warned by an angel to depart like a fugitive from his native country to Egypt. Many other instances of the like nature you may find in the life of Christ, from which, with a little virtuous industry, you may reap the greatest benefit and instruction. Learn then to curb the transports of prosperity, by reflecting that they are in general but the forerunners of adversity. Be firm in tribulation in consideration of the tranquillity and happiness that are to succeed them. For it is the dispensation of Providence to chequer afflictions with intervals of pleasure, the better to nourish our hope, and preserve us from being borne away by an overwhelming tide of troubles, and to intersperse tribulations amidst our felicity, that we may not be elated by it, but remain always in fear from the consciousness of our miserable condition. All this did our Lord for our instruction, and to conceal himself from Satan. Lose not the benefit of it for want of reflecting thereon.

Secondly, be mindful, that he who enjoys benefits and prosperity from the gift of God, has no right to prefer himself to those who are not blest in the same manner: and such as are less profusely favored with them, ought not to be dejected, or envious, in view of such as are. This, I take occasion to observe from the angelical visit which was paid to Joseph, not to his blessed spouse Mary, though she was so much superior to him. So, when we find St. Joseph, though so eminent in the sight of God, favored but in a dream with an angelical visit which was so much more to be coveted in the full enjoyment of the senses; we should learn not to be ungrateful to God, for the gifts of his bounty, by murmuring when they are not so extensive as our desires.

Thirdly, consider that it is by the special permission of the Almighty, that the elect are harassed by troubles and persecutions. It was doubtless no small affliction to the parents of Jesus that his life was sought after. For what more terrible news could be brought to them? It is true, they knew

him to be the Son of God ; but that was not sufficient to ward the inferior part from despondency.
Why, might they not have said, why, O Lord, since
thou art Almighty, should it be necessary to fly
with thy Son into Eygpt? Art thou not powerful
enough everywhere to preserve us unhurt? Why
should we be reduced to the painful necessity of
fleeing from our native land to a distant and unknown country, through rough and dangerous ways!
Add to this, that the divine infant was in an age
too tender, seemingly, for so laborious a journey,
being yet but two months old: and his parents unfit
for the fatigues as well as dangers of the road ; the
one, on account of her being so young, the other,
by reason of his age, and both, for want of necessaries to travel with, which their extreme poverty
denied them. If these were not matters of excessive
affliction, what are? Do you, therefore, when in tribulation, arm yourself with patience, nor expect
from your divine master those privileges which he
did not reserve for his mother, or himself.

Fourthly, consider his ineffable benignity. How
soon and how patiently does he submit to persecution for your sake, and to banishment from his own
country ; rather choosing meekly to fly from the
tyranny than to punish the tyrant: more solicitous
to prevent the commission of a crime, than to exercise his vengeance on the criminal. O how profound
is this patience and humility! He will neither do
injuries nor return them ; and therefore, meekly
contents himself with avoiding their consequences!
Thus does it behoove us to behave in regard to such
as abuse, ill-treat, or persecute us. Instead of making a like return, instead of loading them with the
effects of our vengeance, let us bear them with patience, and endeavor to avoid the rage of their

malice; nay, let us pray for them, and return them
good for evil, after the example which our divine
Master has elsewhere set us.

KING HEROD MURDERS THE INFANTS OF BETHLEHEM.

In fine, our Lord submitted to flee from the face
of his vassal, his servant, his slave; nay, from a
devil incarnate. In this journey he was borne along
by his mother in her tenderest youth, and by St.
Joseph, a feeble old man, through a rough, wild,
pathless, unfrequented, tedious length of road, to
Egypt; which requires a fortnight for a courier to
perform the journey; and they, perhaps, were some
months in effecting it. For, if we may credit tradition, they crossed that desert in which the children
of Israel remained forty years. And what hunger
and thirst must they not have endured before the

end of their journey? For how should such poor
and feeble persons be able to carry with them the
supply of provisions necessary for so long a journey?
And if they did not, where could they be supplied
in so trackless and uninhabited a wilderness? And
where, think you, could they find shelter from the
hardness of the ground, and the inclemency of the
air, to repose themselves by night, amidst a waste,
where houses might seem useless for want of inhabitants? Compassionate, therefore, these illustrious
sufferers, who must doubtless have labored under
many great and tedious difficulties and hardships,
as well in their own persons as in that of the divine
babe they carried with them. Accompany them in
mind, and share with them, the heavy toil of carrying the blessed infant; and wish to alleviate, as
much as possible, their excessive fatigues. Grudge
not to bear a little affliction and penance for yourselves; since so much has been borne for you by
others, by such great personages; nay, and so many
times. I will not give you, pious reader, any detail
of what happened to them on their way to Egypt;
all the idols in the country fell in pieces. They
travelled as far as Heliopolis, and there renting a
little cottage, dwelt for seven years in that place, in
the quality of poor, indigent, homeless strangers.

And here, devout Christian, we enter into an ample
and beautiful field for pious and tender meditation:
and therefore, attend diligently to the following reflections. Whence, and by what means, could they
procure even a homely subsistence for so long a
space of time as they remained in this country? Did
they content themselves, think you, with the idle
occupation of begging? No! we are informed by
several sacred writers, how ingenious as well as
industrious our blessed Lady was at sewing and

spinning, and that she was extremely assiduous in working for the support of her beloved Son and spouse. They were all constant lovers of poverty from the beginning, and continued so to the end of their immaculate lives.

Now, may we not suppose, that she was reduced to go from house to house to solicit for work? For how should the neighborhood know either her wants or her inclination to be employed, unless she did so? And yet, what reluctance must not this pattern of modesty have felt, in being obliged to expose her virginal bashfulness to the loose looks of curious and shameless gazers, by going abroad! Which, nevertheless, we may conceive she could not avoid doing, without taking her beloved spouse and help-mate from his labors, who, no doubt, was busy on his side in earning as much as old age would permit him, to aid his sacred spouse to support the blessed Jesus, till he came to an age to lessen their labor by his own. Indeed, when he came to the age of youth, we may without absurdity believe, that he partook of his mother's blushes, and shared in her labor, by carrying home the work as she finished it, and soliciting for more; for what other messenger can we suppose she had? So may we imagine, that often-times the frugal Virgin, to buy necessary food for him, was forced to send for the money which remained due to her for work unpaid, or to importune and implore for part of it at least. What humiliation must it not be for the Son of God to be sent on such errands? What must not her confusion be, to be reduced to send him on it? And, when the sacred youth carried home the labors of his parent to such as had employed her, and requested the fruits of her industry from them, might he not often meet with some riotous, abusive, noisy person, who, instead

of money, paid him with ill language, and shutting
the doors against him, sent him home empty? How
many such insults are not daily practised towards
poor and helpless strangers! And can we suppose
that Christ escaped them, who went thither in search
of them? How often has he come home hungry, as
children are wont to be, and, asking his mother for
bread, had the mortification to hear her answer him
with a sigh, that she had none to give him! What
anguish must she not feel on such occasions! With
what tender words would she try to appease his hunger and console him! With what redoubled industry
would she not labor to procure him the food he
called for! And how often has she not defrauded
her own mouth, and robbed it of its meal to spare
one for him! These, and such like points, are exceedingly pleasing as well as useful to meditate on, concerning Christ and his blessed mother. I have here
paved the way for you to do it. It is now your business to reap the advantage, by extending and pursuing with devotion such pious thoughts as these,
in order to become little with the little Jesus. Scorn
not therefore to reflect on the most humble and
minute circumstances that may be conceived to have
attended him, however childish they may appear in
the eye of worldings. For they are most evidently
capable of adding force to our devotion, and new
warmth to our love, to inflame our affection, to excite our compassion, to confer new purity and simplicity on our manners, to nourish in us a strong
desire for poverty and humility, to keep up in us a
certain familiarity of practice of the virtues we observe in these divine personages, to create in us a
kind of similitude and conformity with them, and
finally, to raise and strengthen our hopes of enjoying
the fruits of that goodness we so much admire and

wish to imitate in them. It is incompatible with
our low state to ascend to the sublimity of God. But
as St. Paul observes, *That which seems foolish of
him, is wiser than the greatest human prudence;
and that which seems weak, surpasses all the power
of man.* Besides, the meditation of these humble
subjects seems capable of abating, if not totally destroying our pride, of weakening our ambition, and
confounding our vain curiosity. So much good
comes from such spiritual employment. See, therefore, and endeavor to become little with the little
Jesus, that you may, without prejudice to humility,
grow up and be great in the same measure as he
was: follow him whithersoever he goes, and keep
your eyes always upon him.

But have you yet reflected enough to gather from
what has been said, how painful their poverty must
have been, and how mortifying to this modest
family? Had they, think you, the best of anything,
anything superfluous, anything curious? No, this
was contrary to a state of poverty; and, therefore,
she who loved poverty so well, would never have
consented to possess anything of this kind. Nay,
so scrupulous was she of giving way to curiosity, or
anything that seemed opposite to poverty or virtuous industry, that she would not at any price, nor
for the sake of any one, so much as put her finger to
rich, curious, trifling, or unnecessary work. No,
she would often say, when such trifles were brought
to her, let them work at this who have not their
time at heart. And how, indeed, could she, in such
a dejected state, afford to idle away so much precious time as is required in the contrivance as well as
working of expensive bawbles, of no signification
even when they are finished? Though poverty was
not the sole motive that kept her from such kind of

work : no, had she been less poor than she really was, she would have refused them alike : since such kind of employments, properly speaking, are but a more dangerous kind of idleness, as may appear from many reasons. First, because they are but an expensive method of wasting and misspending time : since all such kinds of labors require many more hours, not to say days and months, to complete them, than they possibly can be worth when finished. Secondly, because they are the causes of vain-glory, in such as work them. O how many fond and self-applauding looks does the worker throw away upon such idle pieces of ingenuity ! That curiously flowered apron, that embroidered mantle, this other trimming so richly woven, so well concerted ! How often, alas, how often does it engross the contriver's thoughts, even when away from it, even at the most sacred occupations ! And when the mind should be employed in studying how to render the soul more pleasing in the sight of God, it has enough to do to contrive, to carry on, to perfect a work of this nature, of no manner of consequence when it is done. This is a weakness the female sex are more particularly guilty of, a weakness so much the more to be lamented in them, as they are insensible, in general, how blameable it is. And yet I make no doubt but that devout sex will soon be convinced of it, if they but seriously reflect on the time they consume, the ill habits they gain, and the mischiefs they do, and all to tax themselves and others with an unmerited applause. Thirdly, these kinds of labors are improper on account of the pride they occasion in the persons they are done for. Experience shows us, that these things are the proper fuel to feed and foment the fire of pride. For, as what is mean and lowly cherishes humility, so what is curious and gaudy nourishes pride and vanity. Fourthly, they are the causes of alienating the soul from God : for St. Gregory very judiciously remarks, "The soul becomes more and more weaned from the divine love, in proportion as its affection for earthly objects increases." Fifthly, they are unhappy incitements to the concupiscence of the eye, one of the three great origins of sin in the world : for such vain objects can be useful to no other end than to attract the looks of the vain. And yet as often as any one takes delight in idle gazing on such vain and empty trifles, whether she be the worker or the wearer of them, so often she offends God. Sixthly, they are but too often a snare and bane to such as behold them ; who may many ways transgress by barely looking on them ; for example, by taking scandal, by coveting them, by envying the possessors of them, by rash judgments, by silent murmuring, or finally, by open detraction.

Think, therefore, how often, and how many ways God may be offended by such curious trifles, or rather laborious idleness, before they are brought to a conclusion ? And consider whether you, O female reader, and every effeminate worker of such needless curiosities, are not guilty instruments of all those evils ! Wherefore, whoever should persuade you to work for them such kind of things, you ought never to comply with their request, because no authority can justify your consenting to the vanity of others ; and whatever can possibly tend to offend God, is absolutely to be avoided. How much more then are you culpable if, of your own accord, you do it, to ingratiate yourselves, more desirous of rendering yourselves agreeable in the sight of man than of God. Leave, therefore, to worldlings such works as are indeed the proper trappings of the world, but held in aversion by God. It is not indeed astonishing that persons of little solidity and less piety should make such vain **amusements** their great business of life ; but what cannot be sufficiently wondered at is, that the more devout part, they, who are desirous of attaining to perfect purity of conscience, should defile themselves with such filth, such mere litter ! When it is plain to be seen how many evils are produced from it, of which it is not perhaps the least dangerous to one, to act so opposite to the spirit of poverty. To conclude in a word, such kind of employments are strong signs of levity, vanity, and inconstancy, in the generality of those who give themselves up to them. Be you, therefore, O spiritual Christian, as apprehensive of such amusements as you would be of playing with the venomous serpent. I would not, however, be thought to condemn all beautiful works of ingenuity. Nothing is more innocent than these pretty productions of fancy, which are designed only for a short relaxation from more intense applications of the mind, but especially such works as are dedicated to the service of God at his altar ; provided they be done without too much affection, delight, or attachment of heart, for that is absolutely to be taken care of. All I mean to decry, are those curious nothings, which tend only to feed vanity, to nourish luxury, to bring poverty to scorn, to enervate devotion, and wean the affections of the soul from the Creator to the creature. Of this kind of curiosities hear what St. Bernard thinks: "Tell me, I beseech you," says he, "what can such vanities avail the body, or what advantage do they bring to the soul ! They are at best, but a poor, empty childish satisfaction." It were hard to invent a severer imprecation on those, who, despising the peaceful enjoyment of pleasant repose, delight in the restlessness of curiosity, than to wish they may be condemned to the possession of whatever they hanker after.

But let us return from this long digression, into which the detestable error of curiosity led me, to contemplate our blessed Lady in Egypt, amidst her labors of sewing, knitting, spinning, etc. Think how diligently, humbly, and patiently she persevered in these exercises, without slackening in the least her motherly care of her divine Son, or the business of her family, still assiduous to her devout exercises of watching and prayer, whenever her necessary occupations permitted her the leisure. Compassionate her, therefore, and at the same time make this useful reflection: that even the Queen of Heaven purchased heaven by violence: and can you then **expect** to obtain **it** otherwise ? It is not improbable, however, that some charitable matrons of her neighborhood, witnesses of her great industry and extreme poverty, might now and then send her some small relief, which she submitted to accept with humility and thankfulness. Though it is equally probable that the holy St. Joseph was as industrious as his great age would permit him, to earn a support for his family at the laborious trade of **a** carpenter. Thus you see what ample objects of compassion rise before you at every step. Pause here awhile: then, requesting the blessing of the divine Jesus and his parent, take leave of these innocent exiles, who, banished without cause from their native land, are reduced to wander, and earn their bread in a foreign country, by the sweat of their brows.

JESUS IN THE HOLY HOUSE AT NAZARETH.

CHAPTER XII.

OUR LORD RETURNS FROM EGYPT.

WHEN the Lord had completed his seven years'
exile in Egypt, an angel appeared to Joseph
in a dream, and bid him carry back the Youth and
his Mother to the land of Israel: for they are now
dead who sought the death of the boy. Joseph
therefore patiently took the child and his mother,
and returned to the country of the Israelites; but
at his arrival upon the borders, hearing that Ar-

chelaus, the son of Herod, reigned there, he began to dread going any farther, till again instructed by the angel he **retired** into Galilee, to the city of Nazareth; **which,** according to the martyrology, was much about the same time of the year as the Epiphany.

Here again, you see, as before, how God often sends his revelations, spiritual comforts, and other graces only as it were by halves, and not according to the fulness of our wishes. This may appear from two circumstances. First, from his sending the angel to Joseph, not openly, but in a dream. Secondly, from the angel's not giving him his whole instructions at once, but at two several times. Indeed the gloss says, that God did so, because St. Joseph, and every one blest in the like manner, must be more certain of their vision from a repetition of it. But be that as it **may,** we ought to set a value upon every the least gift of heaven, and be grateful for it, since we ought to assure ourselves that God disposes everything on his part for our greatest benefit.

But now let us accompany our Saviour on his return from Egypt. Be you, devout reader, very attentive to it; it is rich in matter of pious meditation. **Return then** mentally to Egypt, with the pure intention of visiting the child Jesus; fancy yourself to find him among other children, with whom he deigns to play for their spiritual good. Imagine that he runs to meet you: for he is all affability, bounty, and courtesy. Fly then to anticipate him, and throwing yourself on **your** knees, adore and kiss **his** sacred feet: then rising, take him into your arms, devoutly embrace him, and dwell a while in this sweet contemplation. Think you **hear** him say to you: "Welcome hither, O devout soul, partake of the joy with me, of our being again at liberty to return to Israel; and since you are come hither at so favorable a juncture, stay with me, and join us in our journey." In consequence of which, express your joy to him, the desire you have of accompanying him always, and everywhere, and the delight you take in conversing with him. Though, as I have already observed to you, these kinds of pious thoughts may, and undoubtedly will, seem childish in the opinion of worldings; yet you know that a devout and frequent meditation on them will yield you a more than common consolation, and dispose you to greater and more sublime subjects. After this, fancy yourself led by our divine Saviour to his parents, who graciously receive, and courteously treat you. Throw yourself again on your knees, and, devoutly revering them, remain along with them.

The next morning when they are ready to set out on their journey, imagine you see some of the most respectable matrons of the city, and the wiser part of the men, come to accompany them out of the gates, in acknowledgment of their peaceful, neighborly, and pious manner of living and conversing while among them. For doubtless they had given notice some days beforehand of their departure, that they might not seem to steal away in a clandestine manner, which might have looked suspicious; now they had not the same reason for doing it as when they fled into Egypt, to preserve the infant Jesus from the hands of a butcher. And now suppose them setting out, holy Joseph, accompained by the men going before, and our Lady following, attended by the matrons. Do you, therefore, take the blessed infant in your arms, and devoutly carry him before her, for she suffers him not out of her presence.

When they are out of the gates, the holy Joseph
dismisses the company, not suffering them to go on
any farther; when one of the wealthiest of them
calls the child Jesus, and in compassion to the poverty
of his parents, bestows a few pence upon **him**; and
the rest of the company, after the example of the first,
do the same.   Compassionate here the confusion of
the divine child, who blushing, holds out his little
hands to receive what the love of poverty has reduced
him to want; pity likewise his holy parents, who
share his confusion with him, and think on the great
lesson here set you, when you see him who made the
earth, and all that is in it, make choice of so rigorous
a poverty, and so penurious a **life, for his** blessed
parents and himself.   What lustre **does** not the
virtue of poverty receive from their practice!   And
how can we behold it in them, without **being** charmed
to the love and imitation **of** the **like** perfection!
After returning thanks to their company, and taking
their leave, they proceed on their journey.   But
how, think you, was the infant Jesus able to go
through the fatigues of so long a way?   When he
went into Egypt, his infancy made it easy **for** his
parents to carry him; but now too big to be carried,
he is yet too little and tender to walk.   Possibly **in-**
deed some tender-hearted neighbor might bestow
on them an ass to carry him on.   Yet, O admirable
Child! O delicate Youth! O Sovereign of heaven
and earth! How soon did you begin, and what
labors did you not consent to suffer for our sakes!
Well might these words prophetically apply to **you**:
I am poor, and subject to labors from my youth.
What extreme penury! What endless toil! What
bodily hardships, and rigorous treatment of yourself
did **you** not assume for our sakes! Should not
this **very** labor of yours we are now meditating on

have sufficed to redeem us? Take then the child
Jesus, O devout reader, and in your imagination
place him devoutly on the ass, conduct him carefully,
and when he is inclined to dismount, receive him joyfully in your arms, and tenderly cherish him, until his
blessed mother comes up, who may be supposed to
walk slower. Then resign the divine child to her
arms, the reception of whom will serve her instead
of repose.

Thus they repass the desert they came through,
where you may frequently compassionate them on
the way, on account of the little rest they receive,
though wasted day and night with fatigue. When
they reach the utmost skirt of the wilderness, they
find there John the Baptist, who already begins to do
penance, though priveleged from sin. It is said, that
that part of Jordan where John baptized, is the same
which the children of Israel passed over, when they
came through this desert out of Egypt; and that John
did penance near the same place. So that it is not
improbable that Christ might find him there on his
return from Egypt. Fancy then you see him joyfully receiving them : who, after remaining with him
awhile, and partaking of his coarse and homely provisions, share with him in return, the sweets of
spiritual recreation, and then depart. You, therefore, at meeting and parting, omit not to pay your
reverence to the Saint, but throw yourself at his feet,
and devoutly kissing them, recommend yourself to
the intercession of this youth, excellent and wonderful in every circumstance of his life. He was the
first hermit, the founder and pattern of all who make
choice of a religious and solitary life : he was an un-
spotted virgin, an excellent preacher, more than a
prophet, and a glorious martyr. After parting from
John, the blessed travellers cross over Jordan, and

call at the house of Elizabeth, where they pass some time in mutual congratulations, spiritual joy, and celestial mirth. Here Joseph being informed that Archelaus reigned in Judea, and admonished in a dream by an angel, they retired to the city of Nazareth in Galilee.

And now we have brought back the child Jesus out of Egypt, at whose return, the sisters, and other relations and friends of our blessed Lady, came to congratulate with them in Nazareth, where they remained and pursued their usual love of poverty. From this time, to the twelfth year of his age, nothing remarkable is recorded of the blessed Jesus. It is said, however, and it is not improbable, that the fountain is still to be seen there, out of which he used to draw water for his mother. For our truly humble Lord often did such humble offices for her, as she had no one else to do them. Here, too, we may suppose, that St. John the Evangelist, who was then about five years old, often came to visit our Lord, accompanied by his mother, who was sister to the Blessed Virgin. For it is written of him, that he died sixty-seven years after our Lord's passion, in the ninety-eighth year of his age; so that at the time of Christ's suffering, which was when he was something turned of thirty-three years old, St. John was thirty-one; and consequently, the one being seven years old at his return from Egypt, the other must be five. Imagine then, you see these holy children conversing together, and contemplate their conversation in such a manner as the Holy Ghost shall vouchsafe to inspire. What will greatly help your contemplation is, to reflect that this John was afterwards that disciple whom Christ loved the most, and conversed the most familiarly with.

THE HOLY CHILD IS FOUND AMONG THE DOCTORS IN THE TEMPLE.

CHAPTER XIII.

OUR LORD JESUS REMAINS IN JERUSALEM.

WHEN our Lord was twelve years old he went
up with his parents to Jerusalem, according
to the law and custom of the festival, which lasted
eight days. Again, then, the divine Jesus undertakes the labor of a long journey, to honor his
heavenly Father on the days consecrated to him ;
for infinite was the love between the Father and

Son. But the joy, which the external pomp and honor paid to his Father gave the holy Jesus, fell greatly short of the affliction and bitter anguish of heart he felt on account of the many crimes by which sinners dishonored him. Thus then was the Lord of the law observant of the law; and thus humbly did the Creator of the greatest mingle with the least of his creatures. When the octave was ended, his parents returning home, he remained in Jerusalem. Here, pious reader, be attentive and render yourself present to everything that passes; you will find the subject equally devout and profitable. I have already told you, that Nazareth, the place of Christ's abode, is about fifteen miles distant from Jerusalem. When, therefore, in the evening, our blessed Lady and St. Joseph, who had taken different roads, met at the inn where they were to put up for that night, the Virgin not seeing the child with her spouse, in whose company she expected him to return, immediately asks him: "Where is the child Jesus?" To whom he answers with equal surprise and concern, "Is he not with you? Alas! I thought he returned in your company; he came not with me, neither know I what is become of him." Shocked at this unexpected, and unlooked for reply, the frightened mother bursting into a flood of tears, cries: "No, ah, no, he came not with me. Alas, alas! is this the care I should have taken of my child? Is all my tenderness come to this?" Then rushing forth distracted with anxiety, she runs from house to house, with all the composure so much grief was capable of: "Tell me, oh! neighbors, tell me, have ye seen my son? Where is my child? For pity's sake, who has my child? Ah, dearest Jesus! where are you? What is come of you, my dear, my only child?" Thus ran the anxious Virgin from place to place, distracted and lost to comfort amidst her grief and care; the blessed Joseph in tears everywhere followed to console her. But what consolation could either of them receive when they found not the divine Jesus? What must their sorrow be, especially hers, whose tenderness must be greater! What could avail the comfort their neighbors, their friends, their relations endeavored to give them? Can aught compensate for the loss of Jesus? Do you, therefore, condole with this blessed couple, whose afflictions must be greater than tongue can express. For which of all the troubles they ever suffered could equal this? Let us not then be discontented, when trouble visits us, since Jesus thought not fit to spare his parents. It is his divine permission that afflictions should come, they are so many proofs of his love to us, and are calculated for our benefit.

The blessed Virgin finding all her searches to no purpose, retires sorrowful to her chamber, and throwing herself on her knees, with tears of humility mixed with confidence, she thus addressed herself to God, her constant refuge and holy comfort: "O God, my Father, my eternal Lord, my all-sweet and benign benefactor! You vouchsafed to bestow your beloved Son upon me, and I, alas, have lost him; nor know I where to seek him. Restore him to me again; oh! restore him to me! Remove, O Father, this bitter heaviness from me, and show me your Son! I have acted incautiously, but I knew not that I did so. Look not therefore on my negligence, but on the excess of my affliction; and, out of your immense goodness, give me back my Son, without whom life would be a death to me. Oh! where are you, my dearest Son? What is come of you? Who enjoys the blessing of cherishing you in my stead?

Are you returned to heaven to your divine Father! For I know you are the Son of God, and God yourself! Why then did you not acquaint me with your departure, that I might once more have embraced you in these arms, and pressed these lips to your divine mouth before I lost you? Or rather, has not some insidious mortal laid a snare for you? For I know you are truly man, begotten of this **flesh of** mine. Too well I remember the hurrying you away to Egypt in your tenderest infancy, to preserve you from the rage of Herod. And too much, too much I dread, you are fallen into the hands of such another tyrant. But, oh, may your heavenly Father preserve you from every harm, my dearest child! Return, oh dearest Jesus, to your afflicted mother; or let me know but where you are, and I will come to you! Forgive this one neglect, and I will never neglect you more. When did I ever offend you, that you should leave me thus? I know you are not unacquainted with the grief that overwhelms me; oh, ease me then, my dearest Son, and delay not returning to me. Did I, ever since I have borne you, eat, sleep, or live without you before? And now I am without you without knowing how. You know you are all my hope, my life, **my** joy, and that I cannot subsist without you. Instruct me then, where you are, or how I may find you."

With these and such like ejaculations, the holy mother of Christ soothed her sorrow till the next morning, when, by break of day, they went forth seeking him round all the neighboring villages; for there were many ways from Jerusalem to the place where they then were. Not finding him this day, they went the next in search of him to other places, and along other ways, enquiring among all their friends and relations; and now, not finding him, the

afflicted mother redoubles her fears and anxiety.
But the third day returning to Jerusalem, they found
him in the temple, sitting in the midst of the doctors.
No sooner did the blessed Virgin cast her eyes on
the beloved child, than, transported with a sudden
and inexpressible joy, she throws herself on her
knees, and with tears of consolation, returns her sin-
cerest thanks to God. The divine youth, seeing his
mother, came up to her, who immediately clasping
him in her arms, pressed, embraced, and sweetly
fondled him. Now she tenderly prints her kisses
on his cheeks, and holding him at her bosom, stands
immovable, unable, as yet, through an excess of
tender transport, to speak to him : till the desire of
possessing him again in safety, stopped the over-
flow of joy, and gave her words a vent. Then, looking wishfully on him, " Why, ah, why, my dearest
Child, have you used us thus? With what grief
have not I and your Father been seeking you!"
" Why," said he, " did you seek me? Know you
not that it behooves me to attend to my Father's
business?" But this they did not understand the
meaning of. The joyful mother immediately informs
her Son of her desire to return to Nazareth. "My
Son," said she, "it is my desire that we go back to
our peaceful home : and will you not console me
with your company thither?" "Yes, O beloved
parent," replies this pattern of obedience, " your
pleasure shall be mine." And what he said he performed, returning with his parents to Nazareth, submitting wholly to their will in all things, as other
children ought to do.

You have beheld then the affliction of the blessed
mother on this occasion ; and now consider the
hardships of her divine Son, during these three
days. Imagine then you see him at the door of some

poor man craving admittance, where he is received, and sparingly helped to food. Thus the poor child Jesus delights to associate with the poor. Next consider him sitting amidst the doctors : where, with a serene, wise, and respectful countenance, he questions them as if he were ignorant of the things he asks : all which he does partly out of humility, partly not to confound them with the miraculous readiness of his solutions.

Here, likewise, you may consider three very remarkable truths. The first is, that whoever wishes to be united to God, must not be attached to parents, friends, or relations, but renounce them. For Christ, when he was intent upon the affairs of his heavenly Father, forsook his beloved mother, and was not to be found among any of his relations. The second is, that no one who leads a spiritual life, ought to wonder, if he is sometimes in a sterility of devotion, and seems to be forsaken by God, since the same thing happened even to the mother of God. Let not such persons then be cast down, but seek and endeavor to find him, by persisting in devout meditation and pious works. The third is, that no one should be tenacious of their own will or purpose ; for though our Lord Jesus has said, that it was proper for him to attend to the work of his divine Father, yet he changed his purpose, and followed the inclination of his blessed mother, and accompanied her and her holy spouse to Nazareth ; where he remained, submissive to their will. In this you may likewise admire his profound humility, of which we shall take more notice hereafter.

THE PREACHING OF JOHN THE BAPTIST.

CHAPTER XIV.

OUR Lord Jesus, therefore, returned from the temple and from Jerusalem with his parents to Nazareth, and lived under obedience with them till the beginning of his thirtieth year. Nor do we find in sacred scripture anything he did remarkable during that time. What then shall we admire in him, or conceive him to have done during so great an interval! For if he did anything worthy admiration, why was it not recorded as well as the rest of his actions? It seems surprisingly strange! But take notice here, that his doing nothing wonderful was a kind of miraculous action. For nothing that attends his life is void of mystery. While he was spending his life in practical virtue, he kept silent, seemingly inactive, and abstracted. This sovereign Master then, who was to teach all virtues, and to point out the path of life, began from his youth, by sanctifying in his own person the practice of the virtuous life he came to teach, and that in a private ineffable manner, unheard of before; that is, appearing in the eyes of the world useless, abject, and simple, as we may devoutly conceive without danger of rashness. Though I do not pretend to affirm anything of this kind, or any other indeed which is not evidently confirmed by the holy scriptures, or the traditions of the Fathers, as I have already declared in the beginning of this work.

Our Saviour then during this space of time, as we may reasonably conjecture, retired, as much as possible, from the company and conversation of men; spending much time in the synagogue, which was the Church of **that** day, where, in the lowest place, he would remain for a long time recollected in fervent prayer to his divine Father. Thence he would return home to his beloved mother and her blessed spouse, whose labor he would often alleviate by his assistance. He would pass and repass amidst the busy world about him, with an air of as little attention to their affairs, as if he did not see mankind: and these would stupidly wonder that so fine a youth should be seen to do nothing worthy their praise. All expected him to make a shining and considerable figure among them. For while he was a boy, he increased equally in age and wisdom in the sight of God and man. But growing up from his twelfth to his thirtieth year, he was not remarkable for any actions either during his youth or manhood above the common sphere: which occasioned an universal surprise, and drew upon him the derision of the public, who used to call him a useless idiot, an insignificant creature, and a stupid mortal, or by some such opprobrious titles. Neither did he apply to any learning, insomuch that it became a kind of proverb to say, that he was but an old minor. Such a life did he lead and persist in, though it brought him into contempt with all men, who looked upon him as mean and contemptible, which he previously foretold of himself by the mouth of his prophet, saying, *I am a worm, and not a man.*

You see then, how much our Lord did, though seeming to do nothing; he rendered himself mean and despicable to all, as I have already said. And certainly I know no greater or more difficult practice in all the duties of life than this. And they, in my opinion, may be said to have reached the very summit of Christian perfection, who are so far advanced in it as to be able totally to overcome the arrogance of their flesh, and truly and unfeignedly to consent to be reputed as nothing, and even contemned **as** mean and insignificant. A victory over one's self of this nature is greater and more glorious than the sacking a strongly-garrisoned town, according to the words of Solomon. "The patient man is better than the strong one, **and** he that conquers his spirit than the conquerers of a city."—*Prov.* xvi. Until you arrive to this point, never flatter yourself with having done anything. For, as in reality we are but useless, even when we have done our best, according to to the words of Christ, till we attain to this degree of humility, we are nothing at all, but a vain and empty mass; which the Apostle very plainly expresses, "Whoever thinks himself to be something, being really nothing, deceives himself."—*Gal.* vi. If you ask why our Lord practiced **this**, I shall answer you, that it was not on his own account, but for your instruction. And therefore, Christian, if you do not profit from so great a lesson, you become inexcusable. For it is an abomination to see a worm, and the destined food for worms, strutting with arrogance, and vainly raising himself, when the Lord of Majesty deigns to stoop to so abject a degree of humiliation.

If any one should deem it an absurdity to believe that our Lord Jesus **led** for so long a time such **a life** of seeming inactivity as here mentioned, and is rather disposed to think the evangelists defective in the accounts they give of him : I answer, in the first place, that the example of so much and such great virtue, cannot properly **be** called a state of inactivity; since it was the most useful lesson he could give us, as being, properly speaking, the foundation of all virtue. Secondly, it is written in the Gospel of St. John, "When the comforter shall come, the Spirit of Truth whom I send to you from the Father, who proceeds from the Father, he will give testimony of me, and ye shall give testimony of me, because you are with me (that is, in the quality of preachers) from the beginning."—*John* xv. And Peter says, at the election of St. Matthias the Apostle, "It is proper out of these men, etc., from the time of our Lord Jesus entering in among us, beginning from the baptism of John, etc."—*Acts* i. "Now he was then beginning about thirty years old." —*Luke* iii. John then had not been his precursor, had Jesus suffered them to preach sooner. Besides, if he or they had begun their mission sooner, how comes it that he was then so little among his neighbors, that they should enquire, "Is not this the carpenter's son?"—*Matt.* xiii. When, in a very short time after, he was commonly called the Son of David. If then he had begun sooner to do anything remarkable, something of it, at least, would have been hinted in holy scripture, and all the evangelists would not have been so profoundly silent about him. This seems to be the opinion of St. Bernard, as I shall hereafter quote him. But however the truth of it may be, I cannot but think it a very pious matter for meditation. It is thus the Lord Jesus forms the sword of humility, as the prophet foretold him: "Gird on thy sword upon thy loins, O thou most powerful!"—*Psal.* xliv. And with what sword was it more proper to conquer the infernal prince of pride, than with that of humility? For we nowhere read of his having engaged him with the weapons of his greatness, but the opposite ones, even at the time of his passion, when he seemed to stand in need of all his immensity. Hence the same prophet bemoans him to his heavenly **Father**, saying, "You have averted from him the **help of** his sword, and **have not** assisted in the battle."—*Ps.* **lxxxviii.** You see then, Christian reader, how our Lord "began first **how to** do, **and** then to teach."—*Acts* i. Designing one day to invite you to the imitation of him, with those ineffable words, "Learn **from me**, for I am meek and humble of heart."—*Matt.* **xi.** This then was the virtue he first chose to practise ; and that not in outward show only, but from the inmost recesses of his heart, for he **was truly** meek and humble **of** heart. He was incapable of fiction, and therefore readily humbled himself to seem and **be** mean and abject in the eyes of men ; insomuch that even after he began to preach his sublime **and heavenly** doctrine, and confirmed it with miracles, their contempt of him continued, and they would often say of him in derision, "Who is this ? **Is not** this the carpenter's son?"—*Matt.* xiii., **with** other like scornful expressions. According to this sense then, it appears how truly the **apostle** said, "He exanimated himself, taking the form of a servant."—*Philip* ii. And not only of a servant, in one sense, by taking human flesh, but **in** the lowest sense of the word, that is, he took the form of a useless servant, by the lowliness and abject manner of his living.

Would you see how powerfully our Lord put on this sword ? Consider his every action, and you will find humility shining in all its lustre. Do but recollect, and you will find it in every action hitherto taken notice of. And in those which follow, you may observe, that he was so far from neglecting the practice of it, that he increases in humility during his whole life, giving us frequent lessons of it to the hour of his death, and even after death, nay, after his ascension. Did not he towards his end wash his disciples' feet? Was he not extremely humbled by the cross he bore on his divine shoulders? Did he not, after his resurrection, when in a glorified state, call his disciples, brethren? "Go," says he to Mary Magdalen, "and tell my brethren, etc."—*John* xx. And even after his ascension, did he not converse familiarly with Paul, and as humbly as if he had been his equal? "Saul, Saul, why persecutest thou me?"—*Acts* ix. Where he does not call himself God, but me. And finally at the great and tremendous day of judgment, will he not, from his majestic and awful tribunal, say, "As long as ye have done it to one of the least of my brethren, you have done it to me."—*Matt.* xxv.

It was not without reason our Saviour showed such a love for humility. He knew that as pride is the foundation of all sin, so humility is the basis of every virtue, and the first step to salvation. It is but a tottering edifice that is not built upon the groundwork of humility. Wherefore, trust not to your chastity, to your poverty, or any other virtue you are possessed of, unless it be accompanied with, and supported by humility. It was Christ then that first laid this foundation, and showed how it is to be acquired, namely, by vilifying and lowering himself in his own esteem, and in the opinion of all the world, and by the uninterrupted exercise of self-humiliation. Go you, then, O attentive Christian, and do the like, if you would be perfectly humble, as becomes a Christian; for humility, self-contempt, and the practice of lowly and vilifying work, must precede all other virtues. In relation to which, thus says St. Bernard: "Humility, which is obtained by

humiliation is the basis of all spiritual structures.
For humiliation is as truly the way to humility, as
patience is to peace, or reading to knowledge. If
you thirst after humility, be not averse to humiliation. For if you cannot stoop to humiliation, you
will never be able to rise to humility." And in
another place: "Whoever means to raise himself
above himself, must set out by thinking meanly of
himself: lest, soaring above his sphere, he fall beneath it, for want of being perfectly grounded in
humility. And, as there is no becoming in reality
great, but by the merit of endeavoring to be little,
therefore, whoever is desirous of rising to perfection, must restrain himself by humility, that humility may raise him." Wherefore, gentle reader,
when you see yourself humbled, rejoice at it; it is a
good sign, and an argument of approaching grace.
"For as the heart is exalted before a fall, so before
exaltation it is humbled."—*Prov.* xvi. For it is
alike written, that "God resists the proud, and gives
grace to the humble."—*Jam.* iv. And a little
farther he adds, "It is doing but little to submit to
the humiliations which come immediately from God,
unless we learn to accept cheerfully those he is
pleased to send us by the means of his creatures."
Learn an admirable example of this from holy David,
who, being cursed by a servant, was too much animated with grace to be moved with resentment of
the injury. "What is there," says he, "between me
and you, oh Sons of Servai."— 4 *Kings* xiv. Oh, true
man according to God's own heart, not moved to
indignation or anger, by the scornful reproaches of
a slave! Well might he say with a safe conscience,
"If I return evil to those that did evil to me."—*Ps.*
vii. Let this much suffice, at present, on the virtue
humility.

Now let us return to the life and actions of Christ, which is and ought to be the mirror of ours, and the principle object of our intention. Be present then, as I have often exhorted you, to all that relates to him. And contemplate that blessed family, small indeed in number, but great in dignity, rich in grace and virtue, but poor and humble in their manner of living. The venerable old man, Joseph, sought with all possible industry, as much employment in his humble profession, as his feeble age would permit him to go through: and our Lady was as diligent at her manual labor, besides the business of her family, which we may suppose was not little, the preparing of food for her divine Son, her blessed spouse, and self, with other domestic labors arising from this, were all done with her own hands, as she was too poor to have any one to help her. Compassionate her therefore for the laborious life she leads; compassionate likewise our divine Lord, who shares with both their most laborious occupations, for " he came to minister, and not to be ministered to," as he himself says.—*Matt. xx.* Fancy then you see him busied along with his beloved parents, in the most servile work of their little mansion. Devoutly imagine you see these three sacred persons sitting at their frugal meals, not made up of dainties or expensive food, flattering to the palate and inflaming to the passions, but composed of the coarse and homely provisions usual among the poorest people. What sublime, what heavenly conversation passes between them! No vain, no idle discourse finds admittance there; but every sentence is holy, full of wisdom, and dictated by the Holy Ghost. O ineffable banquet, where the mind is no less substantially nourished than the body! After their meals, all retire to prayers, each to their little separate chambers ; our blessed Lady to hers, St. Joseph to his, and our Saviour to his. Follow our divine Lord in your mind, and view him devoutly persisting in fervent prayer to his heavenly Father. In this little cell, after spending the greatest part of his nights in heavenly contemplation, he reposes the remaining part on the ground, as meanly as the poorest of his creatures. Thus do you each night endeavor to accompany him in your mind. O concealed divinity ! why do you thus afflict that precious, that innocent body so continually, when the fatigue of one such night might suffice to redeem the whole world ? Did the excess of your love urge you to all this ? Such was your ardent zeal for the lost sheep you came to convey to heaven on your divine shoulders ! Must you, O King of Kings, eternal God, who supply the wants of all, who afford all persons of all stations what is requisite for them ; must you, I say, be subject to poverty, meanness, and hardship, watching and fasting, and must every circumstance of your life be attended with severity ? What then shall become of those who seek nothing but ease, luxury and vanity ? Surely we did not learn this kind of empty pursuits from this mortified master ! Are we then wiser than he is ? No, he has taught us both by word and by example, humility, poverty, mortification of the flesh, and exercise of the body : let us then improve from the lessons of this sublime teacher, who neither will nor can deceive. And, according to the Apostle's advice, "having food and raiment let us be content with them."—*Tim.* vi. And make such use of them as proper necessity requires ; but not to superfluity ; at the same time, carefully and constantly attending to the spiritual study and exercise of other Christian virtues.

JESUS IS BAPTIZED BY JOHN IN THE JORDAN.

CHAPTER XV.

THE BAPTISM OF OUR LORD JESUS CHRIST.

OUR Saviour, after having lived so painful and abject a life until he was completely twenty-nine years old, when he entered into his thirtieth year, said to his mother, "The time is now come for me to glorify God and manifest my Father, by appearing in the world, and working the salvation of man, for which he sent me. Be of good heart, therefore, O beloved mother, for I will soon return to you." Then kneeling to her, as a man and her son, the great master of humility asks and receives her blessing. Then she kneels to him as God, receives his blessing, and tenderly embracing him, with tears, thus addresses him : "Go, my blessed Son, go with the blessing of your divine Father and mine, be mindful of me, and hasten to return to comfort me." Thus then the blessed **Jesus** respectfully taking leave of his beloved mother and her venerable spouse, sets out from Nazareth towards Jerusalem by the way of the Jordan, where he found John baptizing. Thus the Lord of the world proceeds alone, for as yet he had no disciples. View him then attentively, in the presence of God, and see him travelling alone, barefooted, through a long and rugged road, and condole with him. O Lord, whither are you going, and by what ways ? Are you not the Sovereign of all the kings of the earth ? Where then, O Lord, are your nobles, your soldiers, your attendants, and equipage ? **Where are** your guards to keep off the populace from approaching too near your sacred person, as other monarchs are wont to have ? Where are the trumpets, the instruments, and royal ensigns ? Who goes before to prepare a palace for your reception ? Where are all the honors paid to the royal worms of this world ? Are not the heavens and the earth filled with your glory ? Why then do you proceed thus inglorious ? "Do not a thousand thousands pay homage to you in your kingdom above, and millions minister to you ?"—*Dan.* vii. Why then do you thus travel alone, a-foot, nay, barefooted ? But ah ! the cause is plain ; you are not now in your kingdom. "For your kingdom is not of this world."—*John* xviii. "You have exanimated yourself, taking the form of a servant."—*Phil.* ii. "You are become as one of us, a wayfarer and a stranger. —*Ps.* xxxviii. Like our fathers, you are become a servant, that we may become kings. You are to conduct us to your own kingdom, putting us in the way that leads thither. Why then, alas, do we go out of it ? Why do we not follow you ? Why do we not humble ourselves, but pursue and delight in vain honors, empty pomp, and passing enjoyments ? It must surely be because this is our kingdom, and that we consider ourselves as natives here, and not as pilgrims ; otherwise, why should we be so much taken up here ? O senseless sons of men, why do you embrace the shadow instead of the substance ? Why prefer ye the dubious and transitory to what is certain and lastingly solid ? Why so earnest in giving up eternity for what is but temporal ! Ah, it is too true, O Lord, that we forget our being but pilgrims and strangers upon earth, otherwise we should find no difficulty in following you. We should be content with what is merely necessary on the way ; and, without burdening ourselves, or retarding our journey with more, follow you, running on after the sweet-scented odor of your perfumes, we should be free from every load, and looking on the transitory things of this life as something behind us, or out of our way, we should neglect and despise them. Thus then our Lord Jesus humbly travels on some days' journey, till he arrives at the river Jordan.

When he arrived at the Jordan, he there found John baptizing sinners, and a great multitude of people, who were come thither to hear his preaching : for they took him to be Christ. Jesus therefore says to him : "I entreat you to baptize me along with these people." John looking steadfastly on him, and knowing him in spirit, with fear and reverence answered, "Lord, I myself need to be baptized by you." "Persist not, John," replies Christ, "but let it be done as I say ; for it is expedient that I fulfil all justice. Conceal, at present, what you know of me, for my time is not yet come. Baptize me, therefore, for now is a time of humiliation, and therefore will I practise humility in its greatest perfection."

Be mindful, then, of the practice of humility ; especially as we shall now treat of it with more particularity. The commentary on this place tells us, that there are three degrees in humility. The first is, to be subject to those above us, and not to prefer ourselves to those who are equal to us. The second is, to subject ourselves to our equals, and not to prefer ourselves to our inferiors. The third and most perfect is, to place ourselves beneath and subject ourselves to our inferiors. This is the degree Christ practised on this occasion, and therefore he fulfilled all humility. You may hence observe how wonderfully Christ advanced in humility, by comparing this with the foregoing chapter. There he contented himself with the appearance of a mean and abject, nay, useless servant ; here he subjects himself to his own servant, depreciates himself, and extols the other. There he humbly conversed with mankind, under the outward appearance of insignificance ; but here his humility is so improved, that he puts on the likeness of a sinner, and is contented to pass for one. For John was preaching penance to, and baptizing sinners, yet our humble Lord Jesus will be baptized in their presence, nay, in company with them. "He came," says St. Bernard, "amidst a crowd of populace to the baptism of John. And he came as one out of the sinful multitude, who was the only one exempt from sin." To judge from those about him, who would think him to be the Son of

God? Who would take him for the great Lord of Majesty: How great is his humility on this occasion? The same humility indeed appeared at his circumcision, when he likewise took on him the likeness of a sinner; but here it shone forth with greater lustre, in proportion to the greater number of spectators. But was there not room to apprehend, that the appearance of a sinner might prejudice him who intended to preach publicly to sinners? Be that as it may, it was not a motive strong enough to hinder this great master of humility from profoundly humbling himself. It was his pleasure to seek scorn and self-humiliation, by appearing what he was not on purpose to leave us a practical lesson. But what use do we make of that instruction, who, on the contrary, put on the likeness of everything but our real selves, purely to deceive the world, that they may praise and honor us?—If we think we possess any good qualities, how solicitous are we to expose them to the eyes of the world; and how industrious are we, on the other side, to cover all our defects, though ever so conscious of being sinners? Where is the humility of this? Is this the use we make of Christ's instruction? In relation to this, hear what St. Bernard says: "There is a humility produced by charity, which helps to kindle it; but there is another humility void of all warmth, which is engendered by self-convicting truth. The latter consists in reflection, the former in affection. For if at the light of truth you look seriously on yourself, without flattery or favor, you cannot help being humbled, and appearing contemptible in your own eyes, from this true reflection, though you perhaps are unwilling to appear so in the eyes of others. By these means you will be humble indeed by the operation of truth, but not by the infusion of char-

ity. For were your heart as sincerely humbled as
your mind is convinced of your deserving to be so,
by the light of that truth which has so faithfully
given you to yourself, you would, doubtless, be
willing that others should discover in you the defor-
mities which self-conviction has shown to yourself.
Though it must be owned, that it is neither advis-
able nor expedient to reveal all that passes within
us, and therefore charity and truth jointly forbid us
to publish such things of ourselves, as may injure
us, or give offence to others. But who can doubt
of your disregard for truth, if, captivated by self-
love, you conceal the truth of your own unworthiness, which you are inwardly convinced of ? You
prove it sufficiently, by preferring to that truth
your own interest and vain honor." And afterwards
he adds : " If then you are really humble with that
true humiliation which truth, the great searcher of
hearts, infuses into the soul, add the humility of
the will to it, and make a virtue of necessity. For
there is no true virtue without the consent of the
will ; which will then be effected, if the desire of
outward esteem in the eyes of your neighbor be
proportioned to the knowledge you have conceived
of the inward state of your soul. For otherwise
you have reason to apprehend, lest the dreadful reproach of David be justly applied to you. ' Because
he hath done deceitfully in his sight, that his iniquity may be found unto hatred.'—*Ps.* **xxxv.**
'Divers weights,' saith Solomon, 'and divers meas-
ures, both are abominable before God.'—*Prov.* xx.
Which means, that having weighed the little value of
your own merit, within your own breast, in the
balance of equity and truth, you measure it outwardly at a different rate, and impose yourself upon
the world for more value than you really are of. Bu

fear God, and let that fear deter you from the guilt of so heinous a crime ; that is, of extolling by an ambitious will, what truth ought to humble within you : for that is opposing truth, and struggling against the will of God. Choose rather to acquiesce with him, and study that your will be ever subject to truth by a devout and submissive humility. 'For shall not my soul,' saith the royal psalmist, 'be subject to God.'—*Ps.* lxi. Neither is it enough to be subject to God only, unless you are likewise the same to all mankind for God's sake ; that is, subject to your superiors, subject to your equals, and subject to your inferiors. In this manner Christ teaches us we must fulfil all justice. Go then to your inferior if you will be perfectly righteous, pay a respect to your inferior, and humbly stoop to those beneath you." Thus far St. Bernard, who says again : "Who is just, but he that is truly humble? For when the Lord of all things would have humbly stooped to his servant, and submitted to be baptized by the hands of St. John : seeing him awed by the Majesty of his Person, Christ spoke thus to him : "Suffer it to be so now, for thus it behooves us to fulfil all righteousness.'—*Matt.* ii. Placing the accomplishment of perfect justice in the perfection of true humility. He therefore that is just, is truly humble ; and this justice in the humble, is plain in this : because, he gives to every one his right ; he robs not another of his property, but gives honor to God and retains abjection for himself." But this will appear more plainly if you will but consider the injustice of the proud and arrogant, who attribute every good gift of God to the rewards of their own merit. In relation to which, St. Bernard again says : "As evil may take its source from the greatest good, when become great, we make use of the divine gifts as if they were not such, without even making God an acknowledgment for them ; so they who seem to have reached the highest degree of grandeur and greatness, on account of the divine benefits they have received, are in truth excessively little, for want of returning thanks due to their supreme benefactor.

"However, gentle reader, I have spared the weakness of your senses in the softening expressions of *great* and *little.* Out of regard to the delicacy of your ears, I have forborne calling things by the real names I think they deserve. I should have said, very *wicked* and very *good.* For it is beyond all dispute, that they are so much the deeper in wickedness, who ascribe to themselves the excellencies they may possess. Nothing, in short, can be more criminal. But should any one say, be this crime far from me, since I know it is the grace of God that makes me what I am, and yet, at the same time, studiously aim at self-praise for the grace which he has received ; is not such a person a thief and a robber? Hear only what he is from the mouth of truth itself : 'From thy own mouth will I judge thee, O wicked servant.'—*Luke* xix. And what indeed can be more execrably wicked than that servant who usurps to himself the praises due to his Lord." Thus far St. Bernard.

Hence you may see that the perfection of all righteousness consists in true humility, which derogates nothing from God's honor, nor attributes that to itself, which is not its due ; neither does it injure our neighbor. For the truly humble is neither rash in judging him, nor prefers himself to any one ; but rather thinks himself inferior to all mankind, and chooses the lowest place among them. Hence St. Bernard again says : "How dost thou

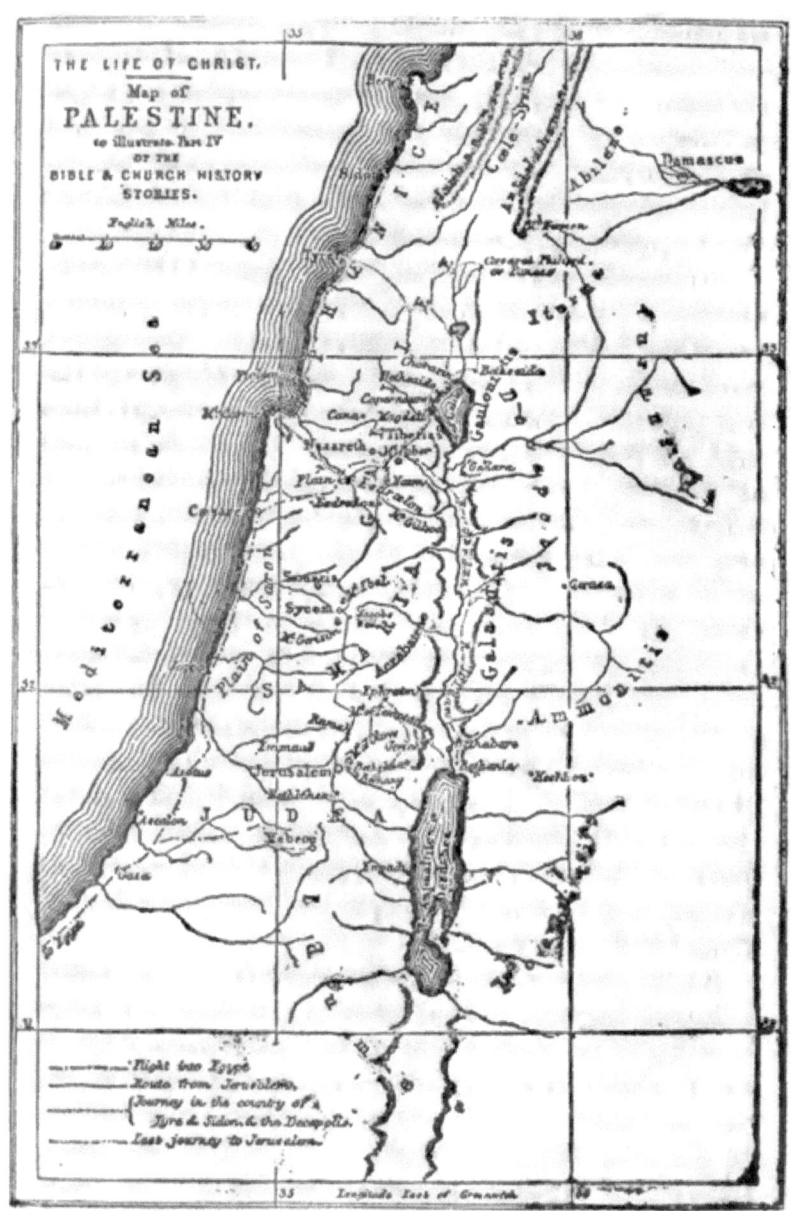

MAP OF PALESTINE.

know, O mortal, but that the very man whose flagitious life and infamous conduct you look upon with horror and contempt, deeming him the greatest of reprobates, and infinitely more sinful than yourself, who live, or at least seem to yourself to live, a sober, virtuous, or pious life : how dost thou know, I say, but that very man may become not only better than those or than yourself in his future practices, and be even now, perhaps, dearer in the sight of God than you? and therefore how do you know but it may be contrary to the divine pleasure for us to place him beneath ourselves, or to refuse him the first honor among us? 'Choose thou,' saith Christ, 'the lowest place, to wit, that you alone may be the lowest of all, and not only not prefer yourself, but even not presume to compare yourself to any.'"— Thus saith St. Bernard. The virtue of humility is again many ways reccommended to us by authentic applauses of the same Saint. "A great mother indeed is humility," saith he, "and a most sublime virtue, which earns that for us which we are taught not to aspire to, enabling us to attain to the knowledge we cannot learn, and to conceive of and from the holy WORD, sublime mysteries not to be explained by words. And why so? Not so much on the account of merit, as of the divine pleasure of the eternal Father of the WORD, the Spouse of the soul, our Lord Jesus Christ, who is God, blessed above all things created." And again : "Humility is a virtue, by which mankind, through a perfect knowledge of his own unworthiness, becomes mean in his own sight." And in another place : "The virtue of humility alone can repair the crime of a breach of charity : and indeed only that virtue is unaccustomed to vain boasting, a stranger to pride, and not given to contention. For he that is truly humble argues not in judgment, nor dissembles any justice." And farther, "Humility reconciles us to God, and pleaseth him greatly when we possess it." Again: "Humility has ever been a special virtue, intimately annexed to the divine grace. For it is ever customary with holy piety, for the sake of preserving humility, to require that the more we advance in perfection, the less perfect we should think ourselves. For even they, who are advancing to the supreme degree of spirituality, retain still something of the imperfections of the lowest, insomuch as they cannot perceive themselves to have attained even the verge of it.

"A beautiful composition is humility and virginity. Neither is that soul little pleasing in the sight of God, in which humility is an ornament to virginity, and virginity adorns humility. What praise is she not worthy of in whom fertility exalts humility, and a birth renders sacred virginity? You have here before you a lesson concerning both the virgin, and the humble: And if you cannot imitate the virginity of the one, imitate at least the humility of the other. Virginity is a laudable virtue, but humility much the more necessary: that is a council; this, a precept: to that you are invited; to this you are obliged. Of that, it is said: 'He that can take, let him take.'—*Matt.* xix. But of this, 'Unless you become as this little one, you shall not enter into the kingdom of heaven.'—*Ibid.* xviii. That, therefore, you are rewarded for; and this, is expected from you. Wherefore, you may be saved without virginity; but without humility you cannot; for where virginity is lost, and has no more the power to please, the tears shed for it by humility may effectually do it. And without rashness, I may say, that the virginity of the sacred Virgin herself would not have been pleasing to God, without humility. For, 'Upon whom shall my spirit rest,' saith the Lord, 'but upon the humble and serene?' Had not then the holy Virgin been humble, the Holy Ghost would not have rested upon her: and had not the divine Spirit overshadowed her, undoubtedly she would not have been pregnant. For how indeed, without him, could she have conceived **by him?** It is clear then, that **when** she conceived by the Holy Ghost, as herself witnesseth, the Lord regarded the humility of his handmaid more than **her** virginity. Whence it follows beyond dispute, that it is humility which renders virginity acceptable. What reply can the virgin vainly elated make to this? **Our** blessed Lady, having as it were, forgotten her virginity, glories only in the abjection of her humility, and you, neglecting this, vainly flatter yourself in the possession of an unavailing virginity. 'He beheld,' saith she, 'the humility of his handmaid.' She! What she? Truly the holy, the pious, and the devout Virgin. **And** are you more innocently pure, more fervently devout than she? **Or can** you presume to think that your chastity is greater or more pleasing to God than hers? Are you able to please without humility when the Blessed Virgin could not? The more honorable your condition is rendered by the gift of chastity: by so much the more do you injure yourself, as often as you soil that innocence of life, with the mixture of pride. Charity, chastity, and humility, have no beauty in themselves, but only in proportion to the beauty they have in the sight of God.

What is more beautiful than that chastity which renders clean the being conceived from uncleanness, changes enmity into friendship, and men into angels? The angel and the chaste man differ indeed in point of felicity, but not of virtue. For if the chastity of the one be happier, that of the other is stronger. It is chastity alone which in this mortal state, represents a kind of immortality. That alone, which, amidst the nuptial solemnities, imitates the **method** of that blessed and heavenly region, where they neither marry nor are married, giving us an **imperfect** relish of the divine and heavenly conversation there enjoyed among the blessed. This frail **vessel** which here we carry with us, and in which we are in danger, chastity sanctifies, not unlike the sweet scented balsams wherewith dead bodies are embalmed and preserved from corruption. It curbs the senses, restrains the faculties of the body, and preserves the whole man from the contamination and loose desires attending idleness. But whatever beauty may appear from the shining ornament of chastity, this, however, is of no value or merit without charity. Nor ought we to wonder at this. For what good indeed can we receive without it? Not faith, though we should remove mountains. Not knowledge, though it be that which speaks with the tongues of angels. Not martyrdom, though by it I should deliver up my body, saith St. Paul, to be burnt. Neither without it can we receive any good, nor with it can we reject any though the most minute. Chastity without charity is like a lamp without oil. Extract the oil, and the lamp will not burn. So take away charity, and chastity will not please. In a word, as chastity avails us nothing without charity, so neither the one nor the other avail anything without humility, nor **can** they truly be called virtues. For it is by humility that we deserve the possession of them both, because to the humble God gives grace. Humility preserves those virtues which we have already acquired; for the Spirit of God reposes only upon the humble and peaceful; it perfects that virtue we are steady in, for virtue is perfected in infirmity, that is, in humility. It conquers pride, that implacable enemy to grace, that source of all iniquity, and rids itself, as well as others, from its insolent tyranny. That alone powerfully resists its malice, and subdues its presumption, being a kind of bulwark and asylum of virtue." Thus far, gentle reader, have I given you many and beautiful commendations of humility from St. Bernard, that great lover of truth and abjection. Endeavor likewise to comprehend the sublime doctrines he gives relating to other virtues, and practice them; but now let us return to the baptism of our Lord.

When John beheld, then, that it was the will of our Lord to be baptized by him, he readily submitted and baptized him. And here, pious reader, cast an eye towards him, and attentively behold, how the Lord of Majesty humbly unclothes himself like a mere mortal, and notwithstanding the coldness of the season, descends thus into the frozen river. Through the immense love he bore us he vouchsafed thus to effect our salvation, by instituting the sacrament of baptism, to wash away the guilt of our crimes. By this he truly espoused to himself not only his whole church, but more especially, in a singular and ineffable manner, the souls of the faithful. For by the faith we promise him in our baptism, we are truly wedded to our Lord Jesus, the holy prophet saying in his person: "I will espouse thee to myself in faith."--*Hosea* ii. Wherefore is this most solemn and ineffable mystery, a work of the greatest service and benefit to mankind? And therefore the holy church triumphantly sings: "This day the church is united to her heavenly spouse: because Christ in the River Jordan washed away her crimes."

And in this most excellent work the three divine persons of the most sacred Trinity, in a singular manner, manifested themselves, and descended: "For the Holy Ghost, as a dove, came and remained upon him, and the voice of the Father was heard saying: This is my beloved Son, in whom I am well pleased."—*Matt.* iii. "In which place," saith St. Bernard: "he said, *Hear ye him.*" Wherefore, saith the Saint: "Begin then now to speak, oh, beloved Jesus, since you are now commissioned to speak from your Father himself. How long, oh divine virtue, and wisdom of God, how long, I say, will you lie concealed amidst mankind, and appear only invested with the infirmities of a mere mortal, and insignificant man? How long, O glorious King, and King of heaven, will you suffer yourself to be called the *carpenter's son*, and even vouchsafe to be thought so? For the holy evangelist St. Luke witnesseth, that 'He was still thought the son of Joseph.'—*Luke* iii. Oh, humility of Christ! how greatly dost thou confound the excess of my vanity; I scarce know anything, and yet flatter myself to know much, and never know when, or how to be silent; but without shame, being indiscreetly forward, and full of vain boasting, I am quick in talking, ready in teaching, and slow in harkening to others. But when Christ remained silent during so long a space of time, and hid the treasures of his divine wisdom from mankind, was it, think you, because he feared the assaults of vainglory from the empty praises of men. What had he to fear from that who was the true glory of his Father? He feared, however, but his fear was not for himself, but for us; he was afraid for us, well knowing the room there was for such fear. For us he was careful, us he instructed more by works than by words, and what he afterwards taught us by word he proclaimed by example: 'Learn of me because I am meek and humble of heart.'—*Matt.* xi. We hear of very little before concerning the infancy of Jesus Christ, and now to the three-and-thirtieth year of his age, we hear of nothing he either did or said. However, from this time he can no longer remain concealed, being thus publicly declared by his Father." Thus far St. Bernard. And this is the authority which I adduced in the foregoing chapter, from which you may understand how our Lord Jesus humbly remained silent so long a space of time for our greater spiritual instruction. And you cannot but observe, in the whole series of what has been already said, the true practice of a profound humility, concerning which, I cannot speak to you but with pleasure, it being a most sublime virtue, and what we stand greatly in need of. And is with so much the more study to be sought, and admired with so much the greater affection, by how much the more our Lord in every action of his life was remarkably solicitous of practising it.

THE TEMPTATION.

CHAPTER XVI.

THE FAST AND TEMPTATIONS OF CHRIST—HE RE-
TURNS TO HIS MOTHER—THE FOUR MEANS TO
ATTAIN TO A PERFECT PURITY OF HEART—THE
GREAT ADVANTAGES OF PRAYER—THE RESIST-
ANCE TO BE MADE TO GLUTTONY—WHY, AND
FOR WHOM GOD WORKS HIS MIRACLES.

OUR divine Lord Jesus, immediately after his baptism, retired into the wilderness, to a certain mountain, now known by the name of *Quarantain Peak*, and there fasted forty whole days and nights, associating, according to St. Mark, with the brutes. Here, then, again contemplate your divine Master: and endeavor to copy from this sublime pattern the many excellent virtues he points out to you in his own practice. To be solitary and retired from the eyes of the world is his greatest ambition; a rigorous abstinence from food is his daily repast; prayer and almost uninterrupted watches are his darling exercise; short and interrupted slumbers, on the hard, cold, bare ground, are his slender repose; and the humble society of brute beasts is all his company. Though the whole life of Christ will appear to have been one continued series of pain and corporal suffering, yet here it seems to be attended with the most afflicting circumstances; and therefore deserves a particular share of your compassion. Pity him, then, and let your pity excite in you a zealous resolution of sharing his hardships, by following the example he here sets you. Four things in this passage are principally to be remarked, which are jointly and mutually conducive to the spiritual exercise of every pious soul: to wit, retirement, fasting, prayer, and mortification of the flesh. And it is chiefly by these that we are to hope to obtain that perfect purity of heart, which cannot be too much coveted, as it includes the possession of every virtue. For purity of heart contains charity, humility, and patience: in a word, an assemblage of every virtuous quality, and an absolute alienation from vice and all its tendencies: because the heart that gives admittance to any one vice, or even suffers in itself the decay of any one virtue, from that moment ceases to be pure. Hence, as we are told in the conferences of the holy fathers of the desert, the whole object of spiritual exercise is, and should be, the acquisition of a perfect purity of heart. For it is by this that every man is to render himself worthy of the beatific vision, as our Lord himself says in the gospel: "Blessed are the clean of heart, for they shall see God." Wherefore St. Bernard says, "That he is the nearest to God, whose heart is the most purified." The natural consequence of which truth is, that to obtain an intimate union with God, we must have a perfect purity of heart.

Now, to obtain this, gentle reader, fervent and assiduous prayer is of the greatest service, as I shall hereafter show you. But what can avail the prayer of one given to gluttony, drunkenness, lasciviousness, and sloth? Nothing. No; fasting and mortification of the flesh are absolutely requisite, although prudence be necessary in the practice of both, indiscretion being the bane of every good action.

Neither does retirement seem of less utility. For,

amidst noise and tumult, how can prayer be performed with that decency which is proper for it?
And who is the mortal so free from danger that
dares give loose to his senses, particularly to seeing
and hearing much without offence to his purity or
innocence of heart? "Death enters by the windows
of our eyes to our souls." And therefore, gentle
reader, follow our Lord to his retirement: that is,
separate yourself, after his example, from the commerce of the world, and be as retired as your station
will permit, if you wish to be united to him, and to
enjoy that beatific vision which is the reward of internal cleanness.

Fly the conversation of all, but more especially
of worldings; fly the novelty of friendships, even
devout ones; shut your eyes and ears to all vain
and transitory objects; and fly, in particular, as the
most destructive poison to the soul, all that may in
the least disturb the peace of your mind and heart.
It was not without reason, that the fathers, for
their habitations, made choice of deserts, and places
remote from all correspondence with mankind, and
recommended to all their pupils to be blind, deaf,
and dumb to the conversation of the world. "For,"
as St. Bernard says to this purpose, "if you are
desirous of becoming sensible of the sweet emotions
of the Holy Ghost; if you have an effectual eagerness to have your soul wedded to God, according
to the prophet, *sit down solitary, and you have
raised yourself above yourself*, by the bare desire
of espousing the Lord of angels. In reality, is it
not above your native meanness to adhere to God,
and to become one spirit with him? Sit down,
therefore, and be solitary as the dove: avoid the
crowds, and have no dealings you can avoid with
the rest of mankind: forget even your country and

the house of your father: *and the King shall be desirous of your beauty*. Endeavor, then, oh, pious soul, to be alone, that you may keep yourself wholly to him, whom you have wholly chosen to yourself. Retire from the public; retire from your own family; retire from your most intimate friends, and even from your necessary attendants. For know that such is the reservedness of your divine Spouse, that he will never indulge you with his company in the presence of others. Withdraw, then, but not so much bodily as mentally. Withdraw, but let it be in intention, in spirit, and with devotion. For Christ your Lord, who is present with you, is so in spirit, and the retirement he expects from you is not so much that of the body as that of the spirit. Though, indeed, it will not be useless for you to retire personally sometimes, if convenience will permit; especially at the time of prayer, as we shall hereafter observe. You may truly be said to be retired and alone, if your thoughts are not employed on trivial things, if you are not affected by what passes in company, if you contemn what the world prizes, if you are fatigued with what your worldly companions hanker after, if you are insensible to ill-usage, and unmindful of injuries: otherwise, you cannot be truly deemed solitary, however personally alone you may chance to be. You see, then, that it is not impossible to be retired amidst a crowd, or to be amidst a tumult, though alone in a desert. Thus, then, however great be the number of people you converse with, you may still be alone if you will but refrain from curious searching into their conversation, or rashly setting up for a judge of it." Thus far St. Bernard. Hence it appears how necessary solitude is, and how fruitless is that of the body, if unaccompanied with that of the mind. However, I must still observe, that corporal retirement is of the greatest service, that the mind may not lose its recollection by exterior objects. Endeavor, therefore, with all due affection and discretion, to imitate, as much as possible, your divine Lord and Spouse, in the great and useful virtues of solitude, prayer, fasting, and corporal mortification.

JESUS, THE SECOND ADAM, WITH THE WILD BEASTS OF THE WILDERNESS.

Learn, likewise. from his associating with dumb creatures, to behave yourself humbly towards all, and to bear with meekness even such as appear to you guilty of misdeeds. To this end, pay often a mental visit to our Lord in his retirement, and observe his manner of conversing there. Every faithful Christian ought to repeat this visit at least once a day, from Twelfth Day to the end of his forty days'

retreat : when, as the Scripture takes notice, he began to be hungry. It was this opportunity Satan
laid hold of to approach him, and try to find out
if he was the Son of God, by tempting him to gluttony. "If," says he, " thou art the Son of God, bid
these stones be made bread." But this **artifice**
could not surprise the Master of all wisdom, who so
rejected it, as neither to be affected by the temptation of hunger, nor leave the tempter room to discover
what he wished to know ; rebuking him with holy
scripture, without asserting **or** denying himself to
be the Son of God. Here let the example of Christ
teach you the duty of resisting the passion of gluttony, which **is the** first victory we ought to begin
with, if we mean to gain a complete triumph over
sin. The man who is overcome by gluttony, is too
weak to cope with any other vice. For, as the com-
mentator upon this passage in St. Matthew says, "He
labors in vain to gain a proper dominion over his
vicious appetites, who **remains a** slave to his own
belly."

The devil, not discouraged by this defeat, took
our Saviour up to Jerusalem, our divine Lord suffering himself to be carried about by the cruel serpent,
who thirsted after his precious blood, as well as
after that of his elect, and patiently enduring such
rough treatment to set us an example of meekness.
Attend, therefore, seriously to the lesson here set
you, and profit by it. When Satan had brought
our Saviour to Jerusalem, he carried him to the
pinnacle of the temple, there to tempt him to vanity;
desirous, as before, of discovering whether he was
the Son of God or not. But here again our Saviour
frustrated his intentions, contenting himself with
confounding the serpent by authority of scripture.
So that, according to St. Bernard, "Our Saviour's

not manifesting his divinity on these two occasions was a sufficient argument with the infernal enemy to conclude that he was mere man ; and therefore it was, that he ventured a third time to try to shake that steadiness which appeared to him to be purely human." Accordingly, the fiend took him to a high mountain, at a little distance from the above-named peak, where, showing him the riches of the world, he endeavored to seduce him to avarice ; but, to his utter confusion, the destroyer was again disappointed and put to flight. See, then, and remember what trials and temptations your divine Lord submitted to, and cease to wonder that you should be tempted also.

Yet think not, pious reader, that these were the only trials he endured. They who reckon but three temptations in the life of Christ must surely be ignorant of scripture, which tells us that "the whole life of man upon earth is one continued temptation."—*Job* vii. And that he endured in the most rigorous manner. For, as St. Paul says, he was *tempted in all, by similitude* to us, though his temptations were but external ; and *without sin*. When he had gained the victory, the angels came and ministered to him. Here be attentive, and devoutly behold our Lord eating, surrounded by the angels who attend him : and endeavor to be present to everything that is here mentioned, the subject being very beautiful, and equally devout.

Here it may be asked, what the angels ministered to our Lord to eat after so long and so rigorous a fast ? This the scripture makes no mention of, and therefore we may suppose this victorious banquet to have consisted of anything of which our devotion shall inspire us with an idea. If indeed we consider the greatness of his power, the question is

solved; because, at pleasure, he could have commanded what he pleased out of all that was created;
or might have created afresh whatever he desired.
But though he made use of his power in behalf of
the multitudes whom he fed twice with a small
number of loaves and fishes, yet we nowhere find
that he ever exerted it for his own or for his disciples' use.   On the contrary, we read that in his presence the disciples were reduced to pluck ears of corn
to relieve their hunger.   So, likewise, when fatigued
with his journey, he sat at the well talking with the
Samaritan, it is not said that he created food, but
that he sent **his** disciples to fetch some from the
neighboring city.   So that it **is not** likely that Christ
was fed in the desert by any miracle, for his miracles
were all wrought in public, and in the presence of
many.   Yet there were none here present with him
but angels; what, then, can we here find to meditate
on?   There were no dwellings here, nor victuals to
be found ready prepared : so that we may conceive
that **the** angels brought thither the food they found
elsewhere prepared.   And why may we not believe
it **to** have been so, when the like happened to Daniel?
For when the prophet Abacuc (*Dan.* xiv.) had prepared the pottage for his reapers, an angel of the
Lord took him by the hair of the head to Daniel,
from Judea to Babylon, that he might eat, and then
brought him back again.   Let us then piously meditate, and rejoice with our divine Lord at his victorious dinner, and with the Blessed Virgin, who
bore a part in his joy, though distant from him.
For we may reasonably conjecture that the heavenly
host who came to pay their homages to our divine
Saviour after his victories over Satan, finding him
pressed with hunger, went in his name to the Blessed
Virgin, his mother, and brought from her the neces

sary food of her own preparing, which they respectfully laid before him to eat.   And with what love,
honor, and devotion, may we not suppose they administered everything to him ; one presenting him
bread, another helping him to drink, another obsequiously tendering to him the fish, or other humble
provision his blessed mother had dressed for him ;
and all jointly entertaining him with heavenly music
and divine canticles.   This done, our divine Lord
dismisses them to their celestial habitation, descends
from the mountain, and prepares to return to his
blessed mother to console her.   And here, again,
behold the Lord of all things undertaking another
laborious journey on foot; and condole with him.
He came by the way of the Jordan, where John beholding him advancing forwards, pointed him out
with his finger, crying out at the same time, " Behold the Lamb of God : behold him who takes away
the sins of the world."—*John* i.   " It is he, it is he
himself, on whom I saw the Holy Ghost descending,
when I baptized him."   And again, the next day,
seeing him walk by the side of the Jordan, he cried
out a second time, " Behold the Lamb of God."
Then Andrew, with another of John's disciples, went
after Jesus : and our divine Lord, anxious of their
salvation, to give them the greater confidence in him,
turned about to them, and asked, " Whom do you
seek ?"   To which they returned, " Where, Lord, is
your habitation ?"   He then took them with him to
the little house he had retired to in those parts ; and
they staid with him the whole day.   After this, Andrew brought with him his brother Peter, whom
Jesus courteously received, knowing well what he
designed him to be.   He then told him, that he
should afterwards be called Cephas or Peter ; and
thus they became acquainted, and in some measure

intimate. Afterwards, Jesus having a mind to go into Galilee to his blessed mother, he left those parts, and set out on his journey.

When he returned home, his holy parents were transported with inexpressible joy: the sacred virgin ran to embrace him, and receive him in her tender and immaculate arms; to whom, and to her venerable spouse, the divine Jesus, reverently inclining, returned his tender expressions of joy with mutual tenderness, and remained with them, as he used to do.

CHAPTER XVII

CHRIST OPENS THE BOOK IN THE SYNAGOGUE.

THUS far, by the grace of God, we have regularly treated the passages of the life of Christ, without omitting any, or at least very few circumstances that may be supposed to have attended him : but I do not design to continue the same hereafter, for it would be too prolix to reduce into practical meditations everything he said and did . Besides, it ought to be our chief study, after the example of St. Cecily, to bear in our breasts the circumstances relating to him. Wherefore, for the future, I shall only collect some of the principal facts to meditate assiduously on, till we come to his Passion; for there nothing ought to be omitted. Neither ought we elsewhere to omit anything wholly, or to neglect meditating on it in a proper place and time. But I do not intend to be so extensive in meditations henceforward, unless occasionally. Let it suffice then, to place before your eyes the bare facts and sayings, on which you yourselves may at leisure piously and

familiarly meditate. For in this seems to consist
the chief sweetness, efficacy, and fruit of these meditations ; that, always and everywhere, you contemplate Christ in some one action or saying of his : as,
when he is with his disciples, when he is with sinners, when he talks or preaches to the multitude,
walking or sitting, sleeping or waking, eating or
ministering to others, healing the sick, or doing
other miracles. In these and such like circumstances consider all his gestures ; but especially contemplate his divine countenance, if you can bring
it to your imagination, which, however, appears
to me the most difficult part of meditation. When
you are thus contemplating the divine face of Christ,
consider whether he looks graciously upon you ;
your conscience will tell you whether you may hope
it or not. Let what has been said in this chapter
serve you to recur to, in whatever I may hereafter
relate, without adding any meditation to it. But
let us proceed to the remaining part of this blessed
life.

After our Lord Jesus returned from being baptized, he persisted in his accustomed humility ; beginning, however, by degrees, to manifest himself in
teaching and preaching in a private manner. For
he is not said to have taken on him the function of a
public preacher during the whole following year, that
is, not till the miracle he wrought at the marriage-
feast, which was on the day twelve-months after
he was baptized. And though he did sometimes
preach, and suffer his disciples to baptize, yet, still
after the imprisonment of the Baptist, he did not
either by himself, or his disciples, wholly apply to
preaching, especially in public. Even in this, giving
us a lesson of surprising humility, by paying such a
respect to John, who was so greatly inferior to him

in preaching, as well as in everything else. He did not begin his mission with noise and ostentation, but humbly and gradually.

One day, therefore, being with the rest of the Jews in the synagogue, he stood up, and read in the book of Isaiah, the following words: "The spirit of the Lord is upon me, wherefore he has anointed me, he has sent me to evangelize to the poor."—*Isaiah* lxi. Then folding the book, he said, "This Scripture is this day fulfilled, in your ears." Behold him then, here humbly taking upon him the office of a lecturer to them, and reading before them, with an affable and serene countenance: thus he lays the Scripture **open** to their understandings, and begins humbly to manifest **himself in** those words, "This Scripture is this day fulfilled;" that is, in other words, "I am he, who is here spoken of." While he was speaking, the whole astonished multitude dwelt on the modesty and beauty of his heavenly aspect, which added efficacy to the divine words **he spoke; for he was** exceedingly beautiful, and inexpressibly eloquent. Of both which the prophet thus sung: "Beautiful of form above the children of men; grace is diffused in thy lips."—*Ps.* xliv.

LEVI IS CALLED TO BE A DISCIPLE, FROM THE RECEIPT OF CUSTOM.

CHAPTER XVIII.

HE CALLS HIS DISCIPLES.

AND now our Lord Jesus began to call his disciples, and to solicit the salvation of our race;
still preserving untouched his former humility.
Peter and Andrew were the first he called; and these
he called three times. The first time of his calling
them was, as above, near the river Jordan, where
they first became a little acquainted with him.—
John i. The second was from the ship, when they
had been catching fish, as St. Luke relates.—*Luke* v.

Then they followed him only with a design of
returning home; but then they heard some part of
his doctrine. The third was likewise from the ship,
when, according to St. Mark, he said to them,
"Come after me, I will make you fishers of men."—
Mark i. "Then, leaving their nets, they followed
him."—*Ibid.* So likewise he called James and John,
at the same places, the two last times; and what
relates to them is contained in the same places
where Peter and Andrew are treated of. He called
also St. John at the marriage-feast, as St. Jerome
says, though it is not mentioned in Scripture. He
called St. Philip, saying, "follow me."—*John* i.
And so he did Matthew.—*Matt.* ix. As to his manner of calling the rest, it is nowhere written. Consider here, then, and behold him in the before-mentioned vocations, and in his conversation with them;
with what affection he calls them, rendering himself
affable, familiar, and sociable with them; attracting them inwardly and outwardly, bringing them
to his mother's, and frequently condescending to
go with them to their houses. He taught them, instructed them, and was equally careful of them as
a mother is of an only son. It is said as a tradition from St. Peter's verbal account that whenever
he slept at the same place with them, if, rising in
the night to pray according to his custom, he found
any of them slightly covered, he would graciously
take the pains to wrap them up warm, having an
extraordinary tenderness for them. For though
they were but men of mean extraction and condition, yet he knew what he had designed them for,
and that they were to be the princes of the world,
and the appointed leaders of all his faithful in the
spiritual war to be waged against Satan. And here,
for God's sake, consider from what small beginnings

the Church took its rise. The Lord would not make choice of the wise and powerful of this world, lest the wonders he was about to perform should be ascribed to their abilities: but reserving these prodigies to himself, redeemed us out of the abundance of his own goodness, power, and wisdom.

JESUS WORKS HIS FIRST MIRACLE AT THE REQUEST OF HIS ....

CHAPTER XIX.

THE CONVERSION OF WATER INTO WINE AT THE MARRIAGE-FEAST.

ALTHOUGH it is uncertain whose marriage this was, that was celebrated at Cana of Galilee, as ecclesiastical history notices, we may, for meditation sake, suppose it to be that of St. John the Evangelist, which St. Jerome seems to affirm in his preface upon St. John. Our blessed Lady was there present, not as a stranger invited thither, but as the head and principal lady of the feast, and the chief manager of it ; so that she was as it were at home, being in the house of her sister, whose elder she was. This may be gathered, first, from the text, which tells us that the mother of Jesus was there, but that Jesus and his disciples were invited thither : which ought to be understood likewise of all the rest of the persons present. So that when Mary Salome, the wife of Zebedee, came to her to Nazareth to tell that she designed to marry her son John, our blessed Lady went back with her to Cana some days before the appointed time of the feast, to make preparations for it, insomuch, that when the guests were invited to it she was actually there. Secondly, it may be gathered from her taking notice of the want of wine ; by which she appears not so much to be a guest, as concerned in the distribution of the entertainment, and therefore perceived the wine to be deficient. For if she had been sitting there as a guest, is it not likely the modest Virgin would have sat by her Son, amidst the men ? And if she had, would she have risen up among them to complain of the want of wine ? Or even had she been seated among the women, had she, think you, been more sensible of the wants of wine than any other of her sex there present ? Or would she have risen from her seat to acquaint her Son with it ? For we cannot suppose, that she called out aloud. All this seems unlikely ; and therefore we may with more probability suppose, that she was present there, not merely as a guest, but rather as one who served and ministered as before-mentioned, for it is said of her, that she

was ever ready and officious in helping and serving
others.

The third is, that she commanded the servants to go
to her Son, and to do whatever else she appointed them:
by which it is plain, that she had a superiority over
them, and that the feast was ordered and disposed
according to her management ; and therefore she was
solicitous, **lest** anything necessary should be wanting.
Hence then, according to this manner, consider
our Lord Jesus at this feast, eating with the rest of
the company, seated not at the head of the guests,
nor amongst the chief of those who were invited, but
in the lowest place, and among the poorest and
meanest, as we may **gather** from his own words:
" When thou art invited to a feast, sit down in the
lowest place."—*Luke* xiv. Wherefore, as it was
ever his custom to teach first by example, what he
afterwards taught by words, it is most likely, that
he took not the first and chief place at this feast,
after the manner of the proud and vain : but rather,
that he chose to sit **in** the lowest seat, among the
more simple and the meaner sort of company.

Contemplate here, likewise, our blessed Lady—
how obsequious and cheerful she is, and diligently
careful that all things might be performed with
great exactness and decency : **submissively** helping
the servants, and showing **them** how, and of what
things they should serve and minister to those who
were invited. And when the feast was almost towards the end, they came to her and said : " There
is no more wine left to set before them." To whom
she answered : " Wait a short time, and I will procure that you may have more." And presently
departing, she went to her Son Jesus, who sat humbly at the lower end of the table, and said to him :
" My Son, they have no more wine, and this, our

sister, being poor, I know not how we shall supply this want." But Jesus answered and said: "Woman, what is this to me and thee?" This answer could not but seem severe to the holy Virgin. But as St. Bernard remarks, "those words were full of mystery, and were given for our greater instruction."

Wherefore, the saint, in this place, speaks to this effect: "Do you ask, O Lord, what is this to thee and to her? Is it nothing to the mother and her Son? Do you ask what it appertains to her, when thou thyself art the blessed fruit of her virginal womb? Is she not the same who conceived without prejudice to her virginity, and brought forth without offence to her modesty? Is it not she, in whose womb you vouchsafed to be enclosed the space of nine months, whose sacred breasts gave you suck, and with whom, at the age of twelve years, you came back from Jerusalem, and was obedient to her? Why then, most beloved Jesus, do you now perplex and grieve her tender soul, saying: 'What is it to me and to thee, O woman?' I already comprehend that it was not to reproach her, or to confound the great modesty of your virgin mother, which made you say: 'Woman, what is that to me and to thee?' For when the servants came to you by her orders, you did without hesitation what she suggested.

"Why then, gentle reader, did he first here make her this answer? Truly for no other reason than for our instruction, and to teach us that they, who having forsaken the world by a thorough conversion to Almighty God, should have no longer a tie to their carnal friends, relations or parents; and that an over solicitude for the supplying of their necessities should not deter them from the daily study and practice of those spiritual exercises belonging to their state and calling. For though as long as we are of the world, there is a duty incumbent upon us to take care of our parents; yet, when we have once forsaken it, so far as even to forsake ourselves with it, we ought upon a much stronger motive to relinquish all temporal care and solicitude for them. To which purpose, it is written of a certain holy monk or hermit, who having quitted the world, and lived a long time a solitary and retired life in the desert, being one day earnestly entreated by his own brother for his advice in some worldly and temporal affair, he calmly desired him to consult another of their brethren who had been dead long before; to whom, when the brother replied, with much surprise at his advice, that his other brother was dead; so am I, answered the monk, also dead to this world, and therefore have nothing to do in it, or with its troublesome affairs. This is what our Lord Jesus meant when he answered his blessed mother, saying: 'Woman, what is that to me and to thee?' Clearly teaching us not to be careful or solicitous for our friends and relations, or even parents themselves, in those things which are contrary to, or inconsistent with the rules religion prescribes to us. This he also confirmed in another place, when, being told by one of the by-standers, that his mother and brethren waited without desiring to speak to him, he said, ' Who is my mother, and who are my brethren?'"—*Matt.* xii. Thus far St. Bernard.

But to return to our subject: The Blessed Virgin was not in the least dismayed or dejected at this unexpected answer of her beloved Son: but full of confidence in his great bounty and goodness, she presently returned to them, and said: "Go to my Son, and whatever he shall say to you, do ye."— *John* ii. They went as she had ordered them: and

having filled the stone waterpots, **which stood there,**
with water, as our Lord had commanded, he again
said to them, "Draw now, and carry to the chief
steward." Here, **first, we may** consider, the great
prudence and wisdom of our Lord Jesus, **in** sending
the wine first to the chief and most dignified person
at the feast. Secondly, we **may** likewise consider,
that our Lord sat not near him, but far below **him,**
when he said : "Take it to the master of the feast."
Whereby it appears, that he held the first place
among the invited, and our Lord Jesus the lowest.
The servants, however, gave the wine to the chief
steward, and to the rest of the company, who openly
declared the manner how **it was** made, they being
eye-witnesses of the miracle ; and his disciples then
believed in him. When the feast was ended, Jesus
took John apart **by** himself, and said unto him,
"Leave this woman **whom** thou hast chosen for thy
wife, and follow me, and I will lead thee to a far
more sublime union and heavenly marriage than
this." Hereupon he immediately left his wife,
and followed Christ, and became his disciple. And
here we may learn many profitable things for our
instruction and example. The first is, that our Lord,
sanctifying by his presence this marriage, gave us to
understand that matrimony is both a lawful and
honorable state, and ordained by God himself.
And in calling St. John from the same, he shows
the spiritual marriage and union of the soul with
God in a single life and a state of virginity, to be
much more excellent and perfect.

After our Lord Jesus had wrought this miracle, he
departed thence, and resolved now to attend to those
things only which regarded the salvation of man ;
and therefore determined thenceforward to preach
his heavenly doctrine openly to all mankind. He

would first, however, conduct his holy mother safely home to her little habitation. Wherefore, taking her by the hand, and being followed by St. John, and the rest of his disciples, they went into Capharnaum, which is near Nazareth; and after some few days, they from thence reached Nazareth. Contemplate here, devout reader, this blessed couple, the mother and the Son. Consider them humbly travelling on foot; and though wearied with the fatigues of their journey, yet united by the strictest ties of love to each other. O what a heavenly couple! Such the **world was** never before blessed with. Consider likewise **his** disciples who reverently follow them, and attentively listen to the sacred doctrine which proceeds from the mouth of their divine master; who was never **idle,** but was ever instructing them in such things as might redound to their welfare. Wherefore we **may** piously imagine, that the abundance of heavenly consolation, which they reaped from such sacred conversation, greatly allayed the toils of their fatiguing journey.

THE SERMON ON THE MOUNT.

As Moses received the law of the Ten Commandments from God, and delivered it to the people from a mountain, so Jesus Christ, the Legislator of the New Covenant, proclaims the eight beatitudes of the New Law, and delivers His doctrine to the people, also from a mountain.

CHAPTER XX.

THE SERMON OF THE LORD ON THE MOUNT, **WHICH** HE BEGINS BY POVERTY.

OUR Lord calling his disciples apart from the crowd, ascended with them to mount Tabor, about two miles distant from Nazareth, to infuse into them his divine doctrine. For it was fit to instruct them first, who were to be appointed masters and leaders of the rest. He taught them many things in that place in a most beautiful and ample sermon: and no wonder a sermon should be such, which was delivered by the mouth of the Lord. He taught them the beatitudes, the dignity of prayer, fasting, alms-deeds, and many truths relating to every other virtue, as appears in the holy gospel. Which I advise you, gentle reader, to peruse seriously and frequently, and to endeavor to enrich your memory with such lessons of spiritual sublimity; but which would require too great a prolixity to consider here; neither is it proper to crowd meditations like these with too many expositions of scripture. However, I shall not entirely drop them, but here and there intersperse some few, and add to them some moral reflections of my own, or of the holy fathers, as occasion, and your instruction may require. Let it at present suffice to observe, that our Lord began this his exhortation with poverty; giving us thereby to understand, that poverty is the first foundation of all spiritual structures. Hence, nothing can be more inconsistent than for Christ, the pattern of poverty,

to be followed by persons loaded with temporal
riches ; since they, whose affections are linked to
such fleeting vanities, are more properly in a state
of slavery than freedom. And they only are qualified for being happy, whose hearts are at liberty.
Therefore it was that Christ told them, "Blessed are
the poor in spirit, etc." For no heart is free, but
that which is linked to God : and they only are so,
whose affections tend only to him. We render ourselves subject to whatever we affectionately love ; and
therefore we ought to love nothing but him, because
subjection to him is the only true liberty. The truly
poor, therefore, may justly be called blessed, who,
for God's sake, contemns all things else. For, by
this means, he becomes, in a great measure, united
to God. Of this great virtue St. Bernard says:

"Poverty is a noble kind of wings that elevate us
in a moment to the kingdom of heaven. The other
virtues flowing from this, obtain us only a promise
of it ; but to poverty, felicity is rather given than
promised : wherefore, our Saviour speaks in the present tense, 'for theirs is the kingdom of heaven.'"
—*Matt.* xii. And a little farther, he adds : "We
see some poor persons sorrowful and pusillanimous,
who would be quite otherwise, were their poverty
such as we are speaking of ; for then they would
consider themselves as princes, and possessors of a
heavenly kingdom. But, alas, the generality of
mankind would be poor, upon condition of wanting
nothing, and love no other poverty than such a one
as is attended with no inconvenience." And elsewhere : "And I," says he, "when once I am exalted
above the earth, may boldly affirm, that I will draw
all things after me ; for if once I put on the likeness
of my brother, I may, without rashness, adopt his
speech ; let not then the rich of this world imagine,

that the brethren of Christ possess nothing but heavenly things, because they hear him say, 'Blessed are the poor in spirit, for theirs is the kingdom of heaven.' No; for they are likewise in possession of the earth; having nothing, yet possessing all things; not begging like paupers, but receiving as masters; so much the more truly masters of all, as they covet nothing. In a word, the whole world, to the faithful lover of poverty, is a fund of riches; because prosperity and adversity are alike subservient and beneficial to him. The covetous worldling yearns after earthly things like a beggar; the faithful lover of poverty despises them like a prince.

"Ask any one of those who with insatiable eagerness pursue worldly gain, what they think of them who, selling what they have to distribute the price of it to the poor, purchase the kingdom of heaven with earthly substance; and whether he looks upon them to act prudently or not? He will, doubtless, approve their wisdom. Ask him again, why he neglects to do himself what he deems well done by others? He will answer, I cannot do it. But why? Truly because tyrannizing avarice will not permit him; because he is not free; because he has neither right to, nor possession of what he seems to enjoy. If they are thine, put them out to interest, purchase with them a solid estate, and with an earthly fund buy an eternal heavenly one. If you are not lord enough of them to have this in your power, I shall deem you not master, but slave to them; the steward, not the possessor." Thus far St. Bernard. Now let us return to our meditation. Consider, then, our Lord Jesus humbly sitting on the ground, with his disciples around him. How affably does he converse with them, as if one of themselves: teaching, and in a beautiful, benign, and pathetic manner, inculcating to them the practice of the above-mentioned virtues. And ever study, as I have before advised you, to contemplate his divine countenance. Cast an attentive eye likewise on his disciples, and imagine you see with what reverence, humility, and fixed attention they observe his blessed aspect, hear his wonderful discourse, and imprint it in their minds: reaping sovereign delight from his words and heavenly looks. In this meditation, endeavor to share their delight with them: attentive, as if you beheld him speaking; and ready to approach with them, in case you should be called; dwelling on this pious subject, according to the lights and graces which it shall please God to bestow on you.

After the sermon is over, behold our Lord Jesus descending from the mount with his disciples, and familiarly conversing with them upon the road; and observe how that little simple congregation follow him, not in any formal order, but as the hen is followed by her chickens; each crowding about him, and struggling to get near him, the better to hear his divine discourse. Think you see the multitude running to meet him, and bringing their sick to be cured by him; for he cured all.

THE CENTURION ENTREATS JESUS TO HEAL HIS SERVANT.

CHAPTER XXI.

THE SERVANT OF THE CENTURION, AND THE SON OF THE PRINCE CURED.

AT Capharnaum, a certain centurion, that is, a captain of a company composed of a hundred men, had a servant who lay sick. Full of faith, therefore, he sent to our Lord Jesus Christ to entreat him to cure him: and our humble Lord answered, "I will come and cure him."—*Luke*. vii. When

the centurion **heard** the answer, he **immediately**
sent back **to him** this message : "Lord, **I am not**
worthy thou shouldst enter under my roof : **say but**
the word, and **my** servant shall be healed." Upon
which, Jesus, applauding his faith, cured the servant at a distance. In the same city lived a prince
or petty king, who went in person to Jesus, beseeching him to come to his house and cure **his sick** son.
But Jesus refused to go, though he acquiesced to
cure the youth. Here consider the merit of faith
in the centurion, and this fresh instance of humility
in our Saviour, who offered himself to go to the
servant, though he refused to go to the pompous
prince. Here you see that no exception ought to
be made to persons. "Our Lord shows more regard to the servant **of** the officer, than to the son of
the king."—*John* **iv.** Thus then it little becomes
us to show any regard in **our** charitable offices to
external pomp and appearance ; it is the goodness,
the right intention, and necessity of the person,
which are to draw our attention. In a word, our
services to **our** neighbor are to be guided, not by
complaisance, but by Christian charity.

THE SICK OF THE PALSY IS LET DOWN THROUGH THE ROOF.]

CHAPTER XXII.

THE PARALYTIC BROUGHT IN TO OUR LORD BY THE HOUSE-TOP AND CURED.

IN the same city of Capharnaum, while our Lord Jesus was teaching in a certain house where Pharisees and doctors of the law, from all parts of Judea and Jerusalem, were assembled to hear him,

some people came thither, and struggled to get in,
with a man ill of the palsy, whom they had brought
on purpose to have him cured by our Saviour.—
Matt. ii., *Luke* v. But finding it impossible to get
in at the door, on account of the great crowd, they
got upon the top of the house, and carried him in
that way and placed him before Christ. Jesus
then, seeing their great faith, said to the paralytic:
"Thy sins are forgiven thee."—*Mark* ix. The
Pharisees and doctors, looking maliciously on, said
to each other, that he had blasphemed, since he
attributed to himself, whom they considered as
mere man, the power of forgiving sins, which belonged only to God. Our benign and humble Lord,
searcher of the hearts and reins of man, answered,
"Why do you think evil in your hearts? That
you may know," added he, "that the Son of Man
has power on earth to forgive sins, I say, arise and
walk."—*Mark* ix.

Here are four things worthy of our meditation.
First, perspicuity of Christ's understanding, who
saw into their hearts. Secondly, that illness is
often the consequence of sin, and that absolution
from this often frees us from that; which may likewise be gathered from the sick man cured at the
fish-pond, whom our Saviour cautioned not to sin
again, lest something worse should befall him.
Thirdly, that great must be the merit of faith, since
the faith of one person may be beneficial to another:
as we have before observed in the case of the centurion's servant, and shall farther see, in the daugh
ter of the Cananean, who was cured by the faith of
the mother. And it is daily verified in the baptism
of infants, who, if they die before the age of discretion, receive, by the faith of others, the earnest
by which they are saved through the merits of

Christ, contrary to the accursed doctrine of some heretics. Fourthly, we may meditate on the goodness of our divine Lord sitting amidst the perverse Pharisees, affably confounding their malice, and working a miracle to try to convert them. Here recollect what I have said on the general subject of meditation.

CHAPTER XXIII.

OUR LORD CURES SIMON'S MOTHER-IN-LAW.

IN the same city it happened likewise that our Lord called in at the house of Simon-Peter, whose mother-in-law was in a high fever. Our humble Lord, informed of it, familiarly stretched forth his sacred hand to her ; and she immediately arose, and ministered to him and his disciples. But what did she minister ? We do not find that recorded. You may then devoutly imagine, that in the house of such poor people nothing but poor and humble viands, such as were soon prepared, were laid before them. Piously fancy too, that you see our Lord himself humbly helping to set things in decent order, in the house of his disciples : these, and such other humble exercises, you may entertain your thoughts with ; for all such, we may reasonably conceive our Lord to have done, who was come to minister, and not to be ministered unto. Thus then consider him familiarly seated at table, under this humble roof, in the midst of this little company of simple ones, and cheerfully partaking of their coarse food, with so much the more pleasure as his beloved poverty presided there.

VIEW OF THE VILLAGE AND LAKE OF TIBERIAS FROM THE SITE OF THE ANCIENT CITY.

CHAPTER XXIV.

OUR LORD SLEEPS IN THE BOAT.

OUR Lord Jesus entering into a boat with his disciples, composed himself to sleep, laying his head on a pillow ; for he might well be fatigued, as he passed his nights generally in prayer, and his days in the toil of preaching. When he was asleep, a sudden storm arising, the disciples were affrighted, and apprehended themselves in danger of perishing, but dared not awake him for some time. At length, however, overcome with fear, they roused him, crying, "Lord, save us, we perish." Our Lord arose, and, chiding them for their little faith, "commanded the sea and the winds, and the storm gave over."—*Matt.* vii., *Mark* iv., *Luke* viii. In these circumstances contemplate our Lord, according to the general rules I have before given you. Add this farther consideration, that though God seems sometimes to sleep to us, and to our concerns, especially in time of tribulation and need, yet we ought to remain firm in faith and confidence, without staggering; for he is ever really awake, and diligently watchful in what regards our good and safety.

CHAPTER XXV.

THE WIDOW'S SON RAISED BY OUR LORD.

AS our Lord was once going towards the city of Naim, he met a multitude of people bearing to the grave the corpse of a young man, the late son of a widow, who followed. The compassionate Jesus, moved to pity at her grief, approached, stopped the bearers, and made them set down the bier: then addressing himself to the corpse, said, "Young man, I say to you, arise." And the youth, who had been dead, arose, and he restored him to his mother; at which all were astonished, and gave praises to God for so great a wonder.—*Luke* vii. Here recur to the general heads of meditation.

CHAPTER XXVI.

OUR LORD RAISES A GIRL FROM THE DEAD, AND CURES MARTHA.

AT the instance of a very considerable man, our Lord Jesus was going with him to cure his daughter. A great multitude accompanied him, among whom was a woman extremely ill, who is re-

ported to have been Martha, the sister of Mary
Magdalen. This woman, acquainted with the wonders he had wrought, said to herself, that if she
could but touch the hem of his garment, she should
be made well. Accordingly approaching, though
with fear, she touched it, and was cured. Our Lord
then said, "Who has touched me?" When Peter
answered, "Lord, you see what crowds press upon
and molest you, and you ask, Who has touched me?"
—*Matt*. ix. Here consider the patience of Christ,
who suffers himself to be thus frequently molested
and pressed by the rude populace. However, our
Lord well knew what he said, and therefore added,
"I know that a virtue proceeded from me."—*Luke*
vii. Martha then manifested her cure, and our Lord
was pleased with curing her, with whom he was
afterwards divinely intimate, and told her, "Thy
faith hath made thee whole." Here again you have
a fresh commendation of faith : here likewise you
see that Christ is willing that his miracles should be
made manifest for the good of the public, and yet is
so humble as to conceal the part he has in them, attributing to the merit of her faith the effects of his
own divine power.

Here too it is worth your notice to observe what
St. Bernard remarks : "Every perfect servant of
Christ," says he, "may be called the hem or lowest part of Christ's garment, on account of the mean
opinion he has of himself." Let them, therefore,
who arrive to this pitch of perfection, perceive that
God hears their prayers, and grants them the cure
of diseases, or other miraculous powers, take care
not to be elated, nor attribute to themselves what
is properly his work, and not theirs. For though
Martha touched the hem with hopes of being cured
by the touch, as she really was, yet the virtue of

the cure came from the Lord, and not from the hem : and therefore he said, "I know that a virtue proceeded from me." Mind this well, and never attribute any good to yourself, for it all comes from our Lord Jesus.

Our Saviour after this went to the house of the great man above mentioned, and finding that the girl, whom he came to cure, was dead, he raised her again to life. Here again recur to the general heads of contemplation I have already proposed to you, and so often mentioned.

CHAPTER XXVII.

THE CONVERSION OF MAGDALEN, AND OTHER THINGS.

OUR gracious Lord, one day, by the invitation of Simon the Pharisee, went to dine with him, which he was accustomed to do, out of his natural courtesy, and the zeal he had for the salvation of souls.—*Luke* vii. Thus the divine Jesus attracted to himself those for whose sakes he came down from heaven, by eating, and familiarly conversing among them. The love of poverty, too, was another motive that induced him to do so. For he was extremely poor, and had received nothing of earthly substance for himself, or those that belonged to him. And therefore this pattern of humility readily and cheerfully accepted of their invitations as occasion required.

Magdalen, who probably had often heard him preach, and inwardly loved him, though she had yet given no proofs of it, chanced to hear of our Saviour's dining at the house of this Pharisee. Wherefore, touched already with a real sorrow at heart for her sins, convinced that he alone could rid her of them, and resolved no longer to delay her conversion, she went immediately to where our Saviour was; and with her eyes and face towards the ground, she passed by the whole company, regardless of all, till she came to her beloved Lord. Then throwing herself prostrate before him, with a certain secret confidence which her inward love for him gave her, with a torrent of tears she began to bathe his sacred feet, sighing, and tacitly saying in her heart, "Lord, I firmly believe, know, and confess you to be my God, and my sovereign; I have offended your divine majesty by many and great transgressions, and have multiplied my sins above the number of the sands of the sea. But, wicked sinner as I am, I fly to your mercy for refuge. I grieve and repent me from my soul, I crave pardon, am prepared to amend, and determined to conform my life for the future to your blessed precepts, without ever departing from them. Oh! reject me not; turn me not away from you; I am sensible I can have recourse to none but you, and you alone I love above all things. Repulse me not, then, but punish my iniquities as you shall think proper; but yet grant me the mercy I sue for." All this while she kept bathing the blessed feet of Jesus with the plenteous flood of her unbidden tears. Hence you may plainly see that our Lord went always barefooted.

At length, the illustrious penitent, with becoming resolution, stopped her tears awhile; and, judging them unworthy to fall on our Lord's sacred feet, she wiped them off with her beautiful hair, which she used on this occasion, because she had nothing more precious with her for that purpose, and because she wished to make those very instruments of her

former vanity instrumental to her present conversion ; besides that, she wished not to remove her
face off the feet of her divine master. When she
had wiped them dry, she devoutly pressed them
with her lips, with fervent eagerness that spoke her
glowing love, and afterwards anointed them with
precious ointments, as they were fatigued with frequent and laborious travelling. Behold her then
attentively, consider maturely her devotion, and
dwell awhile on her love to Christ, and his love to
her · and endeavor to be perfectly present at this
entertainment, which was very solemn in every circumstance. Contemplate likewise the divine Jesus,
how benignly he receives, and how patiently he
bears with all she does. **He** suspends his dinner
till she has done weeping and anointing his feet ;
and all the guests are in suspense at the novelty.
Simon could not help judging our Lord in his mind ;
thinking he would not have suffered such a woman to
approach him if he had been a prophet, and had
known who she was. But our Lord soon showed his
prophetic power, by answering Simon's thoughts
with a parable of the debtor. And openly to show
that love is the great end of all, concluded by saying, "Many sins are forgiven her, because she has
much loved."—*Luke* vii. And then turning to her
said, "Go, in peace." O delightful and pleasing
sentence ! How gladly did Magdalen hear it, and
how joyfully retire ! And now truly converted, she
led ever after an innocent, holy life ; and firmly adhered to the service and honor of him and his
blessed mother. Contemplate, therefore, gentle
reader, these circumstances with all the devotion you
can summon, and labor to imitate this charity,
which is so highly approved by our Lord Jesus, as
well by acts as words.

Here then you have an express proof that charity works a perfect peace and reconciliation between God and sinners. Hence it is that St. Peter tells us, that "Charity covers a multitude of sins."—1 *Peter* iv. As charity then is the soul of every virtue, and none are pleasing to God that are not inflamed with charity, I shall quote some authorities to induce you to aim at the acquisition of this great virtue, in order to render yourself acceptable to the blessed Jesus.

St. Bernard, then, says of it: "This excellent gift, charity, must needs be of incomparable worth, since the divine spouse is so earnest in enforcing it to his new bride. In one place, saying, 'In this all shall know you are my Disciples, if you have love for one another.'—*John* xiii. In another, 'I give you a new precept, that you love one another.'—*Ibid.* And again, 'This is my commandment, that you love one another.'—*Ibid.* xv. Praying elsewhere, that they become one, as he and the Father are one." A little lower the saint adds: "What can we imagine comparable to this, which is preferred even to martyrdom, and to a faith sufficient to move mountains? Thus then when I say to you 'Peace be with you,'—*John* xx.—I mean, may your peace proceed to you from within yourselves, and then all that may seem to threaten you with disturbance from without, will neither have power to fright nor offend you."

The same saint tells us: "The value of every soul is rated by the measure of its charity: as for example, the soul that has much charity is great and vast; that which has but little, is small and diminutive, nay nothing; for, as the Apostle in his first epistle to the Corinthians, chap. v., tells us, 'If I have not charity, I am nothing.' However, if it begins to possess even so slender a portion, as to love where it is beloved, to salute brethren and those who salute, we cannot say that soul is absolutely nothing. I will allow a soul to be not quite nothing, if at least it returns love for love, and cultivates social charity. And yet, according to our Lord's words, 'how much more than nothing does it do ?' I cannot then, by any means, think a soul great, but rather very little and very contracted, when I discover so slender a portion of charity in it : but if it grows up and improves so, passing the narrow limits of so contracted a charity, to reach with liberty of spirit the utmost bounds of gratuitous bounty, by extending itself with profuseness of good-will to every neighbor, and by loving all as itself ; can we any longer say to it, what dost thou do more ? For a soul that dilates itself thus much, must have a heart capacious enough to contain all mankind, even such as it is not tied to by blood, hopes of interest, or any other obligation, save that of which the Apostle speaks, 'Owe nobody anything, but that ye love one another.' However, if you will make farther advances towards the pious invasion of the kingdom of charity, and are desirous of carrying your conquest to its farthest confines, open the bowels of your compassion to your very enemies, do good to those who hate you, pray for those who persecute and revile you, and study to be peaceful to those who hate peace. Then, then, indeed, the altitude and extent of the heavens and of your soul are alike, and their beauty the same. Then will be fulfilled in you what is sung of God, 'extending the Heavens as a skin.'—*Ps.* ciii. And in this heaven of your soul, grown to so miraculous a height, width, and beauty, the Most High will delight to dwell, to expatiate and manifest in it his immensity and glory.'' Thus far St. Bernard.

You see then, pious reader, how useful and necessary a virtue is charity, without which it is impossible to please God, and with which every one is
sure to be agreeable in his sight. Study, therefore,
with all your heart, with all your mind, and with
all your force to possess it. For this possession
will enable **you** to bear with constancy, courage,
and cheerfulness, the greatest hardships and sever-
ities for the sake of God and your neighbor.

CHAPTER XXVIII.

JOHN SENDS HIS DISCIPLES TO JESUS.

THAT glorious soldier and precursor of Christ,
St. John the Baptist, was fettered in prison,
by order of Herod, for the defence of truth, in re-
proving him for detaining the wife of his brother.—
Matt. xi. Here it **was** that, desirous of committing
his disciples to the care of our Lord Jesus, he
thought of sending them on a message to him ; that,
hearing the words of this divine oracle, and seeing
the wonders he wrought, they might be inflamed
with the love of him, and become his followers.
Accordingly he despatched th·m to Jesus, whom
they asked in the name of John, ' Is it you who are
come, or **are we** to expect another?" Our Saviour
was then amidst a great multitude. Behold him
then, attentively, and see with what a pleasing aspect he receives the messengers of John, wisely answered them, first in deeds, and then in words. In
their presence, then, he cured the deaf, the dumb,
and the blind, wrought many other miracles,
preached to the people, and then among other things

said to these envoys, "Go, relate to John what you have heard and seen." They gladly performed their embassy, and related all to John, who as gladly received the joyful tidings. And after the death of John these disciples firmly adhered to Christ. After their departure our Saviour bestowed great encomiums on John to the multitude, as that he was a prophet, nay, more than a prophet, and that greater than he had not appeared among the children of men, etc., as you may find in the gospel. Contemplate, then, our divine Lord in every situation, whether preaching or teaching, or doing aught else, as I have already counselled you so often.

JOHN THE BAPTIST IS BEHEADED IN PRISON.

CHAPTER XXIX.

THE DEATH OF ST. JOHN THE BAPTIST.

HERE we may pause awhile in meditation on the glorious end of St. John the Baptist. When the impious Herod and his infamous adulteress had perhaps already plotted the death of the Baptist, that they might escape the reproaches due to their criminal intercourse, it happened that at a public entertainment, Herodias, the wretched fruit of their incestuous bed, danced so much to the satisfaction of Herod, that he promised her for a recompense the head of John ; and in consequence of this grant, he was beheaded in the prison. Behold here, how great a man is put to death, and how basely and ignominiously he is murdered by the iniquity of a reigning tyrant. Oh, great God, how did you suffer this ! What can be the cause of the death of so great a man, one of such perfection and sanctity as to be taken for Christ ?

But if you would digest this well, consider first the baseness and barbarity of his murderers, and then meditate on the singular greatness and eminence of John, and you will find fresh matter for surprise. You have already seen above, the many and great encomiums bestowed upon him, by our divine Saviour ; now hear what applauses St. Bernard gives him in his panegyric on him : ''That Mother and Mistress of all Churches, the Roman Church, of which it is said, I have prayed for thee, Peter, that thy faith fail not, received her consecration and badge in honor of St. John the Baptist, next after the name of our Saviour. It was indeed fit that the singular friend of his beloved spouse should pass thither when she was to be raised to her sovereign dignity. Peter was crucified, Paul was beheaded, but the preference of dignity was still given to the precursor. The purple of Rome in the blood of martyrs, the sovereign honor belongs to that holy patriarchate. Still, John is everywhere greater, singularly wonderful in all things, and above all. Who was ever so gloriously proclaimed ? Who was so amply replenished with the Holy Ghost in the womb of his mother ? Whose nativity does the Church solemnize except his ? Who was ever so fond of the solitude of a desert ? Who was ever known to converse so sublimely ? Who was the

first preacher of penance, and the kingdom of heaven !
John. Who baptized the King of Glory? John.
Who plainly revealed the sacred mystery of the
Trinity? John. To whom did Christ ever give
testimony but to John? And finally, to whom, after
Christ and his Mother, does the Church pay so much
honor as to John? John is a patriarch, nay, the
last, and head of all the patriarchs. John is a
prophet, nay, more than a prophet; for him, whose
coming he foretells, he points out with his finger;
John is an angel, and the chosen among angels;
our Saviour testifying it of him, saying: 'Behold I
send my angel, etc.'—*John* 1. John is an apostle,
and the first of apostles and their prince; and the
first of God's messengers; John is an evangelist and
preacher of the gospel; but the first in that office:
John is a virgin, nay, the illustrious pattern of all
virgins. The titlespring of purity, and mirror of
chastity: John is a martyr, and the encouragement
of other martyrs, and the soul of martyrdom from
the birth to the death of Christ: he the voice calling
out in the wilderness, he, the fore-runner of the
judge, and the herald of the DIVINE WORD. He is
Elias, and till his coming, the law and the prophets
were so many lamps that beamed forth brightly and
warmly their beneficent influence. I pass over in
silence the proficiency he made in angelic perfec-
tions, by which he not only imitated every degree
of that heavenly hierarchy, but even emulated the
highest in seraphic wisdom and virtue." Thus far
St. Bernard. Now hear that holy archbishop of
Ravenna, St. Peter Chrysogonus, in a panegyric on
the day of his decollation:

"The life of the Baptist," says he, "is the school of
virtue, the mastership of life, the plan of sanctity,
and the model of justice, etc." If, therefore, you

compare the excellence of merit, and eminence of dignity in John, with the littleness and grovelling baseness of those who beheaded him, you cannot help being surprised. What, shall a common executioner, the basest of the human race, be empowered to take away the life of so great, so good a personage, as if he were the meanest and most execrable highwayman or murderer! Behold him, then, with reverence and concern: how readily he stoops his neck to the command of this vile and reprobate butcher; how humbly he bends his knees, and giving thanks to God, lays his neck on the block, and patiently receives on it the repeated strokes of the barbarous executioner. Thus departs the Baptist, that intimate friend, near relation, and familiar servant of our Lord Jesus Christ. Oh! what a confusion is this for us, who, at the least visit of a trivial adversity, lose all sight of patience. John, innocent John, meets death, and such a death, with cheerfulness; and we, stained with the spots of sin, and worthy the divine indignation, are unable to sustain the least contradiction or indignity, though but in bare words.

Our Saviour was absent from the city, when John was beheaded, though still in Judea. But when his death was published, our divine Lord wept for him, as did his disciples, and the Blessed Virgin, who had nursed him in his most tender infancy, and who still loved him with extreme affection. Our blessed Redeemer, however, consoled her, with telling her, that it was expedient that he should die for the defence of the justice of his heavenly Father, that he would soon receive the reward of his sufferings in heaven: and that it was not the will of the Almighty to protect his saints from death, since they are not designed for this world: their kingdom

and country not being earthly but celestial; that
John was freed from the chains of the body, and

THE DAUGHTER OF HERODIAS BEARS THE HEAD OF JOHN THE
BAPTIST TO HER MOTHER.

the powers of death had no more force to retain
him on earth, or to detain him from the kingdom of
heaven, whither he would soon be transferred to reign
with the Father. He then exhorts his blessed mother
to be of good heart, as all was well with her beloved
Baptist.   Soon after this Christ retired from these
parts to Galilee.   Dwell, gentle reader, on the preceding subjects, endeavor to render yourself present
to them, contemplate them devoutly, and when you
have completed your meditation on these heads, as
God shall be pleased to inspire you, proceed to
others, and follow your blessed Saviour, step by step,
whithersoever he goes.

JESUS DISCOURSES WITH THE WOMAN OF SAMARIA.

CHAPTER XXX.

THE CONFERENCE OUR LORD JESUS HAD WITH THE
SAMARITAN WOMAN, AS HE SAT, BEING FAINT
AND WEARIED, BY THE SIDE OF THE WELL TO REST
HIMSELF.

IT happened upon a certain time, that as our Lord
Jesus was going from the country of Judea into
Galilee, he passed though the country of Samaria,
and being wearied with the fatigue of his journey,
which was the space of about fifteen miles, he sat
down to rest himself by the side of a well in the

way, which is called the well of Jacob. Consider here, pious Christian, thy God, and contemplate awhile how he is pleased to condescend to be tired and faint for thy sake. He frequently travelled, was often wearied, and his whole life was laborious, painful, and full of troubles.

While our Lord sat thus by the well's side, his disciples went into the next town to provide meat to refresh themselves : in the meantime, there came a woman of that country, whose name was Lucia, to draw water from the well ; with whom our Lord began to discourse, and to manifest himself unto her, talking of many great and sublime mysteries. What the particulars of this discourse were, how his disciples returned again unto him, and how, by the woman's relation of him, the people of the city came out to him, and detained him with them for many days together, and how, at last, he departed from them, I shall wholly omit, and pass by at present, it being clearly set forth at large in the gospel of St. John, to which I refer you, there steadily to contemplate every action of our Lord Jesus. For concerning the doctrine, which, for our instruction, may be gathered from this part of sacred history, there are many things concerning our Lord Jesus which are worthy of our greatest notice and attention. And first his great meekness, that our most humble Lord would vouchsafe to remain alone, while his disciples were gone into the city to buy provision.

Secondly, he disdained not to converse with that low and simple woman, and to treat with her of such sublime and sacred mysteries, as though he had been discoursing of them in the presence of the most learned and wise men. This ought to reprove and confound the pride of the more learned, who imagine

their labor and pains to be lost, in bestowing their words, swelled with vanity, upon a few or only on one person, esteeming so slender an audience unworthy to receive the exposition of their sublime doctrine. Thirdly, we may consider his great poverty, mortification of the flesh, and humility : his disciples brought him meat from the city, and desired him to eat : but where did he eat? Without the city, in the open air, and at the well's side, drinking of the water to quench his thirst. And in this poor and humble manner, being weary, faint, and hungry, he refreshed himself. Neither are we to imagine, that it was only once, or by chance, that this happened to him, but that it was his usual custom to do so. For we may well suppose, that our most humble Lord travelled through all the countries in the same manner, and that, though ever so faint and wearied, he oftentimes took his small refection, outside of the towns and habitations of the people, near some well or river, having neither delicate meats, curious plates, or delicious wines ; but the pure element from the river or fountain, was his chief and only liquor. He who makes the vineyard abundantly fruitful, the springs to flow with plenty, and gives life to all that move in the waters, was humbly contented, like another poor man, with bread and water only, upon bare ground. We may likewise contemplate how **intent** our Lord Jesus was **in the study of** heavenly things, and of **such as regarded more** the soul than the body ; for being **asked by** his disciples to eat of those meats which they **had brought** him, he answered them, saying : "I have meat to eat, that you know not—my meat is to do the **will** of him that sent me."—*John* iv. Wherefore he waited till the people of the city came, that he might preach to them ; desiring first to per-

form that which appertained to the nourishment of
their souls, before that which belonged to the re-
freshment of his own body, notwithstanding the
great necessity he had for it. Contemplate well
these things, and endeavor with all your study to
imitate his virtues.

THE DISCIPLES PLUCK THE EARS OF CORN ON THE SABBATH DAY.

CHAPTER XXXI.

THE DISCIPLES OF OUR LORD PLUCK EARS OF CORN
AND EAT THEM, THROUGH HUNGER, ON THE
SABBATH.

AS the disciples of our Lord Jesus passed through
the fields with him on the Sabbath-day, where
corn was growing, they plucked some of the ears,

and ate them through hunger. The Pharisees, who watched every word and action of our Lord, that they might find an occasion of accusing him of some breach of their law, reproved him and his disciples for it, saying: "Thy disciples do that which is not lawful to do on the Sabbath-day."—*Matt.* xii. But our Lord, to excuse them, first brought the example of David and his companions, who, when they were hungry, eat the bread of proposition. "Have you not read," said he, "what David did when he was hungry, and they that were with him : how he entered into the house of God, and did eat the loaves of proposition, which were not lawful for him to eat, nor for them that were with him ; but for priests only?" Secondly, that the priests of the law, on the Sabbath-day, circumcised and offered sacrifice ; which are both corporal works. "Have ye not read in the law," said he again, "that on the Sabbath-days the priests in the temple do break the Sabbath, and are without blame?"—*Ibid.* And what might have served for the greatest excuse, was, that the Lord of the Creation was himself present there, who was the author and master of the law, and therefore could give them leave to break it.

Let us now devoutly consider, and take compassion on the great poverty of the disciples, though in company of their Lord, who is the sovereign God and Master of all things. If we duly reflect on it, we cannot but be inspired with the love of poverty and corporal suffering for his sake. For is it not strange to think that they, who, by a singular prerogative, were chosen to the sublime degree of the apostleship, and made the princes of the world, should be obliged by hunger to eat the ears of corn as if they were not men, but irrational animals ; and this too, in the presence of him, who is the Creator

of all things, and who bountifully feeds and provides
for every creature ; and yet he sees them suffer such
want without bestowing any relief, as if he were not
able to help them ?   But our most gracious and merciful Lord, who wrought all things for **our greater**
example, and for the good of **our** salvation, **suffered**
them to be thus needy and poor, for the accomplish-
ment of his great designs ; as he himself also had
assumed the nature of man, with all the infirmities
incident to it, but yet without sin.   Wherefore,
though he had compassion on them in this their hun-
ger and distress, inasmuch as he was moved unto it
by the tender love he bore them ; nevertheless, **he**
was pleased with it, **as** he saw the good-will with
which they suffered, **out of** pure love and affection
to him.

And here all such as have forsaken the world for
the love of **our** blessed Lord, have a perfect model
from which they may copy all those virtues which
are necessary for them to follow ; viz. : patience in
distress, **true** poverty of spirit, and the virtue of
abstinence, contrary to the vice of gluttony. And
first, as to patience in all our necessities and wants :
seeing that the disciples of our Lord Jesus, who had
quitted all they possessed to follow him, suffered
with cheerfulness and patience such great distress
in his presence, whom they saw feed and relieve
miraculously many thousands of other men, how
much **more** ought we to be patient **in the like** necessities, when it shall please his divine goodness to
afflict us with them ? We are neither so deserving
his favors as they were, nor are we so perfectly established in his love ; but on the contrary, have
deserved, for our impatience and ingratitude to so
bountiful a God, much greater punishments, and
many more wants than his goodness permits us to

suffer, who, perhaps, has never yet permitted us to know any want at all.

Secondly, as to what relates to a perfect state of poverty: you are to understand that the poverty of our Lord Jesus far excelled in perfection, beyond any comparison, the voluntary poverty of any other person. For the poverty of those who, for the love of Christ, have forsaken all the riches and preferments of this transitory life, is generally in great **repute** with worldlings, and is commended and esteemed **by** them as a sublime and noble virtue. But the poverty of our blessed Lord was held in **contempt** by all; inasmuch as it was unknown to the world, that he voluntarily submitted to it; wherefore they esteemed it to be of mere necessity, **and** what he could not avoid, as seems to appear both in him and his disciples, who were obliged by hunger **to** pluck and eat the ears of corn; and that poverty, which we suffer not by choice, but through necessity, is too often reckoned a contemptible thing, so likewise was that of our blessed Lord; for such as knew him, saw that he had neither house nor habitation wherein to repose or to put his head, which drew upon him the contempt and derision of all that beheld him. This we may gather from the too general practice of mankind, who conceive the utmost contempt for the poor and distressed; but if, with patience and resignation, they submit to the divine will, they are in reality most worthy and pleasing in the sight of him who left them **his** glorious example: hence, it is a most dangerous and execrable sin **to** despise any man in his poverty or misery. The truly poor, however, are not those only who have forsaken all temporal riches, and make an outward show and profession **of** voluntary poverty, but they, who to this add the poverty of the spirit, that is, desire no plenty, nor seek any more comfort in the perishable goods of this life, than just as much as may suffice to support the infirmities of nature. For, if he that is poor remains so only for want of an opportunity of enjoying the goods and plenty of fortune, such a one has no share in the holy poverty of our Lord Jesus, but rather lives in poverty, misery, and distress in this life, without any merit of an eternal reward in the next. This is the true description of a perfect poverty, concerning which virtue St. Bernard speaks at large in his sermon upon the nativity of our Lord Jesus.

Thirdly, as to the virtue of abstinence, we may find most powerful examples of it both in the disciples of our Lord, and in our Lord Jesus himself. Gluttony is a vice against which we must struggle during our whole life. This we are taught by the holy fathers, who, by long experience, were true judges of the nature of its dangerous and repeated assaults. St. Bernard especially in many places tells us with what assiduity we ought to shun that vice and give to the body only so much nourishment as is necessary for its support. Whatever we allow it more than this, by feeding our lust, and exceeding our present necessities, exposes us to the danger of death, both soul and body. By yielding to this passion, our virtue is so often overcome, that like irrational and senseless brutes we prefer the gratification of our greedy appetites, to every other consideration, which gives rise to many disorders and infirmities. Thus our health is impaired, and not only the body remains indisposed to serve God, but even the soul is so much defiled that it cannot recur to him with becoming purity and cleanliness of heart.

Seeing then, that the vice of gluttony is so dangerous in its consequences and so much condemned by the fathers, we must endeavor to shun it as much as is in our power, and obtain the virtue of abstinence, which we may learn from the example of our blessed Lord, of his disciples, and other saints. They have taught us to subdue our flesh, and keep it in subjection by temperate food, and such a degree of abstinence as may be guided by the virtue of discretion, which, as St. Bernard saith, "is not only a virtue itself, but the director of all other virtues; inasmuch as where this is wanting, that which may seem to be virtue, is only vice." St. Gregory saith that, "Discretion is the mother and preserver of all other virtues." Now discretion, in relation to abstinence, and the nourishing of our bodies, consists in this, as St. Augustine teaches in his book of confession, that a man ought to use the same moderation in eating and drinking for the nourishment of his body, as he would use in taking of a medicine for the cure of an infirmity. For as in taking physic we should take such a portion or quantity as is sufficient for healing our sores, or the curing our disease, so likewise, as hunger and thirst became the infirmities of mankind, by the transgression of Adam, meat and drink, which are medicines appointed for the curing of these infirmities, ought to be taken only in such proportion as is conducive to that end.

The above may suffice of the virtue of abstinence, and the vice contrary to it, which is gluttony, which I have here taken occasion to treat of, from the hunger our Lord Jesus and his disciples sustained, and the poorness of their small refection, who, for our example, both here and in the desert, began vigorously to oppose and fight against the sin of gluttony.

CHAPTER XXXII.

THE JEWS, HAVING DRIVEN OUR LORD JESUS OUT OF THE CITY TO THE TOP OF A STEEP MOUNTAIN, ENDEAVOR TO THROW HIM DOWN THENCE.

WHEN our Lord Jesus was again returned to the city of Nazareth, the Jews desired to see him work some miracles; but our Lord showed them, by many reasons, how unworthy they were of such signs. Being vehemently enraged against him, they drove him out of the city; and our most humble Lord, closely pursued, meekly fled before them. Their fury was so much increased and kindled against him, that they drove him to the top of a high mountain, that they might thence have an opportunity of throwing him down headlong. Our Lord Jesus, however, by the power of his sacred divinity, passed through the midst of them, and went his way; for the time was not yet come in which he had chosen to die. Contemplate him here, devout reader, flying from his enemies, and hiding himself under a rock, to save himself from their fury; compassionate him in his sufferings and endeavor to follow his steps, in the practice of humility and patience

---

CHAPTER XXXIII.

THE MAN WITH A WITHERED HAND CURED BY OUR LORD JESUS.

AS our Lord Jesus was teaching in the synagogue on one of the Sabbath-days, there was a certain man whose wright hand was withered, whom our blessed Lord made **stand in** the midst of the doctors,

and said to them, "Is it lawful or not to do good on
the Sabbath day?" But they made him no answer.
He therefore said to the man: "Stretch forth thy
hand," and it was immediately restored.

Our divine Saviour was oftentimes pleased to
work miracles on the Sabbath, to confound the per-
fidiousness of the Jews, who interpreted the law
according to the letter; which he would have to be
observed according to the spirit. The law did not
forbid the performance of good works: and acts of
charity were not forbidden to be done on the
Sabbath-day; but the committing of sin, and servile
works. They, however, pretending to be greatly
scandalized, conspired against him, and said: "This
man is not of God, for he keeps not the Sabbath!"
Our Lord Jesus, notwithstanding, did not desist from
working miracles on the Sabbath; but rather performed them more frequently, on purpose to unde-
ceive them, and convince them of their error. Consider him then, pious Christian, in the exercise of
the above-mentioned good and charitable actions;
and according to his example, never omit the doing
any good work on account of others being unjustly
scandalized: for the fear of such scandal ought
never to make us desist from those works, which
are necessary for the salvation of a soul, or are helps
to its spiritual advancement in perfection. Although
it is true, in order to avoid giving scandal to our
neighbor, according to the prescription of perfect
charity, we should sometimes abstain from some
temporary satisfaction of the body rather than
offend him. Wherefore the apostle to the Romans
says: "It is good not to eat flesh, and not to drink
wine, nor anything whereby thy brother is offended, or scandalized, or made weak."—*Rom.* xiv.

JESUS MULTIPLIES THE FIVE LOAVES AND TWO SMALL FISHES.

CHAPTER XXXIV

THE MULTIPLICATION OF THE LOAVES, AND HOW OUR
LORD JESUS PROVIDES FOR THOSE WHO TRULY LOVE
HIM.

THE Holy Scripture tells us, that at two different times our Lord Jesus wrought the miracle
of the multiplication of a few loaves, with which
he not only fed, but fully satisfied many thousands
of people. Do you, however, Christian reader, reduce them both to one meditation : and attentively

consider the words and actions of Christ our
Saviour, as they are related in the holy gospel.
"I have compassion," saith he, "on this multitude,
because now three days they have continued with
me. Neither have they what to eat, and if I dismiss them fasting to their homes, they will faint in
the way : for some of them came from afar off."—
Mark viii. After which, he multiplied the loaves,
and they all ate and were satisfied. If we duly consider these words, together with the miracle he
performed, we shall find for our spiritual instruction,
many good motives to love and praise his holy name :
and more especially for that our Lord Jesus here
showed himself to be most singularly good and
merciful, most kind and courteous, most discreet and
circumspect.

And first, that he was most merciful, appears in
the words he spoke, saying, "I have compassion on
the multitude." Whereby it is plain, that it was
his pure mercy alone that moved him to feed and
satisfy them in their great hunger and necessity ;
for, as the royal prophet witnesseth, "All the earth
is full of his mercy."—*Ps.* xxxii.

Secondly, he plainly showed his wonderful kind-
ness and courtesy in the words which immediately
follow : " For lo," saith he, " now these three days
they have continued with me, having nothing to
eat." Holding himself, as it were, obliged to them
for remaining with him those three days, when indeed, on the contrary, it was for their own good and
advantage, and not for his ; save only, that out of
his endless bounty, his desire was, as he himself
affirms in another place, to dwell with the sons of
men, and be conversant with them for their salvation : for they that follow him by a good life, and
are desirous to harken to his doctrine, and keep his

commandments, he most singularly loves, and
never withdraws his bountiful hand from them, but
ever succors and relieves them in their necessities.

Thirdly, our blessed Lord showed his great discretion and circumspection, for seeing that many of
the people were come to him from distant parts, and
considering their necessities, and that it was dangerous to dismiss them again fasting, he said, "If I
dismiss them fasting to their home they will faint
in the way." Consider how full of sweetness and
heavenly comfort were these words. The same daily
happens to us. For we have not of ourselves wherewith to sustain either body or soul, unless he pleases
to give it us; and we should faint in our way,
should he leave us to ourselves, for without him we
cannot attain to any spiritual blessing, so that we
have no reason to glory in ourselves when we experience any comfort in our spiritual exercises:
since it is not our own, but all comes from him.
And therefore, if we duly reflect, we shall find that
the true servants of God, the more perfect they
were in a holy life, the nearer to God, and the more
excellently rich in the gifts of his divine grace, so
much the more humble were they in their own eyes,
attributing nothing to themselves but misery, wretchedness, and sin. For the nearer any one approaches
to God, the more he is illuminated: and therefore
more plainly discovers the great goodness and mercy
of God, so that pride and vain-glory, which proceed
from ignorance and spiritual blindness, can have no
place or residence in his soul: for he can have no
reason to be proud who truly knows God, and
thoroughly examines into his own state. But to
return! It is certain, that we come from afar off when
we come to God; this I speak in regard to myself,
and to such as are like to me, who have gone so far

astray from God by the sins we have committed. Wherefore, whoever returns again to him may be truly said to come a long way. But after Christ had spoken the above-mentioned words, he proceeded to deeds.

Behold him then, pious reader, how he takes the loaves in his hands, and having given thanks to God, gives them to his disciples to set before the multitude, and multiplied them in such a manner in their hands, that every one ate as much as he desired, and there still remained many baskets full of fragments. Consider likewise, how he looks on them while they eat, and is pleased in beholding the satisfaction they receive from this refection. And they, at the same time, admiring the wonderfulness of this miracle, fed both their minds and bodies, rendering praise and thanksgiving to their benefactor, and with joy repeated to each other the wonderful works of his mercy. Whether the Blessed Virgin was present or not, the holy scripture makes no mention: do you, however, Christian reader, meditate on this subject, in the manner your devotion shall direct you, and God shall please to inspire.

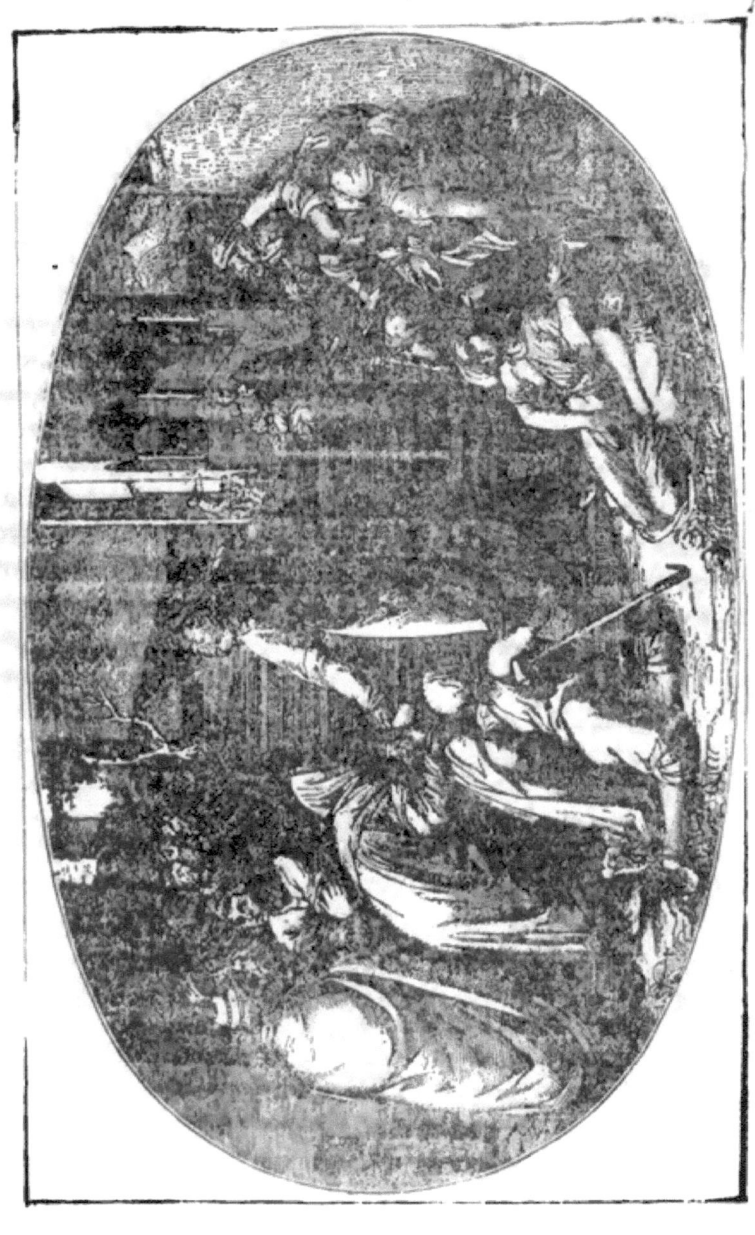

JESUS HEALS THE SICK AND THE INFIRM.

CHAPTER XXXV.

OUR LORD'S FLIGHT WHEN THEY WOULD HAVE MADE
HIM KING : AND AGAINST WORLDLY HONORS IN
GENERAL.

WHEN our Lord had fed the multitude, as
mentioned in the preceding chapter, they
sought to make him king. For they considered that
he was capable of supplying their wants, and therefore they wisely concluded that they could not be
in want of anything under such a king. But our
Lord Jesus, knowing their design, fled impercep-
tibly from them to the mountains, so that they could
not find him. Christ then would not accept temporal
honors. And observe how truly and unfeignedly
he labors to shun them ; he sends his disciples by
sea, and goes himself up to the mountains, that, if
they should persist in searching for him, as they
would probably do, by following his disciples, they
might look for him in vain among them. The disciples, indeed, would not have left our Lord, but
that he compelled them to do so. It was undoubtedly a pious disposition in them to desire to remain
with Christ : but more pious yet to leave him for a
time out of obedience to his will. Observe then
and meditate with what inward regret they depart
from him, but not till he urges them to it, by signi-
fying it to be his divine pleasure ; after which they
comply. and to show their humility and entire submission to his commands, go on board the vessel

without him, however perilous and grievous it be to them. Thus does Christ act daily with us in a spiritual manner; by our own good-will we would never have Christ absent from us, but his pleasure is otherwise; he comes into our souls, and is absent, at times, when he pleases, but always for our good. Hear what St. Bernard says upon this subject: "After the divine spouse has been sought for with continued vigils and prayers, and copious floods of tears, when he seems to be within reach of his pursuing spouse, he again escapes; and again coming up to his weeping pursuer, suffers himself to be taken, but not retained, flying as it were from her arms in the very minute when she embraces him; yet if the faithful soul devoutly persists in her pursuit of him with prayers and tears, he will again, at length, return to her, and, 'not disappoint her of the wish of her lips.'—*Psal.* xx. But again will he disappear, and remain unseen, till again he be sought after with the whole affection. Thus while the soul is confined to this mortal body, it has frequently the joy of its spouse's presence: but that joy is not complete, since, though his visitations rejoice her frequently, the frequent vicissitudes of absence give her equal pain. And this the beloved must endure, till, having thrown off her corporal burden, she shall be able to fly, raised on the pinions of her wishes, wafted over the plains of contemplation, and rapidly following her heavenly spouse whithersoever he goes. Neither shall every soul attain to this, but such only as by extraordinary devotion, vehement desire, and tender affection, proves herself a true spouse of Christ, and worthy that, taking upon him the form of a spouse, he should visit her in the nuptial ornaments of his grace." And elsewhere the same saint says, "Per-

haps he therefore withdrew himself, that he might
be recalled the more earnestly, and the more ardently retained. For thus he once feigned to be
going farther, not that he intended to do so much,
as to be invited to stay, with that tender solicita-
tion, 'Stay with us, for it is growing late in the evening.'"—*Luke* xxiv. And immediately he adds,
"This kind of pious feint, or rather salutary dispensation of Providence, which the incorporal word cor-
porally expressed to the body, the spirit frequently,
in a special manner peculiar to itself, makes use of to
exercise a truly devout soul. Passing by, he means
to be stopt : going away he is willing to be recalled :
his departure is a dispensation of Providence : his
return is ever the purpose of his will ; and both
are the effects of infinite wisdom, the great ends of
which he alone can fathom.

"Experience shows that the soul is frequently ex-
ercised with these vicissitudes of the absence and
presence of the divine word, and he himself spoke
as much : 'I go and I return to you.'—*John* xiv.
And likewise, 'A little while you shall not see me,
and again a little while and you shall see me.'—
Ibid. Oh, the little while, and no little while ! Oh
the short space, and tediously long duration !
Beloved Lord, do you call it a little while when we
are not to see you ? With humblest submission to
your sacred words, O Lord, it is a long, a tediously
long, and heavy age to lose sight of you but for an
instant. Yet both are true in different sense. An
age of your absence is but a little while, if our merit
only be considered ; but if compared to our wishes,
every moment is a tedious age. This the prophet
hints at, saying, 'If he should delay, wait for him :
because he will come and not tarry.'—*Hab.* xi. How
will he not tarry, if he should delay coming: un-

less it be that his coming will be expeditious with
respect to our deserts, though slow with regard to
our desires? Now the amorous soul is wafted by
desire, and drawn on by affection, overlooks its
merits, shuts its eyes to dazzling majesty, opens
them to spiritual joy, fixes its hope in salvation, and
in that confidently proceeds. Made intrepid at
length by hope, she boldly recalls the divine word,
and confidently invites the object of her delight,
calling him with unusual liberty, not her Lord, but
her beloved spouse. 'Return, my beloved, return.'"—*Cantic.* 1. And in another place, the
same saint says, "God never ceases to exercise with
such vicissitudes those who lead a spiritual life, or
rather those whom he intends to lift to spirituality;
visiting them betimes, and early proving them."
Thus far St Bernard.

You have seen then, gentle reader, how our Lord
Jesus alternately visits the soul, and departs from it
in a spiritual sense; and how the soul ought to behave under either circumstance. She must earnestly
and fervently solicit his return, yet patiently bear
his absence, after the example of his disciples, who,
out of obedience, enter the vessel without him, and
bear up against the storms that threaten, with hopes
of his succor to deliver them. But now let us return
to our Lord Jesus. When the disciples had put off
to sea, he went up alone to the mountains, and thus
escaped the hands of them who sought him. You
see with what care and study our Lord fled from the
honor of a worldly crown. And what did he this
for but to set an example for you to follow? His
flight then was not so much for his own sake as
for ours. For he well knew what rashness the
ambition of worldly honors must hurry us into.
For such honors are the greatest snare, that can be

laid to entangle us, and the strongest battery that can be planted for the subversion of our souls, whether it consists in the possession of power, ecclesiastic or secular, of authority, or learning. For it is almost impossible for men to delight in honors, without standing in imminent danger, and tottering, as it were, on the brink of a steep precipice : nay, rather should I say, without already rolling down, and that for many reasons. First, because the mind that is once delighted with honors is wholly engrossed by them, and thinks of nothing but preserving and improving them ; and St. Gregory, in his 30th Homily, observes, "that every one is so much the more alienated from the love of the Supreme Being, as he is delighted with inferior objects."

Secondly, because he is quite taken up with procuring a multitude of friends, acquaintances, and correspondents, by whose means and assistance he may add to his honors, and consequently must comply with many things incompatible with conscience and God's pleasure, out of mere complaisance to them, from whose friendship he expects such advantages. Thirdly, he envies those who are possessed of the honors he covets, and generally detracts from their merit, and thus falls into envy and scandal. Fourthly, he thinks himself, and would have others esteem him worthy of honors, and thus becomes vain and arrogant : when, according to the Apostle, "He who thinks himself something, when he is really nothing, deceives himself."—*Gal.* vi. And therefore Christ says, "When you have done all things well, say, we are useless servants."—*Luke* xvii. But when does an ambitious man say this ? Fifthly, he walks not according to the spirit, but according to the flesh ; and has not his heart raised and united to heaven, but leaves it loose and dissipated with a

variety of earthly objects. And sixthly, when once
a man suffers in himself a relish of ambition for
honors, he is so allured by them as never to be
satiated, but daily hankering after new ones, the
more he obtains, the more he desires to obtain, because he vainly conceits himself to be as honorable
and worthy in the esteem of others, as he is in his
own. Thus does he deliver himself up a prey to
ambition, the worst of vices, and the mother of
many. But to convince you of the malice of this
vice, let St. Bernard speak for me.

"Ambition," says he, "is a subtle evil, a secret
poison, a hidden pestilence, the author of all guile,
the mother of all hypocrisy, the monster-getting
parent of rancour, the moth of all virtues, the cancer-
worm of sanctity, the hardener of hearts, creating
diseases from their cures, engendering sickness from
medicines, and destroying all whom it basely sup-
plants, as a concealed enemy undermines a city, to
involve its inhabitants in its ruins. And what nourishes this dangerous vermin but the dissipation of the
mind, and the forgetfulness of truth ?—And what discovers this lurking traitor, and unkennels this worker
of darkness, but the light of truth ? Such is that truth
which says, 'What does it avail a man if he gain
the whole world, and lose his own soul?'—*Matt.* xvi.
And again, 'The powerful shall suffer powerful torments.'— *Wisd.* vi. It is this same truth that makes
a man reflect, how trivial is the comfort in ambition,
grievous the judgment attending it, how brief its enjoyment, and how obscure its end. And therefore
the third temptation, which Satan tried our Lord with,
was ambition, when he proffered him all the kingdoms
of the earth, if he would fall down and adore him.
You see then, that ambition is the worship of the
devil, for which he promises his adorers in recom-

pense, to lead them to worldly honors and glory."
In another place the saint says, "We are fond indeed of rising, and covet to be exalted. For we are
by nature noble creatures, and of a certain greatness
of soul, and therefore it is natural in us to wish to be
elevated. Yet woe to us if we follow him, who says,
'I will sit on the mount of the testament, in the skirts
of the north.'—*Isaiah* xiv. O wretch! in the skirts
of the north! that is too frigid a mount; however
you may covet power and eminence, we will not follow you thither. Yet how many to this very day follow your foul and fatal steps, **nay,** how few escape
being enslaved by the lust of power! Oh, unhappy
creatures, whom do you thus follow? Who is your
guide? Is not this the mount to which **the** angel
ascended, and fell a devil? **Are you not aware that**
after his fall, tortured with envy, **and wickedly**
anxious to supplant mankind, he showed them a like
eminence, telling them, 'You shall be like Gods,
knowing good and evil.'"—*Gen.* iii. And a little
after the saint **adds,** " Such the power of ambition,
that it can rob an Angel **of** angelic felicity. So the
ambition of knowledge stripped man of the glory of
immortality. **If a man try to ascend** the steps of
power, how many opponents, think you, will he
meet with, how many repulses, and how difficult a
road will he find? And suppose he should attain
the summit of his wishes, what has **he** gained?
'The powerful shall be powerfully tormented.'—
Wisd. vi. So that it is needless to enter into a
detail at present of the solicitudes **and** anxieties
which power produces. One ambitious of useless
knowledge, what labor must he not go through,
what anxiety of spirit, **and** still shall hear, *though
thou burst thyself*, *thou shalt not overtake it*. His
heart shall be bathed **in bitterness**, as often as he

sees one whom he thinks himself inferior to, or fancies that others do. What if he swells himself with conceit? 'I will destroy,' says the Lord, ' the wisdom of the wise, and reprove the prudence of the prudent.'—1 *Cor.* i. But I shall say no more, as you have seen, I fancy, how much the height of ambition, and the thirst of knowledge and power, is to be shunned by such as are any ways terrified at the fall of one angel, and the ruin of man. 'Mountains of Gelboe, neither snow nor rain shall fall upon you.' Yet what shall we do? It behooves us to ascend ; we are born, and imbibed with a desire of elevation : who then shall teach us a salutary ascent? Who but he who tells us, that he who is descended, he likewise is ascended? It is to him we are to apply to learn the right ascent, that we may not follow the footsteps of that evil guide, or rather seducer. For seeing that no one ascended, he, the Most High, descended ; and by his descent, secured to us an easy and safe ascent. He descended from the mount of power, in suffering himself to be encircled with the infirmities of the flesh ; he descended from the mount of science, in the simplicity of his preaching, to save all such as should sincerely believe. In reality, what can seem weaker than the little tender body and limbs of an infant? What more void of science than a child? Who less powerful than one whose limbs are nailed to a tree, and whose very bones are enumerated? And who would be thought less wise than one who should voluntarily part with his life, and make satisfaction for damages he had not committed? Thus you see how much he who descended, lessened and lowered himself beneath wordly power and wisdom. Nor could he ascend higher than he did in charity and goodness. But where is the wonder that Christ should climb by

descending, when we have seen men and angels
precipitated by attempting to rise." The same
saint elsewhere says, "Oh, the perverse ambition
of the sons of Adam ! Though it be a laborious task
to ascend, and an easy matter to descend, they
climb with levity, and descend with difficulty ; prone
to honors, and even to ecclesiatical dignities, a
weight too formidable for the very strength of ar.
angel. But to follow you, dear Jesus, no one is
ready : and few can be dragged, much less led by
your precepts." Thus far St. Bernard. From what
has been said, you may gather, gentle reader, how
much it behooves you to fly wordly and false honor,
and how certain it is, that true honor is to be attained only by humility.

But if some should flatter themselves with the
specious but vain pretext that their love and ambition for learning and honors are but for rendering
themselves more serviceable to their neighbors in
the affairs of their salvation ! St. Bernard will
answer them : "Oh ! that they who have thus am-
bitiously seized those honors, would but use them
with a fidelity equal to the confidence with which
they thrust themselves into them !" But I wish it
may not prove impracticable to gather the sweet
fruits of charity from the bitter plant of ambition.
Now to have that thorough contempt for honors which
they really deserve, requires more than an ordinary
share of the sublimest virtue. St. John Chrysos-
tom observes, " to be in the midst of honors, and
make a right use of them, is like a man conversing
with a very beautiful young creature, and making
a law to himself, never to cast a loose look on her.
A man therefore undoubtedly stands in need of the
greatest fortitude of mind to make a proper, and
none but a proper use of the power and honors conferred upon him. ..

ST. PETER BEGINNING TO SINK CRIES OUT FOR HELP.

CHAPTER XXXVI.

OUR LORD PRAYS UPON THE MOUNT; AND, DESCEND-
ING, WALKS ON THE WATERS: SOME REFLECTIONS
ON PRAYER.

AFTER the disciples had gone on board, and set
sail, our Lord went up a high mountain, and
remained there till the fourth watch of the night, in
fervent prayer to his eternal Father. Whence you
see that our Lord frequently spent his time in prayer,
and often the whole or the best part of the night.
Behold him then in this devout exercise, how he

humbles himself before his divine Father, and like
a good shepherd, solicits for us his flock; and this
in a state of mortification, of watching, and retirement.—And why principally does he do this, but to
set us an example of prayer, as he elsewhere recommended it to his disciples both by word and example.—1 *John* ii. He told them, *It is necessary
to pray, and never cease:* proposing to them the examples of the judge and the widow as related in
Luke xviii., to exhort them to confidence in prayer
and to perseverance in importuning; to which he
added another example, of the friend who lent the
loaves to his friend, merely to avoid being any
longer solicited. And all this was purposely meant
to inculcate on us the virtue of prayer. And indeed,
it is a virtue of the greatest importance towards obtaining all that is useful, and removing all that is
hurtful to us.

Would you obtain patience to bear up against adversities, be assiduous in prayer. Would you obtain
strength to overcome trials and temptations, be assiduous in prayer. · Would you become acquainted
with the subtle deceits of **Satan** in order to avoid
them, would you cheerfully persist in the service of
God, and tread the paths of mortification and affliction for his sake; would you renounce all carnal desires, and wholly betake yourself to a spiritual life,
be assiduous in prayer. If you wish to destroy evil
thoughts, be a man of prayer. If you are desirous
to enrich your mind with holy reflections, and your
heart with virtuous, fervent, and pious desires, be a
man of prayer. If you are willing to strengthen
your good purposes with manly resolution and
steady perseverance, be a man of prayer. In a word,
whether you mean to extirpate vice from, or implant
virtue in your breast, make prayer your constant

study.   For it is by prayer you receive the unction of
the Holy Ghost, who instructs the mind in all things.
It lifts a man to contemplation, and brings the soul
to the embraces of her heavenly spouse.   Such is
the power and efficacy of prayer.   In confirmation
of which, without recurring to any of the numerous
testimonies in holy writ, it is sufficient to recollect
the many ignorant and illiterate persons who by
prayer have obtained, and still daily obtain these
fruits.—Wherefore it highly concerns all, if they
mean to be Christians, to give themselves up to the
exercise of prayer, but this is more especially incumbent on persons in a religious state, who are supposed to have more leisure.

To this, gentle reader, I strongly exhort you:
make it the principal business of life, after the
necessary occupations of your state are complied
with, to attend to prayer.   Let it be your delight;
and take pleasure in nothing so much as in conversing
with God: which is done by prayer.   But, that
you may have the advice of a more able counsellor
than I am, to determine you, hear what St. Bernard
says on the subject:

"They," says he, "who make prayer their frequent study, are sensible of what I say.   Oftentimes we approach the holy altar with a coldness of
devotion, and kneel down to prayer with a froward-
ness of heart; but, persisting in it, we suddenly
feel ourselves replenished with grace, the breast is
nourished with the heavenly aliment, and the whole
interior expands to the inundation of piety."

And again in another place he says: "As often
as I talk of prayer, methinks something inwardly
says to me, whence is it that of all who persist in
prayer, there are so few who are sensible of its fruits!
—We seem to return from it just as we went to it;

no one gives us any answer, or makes us any grant. But follow not your own experience ; rather let faith direct you : for faith is ever true, but experience often otherwise. Now does not the truth of faith tell us by the mouth of Christ, 'Whatever ye ask praying, believe that ye shall receive, and it shall be done unto you.'—*Mark* ii. Let none of you then, brethren, despise or think lightly of his own prayer ; for he to whom we pray does not. Scarce has our prayer gained utterance, when it is recorded by him ; and one of the two we may infallibly depend on, that he either will grant what we ask, or what is more useful. We ourselves are ignorant what it most behooves us to ask ; but God compassionates our ignorance, and still receives our prayer, so as to grant us what is better for us, instead of the useless or pernicious favors we solicit. So that prayer is never barren, provided it be made with the requisite condition mentioned by the Psalmist, that is, delight in God. 'Delight in the Lord, and he will grant you the petitions of your heart.' "— *Ps* xxxvi.

A little farther on he adds, "Observe that such are called the petitions of the heart, which reason dictates as judicious ones. Neither have you cause to complain, but rather to return God thanks with sentiments of the utmost gratitude, since such is the great care he takes of you, that when you ask what is useless, or perhaps detrimental to you, he grants you something better in the stead of it : like a tender parent, who gives a child bread when he asks it, but gives him not a knife for asking. You are to take notice, that the petitions of your heart are wholly contained under these three heads, nor can I see aught which a good man can covet that is not included in them, namely, the goods in this life, which are those of the body and those of the soul, and are two of the three heads; the third is the beatitude of eternity. Wonder not that I include the goods of the body among the blessings which we are to ask of God; for corporal gifts are no less his than those of the spirit, and therefore are to be asked of him, as far as is necessary or conducive to the spiritual; for example, we may, nay ought to ask and hope for the necessary support, to enable us to serve God. But our greatest solicitude, our most fervent and pious importunity, ought to be for obtaining virtue, and the grace of God for our souls in this life, and glory in the next, where both body and soul will be crowned with complete felicity."

And a little farther he says, " Let prayer then for temporals be confined to absolute necessaries: let prayer for the spiritual profit of the soul be free from all impurity, and directed wholly to the divine pleasure: but let prayer for eternal happiness, with all due regard to humility, be bold and daring, with presumption on God's mercy alone." " He that would pray apart, and with fruit," says the same saint, " must choose not only his place, but his time. The time of fasting is certainly the fittest, especially when the night hushes nature into a profound silence, for then prayer will be both purer and more free. Rise, according to the prophet Jeremiah, 'Rise in the night, in the beginning of your vigils, and pour out your soul like water in the presence of the Lord your God.'—*Lam.* ii. How securely does prayer ascend by night, when no witnesses are by but God and his angel, who presents it at the altar of Heaven! How grateful and pleasing does modest secrecy make it appear in the eyes of the Almighty! How serene and undisturbed does it reach his ears, when removed from noise and hurry! And finally, how pure and sincere must it be when unsullied with worldly solicitudes, and not tempted by public applause and flattery? It was for this reason that the spouse in the Canticles retreated to the privacy of her bed-chamber, and to the stillness of the night, to seek her spouse, the divine word, that is, to pray. For in reality they are one and the same thing. Since, otherwise, you cannot be properly said to pray, if in your prayers you seek aught beside the divine word, or on his account, for he contains all you can seek. In him are the remedies for all diseases, supplies for all necessities, helps for all defects, and variety of perfection. In him, in short, you may find whatever is necessary, fit, or useful. It is needless and useless, therefore, to ask anything besides the divine word, who himself contains all things. For even if we should, when necessity requires, ask of God any temporal favors, provided we ask them as we ought, for the sake of the divine word, we cannot so much be said to ask the temporals as the word, for whose sake we asked them." Thus far St. Bernard.

Here, gentle reader, you have the beautiful sentiments of St. Bernard, a man endowed with a sublime contemplative genius, a fervent spirit of prayer, and a refined taste for spiritual pleasures. Reflect on his words, that you may take pleasure in them ; it is for this purpose that I quote them so frequently, for they are not only full of spirit, but highly eloquent and pathetically moving to the service of God. He was a man equally eminent for wisdom and sanctity ; endeavor, therefore, to imitate him by putting in practice the pious counsels he gives. By this means will I accomplish the purpose I had in view in referring to him so often. But let us return to our Lord Jesus.

While our Lord was praying on the mount, the
disciples were at sea in the greatest dismay and
affliction, the wind being contrary, and the vessel
harassed with tempestuous weather. Behold, then,
and compassionate them amidst this severe tribulation. They are attacked by a storm, in a dark night,
and without their Lord. A severe trial indeed! At
the fourth hour of the night, our Lord descended
from the mount, and walking on the waves, came
up to them. Contemplate here our Lord, who,
fatigued with long watching and praying, descends
barefooted from this steep and perhaps craggy
mountain, and walks upon the water as on dry land!
Thus the watery element knew and confessed its
Creator. When he drew near to the ship, his disciples saw him, and taking him to be a shadow or
spectre, screamed out: but our gracious Lord, unwilling to terrify or afflict them any longer, said to
them, "I am here, be not afraid."—*Matt.* xiv. Then
Peter, confident of the Lord's power, began, with
his leave, to walk likewise on the waters; but de-
sponding, was about to sink, when our Lord stretched
forth his right hand, and saved him from sinking.
The gloss upon this place tells us, that our Lord
made him walk on the waters, to give him proof of
his divine power; and suffered him to sink, in order
to remind him of his weakness, and not proudly to
presume himself on an equality with him.

Our Lord afterwards entered the vessel, the storm
ceased, and serenity ensued. The disciples received
him with reverence, rejoiced, and felt more perfect
tranquillity than before. Contemplate him and his
disciples in every one of these passages, which are
rich in matter of devotion. You may likewise draw
from them the moral reflection, that our Lord frequently does the same with us in a spiritual sense,

suffering his beloved to be inwardly or outwardly afflicted in this world, "because he scourges every child whom he accepts."—*Heb.* xii. "For they," the Apostle adds, "who are out of discipline, are not legitimate children, but bastards." It is necessary, therefore, for us to undergo trials and afflictions in this life ; because from them we gain knowledge and acquire virtue, and learn to keep them when acquired ; and what is more, we build all our hopes on them of future and eternal rewards. For which reason we ought not to repine and be impatient under them, but to love and cherish them. But because the advantage of tribulation is great, and yet unknown to many, we therefore look upon them as difficult, nay, insupportable. Therefore, gentle reader, that you may be instructed to bear them as you ought, I will, according to my custom, bring you the authority of St. Bernard. "Tribulation," says he, "is useful, it works a trial, and leads to glory. 'I am with him,' says the Lord, 'in tribulation.' Let us give thanks then to the Father of mercies, who is with us in tribulations, and consoles us in every affliction. For, as I said, tribulation is a necessary good, which is changed into glory, and terminates in joy : a long, an ample, a plenary joy, which no one shall snatch from us. Tribulation is necessary ; and this necessity brings forth our crown. Let us not despise this seed brethren ; it is a small one indeed, but great in the fruits it is big with. Grant it to be tasteless, grant it to be bitter, even grant it to be a grain of mustard. Let us not look upon the outside, but upon what is contained in it. What you behold of it is temporal, the rest which you cannot see, eternal." And lower down, he says : " 'I am with him in tribulation,' saith the Lord, 'and I shall require no other merit than tribulation.' How good then is it to adhere to God. I will do so then, and ever place all my confidence in him, for that he says, 'I am with him in tribulation; I will free him and glorify him.'—*Ps.* xc. 'My delight,' says he, 'is to be with the children of men.' He came upon earth to be with those who are sad at heart, and to be with us in our tribulations. But there shall come a time when we ourselves shall be lifted to meet Christ in the air, and thence to remain forever with our divine Lord, provided we, in the meantime, endeavor to have him with us here. O Lord, it is good for me to be troubled, so thou be but with me. Nay, infinitely better is it than banqueting or triumphing without thee. The furnace tries the potter's vessels; and tribulation tries the just. What are we afraid of? Why do we despond? Wherefore do we fly the furnace? Does the fire rage? No matter; the Lord is with us in tribulation. If God is with us, who dare be against us? What does it import who it is? If he has but hold, who shall make him quit his hold? Lastly; if he glorifies, who has power to humble?" "Let us not, then," says the same saint, "glory in hope alone, but even in tribulation. 'I will gladly glory in my weakness, that the strength of Christ may dwell within me.' says St. Paul.—2 *Cor.* xii. O desirable weakness which is rewarded with the strength of Christ! Ah, who will give me not only to be weak, but even to faint, and be lost to myself, so I be but strong in force of the Lord of forces. For strength is perfected by weakness, and virtue gathers force from infirmity, as the same Apostle says." And again; "when I am weakened then I grow strong." "It is for this reason," adds St. Bernard elsewhere, "that the spouse in the Canticles calls her beloved not a bundle, but a little bundle ; for that love makes every burthen light, and every grievance portable. Well might she call him little, for 'a little one was born to us:' But more especially for that 'the sufferings of this world are not to be compared to the future glory which will be revealed in us,' if we credit St. Paul.—*Rom.* vii. 'For our present momentary light tribulation will, on high, work in us an eternal weight of glory beyond measure,' as the same Apostle says.—*2 Cor.* iii. And that will one day be a heap of glory to us which is now but a little bundle of bitterness. And may it not truly be called a little bundle, since Christ himself tells us, that his yoke is sweet and his burthen light ? Not that it is light in itself ; for the bitterness of death is a severe and dreadful trial, if it be considered only on his own account, yet love makes it seem light and easy."

The same saint elsewhere says, "If we cast an eye over the whole Church, we may easily observe, that the spiritual members of it are much more combatted than the carnal. This is the craft of pride, envy and malice, always to disturb the most perfect : according to the words of the prophet, 'his food is of the chosen sort.'—*Abac.* i. Nay, it is the dispensation of Divine Providence that it should be so ; not suffering the weak to be tried beyond their strength, but drawing even advantage from temptation ; while the more perfect but increase the number and glory of their triumphs over their enemy, in every fresh trial they undergo. With much more eagerness and warmth the adversary struggles to defeat the Church's right wing rather than her left ; not laboring so much to defeat the main body of their forces immediately, as indirectly to weaken it by wasting its very soul." "Now," adds the saint, "there all our resistance is required, where necessity urges most, where the weight of war hangs heaviest, where the battle is the warmest, and the combat most pressing."

Again he adds: "This is the great grace of God to his Church ; this his mercy toward his servants ; this his regard for his elect, that covering her left wing to spare and connive at its weakness, he heads and supports her right ; hence the prophet, in the person of the Church, says : 'I took care to have the Lord always before me, for he is at my right hand that I may not be moved.' "—*Ps.* xv. And again : "O good Jesus ! be thou always on my right ; take hold of my right hand, for I know that no adversary can affect me, if no iniquity sways me. Let my left be harassed and mutilated ; let it be assailed with injuries and aggravated with insults : I willingly sacrifice it, so I be under your custody and protection, so that you stand at my right hand."

And elsewhere, "It is one thing," says he, "to be actuated by virtue, another to be ruled by wisdom : it is one thing to be absolute in virtue, another to be delighted in sweetness. For though wisdom be powerful and virtue sweet, yet, to give words their true meaning, vigor belongs properly to virtue ; and serenity of soul, with a kind of spiritual sweetness, is the certain mark of wisdom. And this I believe the apostle meant, when after many fine counsels relating to virtue, he adds, 'that wisdom consists in sweetness in the Holy Spirit.' To resist then, to repel force with force, which are properties strictly belonging to virtue, are undoubtedly attended with real honor : but that honor a very laborious one. For there is a great difference between the painful defence of their honor and the quiet possession of it. In short, to be actuated by virtue, and to be in full enjoyment of virtue, are two things.

Whatever virtue produces, wisdom **enjoys**: and what wisdom disposes and resolves, **virtue moderates,** and puts in practice. 'Write wisdom in your leisure,' says the wise man.—*Eccles.* xxxviii. The leisure then of wisdom is business; and the more wisdom is at leisure, the **more** active **it is in** its proper sphere. On the other side, virtue **shines** the brighter **for exercise**: and to be properly **active, is** the **proof of virtue.** So that if any one should define wisdom to be the love of virtue, I cannot see **how** he would be wrong. For where there is love, labor becomes sweetness, **and** therefore, perhaps, wisdom, which in Latin is *sapientia,* takes its etymology from *sapor,* relish, as a kind **of** quality or ingredient added to virtue, which gives a relish to that which would otherwise be merely tasteless and insipid. Nor should I think it amiss to define wisdom, the relish of good. It belongs then to virtue," adds the saint, "to bear troubles with fortitude; but to wisdom, the rejoicing in tribulations. To comfort your heart and sustain the Lord, is the part of virtue; **but to** taste and see that the Lord is **sweet, is that of wisdom.** And that the properties of both may the better appear from nature itself, let **it** suffice to observe, that **modesty** of mind is **a** certain proof of wisdom, as constancy is of virtue. **And right it is** that **wisdom** should follow virtue, since virtue is a kind of **solid** foundation on which wisdom raises the superstructure."

In another place, he **says,** "Happy the man who directs the sufferings and passions with a view of justice, so as to bear all he suffers for the Son of God, **without** complaining at heart, but with praise and thanksgiving. He who carries himself thus, properly **takes** up his bed and walks. Our bed is our body, **in** which before we were languishing, subservient to our unruly desires and lawless appetites. We then take up this bed when we compel it to obey the spirit." "The spirit," says the same saint, "is truly manifold which inspires, so many different ways, the children of men in such a manner, that no one can abscond, or screen himself from its heat. Insomuch that it is given them for their use, for miracles, for salvation, for help, for comfort, and for fervor in devotion. For the use of life it is given to the good and bad; and yields alike to the worthy and the unworthy abundance of advantages, without any limits prefixed to it: and therefore he would be highly ungrateful, who should deny or not acknowledge these benefits of the spirit. It is given for miracles, in the many signs, prodigies, and wondrous virtues it operates by the hands of some. It was the spirit operated so many marvellous works in antiquity, and which confirms our faith in old miracles, by the daily new ones it manifests to us. But as the gift of miracles is not always useful to the operator of them, therefore the spirit is likewise given to salvation, as when, with all our heart, we turn to the Lord our God. It is given for help, when, in the midst of our struggles with trials of trouble, it assists our weakness. And, when the spirit gives testimony to our spirit that we are the children of God, that inspiration is given us for our comfort. Finally, the spirit is given for fervor, when breathing strongly into the hearts of the perfect, it kindles a powerful flame of divine charity, by the means of which, in the hope of the children of God, we glory in tribulations, deem scandal an honor to us, rejoice in the injuries done us, and are transported with pleasure when loaded with contempt. To all of us then the spirit is given for salvation, but not alike for fervor. There are but few replenished with this spirit; but

very few, who covet and pursue it. We are content
with our own narrowness; and neither labor to
breathe the breath of liberty, nor even so much as
aspire to it." Thus far St. Bernard.

You have seen then, gentle reader, the many and
beautiful reasons which the saint gives, to show how
necessary afflictions are for us. Wonder not, then,
that our Saviour should suffer his disciples, whom he
loved so tenderly, to be harassed with tempests,
tears, and afflictions, since you see the great useful-
ness of them. We frequently read of their being
agitated with storms and contrary winds, but never
read of their being once shipwrecked. Which ought
to serve you as a lesson to stand firm, patient and
cheerful, amidst the contradictions and trials you
may meet with: and so to exercise yourself in the
practice of the spirit, as, filled with its fervor, to
covet sufferings for the sake of our Lord Jesus Christ,
who chose this way for himself and his followers,
and was the first to tread it before us.

THE WOMAN OF CANAAN ENTREATS JESUS IN BEHALF OF HER
DAUGHTER.

CHAPTER XXXVII.

CHRIST RELIEVES THE DAUGHTER OF THE WOMAN OF
CANAAN, WHO WAS POSSESSED WITH THE DEVIL:
AND HOW OUR ANGEL GUARDIANS FAITHFULLY
ASSIST US.

AS our Lord Jesus was going about exercising
in the most laborious manner the functions of
preaching, and curing the infirm, there came to him
a woman of Canaan, of the race of the Gentiles, be-

seeching him to heal her daughter, who was possessed with the devil. This woman's faith was so
great, that she firmly believed, and without hesitation, that he could do it. Notwithstanding our Lord
at first made her no answer, she persisted, and continued to cry out, and to beg of him to have mercy
on her : insomuch, that his disciples, compassionating her cries, earnestly entreated him in her behalf.
And, when our Lord at length made answer, that
"it was not good to take the bread of the children,
and to cast it to the dogs ;" she, with profound
humility, replied, "that the dogs also eat of the
crumbs that fall from the table of their masters."
Wherefore, she was thought worthy to be heard,
and was granted what she petitioned for.

Consider here our Lord Jesus and his disciples,
and have recourse to the general heads of meditation,
as I have before prescribed to you. Reflect, however, at the same time, on the virtues of this woman,
and endeavor to profit by them, which were chiefly
three. The first was, her great faith, which even extended to her daughter, and for which she was
praised by our Lord. The second was, her persevering prayer ; for she was not only persevering
but importunate : which importunity is also acceptable to God, as I have before showed you. The
third was, her profound humility ; for she neither
denied herself to be included in the comparison
which our Lord made, nor thought herself worthy
to be reckoned among his children, or to have the
bread itself, but was content to receive the crumbs
alone. She greatly humbled herself, and therefore
obtained what she sought for. The same will happen to you if, with a sincere, pure, and faithful
mind, persevering in prayer, you humble yourself
before God, esteeming yourself unworthy to receive

any good from him, you may then assuredly expect
to obtain what you **ask for**. And as the apostles
interceded for the Cananean **woman,** so will your
angel guardian intercede **for** you, and offer up your
prayers to the Almighty. **Upon** this head hear St.
Bernard : .

" Often **when** my soul has been sighing, **praying,**
and tormenting itself with anxiety for its **heavenly**
spouse, and **that** the dearly desired, and **so** much
sought after, has, in his own mercy, condescended to
meet **her,** I **thought** she might, from her own experience, **repeat that** sentence of Jeremiah : ' Thou
art **good, O Lord,** to such as hope in thee, to the soul
which seeks **thee.'** The very angel who accompanies
our heavenly **spouse,** is the previous minister of the
secret salutation ; with what **joy,** with what delight,
with what **transport, turning** to our Lord, does he
say : ' I render thanks to thee, O Lord of Majesty ;
because thou hast given him his heart's desire, and
hast not withholden the request of his lips.'—*Ps.* xx.
He it is who sedulously, and in every place, as
a constant pursuer of the soul, never ceases to
admonish it by continual suggestions, saying :
' **Delight** thyself in the Lord, and he will give thee
the desires of thy heart.' **And** again : ' Wait on
the Lord, and keep his **ways.** Though **he** tarry,
wait for him, because he will surely **come, he will**
not tarry.'—*Hab.* ii. And to the Lord he says : '**As**
the hart panteth after the fountains of water, so
my soul **panteth** after thee, O God.'—*Ps.* xli.
' He hath **desired** thee in the night, and thy spirit
in the inmost recess **of** his heart. From **the** morning he hath watched **unto** thee.' And again : ' The
whole day he hath stretched out his hands unto thee.
Dismiss him. for he crieth after thee. Return, O
Lord, and vouchsafe to give ear. Look down from

Heaven and behold and visit the forsaken.' The
faithful paranymph, who is conscious, without envy,
of the natural love between the soul and her spouse,
seeks not anything for himself, but only the glory
of his Lord. He passeth mutually between the
heavenly spouse and his beloved, offering her vows,
and bringing his gifts, exciting her to love, and
moving him to mercy. Sometimes also, though
seldom, he renders them present to himself; either
attracting her, or inviting him, for he is familiarly
known in the sacred mansion of Heaven, nor fears
a repulse, as he sees daily the face of the heavenly
Father." Thus far St. Bernard.

"WOE UNTO YOU, SCRIBES AND PHARISEES."

Jesus openly, in the hearing of His Disciples and the People, taxes the Pharisees and Scribes with their hypocrisy and their secret vices.

CHAPTER XXXVIII.

THE PHARISEES, AND OTHERS, SCANDALIZED AT THE WORDS OF OUR LORD JESUS.

WE ought never to wonder that some take occasion of scandal at our words and actions, though they be ever so good and perfect; seeing that this often befell our Lord himself, who could not err in word or deed. For it happened at a certain time that the Pharisees asked our Lord, why his disciples did not wash their hands before they ate? Our Lord answered and reproved them for having more regard to the outward cleanliness of the body, than the inward purity of the soul. At which answer they were scandalized; but our Lord regarded them not.

At another time, as he was teaching in the synagogue, some of his disciples, being too worldly-minded, did not understand him, and went away. But to his chosen twelve he said, "Will ye also go away?" Peter, in the name of the rest, answered: "To whom shall we go? Thou hast the words of eternal life." Consider him in these and the like things; how he speaks with authority, and teaches with true doctrine, having no regard to the scandal of the weak and simple: wherefore we must observe, first, that we are not to depart from the virtue of justice on account of another being scandalized. Secondly, that we ought to be more careful for the inward purity of our hearts, than solicitous for the outward cleanliness of the body, which our Lord, in another place, more expressly recommends, saying, in St. Luke, that "we must live according to the spirit:" so that the words of our Redeemer should not seem strange to us, as they did to those disciples who, when he said in St. John, "Unless you eat the flesh of the Son of Man," etc, could not bear to hear them; and therefore, being scandalized, departed from him, but we should rather acknowledge them to be the words of eternal life; that, together with the twelve that remained with him, we may endeavor perfectly to imitate him.

CHAPTER XXXIX.

THE REWARD PROMISED BY OUR LORD JESUS TO THOSE WHO FORSAKE ALL FOR HIM.

ST. PETER, the prudent and faithful disciple of our Lord, on a certain occasion asked him, in the name of the rest of his brethren the apostles, what reward they should have who had quitted the world, and all things in it, for the love of him. Our Lord, amongst other things, answered, "That they who should forsake all worldly things to follow him, should receive a reward of a hundred-fold in this world, and life everlasting in the next." Consider well the greatness of this reward, exult with the utmost joy, and render praise and thanksgiving to God, who has placed thee in a state to negotiate so advantageously for thyself as to be able to gain a hundred for one, and, withal, eternal life. This hundred-fold, however, is not to be understood of temporal things, but of spiritual ones only; that is, of inward consolation,

and heavenly virtues, which we shall prove by experience, and not acquire by knowledge. For when
the soul begins to have a true relish for the virtues of
poverty, charity, patience, and other Christian perfec-
tions, and takes pleasure and delight in the constant
practice of them, may it not be truly said of her,
that she has received a hundred-fold? And if at
length she still rises to more sublime degrees of perfection, so as frequently to partake of the inward
visits of her divine and heavenly spouse, may it
not be again affirmed with truth, that she has received a thousand-fold for all, whatever it may be,
that she has given up for his sake? You see then
the veracity of the words which were uttered by
Eternal Truth, who never fails even in this world,
to reward the soul that is truly devoted to him with
an hundred-fold, and this not once, but frequently;
affecting it often with so deep a sense of his divine
love as to make it esteem as the merest dirt everything it has forsaken, and the whole world itself,
for the sake of obtaining possession of its divine and
heavenly spouse. But that you may be more amply
instructed in relation to this hundred-fold gift of the
gospel, and may reap more benefit from it, hear
what St. Bernard says on that head: "If any
one," says he, "should say, show me the hundred-
fold that is promised, and I will freely quit all
things of this life to obtain it. But why should I
show it? Since faith, which has human reason for
its voucher, can have no merit. Will you sooner
give credit to the evidence of man than believe the
promises of God? You err by diving too deeply into
the hidden mysteries of the Lord. Unless you believe, you cannot understand. It is a hidden
manna; and in the apocalypse of St. John, a new
name is promised that shall overcome: a name

which no one knows but he that receives it.'' And again he says : ''Does he not possess all things to whom all things are turned to good ? Has he not received a hundred-fold who is filled with the Holy Ghost, and possesses Christ in his breast ? Or rather, shall we not say, that the visitation of the Holy Ghost, and the presence of Jesus Christ, far exceed the hundred-fold gift of any other thing ? 'Oh ? how great is the multitude of thy sweetness, which thou hast laid up for those that fear thee, which thou hast wrought for them that trust in thee !' saith the royal Psalmist.—*Ps.* xxx. Observe here how the soul breaks forth into the remembrance, of the abundance of spiritual sweetness, and how, in endeavoring to express herself, she multiplies her words. 'How great,' saith she, 'is the multitude,' etc. This hundred-fold, therefore, is the adoption of children, the freedom and first-fruits of the spirit, the delight of charity, the glory of a good conscience, and the kingdom of God which is within us. It consists not in meat or drink, but in the justice, peace, and joy of the Holy Ghost. A joy indeed, not in the hopes of a future glory, but rather in the present suffering of tribulations. This is that fire which Christ would have vehemently to be enkindled. This is the virtue which made St. Andrew so cheerfully embrace the cross he was to die on, St. Lawrence despise the butcheries of his cruel tyrants, and which made St. Stephen, at his death, pray for those who stoned him. This is that peace which Christ left to those that should follow him, for it is 'a gift, and peace to the elect of God.' It is the peace of the father, and a gift of future glory. It exceeds all sense, and is not to be compared with anything under the heavens, or whatever is desirable in this world. This is the plentiful grace of devotion, and the holy unction teaching us all those things, which they prove who have experienced them, and they who have not experienced are ignorant of." Thus far St. Bernard.

Rejoice then, and be glad, and as I have said before, render thanks to God, that he has called you to receive this hundred-fold, and invited you to enter often into the paradise of joy, which by the study and exercise of prayer, you may hope to obtain.

CHAPTER XL.

OUR LORD JESUS ASKS HIS DISCIPLES WHAT THE JEWS SAY OF HIM.

AS our blessed Lord was coming into the quarters of Cæsarea Philippi, he asked his disciples what the Jews said of him, and likewise, whom they thought him to be, and other things. Some of them answered, and said: "Some take you for John the Baptist, others for Elias, and others for Jeremiah, or one of the Prophets." But Peter, for himself and the rest, answered: "Thou art Christ, the Son of the living God." And our Lord said to him: "Thou art Peter, and upon this rock I will build my Church, and the gates of Hell shall not prevail against it." At the same time he gave him the keys of Heaven, the power to loose or bind upon earth. Behold here, then, pious reader, our Lord and his disciples, and contemplate them according to the general rules before given you. And observe, moreover, that Peter, whom Christ so exalted above the rest, was a little after called Satan by the same Christ, because through the too great attachment which Peter had to the visible presence of Christ's

humanity, he endeavored to dissuade him from suffering, and from going through his passion.   Do you
likewise follow the example of Christ, and esteem
them to be your enemies, who endeavor to draw you
from the practice of spiritual exercises, for the sake
of any temporal good or corporal gratification.

THE TRANSFIGURATION.

CHAPTER XLI.

THE GLORIOUS TRANSFIGURATION OF OUR LORD JESUS ON MOUNT TABOR.

OUR Lord Jesus, desirous to strengthen his apostles in the steadfast belief, both of his divinity
and humanity, first showed them that he was perfect

man, by living among them as a man; and that he was also perfect God, by the wonderful miracles he wrought, which far surpassed the power and nature of a pure man. He had likewise farther told them, that, as man, he should suffer a most painful and opprobrious death; and afterwards rise again gloriously to life, as he was God. After all this he concluded, and said, that there were some of them then present, who should not see death till they had first seen the Son of Man, who was himself, coming in his kingdom; that is to say, beheld him in his glorious transfiguration, and saw his sacred humanity resplendently shining with a wonderful brightness, as they should afterwards behold him in his heavenly glory.

To this purpose, therefore, about eight days after, he took with him three of his disciples, Peter, James, and John, and went up to the top of a mountain called Tabor, and was there transfigured before them; that is, he was so altered and changed from his common appearance, that he put on that beautiful and glorious form, in which he was to appear seated in the high throne of Majesty, so that his face and countenance became bright as the sun, and his garments were as white as snow.

And presently there appeared Moses and Elias speaking with him concerning his sacred passion, which he was to undergo in Jerusalem, and said: "Lord, it is not expedient for thee to die, because one drop only of thy precious blood is sufficient to redeem the world." But our Lord Jesus answered, "The good pastor giveth his life for his sheep: so, therefore, it behooves me to do." The apostles remained ecstatic amidst this glorious vision: and St. Peter above the rest, being forgetful of all earthly things, was desirous of remaining there in possession of that glance of bliss, and therefore said, "Lord, it is good for us to be here: if thou wilt, let us make here three tabernacles: one for thee, and one for Moses, and one for Elias."—*John* xvii. But as the holy Evangelist takes notice, "He knew not what he said" in desiring to continue with our Lord Jesus in that place of bliss, before he had suffered that painful death, which he had before told them he was first to do. The Holy Ghost, likewise appearing in the brightness of a cloud, overshadowed him, and out of the cloud there came a voice from Heaven, saying, "This is my beloved Son in whom I am well pleased, hear ye him." The apostles, trembling with fear at this voice, fell flat, with their faces to the ground: but our Lord Jesus raised them, and bid them not to fear: and lifting up their eyes, and looking around them, they saw none but him alone. Contemplate well these passages, and endeavor to render yourself present, by devout meditation, to the things already said, because they contain most great and sublime mysteries.

THE TRADERS AND MONEY CHANGERS ARE DRIVEN OUT OF THE
TEMPLE.

CHAPTER XLII.

THE BUYERS AND SELLERS CAST OUT OF THE TEMPLE.

OUR Lord Jesus, at two several times, cast the
buyers and sellers out of the temple; which
action, of all the miracles he wrought, seems the
most strange and wonderful. For when he performed other miracles among them, in which he
evidently declared the power of his Godhead, those
perverse people, the scribes and Pharisees, blasphemed and contemned him for them: but at this

time, though there were great multitudes **assembled**
together in the temple, they had not power to resist
or withstand him; while he, with a scourge made
of cords, drove them all out before him. The
reason of this was, that his inward zeal and fervor
being vehemently enkindled in seeing his heavenly
Father so much dishonored, especially in that place
where he ought to have been the most honored and
worshipped, made him appear to them with a terrible and dreadful countenance, so that they were
affrighted, and had not power to resist him. Consider him here attentively, and compassionate him,
for **he** is full of compassionate grief: but, at the
same time, fear him. For it is a dreadful example
that ought to be considered by all men; but more
especially by such as have any office or authority in
the Church of God, and by all religious persons
who are placed in the house of God, to serve him
in devout prayer, and other holy and spiritual exercises. For if such idly busy themselves, and med-
dle with worldly affairs, they may justly fear the
wrath and indignation **of God** against them, and
apprehend the danger of being cut off from his
grace in this life, and cast out of his eternal glory
in the life to come.

JESUS HEALS THE PARALYTIC AT THE SHEEP POOL.

CHAPTER LXIII.

THE SICK MAN THAT WAS HEALED AT THE WATER IN JERUSALEM, CALLED PROBATICA PISCINA.

THERE was in the city of Jerusalem a standing pool of water, in the nature of a pond, in which the sheep were washed that were to be offered in sacrifice. In this place also, according to the opinion of the Fathers, afterwards lay hidden the wood of the holy cross. This water was stirred once

in every year, by particular appointment of God, by
an angel, and the sick person that first descended
into it after its being stirred was immediately healed
of his infirmity: on which account great numbers
of sick people remained continually near the water,
expecting it to be moved by the angel. Among
these there was one lying on his bed, who had been
ill of the palsy thirty eight years, whom our Lord
healed on the Sabbath-day. Here, according to
your usual method, consider how humbly our Lord
approaches the sick man, and speaks to him. For
in this action there are three things worthy of the
greatest attention.

The first is, our Lord Jesus asked the sick person
whether he would be healed or not? By which we
are given to understand, that our Lord, without our
consent, will not bestow salvation upon us. Wherefore all stubborn and sinful persons, who neither
desire, nor yet will give consent to such internal mo-
tions as God inspireth them with for their salvation,
are undoubtedly without excuse. For as St. Augustine saith, "He that made thee without thee, cannot
save thee without thee."

The second thing which is to be observed is, that
we ought to be careful after we are freed and cleansed
from sin, not to fall wilfully into it again, lest our
crime, for so doing, should be punished by our Lord
with more severity. Wherefore he said to the sick
man whom he had restored, "Go thy way and sin
no more, lest worse happen unto thee."

The third thing we ought to consider is, that wicked
men usually misconstrue the good works of others,
and look upon them with an evil eye: but good men
do the contrary. For thus the Jews, full of envy,
when they saw the sick man miraculously cured by
our Lord Jesus, and carrying away his bed on the

Sabbath, immediately told him, "That it was not lawful to do it on that day ;" to whom he answered, "That he who had made him whole, said to him, take up thy bed and walk." Before this, they asked him not who it was that had healed him, but began to carp at what displeased them, and what they thought reprehensible and took no notice at all of the good work which was commendable and so manifestly wrought before them. This is the manner of all wicked men, to turn everything to the worst, which good men convert to the best. For they who lead a spiritual life interpret all things in the best manner, to the honor and glory of God, whether prosperity or adversity, knowing that everything which comes to pass is through his holy will or permission ; and therefore judge the best of, and reap thence great increase of merit, as St. Bernard teaches, saying, "Pry not too far into other men's lives, nor rashly judge of their actions. Think no evil of thy neighbor, but if thou see anything that is bad, excuse at least his intention if you cannot his works: imagine the cause to be ignorance, inadvertency, or an accident. And if his crimes are beyond all dissimulation, say at least to yourself, it was the effect of a violent temptation: had it been as powerful in me what destruction would it not have wrought?" Thus far St. Bernard. That the good reap benefit from all things, even from their own and other men's sins, from the things most hurtful, and from the works of the devil himself, the same saint thus argues: "Though the irrational and animal part cannot attain to what is spiritual, yet it must be owned that, by the bodily service it does, it very much helps those to obtain it, who turn the use of all temporal and worldly things to the eternal advantage of their souls, by making use of the things of this life, as if they used them not." And again:

"Though there are some creatures which are found not only useless, but inconvenient, and even pernicious, yet it is certain that they contribute to the good of temporal and worldly men. For they have ever something that may turn to the good of those, who, according to their resolution, are called saints, if not by affording nourishment or performing their due office, at least by exercising their mind by the help of him, who is always ready to those who make use of their reason, helping them to make a proficiency in good discipline ; by whom also, 'The invisible things of God are seen, being understood by those things which are made.'—*Rom.* i.   In short, he that has grace enough to take all things in good part, and to suppose that all which God sends is for the best, shall be enabled to suffer many trials and tribulations, with little pain ; and by daily exercise obtain at length so great a peace and tranquillity of mind, that seldom or never anything shall offend or molest him, but that shall be verified in him, which the wise man saith, 'Whatever shall happen to the just man it shall not make him sorry.' "—*Prov.* xii.

JESUS IN THE HOUSE OF MARTHA AND MARY.

CHAPTER XLIV.

OUR LORD JESUS RECEIVED BY THE TWO SISTERS, MARY
AND MARTHA; AND OF THE TWO SORTS OF LIVES
SIGNIFIED THEREBY.

IT happened on a certain time, that our Lord Jesus
went with his disciples to the city of Bethania, to
a house named the castle of Martha and Mary. And
they, whose love and affections were wholly placed
in him, were exceeding glad at his coming, and received him with all possible joy and respect. Martha,

the eldest sister, who had the care and government of
the house, went immediately to provide meat for him
and his disciples, but Mary her sister, forgetting as
it were, all corporal food, and desiring to feed her
soul with the fervent love of her dear Saviour Jesus,
sat herself on the ground, beside his feet. And as
our Lord, who was never idle, was talking according
to his usual custom, of those things which regard
eternal life, she, with her heart and thoughts fixed
on him, attentively listened to his blessed words, and
took a pleasure beyond expression, in the exposition
of his heavenly doctrine. Martha, who was busy in
making ready the provision for our Lord and his disciples, seeing her sister sitting idly as it were at his
feet, was troubled at it, and therefore complained to
our Lord, and begged him to bid her sister to rise
and help her.

Mary, at the voice of her sister, awakened as it were
from the depth of a sweet sleep, and fearing she
would be deprived of that sweet contentment and
quiet repose in which her soul was being, always
obedient to the will of God, said nothing, but reverently bowing down her face to the ground, humbly
waited to hear what our Lord would say to her. Our
Lord answering in her behalf, said unto Martha:
"Martha, Martha, thou art careful and art troubled
about many things: but one thing is necessary.,
Mary hath chosen the better part, which shall not
be taken away from her."

At this answer of our Lord Jesus, Mary was greatly
comforted, and sat with more confidence at his sacred
feet, pursuing with perseverance her former purpose. But at length, when all was ready for his refection, and he had done speaking, she arose, fetched
water to wash his hands, and remaining there present,
diligently served him with all things he wanted,

Consider here attentively, pious reader, our Lord entering this house, and with what extreme joy they receive him, together with all that passed as before-mentioned, because thence you may gather most beautiful matter for your devout meditation.

You must know then, that by these two sisters, the Holy Fathers understand two different states of life, the one active, the other contemplative. To treat of these would be a subject of great extent, but though I am convinced that it is not necessary to dwell long upon it, I will, nevertheless, say something on that head: first, because St Bernard in many places has largely treated of it; and secondly, because it is a subject most useful, full of all spiritual comfort, and very necessary. According to this two-fold manner of living we all proceed, but how we ought to act, is a matter we are ignorant of; which is unfortunate and dangerous, especially to men of religious lives.

The active kind of life is emblematically represented in Martha: which active life itself is divisible into two parts. The first is, that by which every one acts chiefly for his own good; correcting, mending, and improving himself in virtue; and next for the good of his neighbor, by works of justice, piety, and charity. The second is, that by which a man is led, though for greater merit's sake, to exercise himself chiefly for his neighbor's advantage, in governing, teaching, and forwarding the conversion of souls: as prelates and preachers do. Between these two parts of active life is the contemplative; and it is disposed in this manner, that every one do exercise himself, first in prayer, sacred studies, and other good deeds and offices of life, with an intention to correct his own vices and acquire virtues; secondly, that he rest in contemplation, seeking solitude, and conversation apart with God; and, thirdly, that by both exercises

inspired and enlightened with true wisdom and goodness, and thence become zealous, give himself up to
the salvation of others.

CHAPTER XLV.

OUR LORD WARNS THE JEWS THAT THE CHURCH
SHALL DEVOLVE ON THE GENTILES, IN THE
PARABLE OF THE HUSBANDMEN WHO KILLED THE
SON OF THEIR LORD.

OUR Lord, zealous for the salvation of the souls
for which he was come to pay down the ransom of life, tried by every means to draw them to
himself, and to deliver them from the jaws of **sin**
and Satan. Sometimes, therefore, he made use of the
most gentle and insinuating means; and at others
of severe and terrifying reproofs: sometimes he recurred to similitudes, sometimes to signs and
wonders; now to prophecies, and anon to threats:
thus varying the means and manner of cure, according to the place and time, and the diversity of
persons.

In this place he reproves the princes and Pharisees,
with severe language, which, however, was so justly
applied, that they took it to themselves. He proposed to them the parable of the husbandmen, who
killed their lord's messengers, sent to them to demand
payment of the fruits due to him, and asked what
punishment was due to such unworthy tenants; they
replied, their lord must destroy the wretches, and let
his vineyard to other husbandmen. Jesus, therefore,

approving their answer, replied to them : the kingdom of God, that is the Church, shall be taken from among you : and shall be given to another people, who will cultivate it : that is, to the Gentiles : of whom we and the whole church are descended To this he added the example of the corner-stone, which signified himself, who was to overthrow Judaism. Upon which, finding themselves to be the persons meant, instead of reforming, they became more exasperated, and quite blinded with malice.

CHAPTER XLVI.

THE JEWS SEEK TO ENSNARE OUR SAVIOUR BY HIS OWN WORDS.

AS our Lord Jesus neglected no means that might conduce to the salvation of the Jews, so, on the contrary, the Jews omitted none to calumniate and destroy him. They thought, therefore, to deceive him, but they deceived themselves with their own devices. They sent to him some of their own disciples, accompained by the servants of Herod, to inquire whether it was lawful for them to give tribute to Cæsar ? By this means, they hoped to bring him under the suspicion of Cæsar and his friends, or render him at least odious to the Jews, believing he could not answer but against himself. But the all-wise searcher of hearts, seeing their malice, answered them, that they must give to Cæsar his own and to God his due ; and told them withal, that they were hypocrites who concealed under fair words a mali-

cious purpose. Thus disappointed in their fraudulent
intentions, they returned with shame.

Here consider attentively our Lord Jesus, according to the general method of contemplation I laid
down for you; and reflect likewise, that Christ will
not allow us to defraud temporal princes and magistrates of their just rights, whether good or bad, be-
lievers or unbelievers. Wherefore, it is a great sin
to refuse payment of the customs and taxes, which
our temporal superiors think proper to lay on us for
the good of the state.

CHAPTER XLVII.

THE BLIND MAN RESTORED TO SIGHT AT JERICHO, ETC.

THE bountiful Lord Jesus, who, out of his immense love for us, came down from his divine
Father's throne to accomplish our salvation, prepared to set out for Jerusalem, to meet his approaching passion, which he had even at this time foretold
to them, but they were too blind in their obstinacy to
understand him. When, therefore, he drew near to
Jericho, a certain blind man, who sat on the way begging, having intelligence from the populace of his pas-
ing by, began to cry powerfully to him for pity. And
though the multitude rebuked him, they could neither
dismay nor silence him. The Lord Jesus, therefore,
out of regard to his faith and fervor, ordered him to
be brought to him, and asked him, "What wilt thou
that I do unto thee?"—To whom the blind man answered, "Lord, that I see:"—which our compassion-

ate Lord granted saying, "See:"—and thus saying, restored him to sight. Consider here attentively, devout reader, the graciousness of our Lord : and at the same time reflect on the great efficacy of prayer, attended with faith and perseverance. Importunity in prayer, you see, does not displease God, but is rather agreeable to him. You have already an instance of this in the Cananean, and elsewhere, and another in the man who obtained the loaves by night through the importunity of prayer. And thus does the Lord grant to all who importune him their just and orderly petitions. For it is to every one alike he says : "What wilt thou that I do to thee?"—Nay, he often grants even more than is asked, as we shall see in the person of Zacheus. Ask, then, like the blind man, without blushing. For why should you blush to serve God, to throw off sin, or to ask the graces necessary for either. To be bashful, is sometimes a virtue, but may oftentimes be a great fault, as St. Bernard observes :

"There is a shame to sin, and a shame to glory. It is a good shame to blush at the thought of sinning or having sinned. And though no human witness be by, you ought with so much the more modesty to revere the presence of a divine one, as you are truly convinced by how much he surpasses man in purity, and that he is as heinously offended at sin as he is distant from it. Such a kind of shame may boldly bid defiance to reproach, and paves a way to glory, by not admitting sin, or at least by repenting of and atoning for it, if committed. But should we be ashamed or grieved to make acknowledgment of our faults ; such a shame is to sin, and deviates widely from glory. For the evil which compunction would fain expel from the heart, this false, this foolish shame, the binder of all lips, suffer not to be banished from it. O sovereign kind of victory to yield to the divine Majesty ; and to find no reluctance in submitting to the authority of his Church ! O strange perversity, **not** to blush at defiling, and yet to blush at cleansing your feet." Thus far St. Bernard.

Whatever may occur to your imagination concerning this blind man, is alike applicable to those other two blind men whom our Lord enlightened at his going forth **from** Jericho, as he did this before his entrance into that city. Of the two former, see St. Matthew, chap. xx., and St. Mark, chap. x., where the name of one of them is mentioned: and that upon their crying out, as this poor man did, they received the same answer, and were cured by our Lord.

ZACHEUS CLIMBS UP INTO THE SYCAMORE TREE.

CHAPTER XLVIII.

OUR LORD GOES INTO THE HOUSE OF ZACHEUS.

WHEN our Lord Jesus, at his entry into Jericho, was passing through the streets, Zacheus, the chief of the publicans, who was informed of his approach, and very desirous to see him, but could not for the throng : at length, being a very little man, he got up into a sycamore tree that he might at least behold him thence.—Jesus therefore, knowing and accepting his faith and desire, said to him, " Zacheus,

make haste and come down, for I must this day abide
in thy house." He immediately came down, received
him with great joy and reverence, and prepared
for him a noble repast. Here you see, Christian
reader, the gracious courtesy of our blessed Saviour,
who grants Zacheus so much more than he presumed
to hope for, or ask. He sought a sight of him, and
Jesus gave him himself. Such is the power of
prayer! And the desire is such! Nay, it is a loud
voice, and an effectual petition. Wherefore says the
Psalmist, "The Lord hath granted the desire of the
poor, and thy ear hath heard the preparation of
their heart." And at the time when Moses was
silent with his lips, and speaking only in his heart,
the Lord said to him, "Why do you cry aloud to
me?"—*Exod.* xiv. Contemplate here our divine
Lord, graciously sitting at table with Zacheus,
amidst a company of sinners, and familiarly conversing with them, in order to gain them over to
himself. Behold, likewise, the disciples, sitting with
the same sinners, and conversing with, and encour-
aging them to good works: knowing it to be the
will of their divine master.

CHAPTER XLIX.

CHRIST GIVES SIGHT TO THE MAN BORN BLIND.

WHEN our Lord went to Jerusalem he saw a
man that was born blind, whose name was
Cælidonius: and stooping down, he made paste of
earth with his spittle, with which he anointed his
eyes, and sent him to the pool called Siloe, to bathe.
The man went, bathed his eyes, and received his

sight. This miracle, which was strictly examined into by the Jews, turned to their confusion.—See the story in the gospel, where it is plainly and beautifully related. Behold here our Lord Jesus, and contemplate him according to the general rules already laid down to you. Here, too, consider the great gratitude of the cured man, who courageously and resolutely defends our divine Lord before the very princes and rulers of the Jews, without sparing them in any way, even before he had the blessing of seeing our Lord. The virtue of gratitude is extremely commendable and pleasing in the sight of God, as its opposite is a detestable vice before him. Of which subject, thus speaks St. Bernard:

"Learn to be thankful for every grace received. Consider diligently the favors heaped upon you, that no gift of God be defrauded of the due return of gratitude and thanksgiving you ought to make, whether the gift be great, middling, or little. Lastly, we are directed to gather the fragments, lest they perish: that is, not to suffer the least benefit bestowed upon us to be forgotten. But does not that perish which is conferred upon the ungrateful? Ingratitude is the soul's worst enemy; it is the destroyer of merit, the disperser of virtues and the exterminator of all good. Ingratitude is a burning gale, which dries up the very spring of piety, the dew of mercy, and the stream of grace."

JESUS CONFESSES HIS ETERNAL GODHEAD.

Jesus declares Himself to be God, and the Scribes and Doctors of the Law take up stones to stone Him, thinking He

CHAPTER L.

OUR LORD RETREATS FROM THE TEMPLE **TO** HIDE
HIMSELF WHEN THE JEWS WOULD HAVE STONED
HIM.

WHEN our Lord Jesus was preaching one day
in the temple, he said, among other things,
"If any one keeps my word, he shall never taste
death." The Jews answered him, "You are then
greater than our father Abraham who died ?" To
which our Saviour replied, "Before Abraham was
made, I am." Which the Jews taking for an impos-
sibility, and an untruth, took stones to stone him.
But he retired out of the temple and hid himself ; for
as yet the hour of his passion was not come. Behold, then, with concern, how the Lord of all is con-
temptuously treated by his vile, unworthy creatures,
and how meekly he gives way to their fury, retreats
amidst the crowd, and, with his disciples, patiently
and **modestly** withdraws **from** the effects **of their
rage, like the** weakest among them.

CHAPTER LI.

THE JEWS SEEK A SECOND TIME TO STONE HIM.

ANOTHER **time, at** the feast **of** the dedication
of the temple, **our** Lord being in Solomon's
porch, was surrounded **by** these ravenous wolves,
who, grinning with their teeth, said, "If thou art

Christ, tell us openly?" To whom the most meek and patient Lamb of God answered humbly, "I tell you so; but you do not believe me." Behold here, then, this affecting scene. He speaks to them with humble affability; and they, with brutal noise and fury, disturb and molest him, and at length, not able to contain the venom in their breasts, take stones to throw at him. Nevertheless, our Lord spoke to them in engaging words, saying, "I have done many good things amongst you; for which of them is it that you would stone me." "Because," say they, "you being a man, would make yourself a God." Observe their unaccountable stupidity. They would know whether he is Christ, and when he proves it to them by words and actions, they want to stone him, without being able to produce one excuse why they cannot or ought not to believe him to be what he really is. But as his hour was not yet come, he got safe out of their hands, and retired to that part of Jordan where John had baptized, which is distant from Jerusalem about eighteen miles. Behold then our Saviour, and consider him and his disciples under this affliction, and mentally compassionate them with all the tenderness you are master of.

LAZARUS IS RAISED FROM THE DEAD.

CHAPTER LII.

THE RAISING OF LAZARUS.

THIS miracle is a famous one, very solemn, and worthy to be meditated on with the utmost devotion. Wherefore, endeavor to render yourself as present in mind to all that is here said, as if you had actually been present when it happened; and freely converse, and not only with our Lord Jesus and his disciples, but with all this blessed family, so devoted to and beloved by our Lord, that is, Lazarus, Mary, and Martha. Lazarus therefore being dangerously ill, and at the point of death, his sisters, who were very intimate with Christ, sent to him to the place whither he had retreated beyond Jordan, saying, "Our brother Lazarus, whom you love, is sick."—They sent him no further message, either because they thought that sufficient to a friend, and an understanding one; or else because they dared not invite him, knowing that the chiefs of the Jews were laying snares for his life. Our Lord Jesus hearing the news, remained silent for two days; and then, among other things, said to his disciples, Lazarus is dead; and I rejoice for your sakes, that I was not there. Observe the goodness, love, and diligence of our Lord, with relation to his disciples. They returned then, and came near to Bethany. Martha, as soon as she was informed of it, ran to meet him, and falling at his feet, said, "Lord, if you had been here, my brother had not died."—Our Lord answered, that he should arise, and thence they began to talk of the resurrection.

Then he sent for Mary, for whom he had a special love; who no sooner knew of it, than she arose, and came to him with haste, and falling at his feet said the same thing. Our Lord, seeing his beloved afflicted and in tears, could not refrain from tears himself, but wept with her. Behold him, then, with the devout women and his disciples weeping; and be moved with the tenderness of the affecting scene.

After awhile, our Lord asked them, " Where have you put him ?"—Not that he did not know; but because, as he was talking to human creatures, he spoke to them in a human manner. They answered him, " Lord, come and see."—And they led him to the sepulchre; whither he proceeded between the two devout females, comforting and condoling with

PRESENT CONDITION OF THE TOMB WHERE LAZARUS WAS BURIED.

them, till they were so consoled as almost to forget and drown all sensations of grief in their attention to him.

When our Lord arrived at the monument, he commanded the stone to be removed, which Martha would have dissuaded him from, saying, that the corpse must smell strong, having been four days dead. But our Lord would have the stone removed. Which done, our Lord Jesus, lifting up his eyes towards heaven, said, "I give you thanks, Father, that you have heard me: I know indeed that you always hear me ; but I speak on account of these, that they may know that you have sent me."—Behold him, then, devout reader, behold him thus praying, and consider his great zeal for the salvation of souls. After this he cried out with a loud voice, saying, "Lazarus, come forth."—And he straight came to life, and started forth from the tomb, but tied as he was when buried. But the disciples untied him, by Christ's direction. Lazarus, when he was untied, and with his sisters, kneeled down, and returned thanks to Jesus for so great a benefit: after which they conducted him home. All who were present were extremely astonished at what they saw, and made it so public, that multitudes, from Jerusalem and all parts, came to see Lazarus : insomuch, that the princes of the Jews, thinking themselves confounded, formed designs against his life.

THE FIG-TREE WHICH HAD NOTHING BUT LEAVES IS CURSED.

CHAPTER LIII.

CHRIST CURSES THE FIG-TREE.

THOUGH, according to historical narration, the
curse of the fig-tree, and the presenting of the
adulteress in the temple, be thought posterior to
Christ's arrival in Jerusalem, yet, as it seems most
proper after that arrival, to employ our meditations
wholly on the passion, and the circumstances relating
to it, I have inserted these two facts in this place.   As
then our Lord Jesus was going towards Jerusalem,
he was hungry, and saw a fig-tree very beautifully

adorned with branches and foliage. Coming therefore
nigh he beheld it more closely, and finding no fruit
on it, he cursed it, and it withered ; to the great
surprise of his disciples. This was mystically done
by our Saviour, who knew it **to** be a time not proper
for such trees to bear. And **he** did it to signify the
curse attending **on** hypocrites and loquacious persons, who are like well ornamented trees without
fruit.

CHAPTER LIV.

THE WOMAN DETECTED IN ADULTERY.

THE perverse Pharisees and princes of the Jews
were perpetually watching, and studiously contriving how **to** surprise Christ by their frauds and
wiles, and **render him** odious to the people. But
their arrows were turned against themselves. As
therefore a woman **had** been caught in adultery, and
was to be stoned according to the law, they brought
her to him **into** the temple, **to** enquire of him what
should be done to her : which they did to perplex
him, that if he should direct the law to be fulfilled,
they might cast upon him the odious imputation of
cruelty and want of mercy : or of injustice, if he
should offer to screen her from the law. But our
all-wise Saviour, seeing the snare; and willing to avoid
it, humbly stooped down, and wrote with his finger
on the ground ; the commentators tell us, that what
he wrote was the sins of the accusers, and this writing
was of such efficacy, that every one was able to read
his own sins therein. When, therefore, our Lord
raised himself again, and said to them "Let him

among you who is without sin, throw the first stone," they departed, astonished and confounded, although Christ, when he had pronounced the sentence, was gracious enough to stoop again, for the sake of his envious adversaries, to save them from confusion. And thus did their duplicity evaporate and come to nothing. After her accusers were gone, our Lord admonished the woman and dismissed her. Contemplate, then, our divine Redeemer in all these circumstances, according to the rule I have prescribed to you in the beginning of this work.

CHAPTER LV.

THE CONSPIRACY OF THE JEWS AGAINST CHRIST ; AND HIS FLIGHT INTO THE CITY OF EPHRAIM.

THE time approaching when our Lord Jesus designed to work our redemption by the effusion of his precious blood, the devil armed his ministers, and sharpened the malice of their hearts against him, even to death ; and the good works of our Lord, especially the raising of Lazarus, but incensed them the more to envy and rage. Whence, able no longer to contain their fury, the high priests and Pharisees held a council, in which Caiphas prophecying, they deliberated upon killing the most innocent Lamb of God. O wicked council ! O reprobate guides of the people, and evil advisers ! Wretches, what are you about to do ? To what excess does your frenzy transport you ? What a sentence is this ! Where is the occasion for your murdering the Lord your God ? Is he not in the midst of you, though you know him not, searching your reins and hearts ?

But thus it is expedient that it should be done as you have desired. His heavenly Father has delivered him up into your hands, by you he is to be put to death, but, alas, his death shall not prove serviceable to you. He indeed shall die and rise again to save his people, but you shall perish from among his people.

The resolution of the council was made public, and our Lord was acquainted with it, but his wisdom, willing to give way to their wrath, especially as everything was not completely fulfilled concerning him, he went to that side of the country near the desert, to the city of Ephraim. Thus flies the humble Lord of the highest heavens, before the face of his most vile and abject servants. Contemplate here our Lord Jesus Christ, and his disciples, under the repeated affliction of a painful and necessitous flight. Meditate likewise how our blessed Lady, his immaculate mother, and her sisters, remained with St. Mary Magdalen, whom our Lord, before his departure, consoles with the promise of his speedy return.

THE WOMAN WHO WAS A SINNER ANOINTS THE FEET OF JESUS.

Jesus, the Legislator of the New Covenant, suffers Himself to be approached by a woman who was a sinner, and graciously pardons her many sins.

CHAPTER LVI.

OUR LORD RETURNS TO BETHANIA, WHERE MARY MAGDALEN ANOINTS HIS FEET.

AS we have seen that our Lord Jesus for our instruction used prudence in retreating from danger, to show us, that according to the exigence of time and place, we ought to decline, with all lawful caution, the fury of persecutors : so now he makes use of fortitude, returning of his own accord, when the due time approaches, that he may meet his passion, and deliver himself up into the hands of his persecutors. And as before he made use of temperance, when he declined the multitude who sought to make him king, now he exerts his justice, when he prepares to demand the honors of a king, and that the people strew branches of palm and olive before him. But how modestly does he receive this honor, sitting humbly on an ass ! Our divine master here made use particularly of these four virtues, prudence, justice, fortitude and temperance, for our instruction. They are called cardinal virtues, that is, principal virtues, because from them all other moral virtues flow.

Our Lord, then, on the sabbath-day, before his triumph of palms, returned to Bethania, about two miles from Jerusalem, where a supper was prepared for him at the house of Simon the leper, where were present Lazarus, Martha, and Mary. It was at that time Mary poured on the head of Jesus a pound of precious ointment, and anointed his head and feet. And what she once did in the same house out of contrition, she now repeats **out of** devotion: for **she** loved him above all things, and could not be satiated **with** honoring **him.**

But the traitor Judas thought a great deal of this, and murmured at it; when our Saviour answered **for** her, and defended her vigorously. Nevertheless, the traitor remained so greatly offended at it, that he from that time took occasion to betray him; **and on** the **Wednesday** following, sold him for thirty **pieces of silver.** Behold then our divine Saviour here supping with his friends, and conversing with them **for** his few remaining days, **until his** passion; but chiefly in the house of Lazarus **and his** sisters, for that was his usual refuge: **there he eat** by day, and there he reposed by night, **with** his disciples. There likewise our blessed Lady **with** his sisters, reposed; whom this devout **family, and** chiefly Magdalen, honored, reverenced, and attended with constancy and affection. Behold then this immaculate virgin mother, struck with excess of fear for her dearly beloved Son, from **whom she** was never apart any more than was absolutely necessary. When our Lord, **in** defending Magdalen from the traitor's murmurings, said, "Pouring this ointment on my body, **she** has done it for my funeral," think you not **that** these words like a dagger, pierced the soul **of the** blessed mother? For what could he say more express to foretell **his death?** So all **were** struck with fear, and full of anxious and disturbing thoughts: talking to each other like persons in the utmost confusion and terror; **none** knew **what** advice to give, or what to take; and all were **in** the utmost terror **whenever** he went to Jerusalem, which, however, he **did** every day: for from this Saturday to the day of **his** last supper, he said many things to the Jews, and wrought wonders openly in Jerusalem. all which I intend to pass in silence, except his riding on the ass, lest our meditation be interrupted ; for we are now on the verge of his passion.

Summon, then, devout reader, all your recollection, that nothing may distract or divert you from the solemn mysteries which precede or attend his passion ; be watchful and attentive to the whole and every circumstance of it, that you may reap the benefit he designs you by it.

JESUS CHRIST RIDES INTO JERUSALEM.

CHAPTER LVII.

OUR LORD JESUS COMES TO JERUSALEM, ON PALM-SUNDAY, RIDING UPON AN ASS.

MYSTERIES were daily wrought, and the Scriptures fulfilled, by our Lord Jesus; and the time drawing nigh, he was desirous of redeeming mankind, through the bitter passion of his sacred humanity. Wherefore, on the next Sunday, very early in the morning, he prepared to go to Jerusalem, in a manner he had never gone before, that he might fulfil the words of the prophet, which were written to that purpose.

When his blessed mother found that he was resolved to depart, she endeavored earnestly to dissuade him from it, and with tender affection said, "My beloved son, whither will you go? Why will you go among those whom you know conspire against you, and seek to kill you? I beseech you therefore not to go among them." And his disciples, and Mary Magdalen, in the same manner entreated him, and besought him to stay: "Go not among them, O Lord," say they, "we pray you: since you know they seek your death, and if you throw yourself into their hands this day, they will secure you, and execute their wicked purpose." O how sincerely did they love him, and how sensibly were they affected at the apprehension of every thing that might hurt him! But he who thirsted after the salvation of man, had disposed it otherwise, wherefore he said: "It is the will of my Father that I should go, come ye also, fear not, for he will protect us, and this night we shall return hither without hurt." And immediately he set out for his journey, and that small but faithful company followed him.

When he came to a certain place in the way, which was called Bethphage, he sent two of his disciples to the city of Jerusalem, and bid them fetch him an ass and her foal, that were tied in the highway, for the use of such poor people who had no beasts of their own. When they were brought, the disciples laid their own clothes, upon them, and our Saviour meekly seated himself upon the ass, and riding in that humble manner, came into the city of Jerusalem. Consider him here attentively, and behold how in this, he reproves the pomp and glorly of worldly vanity. The beast he rode was not decked with rich furniture : instead of golden trappings, embossed saddles, and curious bridles, all the ornaments consisted of poor clothes, and a hempen halter, though he was '' King of kings, and Lord of lords.''   Now when the people heard of his coming, through the fame of raising Lazarus from the dead, they went out to meet him, and re-ceived him as a king, with joyful hymns, and songs : and showing great tokens of gladness for his arrival, they strewed the ways with boughs and branches of the trees, and spread their clothes under the ass's feet as he passed.   But notwithstanding this, he mingled tears with their joy ; for when he beheld the city, he wept over it, saying, 'If thou hadst known, and that in this thy day, the things that are to thy peace : but now they are hidden from thy eyes.   For the days shall come upon thee ; and thy enemies shall cast a trench about thee and compass thee round, and straiten thee on every side, and beat thee flat to the ground, and thy children who are in thee ; and they shall not leave in thee a stone upon a stone, because thou hast not known the time of thy visitation.''

It is manifest in scripture, that our Lord Jesus wept three different times.   Once at the death of Lazarus, to show the wretched state of mankind, who incurred the pain of death through the offence of their first parents.   Secondly, he wept on this day for the blindness and ignorance of men, namely, for the people of Jerusalem, who would not know the time of their glorious visitation.   Thirdly, he wept in his passion, in beholding the malice and perversity of man's heart, and considering that his passion being sufficient for the redemption of all the world, yet many would not partake of it.   Concern-ing this last weeping, St. Paul in his epistle to the

Hebrews says this, speaking of the time of his passion: "Who with a strong cry, and tears were heard for his reverence."—*Heb.* v. We are taught then from sacred text, that Christ wept these three times. But the holy Church relates that he wept a fourth time; that is, in his tender infancy, and therefore she sings, "The tender infant, as he lies in the cold manger, shakes and cries." This he did to conceal from the devil the mystery of the incarnation.

Now our Lord Jesus weeping on this day so abundantly over Jerusalem, and with so sorrowful a heart, both for the eternal damnation, and also for the temporal destruction and ruin of that city, his holy mother, with all the apostles, could not refrain from weeping also.

Thus rideth our Lord upon that humble beast, having, instead of princes, and nobles, his poor disciples about him, together with his mother, and some other devout women, who both with fear and reverence devoutly followed him. He entered Jerusalem in triumph, being honored by all the people, whose shouts and acclamations put the whole city in great commotion. Our Lord went first into the temple, and a second time cast out the buyers and sellers. He stood openly in the temple, preaching and answering the questions of the Scribes and Pharisees all the day, till it drew towards night. But notwithstanding the great honor which before they had done him, yet they permitted him and his disciples to remain the whole day fasting, there being none among them that invited him to eat or drink. And when night was come, he went with his disciples to his homely lodging at Bethania, departing privately from the city with his small company, who, in the morning, had entered publicly with such great honor.

Hence we may learn how little regard is to be paid to worldly honor, which lasteth so short a time, and so slightly vanisheth away.

CHAPTER LVIII.

WHAT OUR LORD JESUS DID FROM PALM SUNDAY TO THE THURSDAY FOLLOWING.

OUR Lord Jesus, the fountain of all charity, desirous to express both in word and deed the perfect charity he bore, as well to his enemies as to his friends, to the end that no one should be lost, but all might be saved, when the end of his life now drew near, and the time of his passion was at hand, labored diligently in preaching the gospel continually to the people ; especially on these days, viz., Palm Sunday and the Monday and Tuesday following. On these days he came very early in the morning into the temple, and preached unto, and taught the people, and disputed with the Scribes and Pharisees, answering their subtle questions, by which they sought to entrap him, and in this manner was he busied from morning until night.

But as it would be too long to treat in particular of all that passed during that time, between our blessed Saviour and the Jews, it being also foreign to the passion, which we are now to speak of ; therefore, passing over all the examples and parables he made use of to reprove and convince them, we will especially consider how the chief priests and Pharisees, perceiving the people to be well disposed towards him, and fearing to execute openly their malicious designs against him, privately and subtly conspired together how they might entrap him in his words, and accuse him of saying something against their law, or against paying the tribute to Cæsar, and thence condemn him as worthy of death. But our Lord, to whom the secrets of all men's hearts are open, knowing their treachery and malice, answered them so wisely, that they were disappointed in their purpose, and were so much confounded, that they durst not ask him any more questions. He then severely reproved the pride, the hypocrisy, the covetousness, and many other wicked practices of the Scribes and Pharisees, saying to them : " Woe be to you, Scribes and Pharisees, who love and seek after worldly glory." Thus he proceeded, rebuking in many ways their evil lives and their wickedness, yet nevertheless he commanded the people to hear and fulfil their doctrine, but not to follow their wicked example. At length he repeated their great ingratitude and unkindness towards him, especially that of the city of Jerusalem, insomuch as he was often desirous to have gathered them under his wings, even as a hen doth her chickens, but they would not, wherefore he forewarned them of their destruction, both temporal and eternal, and thus leaving them, went out of the temple, and with his disciples and many others of the Jews that believed in him, went to Mount Olivet, where he taught them how to prepare for their latter end, and told them of the day of judgment, in which the good should be placed at the right-hand of God in everlasting life, and the wicked on the left-hand, in perpetual misery and torment.

Thus did our Lord put an end to his public preaching to the Jews, on the Tuesday night before his passion ; after which he said to his disciples in private, " Know ye, that after two days, the Son of

Man shall be betrayed into the hands of sinners to be crucified." Oh, what a sorrowful speech was this to all his faithful followers! But the horrid traitor Judas was glad to hear it; and consulted within

JUDAS BARGAINS TO BETRAY HIM FOR THIRTY PIECES OF SILVER.

his heart, by the instigation of the devil, who had entered into him, how or in what manner by his death he might satisfy his covetousness. For this purpose he slept not that night, but early on the morrow, which was Wednesday morning, when the chief priests and scribes were assembled together in the house of Caiphas, Judas went to them, and offered, for a reward, to deliver him into their hands. Wherefore they being glad of the offer, agreed to give him thirty pence: and thus was the death of our Redeemer effected through covetousness, treachery, and malice. Hence did that wicked traitor recover the price of the ointment which before he had murmured at as lost, and from that time he sought an opportunity that he might betray him.

This was the wicked doings of the accursed Judas and the Jews on the Wednesday following. But what, may we imagine, did our Lord Jesus and his blessed company? He went not into Jerusalem, nor appeared publicly among the Jews on that day, but spent his whole time in prayer, and armed himself for the redemption of mankind, which he came to accomplish; praying not only for his friends that believed in him and loved him, but also for his professed enemies; fulfilling now in himself the holy perfection of charity, which before he had taught his disciples, in bidding them to pray for their enemies, and for those that should persecute and hate them.

Our Lord Jesus knowing the malice of Judas, this wicked traitor, and also how the Jews were bent against him, prayed to his heavenly Father for them. And as it was the last day that he was to dwell and converse so familiarly with his holy Mother and his apostles, he comforted them with his holy word, as he was wont to do; but he did it the more especially now, to strengthen them against the great sorrows they were to suffer at his passion. And he comforted his blessed Mother and St. Mary Magdalen in a more particular manner, who continually thirsted to drink in the fountain of his holy grace, of which may he, of his infinite bounty and love, make us all partakers.

JESUS INSTITUTES THE HOLY SACRIFICE OF THE NEW LAW.

CHAPTER LIX.

OUR LORD'S SUPPER THE NIGHT BEFORE THE PASSION : AND OF MANY CIRCUMSTANCES RELATING TO IT.

WHEN the time was come in which our Lord
Jesus had disposed all things for the working
of the salvation of his people, and redeeming them,
not with corruptible gold or silver, but with his most
precious blood · before he departed, by death, from
his apostles, he would first make them a memorable
supper, which might serve for a future token, and

might fulfil those mysteries which till **then had not** been fulfilled.

This supper was truly magnificent, **and the things** great and wonderful which our Lord **Jesus wrought** at it for you. Concerning which, four things chiefly occur, which are most worthy your devout meditation. First, the supper itself. Secondly, his washing the feet of his disciples. Thirdly, the institution of the sacrament of his blessed body and blood. And fourthly, the composition of a sublime sermon by our Lord Jesus. All which we will treat of in their order.

First, then, consider, **how Peter and** John were sent by our Lord to a certain friend **on** Mount Sion, where there was a large room, to prepare the supper, or Pasch. Our Lord himself, with **the rest of** his disciples, entered the city on Thursday, when **the** day was almost spent, and repaired to the same place. Behold him, then, pious reader, standing amidst the apostles, and discoursing on heavenly subjects, while, in the meantime, the Pasch was preparing by some of the seventy-two disciples. When all things were ready, the beloved **St.** John, **who** was most familiar with our Lord, and who was diligent in seeing **that** everything should be in order, came to him and said, "Lord when it pleaseth thee to sup, all things are ready." Wherefore, our blessed Saviour, with his twelve apostles, went up ; and John went also next to him, for there was none who loved him more truly, or that was more beloved by him in return : for when our Lord was taken, John followed him when the rest of the disciples fled, and was present at his passion, nor did he desert him either in his crucifixion, his death, nor even after his death until his burial : at this supper also he sat next to him, although he was the youngest of the apostles.

All having entered the small supper chamber, wash their hands, and standing around it, devoutly bless the table. Consider them attentively in all these things. According to ancient usage they sat on the ground around the table, which was placed thereon ; being composed of many boards joined together, its form is believed to have been squared ; I saw it at Rome, in the Church of St. John Lateran, and I measured it. The length of each side is about two *brachia* and three *palms*, so that although the space was small, three disciples are supposed to have sat at each side, and our Lord Jesus humbly at one corner. By this circumstance all were enabled to eat out of the same dish, and on this account it was that the disciples did not understand him when he said, "he that dippeth his hand into the dish with me shall betray me." The table having been blessed by the hand of our Lord, they all took their seats round it, and John sat next to Jesus. The Paschal Lamb was then brought to them, and you may either suppose them to have received it sitting in the manner I have mentioned, or to have eaten of it standing erect, with their staves in their hands, and thus fulfilling literally the precept of the law. In this case, however, you must imagine them after an interval to have sat down again, which may be known to have been the case from various passages in the Gospel, for in any other position John could not have reclined on our Lord's breast. The Paschal Lamb having then been brought in on a dish, was received by the true and immaculate Lamb of God, our Lord Jesus, who being in the midst of his disciples like a servant or steward cut it in pieces and offered it to them with alacrity, kindly pressing and urging them to partake of it. Whilst they were thus engaged, he declaring his mind to them more

explicitly than he was wont, said, among other
things : "With desire I have desired to eat this Pasch
with you before I suffer ; but yet, behold, the hand
of him that betrayeth me is with me on the table."
This sentence like the keen sword pierced their
hearts ; they ceased eating, and, looking at one another, full of surprise and consternation, each one
enquired anxiously, "Lord, is it I?" Contemplate
them then at this juncture, and sympathize both
with them and with our Lord Jesus, for their affliction is great. The traitor, however, in order to divert
attention and suspicion from himself, ceased not from
his occupation, but continued eating. John then, at
the insitigation of Peter, enquired of our Saviour,
who was about to betray him, on which our Lord
familiarly informed him as he would an intimate
friend. John, astonished and stung to the heart by
such perfidity, turned towards him and reclined on
his breast. To Peter, however, our Lord did not
communicate it, because, as St. Augustine observes,
had he known the traitor, he would have torn him
to pieces with his teeth. By Peter are signified active, and by John contemplative Christians, and from
this fact you may learn that the latter, although to
all appearance unoccupied, neither cease from their
interior acts of devotion, nor yet seek to have the
offenders against their Lord punished ; but, inter-
nally lamenting the crime, approaching more nearly
and clinging more closely to God, seek a refuge
from affliction in his love, and leave all things to the
disposal of his divine providence.

After this our Lord Jesus arose from the table,
accompanied by his disciples, who were ignorant of
whither he wished to go. He descended to a lower
apartment in the same house, as those who have seen
the place suppose, and there causing all of them to

sit down, he ordered **water to be** brought to him, laid
aside his garments, girded himself with a towel, and
proceeded **to wash** their feet.   Peter, astonished at

JESUS WASHES THE FEET OF HIS DISCIPLES.

the proposal of an action which to him appeared so
unbecoming, positively refused to allow of its performance on himself; but hearing the threat of
Christ, that he should have no part in his glory if
he permitted him not to do it, he humbly consented
and submitted to his divine pleasure.

Here, pious reader, let us devoutly consider the
humility of our Lord Jesus, and be diligently attentive to all that follows, it being a subject of great
wonder and admiration: for what a sight was it to
behold the King of Heaven and the Lord of all majesty humbly stooping himself to, and kneeling down
at the feet of poor fishermen, who were sitting; to

behold him washing their feet, wiping them with a towel, and devoutly kissing them! And what much more exalts his humility is, to behold him performing this mean office to Judas, the traitor, who was to betray and sell him. Oh, perverse and wicked wretch! Oh, hard and cruel heart; more hardened than stone, and more impenetrable than the diamond, which is neither moved at so much humility, nor melted or become soft with the heat of such great charity; and who trembleth not with fear at the presence of so great a majesty on his knees before you, but, on the contrary, you persist still in your wicked design of betraying and seeking the destruction of him, who is innocence itself, and whose bounty and ineffable goodness you experience even to the last. But, woe to you, oh wretch! who still remaining inflexible, will infallibly bring forth what you have most execrably conceived, and in the end, not he, but you shall perish. It is undoubtedly a subject of great astonishment, to consider the ineffable bounty and meekness of our Lord Jesus, and to see the notorious obstinacy and malice of the wicked traitor Judas.

When this ceremony was ended, he again returned to the same place where he had supped; where all being seated as before, he began to exhort them all to imitate the example he had given him. Wherefore, we may here contemplate how our Lord Jesus Christ left us this night of his passion an example of five sublime virtues; that is, of humility, as we have seen in his washing of his disciples' feet; of charity, in the institution of the adorable sacrament of his body and blood, and in the sermon he then made, which is full of charitable admonitions; of patience in bearing with his wicked traitor, and suffering many reproaches when he was taken and led as a thief to judgment; of obedience in going to suffer, and meeting an opprobrious death, to fulfil the will of his **Father**; and of prayer, by praying three different times in the garden of Gethsemane.

Let us then endeavor to imitate him in these virtues; and hence proceed to a consideration of the third point, that is, of the institution of the most adorable sacrament of the Eucharist. And in relation to this, we cannot behold without astonishment that most beloved condescension and sublime charity, with which he vouchsafed to give himself **to us**: ordaining that sacrament **as a means** whereby he might leave us that divine and heavenly **food** of his sacred body **and blood**. Wherefore, after he had washed his disciples' **feet, to show** them the ending of the sacrifices of **the Old Law**, and the beginning of the New Testament, **and** to make himself **our** only true sacrifice, he took bread into his blessed hands, and lifting up his eyes to his heavenly Father, he blessed it, and instituted the sacrament of his body, and giving it to his disciples, said, "Take ye and eat, for this is **my** body which shall **be delivered** for you." And in the same manner he took the chalice, and said, "Drink ye all of this, **for** this is my blood which shall be shed for you, and for many, in the remission of sins."

Here, Christian reader, attentively consider how devoutly, how diligently, and how truly our blessed Lord Jesus changed the substance of the bread into his precious body, and afterwards, with his own blessed hands, distributed it himself to that beloved and holy company, enjoining them to keep it as a memorial of his love, saying, "Do this in remembrance of me." This is that sweet and precious memorial which renders man's soul most grateful and pleasing to God, as often as it is worthily received : and therefore the consideration of this most excellent gift of love ought to inflame our souls with love, and wholly transform us into the giver. For what could he have given us more dear, more sweet, and more precious than himself? He whom we receive in the sacrament of the altar, is the selfsame Son of God, Christ Jesus, that took flesh and blood, and was born of the Virgin Mary, and suffered death on the cross for us, rose the third day from death to life, ascended into heaven, sitteth at the right hand of the Father, and shall come again at the last day, to judge both the living and the dead, in whose power is both life and death, who made both heaven and hell, and finally, who can either reward us with the joys of the one, or punish us with the eternal pains of the other : he, the selfsame God and Man, is contained in that small host in the form of bread, which is daily offered to God the Father. He is our Lord Jesus Christ, Son of the eternal and living God.

Touching the fourth and last point to be considered, let us now behold how this sovereign Master, after this institution, made to his disciples a most beautiful sermon, full of heavenly sweetness, and of divine love and charity. For having given to them that blessed sacrament, and amongst the rest, also to the wicked traitor Judas, he said to him : "That which thou doest, do quickly."—*John* xiii. And immediately that accursed monster went to the chief priests, to whom he had sold him on the Wednesday before, and asked them for help to apprehend and take him.

In the meantime he made the said sermon, which he preached to his disciples, giving them his *peace*, and chiefly recommended to them three principal virtues above all others ; that is, *faith, hope,* and *charity*. On charity he expressed himself in these words, saying: "I give you a new commandment, which is, that you love one another: for by this shall all men know that ye are my disciples, if ye love one another." And again: "If you love me and keep my commandments; and whosoever loveth me, and keepeth my sayings, then shall my Father love him, and we will come to him and dwell with him." And in many other places he particularly recommended to them this charity as a worthy legacy, which he would now bequeath to them in his last will and testament.

Secondly, he established them in faith, and confirmed them more strongly in the belief of his divinity, saying, "Let not your hearts be troubled, and fear ye not, as ye have believed in God, so believe in me also." Further showing them that the Father and he were one; and that though as man he was less than his Father, yet he was equal with him as he was God: and therefore he reprehended Philip, who asked him to show them the Father, saying, "that he who saw him, saw the Father." And in the conclusion of this point; he said, "If ye believe not that I am in the Father, and the Father in me, yet at least believe me for the works that ye have seen me do, because no other could do the works which I have done."

Thirdly, he comforted them in hope many ways. And first, as to the effects of prayer, he said, "If ye abide in me, and my words abide in you, whatever ye ask it shall be given you." Again he armed them in regard to all manner of tribulation, and the contempt of the world, saying, "If the world hate ye, you know that it hated me before you." Thus comforting their hope with patience in time of persecution, **by** his own example, who was their Lord and Master.

Lastly, he fortified them, **lest** they should despair **by** reason of his leaving them, telling them that they should conceive great sorrow for his absence for **a** short time, in regard to the death he was to suffer ; but that afterwards that sorrow should be changed into unspeakable joy, **by means** of his glorious resurrection **from** death, **and** his ascension to his Father, **and by** the coming of the Holy Ghost, whom he would **send** to comfort them in all their afflictions, and **teach them** all truth. **And** he concluded with these words, saying, "**All this** I have spoken to you, that ye might have peace **in me.** In the world you shall suffer much sorrow **and** affliction, **but be of good** heart, for I have overcome the world." Which **was** the same as to say, "and so shall **you through** my grace."

After **this** our Lord Jesus lifting up **his** eyes towards heaven, and addressing himself to his Father, said. *Father,* **keep** *them whom thou hast given me. When I* **was** *with them I kept them. But now I come to thee. Holy Father,* **for** *them do I pray : not for* **the world,** *and not for them only do I pray, but for them also, that by their word shall believe in me. Father, whom thou hast given me, I* **will,** *that where I am, they* **also** *may be with me, that* **they** *may* **see** *my glory.* These, with many other things most moving and piercing, he spoke in the presence of his disciples. And it is certainly surprising to imagine how they, who loved him so tenderly, could possibly bear to hear them without melting with grief and sorrow. And doubtless whoever hath grace deeply to examine and dwell by devout meditation upon the sweet doctrine of our Lord and Saviour, cannot but be inwardly kindled with his divine love in beholding such great charity, benignity, goodness, and other things he was pleased to show this night of his sacred passion. Consider him while he speaks, behold in how affable, devout, and effectual a manner he imprints on the hearts of his disciples all he relates to them, and in some measure feeds their souls with the pleasing aspect of his divine countenance. Consider likewise the disciples, how sorrowful they stand to hear him, hanging down their heads, fetching deep sighs, and bitterly weeping; being full of extreme sorrow and affliction, as Christ himself bears witness, saying, "Because I have spoken these things, sorrow hath filled your hearts." And among the rest consider St. John, who above all was most familiar with our blessed Lord, how attentively he beholds his beloved master, and with a most tender anxiety takes particular notice of every word he says.

At length, among other things which he spoke, he said to them, "Arise, let us go hence." Oh, what fear, may we not well imagine, did then seize their hearts; not knowing as yet whither, or in what he would go; believing that the time was now come, in which they were to be separated from him. They arose, however, and followed; each striving which should be nearest to him, and all flocking round him, as her chickens around the hen; they crowded in upon him, first one, and then another, through the earnest desire they had of being near him, and hearing his divine doctrine; all which he, with great patience and benignity, suffered them to do. At last, having ended what he had to say to them, he brought them unto a garden on the other side of the brook Cedron, and there fixing himself in prayer, he waited for Judas the traitor, and the rest that were to apprehend him, as we shall see in that which follows of his passion.

THE AGONY IN THE GARDEN.

CHAPTER LX.

THE PASSION OF OUR LORD JESUS CHRIST; AND HIS PRAYER IN THE GARDEN.

IT is now time for us to enter upon the subject of the passion of our Lord Jesus. But whoever desires to glory in the cross and passion of Jesus Christ, must devoutly apply himself to the pious and frequent meditation of it; the mysteries of which, as well as every other thing that was done relating to it, if they were truly considered with all the attention of the mind, **would**, undoubtedly, transform **each** votary into **a** new **man**. Wherefore, pious reader, banishing from **your** heart all the **vain** and troublesome cares of this life, and all sorts of wandering and distracting thoughts which may hinder your attention, and disturb the tranquillity of your soul, endeavor, as far as possible, to render yourself attentive, as if present at the dismal tragedy of this sorrowful and bitter passion.

And first then, behold, how our Lord Jesus went over the brook Cedron into a garden, whither he was **often used to resort** with his disciples to pray. He took **with him** three of his most beloved disciples, Peter, James, and John, and telling them that his heart was heavy and sorrowful, **even unto death,** he bid **them** watch with him in **prayer.** And then going about a stone's cast from them, and throwing himself on his knees, he made his devout and humble prayer to his Father. We read that he often prayed thus: but he then prayed for us, as our advocate; but now he prayed for himself. Have compassion on him, and admire his most profound humility; who being God co-eternal **and co-equal** with his Father, **forgets, as it were,** his being so, and prays like **men, humbly** offering **up** petitions **to his Father, thus truly** expressing **his** most perfect and submissive obedience to him. But what does he pray for? He prays to his heavenly Father, to take from him, if possible, the bitter chalice of his approaching passion, and that he might not die that cruel death of the cross, if it could any ways be agreeable to his divine will. But his prayer **was** not heard in this; since his Father would have him to die, and would not spare **him,** though his true and only Son, but thus delivers him up for us all. "For God so loved the world, that he gave his only begotten Son."—*John* iii Our

Lord Jesus, therefore, submitted to this obedience, and faithfully fulfilled the divine will of his Father. Consider, likewise, the unspeakable charity both of the Father and Son towards us. It was for us that this death was inflicted upon him ; and he suffered it through the excess of the love he bore us. Wherefore, our blessed Lord prays still to his heavenly Father, saying, "Most merciful and gracious Father, full of pity and compassion, I beseech you to hear my prayer, and despise not my supplication : attend unto me and hear me. I am sorrowful in my affliction : my soul is troubled within me, and my heart is afflicted. Incline your ear towards me, and hearken to the voice of my supplication. It pleased you, O heavenly Father, to send me into this world, to satisfy for the sin of man committed against us ; and presently I was ready at your command, and said, lo, I go : and I have farther declared your word and truth to them, dwelling among them, in many troubles, from my youth fulfilling your will in all you have commanded me, and am also ready to accomplish to the utmost those things which are to be done for their redemption ; yet you see, O most beloved Father, how maliciously my enemies have conspired against me ; I have ever done them good, and bestowed benefits on those that hated me ; and they have again rewarded me with evil for good, and returned me hatred for evil ; and at this present time they have corrupted my disciple, who hath sold me to them for thirty pence, and made him the instrument to destroy me. O Father, if it be your will, take from me, I beseech you, this bitter cup of my passion ; but if not, your blessed will be done. If they will not acknowledge me for your only Son, yet, as I have ever lived a righteous and innocent life, and wrought so many good works amongst them, they ought not to be so cruel and maliciously bent against me. Remember, oh, heavenly Father, that I have always stood before you to speak good for them, and to turn away your wrath from them. And shall good be recompensed with evil? For they have digged a pit for my soul, and prepared a most shameful death for me. Wherefore you, O Lord, who see all things, be not silent, forsake me not, but rise up to help me: for great tribulation is near at hand, and there is no other that can deliver me. My adversaries are all before you that seek my soul: and my heart hath expected reproach, and I am full of heaviness."

This done, our Lord Jesus came again to his disciples, and finding them heavy with sleep, he awakened them, and bid them to watch and pray; this he did also a second and third time; and then returning again to prayer, he said as before, and added, "Oh, most righteous Father, if it be so that you have absolutely ordained that I must suffer a most cruel death on the cross for man's redemption, your most holy will be done. But first I recommend to your care, my beloved mother, and my disciples, whom hitherto I have always taken care of." And while he was thus fervent in his holy prayer, his most precious blood gushed forth like sweat, from all parts of his sacred body, and ran down upon the ground, through the extreme violence of his bitter agony. Here is a subject of grief and sorrow, which ought to be sufficient to move the hardest heart to compassion at the anguish and pain which our blessed Lord Jesus suffered at that time for our sake. For by virtue of his divinity, he foresaw all the pains and torments which were to be inflicted upon him, and therefore, according to his humility, his tender body trembled with fear, and fell into a most violent and bloody sweat. Let us learn hence to check our frequent impatience by recollecting, that our Lord prayed three times to his Father before he received an answer.

Now at the third time, when he was in the most profound anguish of spirit, behold an angel from God, the prince of the celestial heirarchy, St. Michael, came down and stood before him, comforted him, and said, "Hail, O blessed Lord Jesus! your devout prayer and bloody sweat I have offered up to your Father, in the presence of the whole court of heaven. We all humbly prostrate before him, have besought him to take from you that bitter draught of your passion : but your heavenly Father answering us, said, 'My blessed Son knows full well that the redemption of mankind, which, out of our sovereign love to him, we so much desire, cannot be conveniently fulfilled without the shedding of his blood ; wherefore, if he is desirous of their salvation, he must die for them.'" To whom our Lord Jesus again replied, "I desire above all things the salvation of man's soul, and therefore, I choose rather cheerfully to suffer death, by which the souls which my heavenly Father hath made to his own image and likeness, may be saved, than not to die, and that those souls should not be redeemed : Wherefore, my Father's will be done." The angel then again replying, said, "Be now of good heart, my divine Lord. and act courageously : for it behooves the high to work great things, and to suffer courageously most severe and difficult trials ; your pains and troubles will soon pass away, and joy and glory shall ever after succeed. And your heavenly Father is, and will be, always with you ; and will keep and preserve from harm, your blessed mother and your disciples, according to your desire."

Our most humble **Lord Jesus rose** up, and meekly
accepted this small comfort from the angel, the
Creator from the creature, reputing himself for
that time **even** inferior to them. Wherefore, he
was sorrowful as man, was comforted **by** the angel
as man, and as man prayed him to recommend him
to his Father, and to the whole court of celestial
spirits.   And thus a third time he riseth from prayer,
with his body covered with blood ; whom you **may**
behold with inward compassion, wiping himself or
bathing **in** the river ; all which is to be devoutly
considered with sorrow **and** compassion, since it
could not possibly be endured without great bitterness and pain.

Here we must observe, that many of **the** fathers
and learned doctors say, that our Lord Jesus prayed
in this manner, not merely for fear of his bitter
passion, but chiefly through the pity and mercy
which he had towards his chosen people, the Jews,
lamenting that they would be lost by not believing
in him, and putting him to death.   For surely it
was most ungrateful in them to crucify him, since
he was of their race ; and was also prophesied in
their law to be the true Messiah, Christ Jesus, who
was to come, and who had farther showed them so
many **signs**, and given them so many proofs of his
singular love.   Wherefore, as some of the holy
fathers say, he prayed after this manner, saying, "O
heavenly Father, if it could stand with the salvation
of my brethren the Jews, and that the Gentiles might,
by some other means, be converted to you, I would
be glad to refuse this bitter passion ; but if otherwise
it be expedient that the Jews be blinded in their
malice, so that others after them may have a more
perfect sight in the faith and true belief of you, **then**
not my will but yours be fulfilled."

There was in Christ at this time four kinds of wills, viz.: The will of the flesh, which would no ways agree to suffer. The will of sensuality; and this murmured and feared. The will of reason; and this consented and was obedient. And lastly, there was in him his divine will; which commanded and passed sentence. And as he was true man, as such he suffered great anguish of spirit, and underwent a most bitter agony. Wherefore, have an inward and cordial compassion for him, and consider attentively every action of the Lord your God.

After this he came to his disciples, and said to them, "Now sleep and take your rest;" for their eyes were very heavy.

Thus the Good Shepherd was carefully watchful and vigilant over his little flock, his beloved disciples. Oh, how great was the love of our sweet Lord and Saviour towards them! For those whom he loved, he loved to the end: so that even in his great anguish and bitter agony, he was careful in procuring their rest and quiet repose.

JUDAS BETRAYS HIS MASTER WITH A KISS.

CHAPTER LXI.

OUR LORD JESUS CHRIST TAKEN AND BETRAYED BY JUDAS.

IMMEDIATELY after, our blessed Lord beheld his adversaries coming with lighted torches and lanterns, and weapons to apprehend him ; and yet he would not awaken his disciples till his enemies came near to him : then he spoke and said, "Rise, let us go ; behold he approacheth that shall betray me."— *Matt.* xxvi. And while he was speaking, that wicked wretch, Judas the traitor, came and approaching him, kissed him. For it is written, that it was the manner and custom of our Lord Jesus towards his disciples, that when at any time he had sent them out, at their returning again, he would receive them with a loving kiss. Wherefore the traitor went before the wicked band, and kissed him as he used to do, and said, "Hail, master."

And here let us behold our Lord Jesus, how patiently and meekly he receives that false and treacherous kiss, from that unfaithful disciple, whose feet so lately he had vouchsafed to wash with his own hands, and whom, out of his unspeakable charity he refused not to feed with the precious food of his blessed body. Consider, likewise, how meekly he suffered himself to be taken, bound, struck, and furiously dragged away, as if he had been a thief, or the most wicked person in the world, void of power to help himself. Contemplate also the great sorrow and inward affliction he had on account of his disciples, who fled and left him in the hands of those ravenous wolves. And on the other side, consider the grief of their hearts, since the cause of their leaving him was not the perversity of their will, but the frailty of their weak nature ; for which they heartily mourn and sigh, like poor orphans, that know not what they do, or whither to go ; and their sorrow was so much the greater, as they knew in what a barbarous manner their Lord and master would be treated and abused.

Those cruel butchers drive and pull him along as they would a beast to the slaughter, and he, like a meek lamb, not opening his mouth, patiently follows them without resistance. First, those vile wretches led him from the brook Cedron, near which place he was apprehended, towards the city of Jerusalem, and that with great haste, pain, and violence having

his blessed hands bound behind him, as if he had
been some grievous malefactor; his garments torn
off, going bareheaded, and bent down, from the
great haste, and the violent pain, they forced him to,
in going.

ANNAS HEARING THE REPORT OF HIS HAVING BEEN TAKEN, COMES
OUT TO SEE HIM.

When he was brought before the chief priests and
scribes, that were then assembled together, expecting his coming, they were rejoiced and glad that
they had apprehended him: they then began to examine him, and to ask many questions, endeavoring to ensnare him; they procured false witnesses
against him, spit in his sacred face, blinded his eyes,
buffetted and derided him, saying, "Tell us who it
was that struck thee." Thus many and different

ways they afflicted and tormented him, and in all
he gave us most singular examples of patience.

At length the chief judges rose up and departed,
having ordered him to be kept in custody under a
loft, in the nature of a prison, where they bound
him to a pillar of stone, as those say who have seen
it, leaving a guard of armed men with him for greater
security ; who, during the whole night, abused and
derided him with many opprobrious and reproachful
speeches, saying, "Do you believe yourself to be
better or more wise than our learned magistrates?
Or can you imagine that they understand not the
law and religion much better than you? How foolish do you appear in taking upon you to reprehend
and teach them, against whom you should not have
presumed to open your lips. Wherefore now your
wisdom appears, in being obliged to suffer that which
all such as you truly deserve ; you are truly worthy
of death, and it would be a pity that you should
escape it." Thus the whole night, sometimes one,
and sometimes another, both with scurrilous language and wicked works, continually reviled and
abused him. And our blessed Lord, with bashful
and modest countenance, patiently bore it all, and
was silent to every scornful word they said against
him ; but with his eyes modestly inclined towards
the ground, made no answer, as if he had been
guilty, and worthy of blame. O most amiable Lord,
into whose hands are you come? This is truly the
hour, and power of darkness, and with what patience
do you suffer it !

Thus stood our blessed Redeemer, bound to that
pillar, till the next morning. In the meantime John,
who had followed him to the high priest's house, went
to the Blessed Virgin, to Mary Magdalen, and other
devout people who were at that time assembled at

Mary Magdalen's house, where our Lord made that memorable supper the night before, and related to them all that had happened to our Lord and his disciples; which when they had heard, they were seized with unspeakable grief, and wept most bitterly. Consider them attentively, and have compassion on them, for they are now in the greatest grief and affliction that ever they were in for their Lord, for they now plainly see and know full well that he will be taken from them and put to a cruel death. Our blessed Lady retired alone to prayer, and said, "O most sovereign, most high, and most merciful Father, I present myself before your majesty, to recommend to your protection my dearly beloved son. O gracious Father, reveal to me whether my son Jesus shall be put to death or not. Be not severe to him, O bountiful Father, who to all others art so good and merciful; for he knows no sin, nor ever committed any evil. O most just Father, if you require his death for the redemption of the world, I beseech you, if possible, to find out some other means whereby to accomplish your design, and that my blessed son's life may be spared, if it be your holy will. And he, out of obedience to you, has abandoned himself into the hands of his enemies, and will not attempt to deliver himself from their power. Wherefore, I beseech you, O heavenly Father, to help him, and to deliver him to me again out of their wicked hands." Thus, or in words to this effect, our blessed Lady prayed for her son in the profound sorrow and grief of her soul, wherefore we ought to accompany her in her anguish, and be moved with compassion towards her in her great affliction.

CHAPTER LXII.

OUR BLESSED LORD IS CARRIED BEFORE PILATE; SCOURGED AT THE PILLAR, AND CROWNED WITH THORNS.

EARLY next morning, the elders and chiefs of the people returned and caused Jesus to be bound, and led with his hands fastened behind him; and thus hand-cuffed, brought him to Pilate, mocking, reviling and insulting him with the most abusive taunts, as he proceeded on the way. Thus went this innocent Lamb, in the guise of a malefactor, hurried by the merciless butchers to unmerited slaughter. As he was going on his way, his blessed mother, St. John, and the holy women who accompanied the virgin, who had left their humble retirement so early on purpose to come to his assistance and comfort, met him at the turn of a street: and what tongue can express the bitter anguish of their souls, at the sad sight of their Lord thus hurried along by an insulting and abusive mob? Or what degree of inbred grief can figure the excess of mutual sorrow this interview begot on both sides? Our Lord could not but suffer extremely through the compassion he felt for his beloved followers, and chiefly for his mother. For he knew full well the bitter grief they felt for him, sufficient to tear their bleeding souls from their convulsed bodies.

He was then brought before Pilate, and the holy women followed at a distance, the thronging rabble not suffering them to approach nearer. Many accusations were laid against him to Pilate, but he, finding all to be groundless, and desirous to rid himself of so odious a prosecution, dispatched him to Herod. Herod was much pleased at this, hoping by this means to see a miracle wrought by Christ; but he could not obtain the least gratification of this sort from Christ, who thought him unworthy even to hear a word from his sacred mouth. Hence, Herod, look-

HEROD WITH HIS MEN OF WAR MAKES A MOCK OF JESUS.

ing upon him as an idiot, caused him to be clothed in a white garment, the usual habit of fools in those days, and thus, in derision, sent him back to Pilate. So that Christ patiently bore to be reputed both a fool and a malefactor by all, without deserving the title of either from any one. Contemplate him, then, as he is led backwards and forwards, with his eyes modestly depressed, hearing the shouts and taunts, receiving the buffets, spittings, and perhaps filth

thrown at him by rude populace, without murmur
or complaint; cast a pitying eye upon him in this
sad plight, and with him compassionate his afflicted
mother and beloved disciples, who follow him as
closely as the mob will permit, till they reach the
palace of Pilate. Here again he is loaded by the
savage brutes with false accusations, which they
utter with the utmost impudence and inveteracy.
Yet Pilate, finding in him nothing that bore the appearance of guilt, sought means to free him from
their hands. Wherefore he says, "I will punish,
and then dismiss him." O Pilate! do you presume

JESUS BY THE COMMAND OF PILATE, IS SCOURGED AT THE PILLAR.

to chastise your Lord and Sovereign? Surely you
are beside yourself thus to dare to inflict stripes on
him who is as guiltless of stripes as of death. Oh,

how much more wisely had you acted to chastise
yourself by his admonition! Pilate, however, was
besotted enough to order him to be most **inhumanly**
scourged.

By his order **therefore, our** most innocent Lord
was stripped naked, **bound to** a pillar, and inhumanly
scourged. Thus was that innocent Lamb, **and that**
most beautiful among the children of men, **shamefully** exposed, naked and abashed, before the whole
populace ; and received with invincible patience the
cruel stripes of his barbarous executioners. So that
the most beautiful flower of human nature, and **the**
fairest and **most** delicate of all flesh, was covered
with stripes, wounds and bruises, insomuch that
from the crown of his head to the soles of his feet,
his most precious blood ran, flowing from all parts
of his sacred **body, in** abundance upon the ground,
being so long **scourged** and beaten that **they** added
wound **to wound, bruise** to bruise, **and stripe to**
stripe· **till at length, the** inhuman spectators being
weary of beholding any longer what the cruel
butchers themselves were wholly tired of, he **was
ordered to** be unbound. He was then loosed **from**
the pillar, on which the stains of his precious blood
are **still** to be seen, as many authentic historians
affirm.

Here, pious reader, let me entreat you to dwell
some **time on** this subject, and attentively consider,
with heart full of sorrow and compassion, the **ex-**
tremity **of his** bitter pains ; and if you find not your
heart moved, **or even** melted with grief and compunction at **the sufferings** of your blessed Lord, you
may conclude that it is more hard and impenetrable
than stone. It **was** then fulfilled of him, what the
prophet Isaiah had **long** before prophesied, saying,
" We have seen him, and there was neither form

nor beauty left, and we esteemed him as a leper, and as one smitten by God, and humbled." O sweet Jesus, who dared to be so bold as to presume to strip you of your garments? Who was it that dared with more assurance to bind you to the pillar? And who, most audacious of all, could persume to beat and scourge you in that cruel manner? But you, O most bright sun of righteousness! you, I say, who withdrew the resplendent beams of your glory, and

THE SOLDIERS CROWN JESUS WITH THORNS, AND BOW THE KNEE
TO HIM AS KING.

who vouchsafed to hide your power and might, so that darkness, and the power of darkness reigned for a time, and your enemies appeared, by your divine permission, more powerful than yourself. It was the excess of your love, and the greatness of our iniquity, which disarmed you of your strength in this conflict. But accursed be that malice which caused you to be thus cruelly tormented.

After this they led him round the place to seek for his clothes, **which** were scattered about **in** different parts, some **in** one place, and some in another, by those barbarous executioners who had stripped him. Here ought tenderness move us to compassion towards him, thus afflicted and trembling **with cold** ; for as the gospel tells us, the weather was sharp and piercing. As he was clothing himself again, **some** of the wicked populace went to Pilate, and said, "This man said, he was king, wherefore, let us clothe him after **our manner**, and crown him **as** such." Then taking him aside, they clothed him in a purple garment : and platting a crown of thorns, they put it upon his head, and with violence **pressed** them into his sacred temples ; giving him a reed instead of a sceptre, they kneeled down and saluted him in derision, saying, "Hail, **king** of the Jews." To all which Jesus made no answer : and like a meek and patient lamb, opened not his mouth. Here behold with melting heart, how often they strike him upon the head to drive the piercing thorns more deeply into his sacred temples, so that they forced the blood from every part, which running down in great abundance, covered his blessed face. Consider how he behaves in every action, and how patiently he bears every insult which they offer to him ; **they deride and** mock him as one **who** would make himself king, **without power** to effect it. **He is** clothed in purple, **carries** a crown of thorns on his head, holds a reed in his hand, and they on their knees, salute him in derision as king, and he is silent, and murmurs not. But, oh miserable and wicked wretches ! how dreadful shall that blessed head appear at the last day, which now you beat and abuse so inhumanly! Neither was all they had hitherto done sufficient to weaken their malice against him; but to add more to his reproach, they brought into the house many of the mob to gaze

THE PEOPLE CRY, "NOT THIS MAN, BUT BARABBAS."

on him; after which they led him out to Pilate, and showed him to the whole multitude; having on his purple garment, his crown of thorns, and a sceptre of a reed in his hand. In this manner stood that innocent lamb, with his eyes modestly depressed before that great multitude, who scoffed and derided him, and with the loudest shouts exclaimed against him, crying out to Pilate, "Crucify him, crucify him."

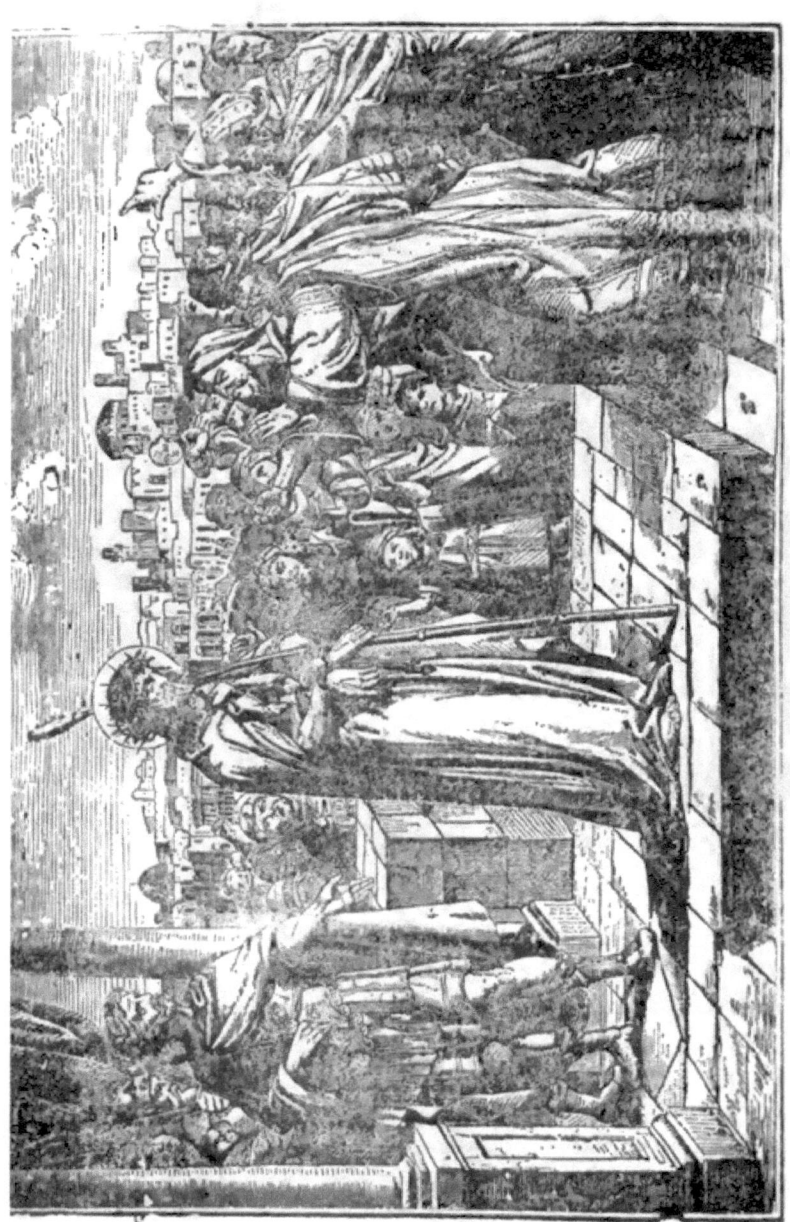

"ECCE HOMO!"—BEHOLD THE MAN.

Pilate desiring to convict the Jews of their hypocrisy and pretence in alleging that Jesus sought to make Himself a King in opposition to Cæsar exhibits Jesus to the multitude with His crown of thorns and the mock purple robe.

PILATE YIELDS TO THE CRY FOR HIS CRUCIFIXION.

CHAPTER LXIII.

OUR BLESSED LORD JESUS IS CONDEMNED TO SUFFER
A CRUEL DEATH ON THE CROSS, AND COMPELLED
TO CARRY THE SAME TO MOUNT CALVARY.

OUR blessed Lord Jesus having been many ways
shamefully reviled, mocked and abused, and
having suffered many cruel torments among them,
the chief men of the Jews continually sought his death,
and stirred up the whole multitude to join them, and

to importune Pilate to have him crucified. At length
that wicked judge, fearing more to incur their dis-
pleasure than to condemn the innocent, passed sentence of death upon him.   Then were the Scribes
and Pharisees full of joy, that they had accomplished
their designs, and attained their wicked ends against
him.   They remembered not the benefits they had
received from him, nor the miracles he had wrought
among them ; they neither pitied him for his innocence, nor were they moved at the cruelty and baseness of the action they were going to commit ; and
instead of ceasing from their wicked purpose, in consideration of the great affliction, sufferings, and reproaches they had already inflicted upon him, they
rejoiced and were glad that their designs were now
near their execution. Wherefore, they revile, mock,
and insult him, who is the true and eternal God, and
hasten, as much as possible, his death.   He is again
carried back to the house, stripped of his mock
purple garment, and left naked before them.   Pause
here a moment, and attentively consider the make
and form of his sacred body : and that you may be
moved to inward compassion towards him. and feed
your soul with devout contemplation, close your
eyes· for a while to his divinity, and consider him
as purely man, and you will behold the most lovely,
fair, innocent, and beautiful among the sons of men
in that doleful condition, full of wounds and bruises,
covered with blood, naked and abashed. seeking
and gathering together his garments. which were
dispersed in different parts of the house. by those
cruel and merciless brutes, and clothing himself
before them, whilst they stand insulting and reviling him, as if he had been the most contemptible
of all creatures, forsaken by God, and destitute of
all help and comfort.   Then consider the profound

and wonderful meekness of him as God and man;
behold how that immense, eternal, and incom-
prehensible majesty stoops to the ground, collects
his torn garments, and bashfully clothes himself before his enemies, as though he was the vilest of men,
their bought slave, under their dominion, and by them
chastised as a base and unpardonable criminal. After
this, accompany him out, and behold how, after he
has put on his clothes, they hurry him away, and
load him with the heavy wood of the cross, which,

JESUS HAS THE CROSS LAID UPON HIS SHOULDERS.

as historians say, measured fifteen feet in length;
this the most meek and innocent Lamb took and
bore upon his blessed shoulders; and thus was he
hurried along by an enraged mob, in company with

two th eves, who were condemned to death ; these
were his companions in suffering.

Oh, sweet and beloved Jesus, how much do these
your enemies debase you, by making you a companion with thieves ! And what is still worse, they
compel you to carry your own cross, which is a
burthen they imposed not upon them. Wherefore,
as the prophet Isaiah saith, "You are not only
numbered with evil doers, but are used worse than
they. Your patience, O Lord, is unspeakable."

And now, devout Christians, with all possible attention and devotion, observe our Lord Jesus, how
he bends under the weight of the cross, vehemently
sighing, and wearied. Take pity on him in this sad
plight of renewed afflictions and calumnies.

THE FIRST FALL OF JESUS UNDER THE WEIGHT OF HIS CROSS.

His blessed and afflicted mother, seeing that she could not get near him, on account of the great concourse of people which pressed about him, went, with St. John and the rest of her companions, a nearer way, to the end that she might meet him at the winding of the street. And when she perceived him coming, bowed down with the heavy load of the cross, which before she had not seen, she was like one beside herself, and half dead with grief, so

JESUS MEETS HIS MOST BLESSED MOTHER.

that she could neither speak to him, nor he to her, by reason of the furious mob which hurried him along with great violence and compulsion. After, however, he had gone a little way, he turned to the women that followed, weeping, and said: "Ye daughters of Jerusalem, weep not for me, but weep for

yourselves and for your children," etc., as is farther
contained in the gospel. And in these two places
were erected two churches in memory of these
things, as they report who have been there, and
seen them. And as Mount Calvary was distant from
the city, he was so tired and faint, that he was not
able to carry his cross the whole way, but fell down
under it with exhaustion. The wicked executioners,
not willing to defer his death, lest Pilate should re-
voke his sentence, as he had before shown some inclination to release him, compelled one Simon, a
stranger, to carry it for him, and Jesus they led un-
burdened the rest of the way, but bound like a thief
to the place of execution.

SIMON OF CYRENE IS FORCED TO HELP JESUS TO BEAR HIS CROSS.

Now, if we attentively consider all that hath been

done to our Lord Jesus, and the many things he hath suffered from the time he **was** first apprehended to this present, we shall doubtless find **therein great** matter of sorrow **and compunction.** For we may truly believe, that from the hour in which he was first taken in the night, till the time of his being crucified, he was in one continual combat, and endured numberless reproaches and injuries, sorrows and detractions innumerable and suffered the most cruel torments among them. For there was no manner of rest given to him but continual trouble and vexation. And here you may dwell, devout reader, for some short review of that which hitherto hath been acted against him : first, how one lays violent hands upon and apprehends him, another binds him tightly with cords, another blasphemes him, another spits in his sacred face, another proposes to him subtle questions in order to ensnare him, another drags him backwards and forwards from one judge to another, another blindfolds his eyes, another buffets him, another strips him of his clothes, another binds him to a pillar, another most cruelly scourges him, another unbinds him and clothes him in a purple garment, another plats a crown of thorns which he presses upon his head, another puts a reed into his hand, another takes it from him, and striking him with it upon the head, drives the thorns further into his sacred temples, another kneels down before him and mocks him, and so of the rest, sometimes one, and sometimes another. Now they **lead** him to Annas, now to Caiphas, then to Pilate, and thence to Herod ; now hither, and then thither, now out, and then in again. And finally, he was dragged and hurried along with great violence, and without rest, till he came to Mount Calvary, which was the place fixed for the period of this doleful combat.

ST. VERONICA WIPES THE FACE OF JESUS WITH A NAPKIN.

CHAPTER LXIV.

OUR LORD JESUS CHRIST IS NAILED TO THE CROSS.

WHEN our blessed Lord Jesus was now come to Mount Calvary, those wicked and merciless butchers began then to effect their cruel work. Be present now with all the attention of your mind to these things, and devoutly consider every particular relating to the Lord your God. Behold with the interior eyes of your soul, some preparing the cross,

some making ready the ropes and cords to bind him,
some the nails and hammers to fasten him, others
preparing the ladder and other instruments, some
digging the hole in the earth to fix the cross in, and
others busy in stripping him, so that this is the third
time of his being stripped, by which his wounds are
again renewed by the violent tearing off his clothes,
which were cleaving to his sacred flesh. His blessed

JESUS IS STRIPPED OF HIS RAIMENT.

mother, when she beheld him thus used, was afflicted
beyond expression. And oh, how full of bitter anguish, indeed, may we well imagine, was her tender
soul, in beholding her beloved and innocent son thus
shamefully abused, and loaded with injuries and insults! Then was he extended upon the cross, as it

lay upon the ground, and with cords stretching **forth** with violence his sacred hands and feet, the cruel slaughterers with long iron nails barbarously piercing them, nailed him fast to it.

Thus was our Lord and Saviour Jesus Christ fastened to the cross, hand and foot, and so excessively strained thereon, that as the royal prophet saith : " All his bones might be numbered :" and his sacred **blood ran** forth in streams from his blessed **wounds** in great abundance : and his arms and legs were so widely stretched with the nails, that he could move no part of his body, except his head. And as his whole weight was supported only by three nails, his pains undoubtedly were great beyond what any heart can conceive, or tongue express. **But still** to add insult to the pangs he suffered, he was crucified between two thieves, and loaded with derision, contempt, and reviling from all parts. Some blasphemed him, others shook their heads, and said, " Fie on thee, thou art he that wouldst destroy the temple of God, and build it up again in three days. Others he saved, himself he cannot save ; and if thou be the Son of God descend now from the cross, that we may believe." And those who crucified him, divided his garments among them before his face. All this was acted in the presence of his afflicted mother, who stood under the cross, and whose tender compassion and tears added much to his sorrow and affliction ; for she **accom**panied **him in her** soul on **the cross,** and inwardly desired **rather to die with** him, than to live any longer without him. **Thus** stood the doleful mother beside the cross of her son. She never turned her eyes from him—she was afflicted and full of anguish with him ; and with many bitter sighs prayed to her heavenly Father, saying, " Oh, heavenly Father, and sovereign Lord of majest**y** without doubt it was foreseen and pleasing to you from all eternity, that my most beloved and innocent son should shed his precious blood, and be crucified for the sins of the world, wherefore it is not proper to ask him of you again. But, most holy Father, you see the bitter torment and anguish of his soul, wherefore I beseech you to ease his pain, and release him, if it be your heavenly will."

JESUS IS NAILED TO THE CROSS.

And her blessed son secretly prayed to his Father for her, saying, "Oh good Father, look down, I beseech you, on my afflicted mother, and behold how deeply she is tormented for me: my crucifixion is sufficient for the sins of mankind; she hath not deserved any such thing, and yet she is with me in heart upon the cross, and bears an equal share with me in my pains. I recommend her to you, beseeching that it would please you to assuage and lessen her grief."

There were also with our blessed Lady the beloved disciple, St. John, and Mary Magdalen, and the two sisters of our Lady, Mary of James, and Mary of Salome, and other friends, standing under the cross, who all, but especially Mary Magdalen, the beloved of Jesus, were very sorrowful, and wept bitterly, and could no ways be comforted, because of the pains of their beloved master: for their sorrow was renewed with his, in the words, or deeds, which were said or done to him.

CHAPTER LXV.

THE WORDS WHICH OUR LORD SPOKE WHILE HANGING UPON THE CROSS : HE YIELDS UP HIS SPIRIT.

OUR Lord Jesus hanging on the cross, ceased not to do, and to speak those things which were for our advantage, even to the last moment in which he gave up his spirit ; wherefore he spoke seven times, as is written in the Gospel.

The first time he spoke was when he prayed for his enemies, saying, "Father, forgive them, for they know not what they do." O wonderful patience, charity, and benignity !

The second was to his mother, when he said, "Woman, behold thy son ;" and to John, "behold thy mother." He would not call her at that time mother, lest the tenderness of the expression should have occasioned her more grief.

The third was to the good thief saying, "This

day thou shalt be with me in paradise." In which words he showed his infinite and unbounded mercy towards us.

The fourth was when he said, "*Eli, Eli, Lamma sabacthani.*" That is to say, "My God, my God, why hast thou forsaken me!" As if he had more plainly said : "My God, you have so much loved the world, that while you give me to death for its redemption, you seem to have forsaken me."

The fifth was when he said, "*Sitio;*"—I thirst ! Which word gave occasion to his enemies to rejoice, and to his mother greater occasion of compassion. And although this word may be understood of thirst for the salvation of souls : yet he truly thirsted for drink ; for by the great effusion of his blood, he had little moisture left within him. Wherefore his cruel butchers, who were studying how they might torment him, took vinegar mixed with gall, and put it to his mouth, that he might drink.

The sixth was when he said, "*Consummatum est :*" It is finished ! As if he had said, "O Father, I have perfectly and obediently fulfilled all the commands you gave me, and all that has hitherto been written of me : wherefore, now, if it pleaseth thee, receive me again to thyself." To which, we may for devotion's sake imagine, his Father replied, "Come, my beloved Son, for you have fulfilled all things completely, and I will not that you suffer any more ; come then and resign your soul into my arms, and repose yourself forever in my bosom."

And then our blessed Jesus began to fail in his sight, after the nature of dying men, and grew faint and languid, sometimes closing and sometimes opening his eyes ; and bowing his head first on one side, and then on the other, till being quite spent, and life failing, he recommended his soul to his Father, cry-

ing out with a loud voice, the seventh time, saying,
"Father, into thy hands I commend my spirit."
With which he yielded up the ghost.

JESUS DIES UPON THE CROSS.

At this strong and vehement cry of our Lord Jesus,
a centurion who was standing by was converted, and
immediately said, "Verily, this man is the **Son of
God ;**" because he heard him cry so loud when he
expired.

Oh, in what a sad and sorrowful condition may we
well suppose was the tender heart of his blessed
mother, when she beheld him to languish in so painful a manner, to cry out, and to die in her presence !
We may easily believe that her spirits failed her, and
that she was ready to give up the ghost with him,
much more than when she met him carrying his

cross. And what can we think of Mary Magdalen, of St. John, his beloved disciple, and of the other two sisters of our Lady? Undoubtedly their sorrow was inexpressible, they were loaded with grief, and overwhelmed with bitterness and tears, without comfort of any kind, and knew not what to do.

Behold now our Lord Jesus hangs dead upon the cross, and the multitude of people return again to the city. But his most afflicted mother, with the other four, remain still near him, feeding their souls with the divine contemplation of their beloved, and waiting for help from God, that they might have him taken from the cross, and buried.

If you also, Christian soul, will behold your Lord in devout contemplation, you cannot but conceive a tender compassion, seeing that from the crown of his head to the sole of his foot there was no part of him left whole; there was no member, nor any sense which had not their extreme pain and affliction. Employ thyself then in the daily study of these sufferings of thy Lord, and make them the frequent subject of thy devout meditation.

CHAPTER LXVI

THE OPENING OF OUR BLESSED SAVIOUR'S SIDE WITH A SPEAR.

WHILE the blessed mother of our Lord Jesus, with St. John, St. Mary Magdalen, and the two sisters of our blessed Lady sat near the cross, with her eyes attentively fixed on her beloved son, contemplating him thus hanging dead between two thieves, forsaken and abandoned, there came many

men from the city towards them ; being sent to break
the legs of those who were crucified, and to kill them
downright, if they were not already dead, that their
bodies might not be seen hanging on the crosses upon
the Sabbath-day. Our blessed Lady, with the others,
rose up to look, and saw them coming, but knew
not for what reason : wherefore their sorrow was
renewed, and their fears increased as they saw
them advance nearer. His blessed mother being
more sensibly affected than the rest, and not knowing what to do, turned herself towards her beloved
son, and said, "My most dear son, to what end, I
beseech thee, do these cruel butchers return hither
again? What more do they intend to do? Have
they not already taken away thy life? I was in
hopes that they were satisfied with what they had
done before to thee while thou wast living: But
now it seems that they have not yet done with thee,
but they will further pursue thee dead. I know
not, my beloved son, how to act, since I am as unable of helping thee now as I was before in deliver-
ing thee from death. I will approach, however,
and stand near the cross, at thy blessed feet, and
beseech thy heavenly Father to render them favorable towards thee."

Hence they all five, bitterly weeping, went and
placed themselves before the cross of our Lord Jesus.
And the multitude, hastily advancing, came with
great shouts and noise, and seeing that the two thieves
were yet living, with great rage they broke their
legs, and killed them, and taking them down, cast
them into a ditch. And then returning they came
to our Lord Jesus. And his blessed mother,
pierced to the heart with grief, fearing they might
do the same to him, in an agony of humility, kneeling down before them, with her arms extended, and

with a loud and compassionate voice, spoke to
them in this manner: "I beseech you, brethren,
for the love of God, most High and Almighty,
that you will no more afflict or torment me in
my most dear son: I am truly his most sorrowful and disconsolate mother, whom you know has
never injured or offended you. And if my beloved
son seemed to oppose you, you have put him to
death for it. What more can your revenge require?
Forbear then to insult him any longer, and I will forgive the injuries you have hitherto done me in his
death and sufferings. But oh, be thus far merciful
in your cruelty; touch not his dear corpse, but suffer
me to carry it whole to the sepulchre. What will it
avail you to break his limbs, who has already expired this hour past?" Thus did the sacred Virgin
persist on her knees, with John and Magdalen,
and the other devout women, weeping and entreat-
ing those inhuman butchers! O sacred Lady, to
what purpose do you thus demean yourself to those
barbarous wretches! Can you hope for any success
with such inexorable savages? Will pity make the
impious relent? Will the merciless give yearnings
of mercy, or pride bend to humility? Alas! your
endeavors are ineffectual; condescension is the aversion of the haughty.

One Longinus, at that time a proud and wicked
man, but afterwards a convert, a saint, nay, a martyr,
stretched forth his lance, and seeming to give ear to
their cries, pierced our Lord's sacred side, when immediately from the wound gushed forth a stream of
water and blood. At the sight his disconsolate mother
fell into a swoon, in the arms of Magdalen: and
while St. John and the holy women were busied in
supporting and restoring our blessed Lady, the impious butchers departed. And now at her recovery,

a new taste of death succeeded the former, when she
beheld her beloved and divine sun, hanging dead on
the cross in such a mangled and deplorable condition.   Oh, how many strokes of death **did not this**
spotless Lady feel on this day !   Who **can** doubt of
their being equal in number to the insults and cruel-
ties used to **him** ?   And thus was fulfilled what Simeon
foretold, that "the sword of sorrow should pierce her
soul."   Thus did one lance, with the same sacrile-
gious stroke, pierce the blessed body of Jesus and
the sacred soul of Mary.

When our blessed Lady was recovered, they all
sat down at the foot of the cross, at a loss what to do
or how to act.   How to take down and where to deposit the holy corpse they could not contrive, for
want of strength and for want of a sepulchre to put it
in.   To depart and leave him on the cross in that
condition, they knew not how to resolve, and to remain there long was neither decent nor safe, for night
was coming on.   What perplexity ! O bountiful God,
how didst thou suffer this thy favorite, this mirror of
all virtues, this our sacred advocate and protectress
to be afflicted ?   Surely it were time she had some
respite from the excess of anguish.

CHAPTER LXVII.

THE DESCENT OF OUR LORD FROM THE CROSS.

AGAIN they saw several persons coming along
the road : these were Joseph of Arimathea,
and Nicodemus, and some persons with them, who
brought instruments to take down the sacred body
from the cross, and a great quantity of myrrh and

aloes to embalm it. This gave them a new alarm, not knowing at a distance but they might be persons coming to offer new outrages to the blessed corpse. Wherefore, they all arose, and immediately falling on their knees, applied themselves to prayer, beseeching God to avert the affliction they seemed again threatened with. At length, however, St. John discovered who they were, and returning thanks to God, they all began to be comforted. Our blessed Lady then dispatched St. John to meet them, who brought them to the cross where the holy women were, and presented them to the afflicted mother of God. Our blessed Lady received them graciously, and with all the joy compatible with her present state of grief. Joseph and Nicodemus condoled with her and the pious company. Then all falling on their knees, adored the sacred relict of our Lord, and after some time spent in devout and humble prayer and religious homage, they all again arose and prepared to take him down from the cross.

While the holy company are busied in their devout offices to Christ, endeavor, pious reader, to be as devoutly attentive to all that passes. Two ladders then are fixed to the cross, one to each arm. And whilst Nicodemus goes up to that on the left hand, Joseph ascends the other on the right, and labors to draw the nail with which that hand is fastened. This was done not without great difficulty, and bruising the divine flesh, for the nails were of an immoderate size. The action, however, was acceptable to God, inasmuch as it was a violence that was unavoidable and done through the utmost purity of intention and liveliness of faith. When Joseph had drawn out the nail, St. John made a sign to him to give it to him with privacy, which when he received, he hid it in his bosom, that the

afflicted Virgin might not see it.   Then Nicodemus
extracted the nail from the left hand, and gave it
likewise to St. John, who joined it devoutly with
the former.   When the nails were thus drawn from
the hands of our blessed Redeemer, Nicodemus descended to draw out that which fastened his
heavenly feet, while Joseph supported the body.
Oh, thrice happy Joseph, who was deemed worthy
to embrace so divine, so inestimable a treasure!
While Joseph held the sacred body leaning on his
arms, our blessed Lady took hold of the hand which
hung down, and pressing it reverently and tenderly

JESUS IS PREPARED FOR BURIAL.

to her face and lips, kissed it, pressed it, and devoutly bathed it with tears.   Oh, nature, what a
spectacle!   Oh, human heart, what must thou be,

not to melt at such a sight! When the nail was extracted from the feet, Joseph descended by degrees, while the others received the heavenly body of our Lord, and reposed it decently on the ground. Our blessed Lady then raised the holy head and shoulders, and placed them on her lap, and the Magdalen prostrating herself, embraced his sacred feet, whence she had once received such a plenitude of grace. All the rest stood round joining their sighs and tears, and bitterly bemoaning the only begotten Son of God, thus disfigured by base, ungrateful man.

CHAPTER LXVIII.

THE EMBALMING AND BURIAL OF OUR LORD.

AFTER a short space, as night was drawing on, Joseph besought our Lady to permit him to embalm and wrap up the sacred body in the fine linen he had brought with him for that purpose. But she knew not how to part with the dear treasure so soon again. "I entreat you, my friends," said she, "rob me not so soon of my dear, my only son, of all that is dear to me in this life; rather, if you are in haste to bury him, lay me in the sepulchre near him. Oh, that I might, dearest Jesus, lie by thee, and never be separated from thee." Tears flowed down her virgin cheeks, and sobs forbid her words an utterance. Silent and sad she viewed the lovely, mangled form; now she examined, one by one, the reeking wounds still fresh and full of clotted blood, now she picked out, with care and cruel anguish, one after another, the long and splintered thorns still buried in his temples: now

she beheld his head, and now his face, composing
the few straggling hairs which blinded inhumanity
had left upon his head and beard ; and washing off
the dirt and spittle from his divine countenance with
floods of tears ; unsatiated with weeping, sighing,
and gazing on the object of her anguish. Thus
fixed, and immovable, the afflicted mother dwelt
on the beloved form of her divine son, and was not
to be removed from him, till St. John, with reverence approaching, entreated her to consider the lateness of the day, and to consent that Joseph and
Nicodemus might do their pious offices in time, to
prevent any insults or calumnies of the Jews. To this
remonstrance the wise and humble Virgin yielded,
remembering well that her dearest Jesus had recommended her to the care of this faithful and loving disciple. And therefore, without contending,
she gave them her blessing, and permission, to dress
and wrap him up. St. John then, with Joseph and
Nicodemus, immediately embalmed the holy body
and wrapped it in the fine linen cloth   While they
were busied about the body, the blessed Virgin still
kept the head upon her lap, and Magdalen was still
officious about his feet. There knelt the illustrious
penitent, almost dissolved with the excess of her
grief, and now on those sacred limbs, which compunction had elsewhere bathed with her tears, unspeakable grief and tender compassion made her
pour a double flood. She beheld those dear feet
cruelly pierced and torn, mangled and bloody, but
could not behold them clearly through the bitterness of her weeping. The Evangelist bears witness
that she loved exceedingly, and therefore who can
be amazed that she should grieve exceedingly, to
see our Lord, whom she thus loved, and to see him
thus mangled, dead, and reduced almost to noth-

ing! Scarce could her breast contain her heart, thus enlarged with panting anguish; nor is it improbable that, if she might, she would have gladly expired at the feet of her dead Lord. This was the ninth and last office she could pay her divine master, and in doing this, how bitterly did she grieve, that she could not do it in the manner she wished. She would fain have laid out the blessed body, anointed, and wrapped it wholly of herself, with that decency and reverence due to it. But neither the time nor place would permit it; for she could not do more at that time, nor in a better manner, than to bathe his venerable feet with her tears, dry them with her locks, kiss them, and reverently wrap them in the linen; this she did, and did it with a diligence equal to her affection.

When the body of our divine Saviour was wrapped up, they all turned their looks towards our blessed Lady to learn her pleasure, and share her parting grief. And she, finding there was now no more time to delay, threw her face on that of her heavenly son. "Oh, precious son Jesus! do I still hold you dead on my lap! And must I, must I then part from you? O cruel, unspeakable, cruel divorce of death. Sweet and delightful was our converse with each other, and free from injury or offence to any, why then do I see you, sweet offspring of my bowels, thus mangled and murdered like a public nuisance? How faithfully, how dutifully, how tenderly did you, when alive, wait on and cherish me: yet what return was I able to make you in this dreadful conflict! Your heavenly Father was able alone to assist you: I could not; and he, for his ineffably divine reasons, would not. Blessed be his holy name alike for all he has done. But why, my only joy, did you abandon yourself? Ah! it was for the

generous love of mankind, whom you came to redeem. Alas, how dear has this redemption cost
you! Yet dear as it has been, as it redounds to
your glory and their salvation, I submit to, nay,
rejoice at it. And if I do grieve, forgive me, all-
bounteous Jesus, forgive me these tears and sighs,
which surely are but due from so lovely, loving,
and divine a son. How can I refrain from tears,
when I behold to what a deplorable condition the
sins of man have brought you? You have neither
sin nor harm in you. But now, alas! our social
converse with each other is broken off. Well, since
it is your will, it shall be mine; and these hands,
in obedience to your divine pleasure, shall bury
your sacred body. And then whither, or to whom
shall I, your afflicted mother, fly for protection?
How shall I live without you? Oh, that one tomb
might contain us both, that we might never be separated in body any more than in mind! Go then,
lovely Jesus! Go to your sepulchre, and since my
body may not be there entombed with yours, my
soul shall still accompany you thither, and there
forever dwell with you. To you, then, I offer and
recommend it. Oh son, oh dearest, oh divine son,
how hard is this separation!"—A flood of tears followed her words, and bathed the sacred face of
Christ more plentifully than those of Magdalen had
bathed his feet. She wiped them off, however, and
kissing his lips and eyes, wrapped up the holy
head in the linen. After which all again falling on
the ground, and paying their adorations, took the
sacred body and bore it to the monument, our
blessed Lady holding up the head, St. Mary Magdalen the feet, and the rest the body.

Near the place where our Saviour was crucified
was a sepulchre, in which they buried our Lord,

with reverence, tears, sighs, and adorations. After he was laid in the monument, the afflicted mother embraced him, and clung to him for awhile ; but

JESUS IS LAID IN THE TOMB.

St. John and the women raised her, and rolled a great stone against the entrance of the monument. Venerable Bede tells us, that this monument was a kind of round mansion, hewn out of a rock beneath, so high that a man could not reach, with his arm perpendicularly raised, to the roof of it. Its entrance stood eastward : and in it our Lord's body was placed in a tomb, on the north side, of seven feet long.

CHAPTER LXIX.

OUR BLESSED LADY'S DEPARTURE FROM THE SEPUL-
CHRE, AND RETURN TO MOUNT SION.

WHEN Joseph of Arimathea had completed
his office of burying our Saviour, and was
about returning to Jerusalem, he came to the Blessed
Virgin, and entreated her, with many solicitations,
to retire to his house, with the companions and
sharers in her grief, offering it, and all he was master
of, to her service and command. But our blessed
Lady graciously returning him thanks, excused herself from going thither, because she was committed
by her son to the care of his beloved disciple John;
who, when Joseph turned to him to beseech him to
prevail upon her to honor his house with her sacred
presence, told them all, that he must lead her immediately to Mount Sion, the place where Jesus
had but the night before supped with his disciples,
and where he himself proposed to remain with her.
Upon which, they forthwith adored at the sepulchre,
and after paying their submission to the holy virgin, and their respects to her company, they went
their way; but our blessed Lady, St. John, and
the devout women remained sometime longer opposite to the sepulchre.

At length St. John remonstrating to our blessed
Lady, that it was neither safe to remain there late at
night, nor decent to enter the city much later in the
day, she humbly arose, and kneeling before the sepulchre, embraced it, saying, "Farewell, my dearest,
best-beloved son; since I may not, must not stay
longer near you, I recommend you to your eternal

Father's all-wise and almighty care." Then lifting her eyes to heaven, with abundance of tears, and heart full of grief, said, "To you, O eternal Father, I recommend this dear deposit of your and my only begotten son. Oh, take under your protection, and guard from every insult his precious body, and with it accept my soul, which I here leave together with it." Then rising, she departed with her companions from the monument.

When they came again to the cross, she kneeled down and adored, saying, "Here died my dear, my precious son ; here he poured out the generous sea of blood for man's redemption." And after her example all did the same. Nor is it without good grounds that we may believe our blessed Lady to have been the first reverer of the cross. When they approached the city, the women veiled her like a widow, wailing, distressed, and afflicted before her, whilst she proceeded with her head and face quite covered, between St. John and St. Mary Magdalen. At their entrance into it, a pious contention arose between Magdalen and St. John ; she pleading hard that our blessed Lady might come to reside at her house, alleging the goodness with which our Lord had honored her in his life-time in resorting to it ; he on the other hand, being desirous of leading the sacred virgin to Mount Sion, where he said she would be safer, and more within the reach of all their friends. Accordingly our blessed Lady determined to go thither, and Magdalen followed her. As they passed through the city many devout persons of both sexes met her, condoled with her, and cried aloud against the injustice done to her divine son, as they accompanied her to the house whither she was repairing When she arrived at the place where she was to remain, turning to her attendants, she returned them thanks, and they submissively bowing, paid her homage and condolence. Our Lady was followed by her two sisters and Magdalen into the house: after which St. John, placing himself at the door, returned thanks to the rest, and on account of the lateness of the evening, dismissed them. But with eyes disconsolate did this childless mother look round the house, where she could no more see the object of all her delight. "O fair and beauteous, O lovely son!" she said, "where art thou now? O John! where is my only son? O Magdalen! where is thy master, that more than parent, who loved thee so tenderly? O beloved sisters! where is my Jesus? Every joy is now fled from me—every sweetness, every pleasing sight now vanishes from my eyes—now he is no more before me. Alas, alas, what agonies he suffered! Alas, how my grief augments whenever I look back and consider him all torn, all bruised, disfigured, sighing, panting, and fainting with thirst, anguish, and violence! What insults, what torments, and what taunts did he not go through! And I, in vain, wished to comfort him. His foes inhumanly abused him—his friends meanly and shamefully forsook him—his poor, his tender mother, wanted power to help him—and his Father, his Almighty Father, would not rescue him. And with what haste was he not hurried to the cruel, inhumanly cruel, unnaturally cruel slaughter! What wretch so vile was ever condemned, and executed with so much injustice, barbarity, and precipitation, as my poor innocent, inoffensive son, Jesus! Oh, my son! in this last and unhappiest of nights wast thou basely betrayed, inhumanly seized, perfidiously condemned, and now cruelly crucified, thou liest unjustly murdered! O dearest Jesus! how bitter is this separation from thee and how insupportable the sad

reflection on thy undeserved, ignominious **death !**"
Thus went on this tender, this afflicted mother, till
St. John at length besought **her** to desist from her
excessive grief, and administered comfort to her. Do
you, amidst your pious contemplation, **wish** to do the
like, devout reader ; obey her, minister **to her,** and
attend and comfort her ; **join** with St. John in preparing something for her refection, and for those who
are with her, **who** are all fasting and faint: And when
you have indulged yourself awhile in this pious,
spiritual officiousness, procure the virgin's blessing,
and depart.

CHAPTER LXX.

MEDITATION **ON** OUR BLESSED LADY'S CONVERSATION WITH HER DEVOUT COMPANIONS.

ON the morning of the Sabbath, they all remained
in **the** house with the doors shut, extremely
afflicted, **and** mourning like orphans for the loss of a
tender parent, without uttering a syllable, but looking
dejectedly on each other, as is usual **on** occasions of
extreme grief, and supplying **their** want of words with
abundant sighs. While thus they sit distressed, **a**
sudden knocking at **the door** alarms and dismays
them, **for** all courage **is** departed from them ; but
John going to the door, finds it to be Peter, and re-
moves their fears by acquainting them with it. Peter,
with the sacred virgin's leave, being admitted, full of
confusion, anguish and repentance, approaches, but
without being able to utter a word. After him came,
one by one, the **rest of** the disciples, weeping and
abashed. At length, when their tears and sighs are
abated, they begin to talk of their deceased Lord.

"O how I blush from my soul," says Peter, "and how well my confused conscience tells me, that I am unworthy to speak in your presence, sacred Lady, or even to be seen by mankind, after having so shamefully denied and forsaken my divine **Master**, who loved me to so great a degree !" In like **manner all** the other disciples, with tears, beating their breasts, and in deep sorrow, accused themselves for having **a**bandoned their Lord in his passion. But the gracious virgin mother consoled them, saying, "Alas! my children, your and my bountiful master, and faithful shepherd, has now departed **from us** for awhile and left us like orphans without a parent. However, I finally trust to his goodness, that he will soon be with us again. And you know how good and indulgent he is, and how much he loves you all. Despair not then, but confidently rely on his goodness for your reconciliation, and depend on his pardon for every fault and offence you have hitherto committed against him ; for he knows full well the frailty of your nature, and the **greatness** of the temptation. By his Almighty Father's permission, such was the fury and outrage of his enemies, that your staying with him could not have been of service to him : therefore, be not discouraged." "Truly, O benign Lady," says Peter, "thus far what you say I hope will in some measure alleviate my offence : it was the very fury you **speak** of which so terrified me as to make me think myself in danger of falling a victim to it ; and that terror it was which made me so shamefully deny my Lord. Nor did I at the instant reflect on the words by which he foretold this denial." Magdalen then inquiring concerning the prediction of our Lord, Peter told her the circumstances of it, and added, that our Lord told them many things at his last supper. Upon which, our blessed Lady desiring to be informed of all the particulars of what her divine son had done and said on that occasion, Peter made a sign to John, and John related the whole particulars. And then, as well concerning this as other occasions, they related among themselves, several things which Christ had taught and practised among them, and thus they passed the whole day in talking of him. O how attentively did Magdalen, and much more our blessed Lady, listen to all this ! O how often did she that day cry out, "Blessed forever be my holy son, Jesus." Behold then diligently, and compassionate them in the extreme affliction, with which this day overwhelms them.—For what a sight was it to behold the queen of Heaven and earth, the princes of the holy church and the director of Christ's people, seized with so great sorrow, and forced to hide themselves in that little house, not knowing what to do, having nothing to comfort them, but only to communicate together, and repeat the former sayings and actions of their divine Lord and master, Jesus. Our blessed Lady, however, remained with a peaceful and serene mind, being always firm and constant in the certain hope of her son's resurrection; in which hope she persisted the whole Sabbath ;* for which reason the Sabbath is a day specially dedicated by the church to her. Her comfort, however, was not wholly free from grief, whenever she thought on the bitter death and sufferings of her blessed son.

Now when the sun was gone down, and it was lawful for them to work, Mary Magdalen, and the other Mary that was with her, went out to buy certain sweet spices to make ointment to anoint the body. For the night before, after they came from the sepulchre, they began to make things ready for

---

* The Sabbath here meant is the Jewish Sabbath, which corresponds to our Saturday.

it till sunset ; after which time they ceased : for, according to the law, they were obliged to keep the Sabbath, from sunset the evening before, till the setting of the same on the Sabbath evening. Behold them now, how they go with sorrowful and mournful countenances, and apply to some devout good man for the spices they had occasion for: and he, tenderly compassionating their affliction, willingly supplied them. Wherefore, choosing the best they could find, they returned home, and applied themselves to compound a precious ointment, after the best manner they were able.

Cast an eye towards them, and behold how they labor for our Lord Jesus : weeping, sighing, and sorrowful ! Our blessed Lady and the Apostles stood looking on, and no doubt, when needful, assisted them ; which done, and night being come, they ceased, and retired to repose, which, we may piously imagine, was very little.

CHAPTER LXXI.

OUR LORD JESUS DESCENDS INTO THE LIMBO OF THE FATHERS.

WE are now to consider what our blessed Lord did on this day of the Sabbath. You are to know, then, that as soon as he expired, his blessed soul descended into that part of hell called Limbo, where the souls of the Fathers were detained, and there he remained with them. During which time they were in possession of glory ; for the vision of God is the perfect glory of the blessed. Oh, how great was his bounty ; how great his love, and how great his humility ! He could, if he had pleased, have delivered his servants by means of an angelical messenger, who might have conducted them to his presence, in whatever place he had chosen ; but this, his infinite love and humility would not suffer him to do. Wherefore, he himself descended ; and, though Lord of all, visited them, not as servants, but as intimate and familiar friends, and remained with them, till near break of day the Sunday following. Think well on this, and endeavor to copy after so great a pattern.

The holy Fathers were in an ecstacy of immense joy at the approach of their Redeemer. All anxiety then gave place to ineffable delight ; and their petitions and solicitations, for a speedy deliverance from this state of captivity, were changed into praises and thanksgiving, for the inexpressible benefit of their redemption. When, therefore, the soul of Jesus advanced towards them, imagine you see the holy tribe assembled together, hastening with transports of the most earnest alacrity to meet him, and crying out to him, "Blessed be the Lord God of Israel, because he has visited, and wrought the redemption of his people." " Raise up your drooping heads, O afflicted fellow captives, for behold your redemption is coming. Rise up, rise up, O Jerusalem, break the chain from off your neck ; behold the Saviour comes to ransom us from our fetters." "Lift up your gates, O princes, and be ye lifted up, O eternal gates, and the King of Glory shall enter in." "We adore you, O Christ, and we bless you, our most loving God." And thus falling down, they adored him with unspeakable joy and gratitude. Thus did they continue in praise and thanksgiving, before our Lord, till the dawn of the third day : at which time our Lord, heading those happy souls, led them glorious and triumphant, from that subterraneous place of their captivity, to that earthly paradise of delights, where those glorious prophets of God, Elias and Enoch, are waiting the coming of Antichrist, whom they are appointed to oppose. Here our blessed Redeemer stajd some time with them; and here they still persisted, in conjunction with those two venerable men, in praising, thanking and glorifying their all-gracious benefactor. At length our Saviour said, that it was time for him to leave them, and to depart, and resume his sacred body, by a glorious resurrection. "Go then," say they, "O divine, O bounteous Redeemer, O King of Glory! complete the merciful work you have so graciously begun, and so divinely carried on; but oh, vouchsafe speedily to return to us, that our joy may be redoubled in the desirable sight of your sacred body, which we have so long and so earnestly desired, and sighed after."

You see then, O devout reader, that you need not want matter for pious meditation during the interval between our Lord's death and resurrection. Hitherto I have made but few and short meditations on the passion of Christ, that the mind might not be taken off from attending to the series of his sufferings; but now it will not be improper to make some serious reflections concerning it. Hear, therefore, what St. Bernard says:

"What think you, O Christian soul? Can you owe anything less than your whole life to Christ, who generously laid down his precious life for you, and bore the most excruciating torments to free you from bearing them to all eternity? Were the lives of all the sons of Adam, the splendor of the angels, and the worth of the whole creation, to be united in one living creature, yet would such a creature be nothing in comparison with his body so stupendously beautiful. Were all the excellent talents of every animated being to be centered in one, what would they be to the superior virtues assembled in his conception from the Holy Ghost, in his birth from a virgin, in the innocence of his life, in the elegance of his doctrine, in the brilliancy of his miracles, in the revelation of his sacraments and mysteries! Were all the torments which nature can suffer to be inflicted on one being, yet would they be nothing in value to what he went through in the series of his life, passion and death. The heavens then are not so high exalted above the earth as his ways are above ours, and his life above our life. Nay, a mere nothing, an unexisting nothing, bears as great a proportion to something, as our life does to his. Nothing can be more excellent than this, nothing is more miserable than that. Our life is all corruption, his life purity itself: ours of no worth, his of immense value. And yet he grudged not to lay down that precious life, to save us from eternal death. O excess of goodness! When therefore we have devoted to him our life, and all that is valuable in it, we still fall short of what he has done for us, and our offering is no more to be compared to his, than the twinkling light of the remotest star to the lustre of the sun, the least drop of water to a great river, a pebble to an enormous mountain, or a grain of wheat to a summer's harvest.

"It was not of trivial matters, that this blessed Redeemer stripped himself for you. He lowered himself, and that not a little, to exalt you: he lowered himself to flesh, he lowered himself to death, and the death of the cross. O who can express this excess of humility, meekness, and condescension in the God of majesty, deigning to put on flesh, to be punished with death, to be disgraced with a cross? Perhaps it may be asked: but could not the Creator have repaired the works of his own hands, without all this difficulty? Doubtless, he could; but he chose to do otherwise, though to his own cost; that the base and detestable crime of ingratitude might no more take root in the heart of man. He suffered, therefore, an immensity of hardships, to stimulate man to pay him the just debt of immense love; and to move him, whom the facility of his creation had rendered ungrateful and indevout, to be grateful and earnest in thanksgiving for his redemption, which was wrought with so much difficulty. How did ungrateful man reason upon his creation! I **was** made indeed out of nothing, **gratis,** but I was made without any expense or labor to my Maker: he said the word, and I was made like all other beings. But now, 'the mouth of them that speak lies was stopped.' And now, O man, the immense cost which God has been at in redeeming you, is as apparent as noon-day sun. Your Redeemer, to ransom you, disdained not becoming, from a sovereign Lord, an humble servant, from infinitely rich, extremely poor, from the immortal word, mortal flesh, from the Son of God, the son of man.

"Consider yourself rightly then, and remember that if you were made of nothing, you were not redeemed with nothing. In six days God created all things, and you among the rest: but he was three and thirty years upon earth, laboring and working your redemption. O how hard did he toil, bearing the necessities of the flesh, the anxieties and tribulations of the spirit, and all the severe trials his enemies could put him to! Did he not heap to himself all the horrors of death, and aggravate those horrors with the ignominy of the cross?

"O how amiable, lovely Jesus, how amiable to me above all things, does thy chalice render thee! that chalice, that bitter, bitter draught which thou vouchsafedst to drink for our redemption! This, this demands, and justly demands, all our affections: this alone ought to engross all our love: this alone should suffice sweetly to attract, justly to win, closely to knit, and forcibly to captivate us to thee. You see then, pious reader, that the author of nature was at no expense in the fabric of the world, in comparison with what it cost the Redeemer of nature to restore it. He only spoke, and the former was made—he only gave his orders, and it was created. But in the latter, his word was contradicted, his actions reprimanded, he was insulted with torments, was punished with death, and reviled with the cross.

"It was the height of infinite goodness in Christ to deliver up his life a prey to death for us; and to pay down from out of his own sacred side, the full ransom due to his eternal Father. In this, how truly did he fulfil what the Psalmist sung of him— 'With the Lord is mercy, and with him plentiful redemption.' Plentiful, indeed, was this redemption, to effect which he poured forth not a single drop, not from one part of his body, but rivers of blood, from several parts.—Think then, O man, on the greatness of your obligation; think on the debt of love you owe him. What is it he should have done, and has not done for you? He has enlightened you, when blind; unbound you, when in chains; set you right, when astray; and reconciled you, when guilty. Who then can forbear running willingly and cheerfully after him who delivers us from errors, and connives at our frailties, who gives us, whilst living, the means to merit, and bestows

on us in death, **the reward of** the merit he gives!
What excuse can any one plead for not running
after the fragrant odor of his ointment? Not
surely that the fragrancy of it did not reach him.
The odor of his sweet-scented life has gone through
the whole earth.   For the whole earth is full of his
mercy, and **the** effects of his mercy surpass all his
other works.   He therefore who is insensible to, or
follows not this fragrant odor, is either totally **dead,**
or totally corrupted.

"The holy spouse in the canticles is not ashamed
of the blackness she borrowed from her spouse, to
resemble whom, is the summit of true glory.   There
is nothing more glorious than to put on the blackness of reproach, which Christ himself put on.
Hence, says the Apostle, with salutary transport,
'Far be it from **me to glory in** anything but the
cross of our Lord Jesus Christ.'   How dear ought
the ignominy of the cross to be to all those who are
so happy as not to be at variance with him who
suffered on it for our sakes?   There is a blackness
in it, we must own, but that blackness is beautiful,
insomuch as it was the form and likeness of our
Lord.   Whom else did Isaiah, in spirit, call **the**
man of sorrows, knowing infirmity, who, 'had
neither form nor comeliness?   Him,' says he. 'we
esteemed stricken, smitten of God, and humbled:
but he was wounded for our transgressions, he was
bruised **for our** iniquities, and **with** his stripes we
are healed.'

"What, fellow Christian!   Did Christ not take
upon him the shame of sin for our sakes, and shall
we be ashamed of being vilified, or reputed black for
his sake?   Look attentively on this vilified Saviour,
disfigured in dress, and clothed with mock garments,
defaced with bloody wounds, defiled with nauseous

spittle, mortified with blows, and pale with death. What more deformed, or blackened, could strike the eyes of his beholders, than he, when, with his arms wide extended on the cross, he afforded laughter to his inveterate enemies, tears to the faithful, and agony to convulsed nature, when he alone was a subject of mockery and sport, who alone was worthy to command respect, and able to inflict terror through the whole universe?

"Meditate, therefore, O pious reader, on the sufferings of that most sacred, crucified body, and see if there is anything there, which does not plead for you to the eternal Father. For you it is that that divine head is pierced with innumerable thorns. 'My people,' saith the Lord by his prophet, 'have covered me all over with the thorns of their sins.' Lest your head should ache, lest your intentions should be wounded, his eyes were closed by death, and the luminaries of the world were at that instant extinct. At the darkening of his sacred eyes, those great lights were eclipsed with the rest, and universal darkness overshadowed the whole earth. And why all this, but that your eyes might be averted from beholding vanity, or being attracted by it.

"Those blessed ears which perpetually hear in Heaven, the exulting exclamation of 'Holy, holy, holy, Lord God of Sabbaoth;' heard upon earth, 'thou hast a devil: crucify him, crucify him.' And all this, that your ears might no longer be deaf to the voice of God, or to the cries of the poor: but deaf to detraction, deaf to discourses injurious to God, or detrimental to your brother, and deaf to every vain and unprofitable sound.

"That divinely beauteous face, the most comely of all amongst the sons of men, was defiled with spittle, disfigured with bruises, profaned with dirt, and exhibited to scorn, that your face might be made fair and shining ; and being confirmed in goodness, might not turn to opposite extremes.

"That blessed mouth which directed angels, and instructed men in heavenly knowledge, which only spoke, and all things were done according to his will, was drenched with vinegar and gall; and why? But that your mouth and heart might thenceforth be enabled to relish the sweets of truth, and confess your God.

"Those heavenly hands, which moulded the heavens and the earth, were barbarously stretched with nails on the cross. Why did your guiltless Saviour submit to this, but to purchase for you the grace of keeping your hands ever open for the relief of the needy and distressed ; and to qualify you to say with the Psalmist: 'My soul is always in my hands?' What we carry in our hands we cannot easily forget, and thus he, who has his soul forever in his hands by his indefatigable industry in good works, cannot be unmindful of it.

"Those sacred feet whose very footstool we ought to adore, because it is holy, were inhumanly trans-fixed with nails, that your feet might not hurry you to evil, but run on in the way of the commandments of your God. 'They have pierced my feet,' says the prophet in the person of Christ, 'they have num-bered all my bones.' For you he sacrificed his flesh and his life, to purchase your body and soul ; and thus he ransomed all you are, with all he is himself.

"Rouse up then, my soul, and shaking off your dust, contemplate this memorable, this incomparable man, this Man-God, whom you see before you in the transparent crystal of the holy Gospel. Consider, my soul, who this is, who proceeds with the majestic air of a monarch, though covered with the ignominy of a despicable slave! He moves with a crown on his head, but his diadem is an instrument of torments, and his sacred temples are transfixed with innumerable wounds from it. He is decked in royal robes, but they are to him badges of scorn instead of honor. He waves a sceptre in his hand, not to command others, but to be struck with it himself. He is adored with bended knees, proclaimed a king, and receives the homage of a numerous multitude, but they are marks of contempt and derision instead of duty and fidelity. His lovely countenance is spit upon, his beauteous cheeks are buffetted, and his honorable neck bends under dishonor.

"Behold, my soul, how this sacred man of sorrows is abused and reviled. He is commanded, all faint and sinking beneath his stripes, to bend his sacred shoulders under the heavy load of the cross, and to bear his ignominy to the place of execution. He is raised on the cross, he is insulted and scoffed at there, and permitted no other comfort than a draught of vinegar, mixed with gall. And in return for all this usage, he only says, 'Father, forgive them, for they know not what they do.' What a stupendous personage is this, who, amidst all his torments and ill-usage, never once opened his mouth to complain of, accuse, threaten, or curse the vile brutes, who are busied in doing him such cruel injustice! But, after all their ill-treatment of him, he breaks forth into such terms of blessing as have no example. What instances of meekness, patience and goodness, can we produce like this?

"But look, my soul, yet a little nearer, and see how worthy he is of all your admiration and pity. Behold him naked, and torn with stripes, suspended by iron nails, on an ignominious cross, between two thieves, plied with vinegar and gall, persecuted to death, nay, even beyond death, with a lance, which rips open his sacred side.—And view him thus pouring forth five rivers of precious blood, from his hands, feet, and sides ! Weep, O my eyes, and'thou, O my soul, melt into tenderness, dissolve into pity for this most lovely of the sons of men, whom thou seest amidst all this meekness, oppressed with every injurious treatment.

"O look down, Lord, eternal Father! look down from your sanctuary above, and behold this sacred offering which our high priest, your holy Son Jesus Christ, offers to you for the sins of us, his brethren, and be propitious to the multitude of our iniquities, and greatness of our malice. Behold the blood of our brother Jesus, crying out to you from the cross, 'Behold, I am crowned with glory and honor.' Earnest he stands, soliciting at your right hand for us ; for he is our flesh, and our brother.

"Look, O Lord, on the countenance of Christ thy Son, who is become obedient to thee, even to death, and let not the marks of his wounds be ever from before thy eyes, that thou mayest always remember the satisfaction he has made to thee for our sins. Would, O Lord, that the sins, by which we have deserved thy indignation, were placed in a balance with the sufferings which thy most innocent son Jesus endured for us ! May every tongue return thee thanks O Lord, for thy great goodness, who sparedst not thy only son, but deliveredst him to death for us, to the end we might have so great, so true an advocate with thee in heaven ! And to thee, O blessed Jesus, what acts of thanksgiving, or what tribute, worthy thy acceptance, can I make, who am but dust and ashes, a vile compound of clay ? For what was there wanting for my salvation, which thou hadst not done ? From the crown of the head to the sole of the foot, thou wast wholly plunged in the waters of suffering and affliction, to draw me out of the same. The waters have entered even to thy blessed soul. Thy soul was separated by death, that thou mightest restore me mine, which I had lost. Wherefore, thou hast bound me to thee by a double debt, that is, by what thou hast bestowed upon me, and by what thou has lost for my sake. I am indebted to thee for my life, which twice thou hast given me; once in my creation, and once in my redemption. Wherefore, I have nothing to offer thee, which more justly is thy due, than my life itself. I cannot find what recompense man can make thee, O Christ, for thy precious soul, which was so much troubled and burdened with affliction. For were the heavens, the earth, and all the beauties belonging to them, in my power, they would all fall short of the greatness of the debt I owe to thee. It is thy gift, O Lord, that I even make thee any part of that return which I owe thee. I ought to love thee with all my heart, with all my soul, with all my mind, and with all my strength; and to follow thy example, who vouchsafedst to die for me. And how shall I be able to do this but by thy help? My soul shall follow close after thee, because her whole strength depends on thee!"

Thus far St. Bernard. But let us now proceed to the resurrection of our Lord Jesus.

CHAPTER LXXII.

THE GLORIOUS RESURRECTION OF OUR **LORD JESUS,** AND HIS APPEARANCE FIRST TO HIS BLESSED MOTHER.

EARLY on the Sunday morning, before the break of day, the soul of our blessed Jesus, accompanied by a glorious tribe of blessed spirits, returned again to the sepulchre where his body lay ; and resuming the same, he arose by virtue of his sacred divinity, and miraculously wert out of the grave without opening it. About th same time, Mary Magdalen, Mary of James, and Mary of Salome, taking leave of our blessed Lady, set out towards the sepulchre of our Lord ; taking with them many precious ointments, which they had prepared for that purpose. The Blessed Virgin in the meantime remained at home, fixed in devout prayer ; which we may piously imagine she made in the following manner : "Most merciful Father, full of clemency and pity, you know that my most beloved and blessed son is now dead and buried, and that he was first cruelly fixed to a disgraceful cross between two thieves ; and that after he had resigned his blessed soul to you, I myself helped to place in the sepulchre his sacred body, which I conceived without blemish, and bore without pain. You know, O Lord, he was all the good I possessed, all I could desire, and the only comfort and life of my soul. But at length he was suddenly snatched from me, being full of sorrow, full of wounds, rent and scourged, and by his cruel enemies shamefully abused and condemned to death ; so that he was forsaken by his disciples, who fled from him ; and I, his disconsolate and afflicted mother, could no ways help him. But now, O Father of mercy, though at that time it pleased you not to deliver him from that cruel and bitter passion, yet, as your holy will is now fully accomplished, and it is in your power to restore him again safely to me, I beseech your divine majesty to do it. Why does he tarry so long ? Send him to me speedily, O most bountiful Father, for my soul can have no peace till I behold him. O my most sweet son Jesus, where art thou now ? What art thou doing ? And why dost thou stay so long before thou comest to relieve me ? Delay no longer I beseech thee, but come ; for thou thyself saidst, that thou wouldst arise on the third day ; and is that day now come ? Rise therefore, my beloved, my joy, and comfort me with thy presence, whom thou hast so much afflicted with thy absence."

As our Lady was thus praying, bathed in a flood of tears which flowed from her lovely eyes, our blessed Lord suddenly appeared, and stood before her robed in white, and with a pleasing and lovely aspect comforted her, saying, "Hail, holy parent." She, surprised with sudden joy, said, "Art thou my blessed son, Jesus ?" and bowing down, she adored him. And he again said to her, "It is I, my beloved mother. I am risen from death, and am now present with you. My sorrows have ceased. I have triumphed over death, and have overcome all my pain and anguish, so that they can never more have any power over me." To whom she answered, "Blessed be thy omnipotent and eternal Father, who has comforted me again with thy presence : may his holy name be exalted, magnified, and praised forever." Thus lovingly conversing to-

gether, our Lord Jesus related to her the things he
had wrought in those three days, after his passion,
and how he delivered the fathers from the prison
in which they were confined.   Wherefore, this is a
sovereign Pasch, this the joyful day of which the royal
prophet spoke, saying, "This is the day which the
Lord hath made ; let us rejoice and be glad therein."

TWO ANGELS IN SHINING ROBES DECLARE HIM RISEN.

CHAPTER LXXIII.

THE COMING OF THE THREE MARYS TO THE MONU-
MENT, AND THE RACE BETWEEN PETER AND JOHN.

MAGDALEN, as we have said before, in company with the two Marys, went to the monument with the ointments.   When they came to the

entrance of the sepulchre, they were concerned **as** to how they should get in; who will roll away the stone for us from the monument, say they? But **no** sooner had they said it, than looking up they saw the stone removed, **and an** angel sitting upon it, who said to them, "Be not afraid." They, however, disappointed of their hopes, by **not** finding the body **of** our Lord, gave little attention to **the** angel; but running back affrighted, told the disciples that our Lord's body was taken away. Upon which, Peter and John immediately arose, and ran to the monument with zeal and anxiety, and the Marys after them. When they came thither, they found not **the** body, but only the winding sheet, and other linen it was wrapped in Wherefore they returned immediately with their eyes bathed in tears, and their hearts rent with affliction. They sought their Lord, but **could** not find him, nor knew they now where or which **way to** seek him.—Compassionate them then, **pious** reader, **in so** great an affliction.

CHAPTER LXXIV.

OUR LORD S APPEARANCE TO THE HOLY WOMEN.

THE Marys, however, remained there, and looking towards the monument, saw two angels standing clothed in **white,** who said to them, "Whom do you seek? Do you **seek** one living among the dead?" But they gave no attention to the angels, nor received any comfort from this vision. For they came not to seek angels, but the Lord of angels. Two of the Marys, therefore, lost and absorbed in **affliction,** withdrew to **a** little distance from the monument, and sat down to soothe their grief. While Magdalen, at a loss what to do, and unable to live without her divine Master, sat sadly pensive and weeping at the mouth of the sepulchre; where again she saw the same angels, who again asked her, "Woman, why do you weep? Whom do you seek?" "They have taken away my Lord," said she, "and I know not where they have laid him." O wonderful operation of love! One angel had told her he was risen : and two others had assured her he was alive; and yet so forgetful is she as to say, I know not. Love, divine love, was the cause of this self-oblivion in Magdalen, for as Origen says on this passage, her soul was not with her, but with her divine master Hence she knew not—that is, she

APPEARS TO MARY MAGDALEN.

knew neither how to hear, remember, nor think without him. Wherefore, while thus she continued weeping, disconsolate, and regardless of all the angel said to her, her divine master, overcome as it were by her excess of love, appeared to her to console her, and said, "Woman, whom seek you? Why do you weep?" At first she knew him not, but inebriated with affection, answered him, "Lord, if you have taken my Lord away, tell me where you have put him." Think then you see this glorious woman with her face bathed in a flood of tears, beseeching, and with every moving remonstrance earnestly conjuring him to tell her where she may find the beloved object she was in search of: for still she hoped to hear some glad tidings of him. How grateful a sight was this to Christ! He therefore again said to her, "Mary!" When immediately coming as it were to herself, and knowing him by his voice, she cried out in a transport of unutterable joy, "Rabbi?" that is, master! "Ah, you are the sweet, the adorable Lord I was seeking with so much eagerness." Then rising, she ran to embrace his feet. But our Lord, to raise her mind to a more celestial affection, and wean her from his earthly presence, said to her, "Touch me not, for I have not yet ascended to my Father: but tell my brethren, I ascend to my Father, and yours." After they had awhile conversed in a celestial manner with each other, our Lord gave her his blessing, and departed : when she, full of joy and spiritual comfort, went to her companions, and told them the gladsome news. They were exceedingly overjoyed at the tidings of our Lord's resurrection : but when they found they were not blessed with a sight of him, they departed homewards with grief and dejection. But as the above-mentioned three Marys were proceeding on their way, before they came to the city,

the benign Jesus vouchsafed to appear to them, saying, "Hail!" No sooner did they hear and see him,
than seized with a joy beyond the power of words to
express, they fell on their faces and adored him
Here again our Lord vouchsafed to enter into a gra-

JESUS APPEARS TO THE COMPANY OF HOLY WOMEN.

cious and ineffable conversation with them for some
time, concerning his sublime mysteries. After which
he said to them—bid my brethren come to me in
Galilee, there they will see me as I foretold them.
Admire here the great humility of our Lord Jesus, in
calling his poor lowly disciples his brethren. This
you see is a virtue, which Christ laid not aside even
after his resurrection. Meditate then devoutly on
those edifying subjects. And, if you be desirous of
reaping full advantage from the contemplation of

them, endeavor to be as present in spirit, as these holy persons were in body.

CHAPTER LXXV.

OUR LORD'S APPEARANCE TO JOSEPH, TO JAMES THE LESS, AND TO PETER.

OUR Lord Jesus, after departing from the Marys, appeared to Joseph of Arimathea, who had buried him, and who was now in prison. For the Jews had seized him and confined him in a jail, with an intent to put him to death after the Sabbath. Our Lord therefore appeared to him, and wiping off the tears and damp from his face, led him out, the doors unopened, as ancient pious tradition informs us. He also appeared to James the Less, who had vowed never to taste any food, till he should see our Lord risen from the dead. To him, therefore, and to those who were with him, he commanded that they should spread the table, then taking bread and blessing it, he gave to him, saying, "Eat, my beloved brother, for the Son of Man is risen from the dead."*

When the Marys returned home, and acquainted the disciples with the resurrection of Christ, Peter, extremely afflicted that he had not seen his Lord, and unable, through excess of love, to rest without seeing him, arose immediately and went alone to the sepulchre, not knowing where else so speedily to find him. While he was proceeding on his way, Jesus appeared to him, and said, "Peace be to you, Simon Peter." Then Peter striking his breast, and

---

* See St. Jerome on Ecclesiastical Writers, tom.

prostrating himself on the ground, in a flood of tears, cried out, "O Lord! O dearest Saviour! I have sinned against thee; I acknowledge my crime in leaving thee in thy distress, and shamefully denying thee thrice." And when his love and grief stopped his words, he embraced his master's holy feet, and tenderly kissed them. Our Lord then raised him, and embracing him, said again : "Peace on thee, Simon Peter : fear not, thy sins are forgiven thee. Thy denial I foresaw and foretold thee, and now I forgive thee. Go and confirm thy brethren in the belief of my resurrection. And be confident thyself, that I have conquered for thee all thy enemies, and even death itself." Thus awhile they stood solemnizing a glorious Pasch in heavenly conversation. After this Peter returned to our blessed Lady and the disciples, and related to them all he had seen and heard. In the Gospel there is no mention made of our Lord's appearing to his sacred mother. I have, however, taken notice of it, first because the Church seems to countenance my doing so, as may appear more plainly in the legend on the resurrection.

CHAPTER LXXVI.

CHRIST'S RETURN TO THE HOLY FATHERS AFTER HIS RESURRECTION.

OUR Lord not having yet visited the holy Fathers after his resurrection, as soon as he departed from Peter, took a numerous retinue of angels, and went to visit them. When the venerable tribe saw him coming towards them, they went to meet him with excessive transports of spiritual

Joy, singing, "Behold, our king comes : let us meet our Saviour! Our mighty beginning, and his kingdom shall have no end! This is a blissful day that shines forth to us! Come all, and obey the Lord." Then prostrating themselves, they adored him : and rising, continued singing with reverence, fervor and joy, his praises, saying, "Thou hast risen our glory : we will be glad and rejoice in thee. Thy kingdom is of all ages ; and thy dominion shall last from generation to generation. We depart not from you ; and you shall raise us, and we will magnify your holy name. Our leader is come forth ; made a high priest forever. This, this is the day which the Lord hath made ; let us be glad and rejoice thereon. The day of redemption has shone forth to us, of ancient reparation, and of eternal felicity. This day throughout the universe, the heavens distil honey ; because the Lord has reigned from a tree. The Lord has reigned, he is clothed with beauty , the Lord is clothed with strength, and hath girded himself. Sing to him a new song, for he has wrought wonders. His right hand and his holy arm hath saved us to himself. For we are his people, and the sheep of his pasture. Come let us adore him." When the evening drew nigh, Jesus acquainted them with his design of going again to visit his poor afflicted brethren, who, after his death, were dispersed like sheep having no shepherd, and were seeking him with the utmost anxiety. "I will return therefore," says he, "to them, that I may console and strengthen them, and will soon come back to release you." Then the holy Fathers, prostrating themselves again, adored him, saying, "Go, Lord Jesus, blessed be thy holy name ; and be all things done according to thy divine word and will."

THE JOURNEY TO EMMAUS.

CHAPTER LXXVII.

CHRIST APPEARS TO THE TWO DISCIPLES GOING TO EMMAUS.

AS two disciples were walking together towards the little town of Emmaus, talking of what had happened in a melancholy manner, and in a kind of despondency about him, our Lord Jesus came up to them, and in the form of a traveller joined in conversation with them ; interrogating, answering, and giving them salutary maxims, as the Gospel relates. at length, suffering himself to be forced, he went in with them, and manifested himself to them. Here, pious reader, contemplate the goodness of Christ. For, first, such is his ardent love for his disciples, that he cannot suffer them long to wander in uncertainty and affliction. Like a faithful friend, a trusty companion, and an affable Lord, he joins with them, enquires the cause of their affliction, and expounds the scriptures to them in such a manner as to cleanse their hearts from all rust of earthly affections, and influence them with divine love. Thus does he daily behave towards us in a spiritual manner. If overcome by any afflictions, perplexities, or languor of soul, we talk of him, he is immediately with us, comforting, enlightening, and inflaming our hearts with his love. Of such excellent advantage is it to us to talk of God in our adversities or tribulation. Hence, says the prophet, "How sweet are thy words to my taste, sweeter to my mouth than honey and the honey-comb." And again, "My heart waxed hot within me, and fire burns in my meditation."

Secondly, behold the goodness of our Lord in feigning that he was going farther, in order to increase their desire of his staying with them, and to induce them to invite and detain him. How gracious was it in him to go with them, to break bread, to bless that bread with his sacred hands for them, and afterwards to reveal himself to them ! Does he not do the same towards us all, as often as we apply to prayer and meditation? Thus then does it behoove us to pray without ceasing

CHAPTER LXXVIII.

OUR LORD APPEARS TO THE DISCIPLES, WHO WERE
SHUT UP ON THE DAY OF THE RESURRECTION.

THE two disciples immediately returned to Jerusalem, and finding all the other disciples, except Thomas, assembled together, they related what had happened to them, where they likewise heard in their turn, a confirmation of our Lord's being risen, and having appeared to Simon. During this conversation, our Lord Jesus himself came into the room, the doors being shut, and saluted them all, saying, "Peace be with you." The disciples seeing our Lord, fell on their faces, and acknowledged their fault in having fled at his passion, they received him with great joy. Our Lord then comforted them, saying, "Rise, brethren, your sins are forgiven you." After which he stood familiarly amongst them, and showed the prints of his sacred wounds. Meantime, the table being spread by his order, he sat down, and eat part of a fish and some honey which was set before him. Then he breathed upon them, saying, "Receive ye the Holy Ghost." O how full of joy and spiritual delight was this interview!

Imagine, too, you see here our blessed Lady; for it was to her that the disciples flocked when they assembled together after the death of our Lord. O with what inexpressible joy is she not filled at the sight of her glorious and triumphant son in the midst of his disciples, and how studious, how pleased, and how devoutly transported is she in doing little offices of reverence and love towards him! And how willing is our Lord to add to her delight by accepting little services from her, and making her returns of honor and affection before his disciples. Forget not, likewise, to cast an eye of devotion towards Mary Magdalen, that favorite among the disciples, that kind of female apostle among the apostles. Fancy you see her as usual, sitting at the feet of her divine master, absorbed in attention to his divine words, and transported with joy whenever she has an opportunity of ministering to him. O how heavenly must this mansion be, and what a blessing to be in it at this delicious moment! O this was a true Pasch! Who must not rejoice to be present at it? And what delight must you not experience in contemplating it? But perhaps you are present at it, without being affected by it. Though if you were truly attentive to the passion, and contemplated it with a sincere feeling of the sufferings of Christ, of his mother, and of his disciples, you cannot but now partake in the joys of their Pasch. The same joys you might renew on every Sunday, if you were careful likewise to renew on the preceding Friday and Saturday, the devout memorial of his passion. For, as St. Paul says, "If you are partakers of his passion, so shall you be of his comforts."

JESUS APPEARS TO HIS UNBELIEVING DISCIPLE

CHAPTER LXXIX.

OUR LORD APPEARS TO THE DISCIPLES ON THE OCTAVE OF EASTER, WHEN ST. THOMAS WAS WITH THEM.

AGAIN on the eighth day after his resurrection our Lord Jesus appeared to his disciples, the doors being shut. And now Thomas, who the time before was not of their company, was present with them. To whom, when they gave him an account of Christ's having vouchsafed them a visit, he answered, "Unless I see in his hands the print of the nails, and put my finger in his side, I will not believe." Christ then, the Good Shepherd, solicitous for his little flock, in compassion to the frailty of this his beloved disciple, stands before them all, and graciously salutes them, saying, " Peace be with you." Then addressing himself to Thomas, he said, " Reach hither your finger and behold my hands ; stretch forth your hand and put it to my side, and be not incredulous, but faithful." Then Thomas, after having touched the wounds of Jesus, falling on his face, said, "My Lord and my God." Thus making reparation for his former unbelief. For now, though he saw but the humanity of our Lord, he confessed his divinity. After this he joined with his fellow-disciples in acknowledging the fault of forsaking so divine a master at the time of his passion. But our Lord Jesus graciously raised him up, bid him be cheerful, and mercifully forgave him all former faults. It was doubtless by special dispensation of heaven that Thomas was permitted to hesitate in faith, that Christ's resurrection might more evidently appear. How glorious does the bounty and condescension of this sweet Saviour shine forth in his conduct towards his weak disciples, and particularly to Thomas, in showing to them his sacred wounds, to remove from their souls every cloud of doubt for their and our advantage! Three great ends he proposed to himself in preserving the prints of his sacred wounds ; that by them he might confirm his apostles and make them firm in the faith of his resurrection : that while he was acting the office of our mediator with his divine Father, he might the more easily appease him, by showing them to his eternal majesty ; and finally, that he might in the day of judgment clear himself to the reprobate, by reminding them of what he had suffered to redeem them, if they would have been redeemed. Our Lord Jesus remains thus awhile with his blessed mother and the beloved disciples, talking with them of the kingdom of God, while they stand listening to his ineffable doctrines, and dwelling on his divine countenance, in raptures of admiration, joy, and love. Observe them standing round him, but our blessed Lady close by his side, and Magdalen in her usual place, at his sacred feet. Do you too stand there reverently, yet at a distance, and perchance your humility, compunction, and devotion may move his mercy to call you nearer to him. At length, however, our divine Saviour left them; telling them that he should thence repair to Galilee, where again they might see him; and departing he gave them his blessing. They remained then awhile together, still hungering and thirsting after him; not satiated with his presence, though greatly comforted.

THE MISSION OF THE APOSTLES INTO THE WHOLE WORLD, ACCORDING TO HIS PROMISE.

CHAPTER LXXX.

OUR LORD JESUS APPEARS TO HIS DISCIPLES IN GALILEE.

THE disciples were no sooner repaired to Galilee, as our Lord had appointed them, than he appeared to them, saying, "All power is given to me in heaven and earth: Go ye therefore and teach all nations: BAPTIZING THEM IN THE NAME OF THE FATHER, AND OF THE SON, AND OF THE HOLY

GHOST : teaching them to believe all those things I have commanded you : and **behold I** am with you always, even to the end of the world."—*Matt.* **xxviii**. After this **they all** humbly adored him, **and re**mained with him for some time with great joy and satisfaction. Consider them well, and contemplate the above mentioned words he spoke to **them** : for they are full of mystery and heavenly consolation. For, first, he showed them that he is Lord of all things. Secondly, he gave **them** authority and **a** command to preach. Thirdly, he taught them the form of baptism. And finally he encouraged and comforted them, by promising always to be with them **to the** end of the world. Consider then the sweet and singular joy **they** receive, and the many great and wonderful **tokens** of love he shows them ; which **being** done, **he** farther gave them his blessing, and disappeared.

CHAPTER LXXXI

HE APPEARS TO THEM AGAIN NEAR THE SEA OF TIBERIAS.

WHILE the disciples remained in **Galilee**, on a certain time, seven of them went out **to** fish in the sea of Tiberias, and having labored the whole **night, they** caught nothing. Here at the break of day, our Lord appeared again **to** them, standing on the sea shore, and asking them if they had taken any fish, they answered him, no. Wherefore he said, "Cast the **net on** the right side of the boat, and you shall find some." They did as he ordered them, and they were not able to draw the net out **for** the multitude of fish. Then John said to

Peter, "It is our Lord." Peter, when he heard it was their Lord, put on his coat, for he was then naked, and cast himself into the sea to come to him ; but the other disciples came in the boat. When they come to land, they saw hot coals lying, and a fish laid thereon, and bread, which the Lord had prepared for them. He bid them likewise bring some of the fish they had taken, and dress them ; and he eat with them on the sea side. And according to his accustomed humility, he ministered to them, he broke the bread and gave it them, and gave them likewise of the fish. The seven disciples, with great alacrity of spirit, conversed with their Lord, and with all submission and respect eat with him, admiring, with hearts full of joy, the affability of his pleasing countenance. They received from his sacred hands the food he gave them, and with no less abundance and spiritual comfort, replenished their souls, as well as their bodies. O what a divine and celestial banquet! Consider well every particular, and endeavor to feed thy soul with them.

When the refection was over our Lord addressing himself to Peter, said, "Lovest thou me more than these?" To whom Peter replied, "Lord, thou knowest that I love thee." Wherefore Christ said to him "Feed my lambs." Our Lord repeated the same question three times, and at every time recommended to him his flock. Whence we may see the singular bounty and care of our Lord Jesus, and especially his exceeding charity and love for our souls, by his repeated recommendations of them to Peter's care. After this he foretells Peter the death he should suffer for his sake, saying, "When thou wast younger, thou didst gird thyself, and didst walk whither thou wouldst. But when thou shalt

be old, thou shalt stretch forth thy hands and another shall gird thee, and lead thee whither thou
wilt not." And this he said to signify that by
death of the cross he should glorify God. After
this Peter desired to know of our Lord, in what
manner John should suffer: and our Lord answered
him, saying, "So I will have him to remain till I
come; what is it to thee?" As if he had said, I
will not that he follow me by the way of sufferings
and passion, as thou shalt; but that he live to a full
and complete age, and end his days in peace. Some
of the disciples understood by that saying, that he
was never to die.

After these things our Lord disappeared, and returned again according to his usual custom, to the
holy Fathers. The disciples remained greatly comforted, and returned soon after to Jerusalem.

CHAPTER LXXXII.

OUR LORD JESUS APPEARS TO MORE THAN FIVE HUN-
DRED DISCIPLES TOGETHER!—SOMETHING RELAT-
ING TO HIS APPARITIONS IN GENERAL.

SAINT PAUL mentions that our Lord Jesus, at
another time, appeared to above five hundred
disciples gathered together: but where, at what time,
or in what manner, is uncertain, it not being recorded in scripture. Yet we may well suppose
that it was with the usual meekness, bounty, and
charity on his side, and with no less joy and comfort on that of the disciples. And hitherto we have
spoken of our Lord's appearing twelve different
times after his resurrection; having omitted two

other apparitions which follow, when we shall treat
of his ascension. But there is mention made only
of ten in the gospel. For it is not written in any
place that he ever appeared to his holy mother; so
that it is only piously believed he did. How he appeared to Joseph of Arimathea, is written in the
apochryphal gospel of Nicodemus. And his appearing to James, St. Paul mentions in his Epistle
to the Corinthians, as he does likewise that to the
five hundred brethren.

We may, however, devoutly suppose, that he appeared several other times; for it is very probable
that our most bountiful Lord often visited his holy
mother, his beloved disciples, and St. Mary Magdalen, comforting those in a more especial manner
who had suffered and been most afflicted at his
bitter death and passion. And this seems to be the
opinion of St. Augustine, when, speaking of the
time of the resurrection, he says, "All things relating to our Lord's appearance after his resurrection are not written! For he conversed with them."
And it is not improbable that the holy Fathers, and
chiefly Abraham and David (to whom the Lord made
a special promise of the incarnation of his son)
came in company with him, to see the most excellent virgin, their daughter, and God's most blessed
mother, who for them and for all others had found
so much grace, and bore the Saviour of the world.
O with what joy and comfort did they behold her!
With what reverence did they bow to her; and with
what alacrity did they praise and honor her.

And here we may consider the great benignity and
charity, and the profound meekness of our Lord and
Saviour Jesus Christ in this, that after his resurrection, and the glorious victory he had gained for us,
he would not leave us, and ascend at once into his

glory, but, as a pilgrim yet on earth, would remain forty days, **and be** conversant among us, to confirm **and** strengthen his apostles in their faith. This **he** might have done by his angels, but such was his unspeakable charity, that he would do it himself, by personally conversing with us for the space of forty days, appearing to his apostles, and preaching to them of the kingdom of heaven. All this hath our most merciful Lord done for us, and yet we reflect little **on it.** He hath always loved us, and still loves us; but yet such is our ingratitude, that we return him not our **love** for his; which is a mark of great unthankfulness in us towards him, notwithstanding the unbounded charity he still has for us.

JESUS ASCENDS INTO HEAVEN TO SIT ON THE RIGHT HAND OF THE
FATHER.

CHAPTER LXXXIII.

THE GLORIOUS ASCENSION OF OUR LORD AND SAVIOUR JESUS CHRIST.

TOUCHING the wonderful ascension of our Lord Jesus, it behooves thee, pious reader, to awaken thy heart, and to render thyself more than ordinarily attentive to all that is here said or done, relating to this subject, if thou desirest to feed thy soul with heavenly comfort, and reap the spiritual unction,

which plentifully flows from the devout contemplation of so divine a subject.

On the fortieth day after his resurrection our Lord
Jesus, knowing that his time was now come to depart
from this world, and to pass hence to **his** Father,
taking with him the holy patriarchs, prophets, and
others, who after his resurrection were in the terres-
trial paradise, and blessing Enoch and Elias, who
remained there still alive, he came to his apostles,
who were gathered together on Mount Sion, which
was the place where he made his last supper the night
before his passion. There were likewise with the
apostles at this place, the Blessed Virgin, and many
other disciples ; **and** our Lord appearing to them said,
that he would **eat with them** before he departed from
them, as a special token and memorial of the love he
bore them. **And as they were all** eating, being full
of joy and spiritual comfort at this last refection of
our Lord Jesus, he said to them, "The time is now
come in which I must return again to him that sent
me ; but you shall remain in the city till you are
clothed with the virtue descending from above ; for
within a few days you shall be filled with the Holy
Ghost, as I before promised you. After which you
shall be dispersed throughout **the whole** world, **to**
preach **my gospel**, baptizing all that **shall** believe **in**
me, so that you shall be my witnesses to the utmost
confines of the earth." He likewise **reproved** them
for their incredulity in not believing **those** who had
seen **him rise, that** is the angels. This **he chose to**
do at the time he was speaking to them of preaching
his gospel, to give them to understand, that they
ought to have believed the angels, even before they
saw him, much sooner **than** they ought to be believed
by those to whom they were to preach, who, nevertheless, would believe them, though **they** should not

see him. This he did, that by knowing their fault they might remain humble; showing them at his departure how much he admired that virtue, and that he: commended it to them in a singular manner. They asked him concerning many things that were to come to pass; but he would not inform them, inasmuch as it was not necessary for them to know the secrets of God, which his Father had reserved in his own power, to fulfil at his own will and pleasure. And thus they continued discoursing and eating together, with great comfort and satisfaction, occasioned by the presence of their Lord; yet their comfort was mixed with some grief, by reason of his departure from them. For they loved him so tenderly, that they could not hear him speak of leaving them without heaviness and sorrow.

And what can we think of his blessed mother! May we not devoutly imagine that, sitting near him, and hearing what he said concerning his departure, she was moved with the tenderness of her motherly affection; and that overcome with grief, which suddenly seized, and oppressed her blessed soul, she inclined her head towards him, and rested it upon his sacred breast? For, if St. John the Evangelist, at the last supper, took this freedom, with much more reason may we suppose her to do the same on this doleful occasion. Hence, then, with tears, and many sighs she spoke to him in this manner: "Oh, my beloved son, I beseech thee not to leave me; but if thou must depart, and return again to thy heavenly Father, take me, thy afflicted mother, along with thee!" But our blessed Lord endeavored to comfort her, and said, "Grieve not, oh, beloved parent, at my leaving you, because I go to my Father; and it is expedient that you remain here a short time longer, to confirm in their faith, such as shall be converted, and believe in me, and afterwards I will come again, and take you with me, to be a partaker of my glory." To whom again our Lady replied, "My beloved son, may thy will always be fulfilled in all things, for I am not only contented to remain here during thy pleasure, but to suffer death for love of those souls, for which thou hast so willingly vouchsafed to lay down thy life: this, however, I beseech thee, be thou ever mindful of me." Our Lord then again comforted her, with the disciples and Mary Magdalen, saying, "Let not your hearts be troubled, nor fear ye anything; I will not leave you desolate; I go, but will shortly return again to you, and will remain always with you." At length he bid them remove from thence, and go to Mount Olivet, because from that place he would ascend into heaven, in the presence of them all: saying this, he disappeared,

His holy mother, with the rest of the company, hastened to the said mount, about a mile distant from Jerusalem, as he had appointed, where our Lord again soon appeared to them. Behold on this day we have two different apparitions of our Lord. Thus being all together, our Lord embraced his holy mother, and she again embraced him in a most tender manner, taking leave of each other. And the disciples, Mary Magdalen, and the rest falling down to the ground, and weeping with tenderness, kissed his blessed feet, and he, raising them up, embraced all his apostles most lovingly.

Let us now, pious reader, diligently consider them, and devoutly contemplate all that is here done: and amongst the rest, let us behold the holy Fathers, who being there present, though invisible, joyfully admire, and inwardly praise the blessed virgin, by whom they received so great a benefit as their salvation. They behold, with pleasing admiration, the glorious champions, and leaders of God's hosts, the apostles, whom our Lord Jesus had chosen from among all others, to conquer and subdue the world, and bring it over to the belief of his holy doctrine.

At length, when the mysteries were all fulfilled and completed, our Lord Jesus began gradually to raise himself up before them, and to ascend by his own virtue and power into heaven. And then the Blessed Virgin, with the rest, fell down and devoutly worshipped him. And our Lady said, "O my beloved, I beseech thee to be mindful of me," and with this she burst forth into tears, not being able to refrain, when she reflected on his departure, yet was she full of inward joy, to see her blessed son thus gloriously ascend into heaven. His disciples also, when they beheld him ascending, said, "Thou knowest, O Lord, that we have renounced all things for thee, wherefore, we beseech thee not to forget us, but be ever mindful of us, for whom we have forsaken all." Then our Lord lifting up his hands, with serene and pleasing aspect, crowned with glory, victoriously ascended into heaven, but first blessing them, he said, "Be steadfast, and fight courageously, for I shall always be with you, even to the end of the world."

Thus, our Lord Jesus, all glorious and resplendently shining, ascended into heaven, triumphantly leading with him the noble tribe of holy Fathers, and fulfilling that which the prophet Micah had said long before his ascension: "And their king shall pass before them, and the Lord at the head of them." So that they all followed him with unspeakable joy, singing canticles of praises and thanksgiving to him, for their deliverance from all sorrow, and their entrance into all joy, and **never-ending** felicity.

And Michael, the prince of God's celestial host, going before, carried the joyful tidings of their Lord's ascending, at which the whole heavenly court of celestial spirits came forth to meet their Lord, and with all worship and reverence, they led him with hymns and songs of jubilation, repeating with inexpressible joy, Alleluia, Alleluia, Alleluia.

Having paid their due reverence to the Lord, and ended the joyful canticles, which related to his glorious ascension, the angels and the holy Fathers began to rejoice together. And what tongue can express, or mind conceive, that which passed between them at **this** happy, happy meeting? **The** blessed spirits first began to congratulate them on their arrival, saying in this manner: "Ye princes of God's people, ye are welcome to our eternal habitation, and **we** rejoice and are glad at your arrival: ye all **are** gathered together, and wonderfully exalted with our God; Alleluia. Therefore rejoice, and sing to him who so gloriously ascendeth to heaven, and above the heaven of heavens: Alleluia."

To which the holy Fathers again joyfully replied, "To you, princes of God's people, Allelnia: Our guardians and helpers, Alleluia: Joy and peace forever, Alleluia: Let us sing and make mirth to our king and our Saviour, Alleluia, Alleluia, Alleluia. Now we joyfully enter into the house of our Lord, Alleluia: to remain forever in the glorious city of God, Alleluia. As sheep of our Lord's pasture we enter his gates, Alleluia: With hymns and canticles, Alleluia: For the Lord of power is with us. Alleluia, Alleluia, Alleluia." For according to the prophet,

"The Lord is ascended in shouts of joy, and the Lord in the sound of a trumpet."

Our Lord Jesus ascended visibly for the greater comfort of his mother and disciples, that they might see him as far as they could. And behold "A cloud received him out of their sight, and in an instant they were present in heaven!" And as the Blessed Virgin and the disciples were still looking up, two angels stood beside them in white garments, who began to comfort them, telling them not to look longer after his body, which they saw ascend so gloriously into heaven, for that they should not see him any more in that form till the Day of Judgment, when he should come to judge the quick and the dead. They bid them return into the city again, and there to expect the coming of the Holy Ghost, as he himself had told them. Our blessed Lady spoke to the angels, desiring them to recommend her to her blessed son ; who profoundly inclining to her, promised gladly to fulfil her commands.—And the apostles and Mary Magdalen recommended themselves in the same manner. After this, the angels departing, they went according as they had been appointed into the city, unto Mount Sion, and waited there the coming of the Holy Ghost.

Our Lord Jesus, in company with that blessed tribe of holy souls, opened the gates of Heaven, which for a long time had been shut to mankind, and as a victorious conqueror, triumphantly entered in, and joyfully saluting his father, said, "O holy Father, I return thee thanks for the glorious victory thou hast given me over all our enemies: behold, O eternal Father, I here present to thee our friends, who till this time have been detained in banishment and in prison! And as I have promised to my disciples and brethren, whom I have left in the world, to send them the Holy Ghost, the comforter, I beseech thee to fulfil my promise, for to thy care and protection I recommend them." The Father raising him up, placed him on his right-hand, and said, "My blessed son, to thee all power is given in heaven and earth, wherefore concerning all thou hast asked, dispose and order as shall seem most expedient to thee."

After this the angelical spirits and holy Fathers, who remained all the time prostrate before the throne of the most adorable Trinity, arose, and with all reverence, resumed their Alleluias and spiritual canticles, and sung joyfully to the Lord.

For if Moses and the children of Israel, after they had crossed the Red Sea, sung a song to the Lord, saying, "Let us sing to the Lord," etc., and Mary the prophetess, Aaron's sister, and other women going out after her, sung to the Lord with timbrels, and with dances, with how much more reason should they do it now, after the victory obtained over all their enemies? And when David brought the ark of the Lord to Jerusalem, the whole multitude of the children of Israel sung to the Lord, and David played before him, on all manner of instruments, on harps, on timbrels, on cornets, on cymbals, "and David danced before the Lord with all his might."—*2 Kings*, 6. With how much more reason did they now do it, when present with their Lord, in the perfect enjoyment of so great happiness? And if St. John the Evangelist, as we read in the Apocalypse, heard a voice from heaven of a hundred and forty-four thousand playing on their harps, and singing a new song before the throne of God and the Lamb, whatever that might represent, I cannot but piously imagine, that it was on this day, more than on any other, fulfilled. They all sing, they all rejoice, and exult with the utmost jubilation, and with shouts of mirth they praise and glorify the Lord, so that the whole heavenly Jerusalem echoes with joyful Alleluias, and canticles of mirth were heard throughout every part.

Never from the beginning of time was there known so solemn a festivity, nor shall ever be again, till after the last and general day of judgment, when all the elect shall meet together in their beautiful and glorious bodies.

And therefore this solemn feast of the ascension, if every circumstance be duly considered, is the greatest of all solemnities, which we shall find to be true, if we briefly consider the rest. The incarnation of God is a great feast, a day of solemn jubilation to us, but not to him, since he was then confined within the narrow compass of the small enclosure of a virginal womb. His nativity was likewise a great feast, and a day of public rejoicing to us. But he was to be pitied, who was born to such great poverty, suffering and penury. His death and suffering was a great feast to us, because our sins were then all blotted out ; but as he suffered most cruel torments, and a most vile death, it was not to him, nor ought it be to us, a subject of joy. The resurrection of our Lord Jesus was a most solemn festivity, both to him and to us, because he appeared as a triumphant conqueror over death, and we remained justified, and in the opinion of St. Augustine, was a more holy feast than the rest, which may be understood of those which preceded it. For the day of the ascension seems still to be more holy and greater than that, for though our Lord rose then from the dead, yet he still remained on earth, the gates of heaven were not yet open, nor were the holy Fathers then presented to his Father, which was fulfilled on the day of his ascension. And if we consider, whatever God wrought before this, he wrought to this end, without which his work would have been imperfect. For heaven and earth, with all things in them, were made for man ; and man was made only for God, and to enjoy him in his glory : to which glory, no one, though ever so just, could ever attain after sin, till this day. Whence you may, in some measure, comprehend how great and wonderful is this day, which may properly he called the solemn and joyful festivity of our Lord Jesus. For on this day was he first seated in glory, in the humanity he had assumed, at the right hand of his Father, and enjoyed a perfect rest from all his labors.

This day is also a feast of great joy and glory to the blessed spirits of heaven ; for on this day they received a new satisfaction, in the sight of their Lord, whom before they had not seen, under the veil of his sacred humanity. And on this day was begun to be repaired the ruins of their heavenly company, occasioned by the fall of their reprobate brethren, some of whose vacancies were filled up by a glorious number of blessed souls, of patriarchs, prophets, and others, who on this day triumphantly entered the heavenly Jerusalem, and took possession of it as their own right and inheritance. Wherefore, as we solemnly celebrate the feast of one saint or martyr who departed this life, and entered the glory of heaven, how much more ought we to do the same for so many thousands, who entered together in company with the Holy of Holies, who is far more worthy all praise, honor and glory, than all the saints and angels together.

This day is likewise a feast of special joy to the Blessed Virgin, inasmuch as she beheld her blessed son Jesus, perfect God and perfect man, crowned with glory and triumph, ascend victoriously to heaven.

It is also a feast of joy to us, for on this day was our nature first exalted above the highest heavens ; and had he not ascended we could not have received the greatest of all gifts, the Holy Ghost, whom he had promised to send us, wherefore he said to his disciples, "It is expedient for you that I go, for if I go not, the Paraclete shall not come to you."

St. Bernard saith, in his sermon on this day, that "The glorious feast of the ascension is the end and accomplishment of all other feasts and solemnities, and a blessed conclusion of the weary pilgrimage of Jesus Christ on earth."

Hence then may you gather, pious reader, that this feast is greater and more solemn than all others, and that soul, which earnestly and truly loves our Lord Jesus, should on this day lift up his mind more fervently towards heaven, and endeavor to receive a greater plenitude of spiritual comfort and joy than all other festivals of the year. For our Lord said to his disciples: "Truly, if you loved me, you would rejoice and be glad, because I go to the Father." Whence it appears from his own words, that there was no day in heaven more joyful than this, which lasted till the following day of Pentecost, and we may devoutly imagine it to have been kept and solemnized in the following manner.—The ascension of our Lord and Saviour Jesus was about the sixth hour. And although the whole court of heaven made a general rejoicing in a manner beyond all expression, yet from the hour of his ascension to the sixth hour of the next day, we may piously imagine that the angels more particularly celebrated this joyful festival. And, in the same manner, on the second, the archangels ; on the third day, the virtues ; on the fourth day, the powers ; on the fifth, the principalities ; on the sixth, the dominations ;

on the seventh, the thrones ; on the eighth, the cheru-
bims ; on the ninth, the seraphims ; which are the
nine orders of holy angels, who continued their joyful solemnity till the vigil of Pentecost ; from which
time, to the third hour of the day following, which
is Whitsunday, the holy Fathers, with the rest of
their blessed company, made the same solemn re
joicings.　Thus, during the space of ten days before
the descent of the Holy Ghost upon earth, they all
continued in an uninterrupted acclamation of praise,
glory, and thanksgiving to God, to whom be continued the same by every creature to the end of the
world, and forever.　*Amen.*

CHAPTER LXXXIV.

THE COMING OF THE HOLY GHOST.

OUR Lord Jesus being ascended into heaven,
his blessed mother, with the disciples, returned
to Jerusalem, as the angels had told them, and with
great joy and comfort, remained there during the
space of ten days in fervent prayer, expecting the
coming of the Holy Ghost.

When the tenth day was come after the ascension,
our Lord Jesus said to his Father : "My beloved
Father, the time of grace is near at hand, be mindful, I beseech thee, of the promise I made to my
brethren, concerning the Holy Ghost." To whom
the Father said, "My beloved Son, the promise you
have made is most grateful in my sight, and I am
well pleased it should be performed ; and as the
time is now come to fulfil it, let the Holy Ghost
descend to replenish, and fill them with his grace,

to comfort and strengthen them, to instruct and teach them, and bestow on them abundance of all heavenly virtues."

The Holy Ghost descended, then, on Whitsunday, in the form of fiery tongues, upon a hundred and twenty disciples, who at that time were gathered together, and filled them with all grace and virtue: by which they were so greatly strengthened and inflamed, that they immediately went forth, and began to preach the gospel throughout the whole world, and in a great measure made it subject to their doctrine.

This day is then the feast of love, for, as St. Gregory saith, it is the feast of him, who is love itself. For which reason, he who truly desires to serve God, should endeavor, in this holy solemnity, to be inflamed with love, or at least to be enkindled with a vehement desire of being so free from any mixture of the love of this world. For, as St. Bernard assures us, "He is greatly mistaken who thinks to unite heaven with earth, the sweet balm of spiritual comfort, with the enjoyments of worldly vanities, or the bountiful gifts of the Holy Ghost, with the deceitful flatteries of the flesh."

Let us, therefore, devout reader, wholly forsake the fleeting vanities of this world, and purify our hearts from all earthly and vain love to creatures, and lead a life of devotion and prayer, as the apostles did, expecting the coming of the Holy Ghost. Thus may we hope to be visited by him, as the apostles were, and to receive all spiritual comfort and grace for our souls.

That we may therefore be able to receive the singular gifts of this divine spirit, and to attain to that bliss to which our Lord is ascended, to prepare the way for us to follow, let us break off all unnecessary engagements with this wretched world, and take no delight in the foul satisfactions of the flesh, nor feed its unlawful desires, but ever earnestly wish, with the apostles, to be separated from it. So that through the grace of the divine Paraclete, the Holy Ghost, we may faithfully endeavor to follow the example of our Lord Jesus Christ in this world, and hereafter to ascend with him into the glorious city of the heavenly Jerusalem ; where he, sovereign king, together with the Father, and the Holy Ghost, one God, in perfect Trinity, liveth and reigneth for-ever, world without end. *Amen.*

THE END.

RHYTHMICAL PRAYER

TO THE

SACRED MEMBERS OF JESUS

HANGING UPON THE CROSS.

ASCRIBED TO ST. BERNARD.

Rendered into English Rhythm

BY

EMILY MARY SHAPCOTE,

TERTIARY OF ST. DOMINIC.

P. J. KENEDY & SONS

Publishers to the Holy Apostolic See

44 BARCLAY STREET, NEW YORK

ST. BERNARD'S RHYTHMICAL PRAYER.

PART I.

I.

O SAVIOUR of the world, I cry to Thee ;
  O Saviour, suffering God, I worship Thee ;
O wounded beauteous Love, I kneel to Thee ;
Thou knowest, Lord, how I would follow Thee,
If of Thyself Thou give Thyself to me.

II.

Thy Presence I believe ; O come to me !
Behold me prostrate, Jesus ; look on me !
How beautiful Thou art ! O turn to me !
O in Thy tender mercy turn to me,
And let Thy untold pity pardon me !

III.

With trembling love and fear I worship Thee ;
I kiss the grievous nails which entered Thee,
And think on those dire wounds which tortured Thee,
And, grieving, lift my weeping eyes to Thee,
Transfixed and dying all for love of me !

IV.

O wondrous grace ! O gracious charity !
O love of sinners in such agony !
    380

S. BERNARDI RHTYHMICA ORATIO.

PARS I.

AD PEDES.

I.

SALVE, mundi salutare,
 Salve, salve, Jesu care,
Cruci tuæ me aptare
Vellem vere, tu scis quare,
 Da mihi tui copiam.

II.

Ac si præsens sis accedo,
Imo, te præsentem credo :
O quam mundum hic te cerno,
Ecce tibi me prosterno,
 Sis facilis ad veniam.

III.

Clavos pedum, plagas duras,
Et tam graves impressuras,
Circumplector cum affectu,
Tuo pavens in aspectu,
 Tuorum memor vulnerum.

IV.

Grates tantæ caritati,
Nos agamus vulnerati ;

Sweet Father of the poor! O who can be
Unmoved to witness this great mystery,—
The Healer smitten, hanging on a tree?

V.

O Gentle Jesus, turn Thee unto me;
What I have broken do Thou bind in me,
And what is crooked make Thou straight in me;
What I have lost restore Thou unto me,
And what is weak and sickly heal in me.

VI.

O Love! with all my strength I seek for Thee;
Upon and in thy Cross I look for Thee;
With sorrow and with hope I turn to Thee,—
That through Thy Blood new health may come to me,
That washed therein Thy love may pardon me.

VII.

O take my heart, Thou loved One; let it be
Transfixed with those dear wounds for love of Thee,
O wound it, Jesus, with pure love of Thee;
And let it so be crucified with Thee,
That it may be forever joined to Thee.

VIII.

Sweet Jesus, loving God, I cry to Thee;
Though guilty, yet I come for love of Thee;
O show Thyself, dear Saviour, kind to me!
Unworthy as I am, O turn to me,
Nor at thy sacred Feet abandon me!

IX.

Dear Jesus, bathed in tears, I kneel to Thee;
In shame and grief I lift my eyes to Thee;
Prostrate before Thy Cross I bow to Thee,
And thy dear Feet embrace; O look on me,
Yea, from Thy Cross, O look, and pardon me.

O amator peccatorum,
Reparator confractorum,
   O dulcis Pater pauperum!

V.

Quicquid est in me confractum,
Dissipatum aut distractum,
Dulcis Jesu, totum sana,
Tu restaura, tu complana,
   Tam pio medicamine.

VI.

Te in tuo cruce quæro,
Prout queo, corde mero,
Me sanabis hic et spero,
Sana me et salvus ero,
   In tuo lavans sanguine.

VII.

Plagas tuas rubicundas,
Et fixuras tam profundas;
Cordi meo fac inscribi,
Ut Configar totus tibi,
   Te modis amans omnibus.

VIII.

Dulcis Jesu, pie Deus,
At te clamo licet reus,
Præbe mihi te benignum,
Ne repellas me indignum,
   De tuis sanctis pedibus.

IX.

Coram crucem procumbentem,
Hosque pedes complectentem,
Jesu bone, non me spernas,
Sed de cruce sancta cernas,
   Compassionis gratia.

X.

O my Beloved, stretched against that **Tree**,
Whose arms divine are now enfolding me,
Whose gracious Heart is now upholding **me,-**
O my Beloved, let me wholly be
Transformed, forgiven, one alone with thee!

PART II.

TO THE KNEES.

I.

O JESUS, King of Saints, I worship Thee;
O hope of sinners, hail! I rest on Thee;
True God, true man, Thou hangest on the **Tree**
Transfixed, with quivering flesh and shaking knee,
A criminal esteemed,—I worship Thee.

II.

Alas, how poor, how naked, wilt Thou be!
How hast Thou stript Thyself for love of me,
How made Thyself a gazing-stock to be!
Not forced, but, O my God! how willingly
In all Thy limbs Thou sufferest on that Tree!

III.

Thy Precious Blood wells forth abundantly
From all Thy open wounds incessantly;
All bathed therein, O God, in agony
Thou standest on the Cross of infamy,
Awaiting the appointed hour to die.

IV.

O infinite, O wondrous majesty!
O terrible, unheard-of poverty!
Ah, who, returning so great charity,
Is willing, Jesus, thus to give for Thee
His blood for Thine, in faithful love for Thee!

X.

In hac cruce stans directe
Vide me, O mi dilecte,
Ad te totum me converte,
Esto sanus, dic aperte,
    Dimitto tibi omnia.

PARS II.

AD GENUA.

I.

SALVE, Jesu, Rex sanctorum,
Spes votiva peccatorum,
Crucis ligno tanquam reus,
Pendens homo, verus Deus,
    Caducis nutans genibus.

II.

O quam pauper! O quam nudus!
Qualis est in cruce ludus,
Derisorum totus factus,
Sponte tamen, non coactus,
    Attritus membris omnibus,

III.

Sangius tuus abundanter
Fusus, fluit incessanter,
Totus lotus in cruore,
Stas in maximo dolore,
    Præcinctus vili tegmine.

IV.

O majestas infinita!
O egestas inaudita!
Quis pro tanta caritate
Quærit te in veritate,
    Dans sanguinem pro sanguine?

V.

O Jesus, how shall I, then, answer Thee,
Who am so vile, and have not followed Thee?
Or how repay the love that loveth me
With such sublime, such awful charity
Transfixed, from double death to set me **free?**

VI.

O Jesus, what Thy love hath been for me!
O Jesus, death could never conquer Thee!
Ah, with what loving care Thou keepest **me**
Enfolded in Thine arms, lest I should be,
By death of sin, a moment torn from Thee!

VII.

Behold, O Jesus, how for love of Thee,
With all my soul I trembling cling to Thee,
And Thy dear Knees embrace. O pity **me!**
Thou knowest **why—in** pity bear with **me,**
And overlook the shame that covers me!

VIII.

O let the Blood I worship flow on me,
That what I do may never anger Thee;
The Blood which flows at every pore from **Thee**
Each imperfection may it wash from **me,**
That I may undefiled and perfect be.

IX.

O force me, best Beloved, to draw to Thee,
Transfixed and bleeding on the shameful Tree,
Despised and stretched in dying agony!
All my desire, O Lord, is fixed on Thee;
O call me, then, and I will follow Thee.

X.

I have no other love, dear Lord, but Thee;
Thou art my first and last; I cling to Thee.

V.

Quid sum tibi responsurus,
Actu vilis, corde durus?
Quid rependam amatori
Qui elegit pro me mori,
    Ne dupla morti morerer?

VI.

Amor tuis amor fortis,
Quem non vincunt jura mortis;
O quam pia me sub cura
Tua foves in pressura,
    Ne morsu mortis vulnerer.

VII.

Ecce tuo præ amore,
Te complector cum rubore,
Me coapto diligenter,
Tu scis causam evidenter,
    Sed suffer et dissimula.

VIII.

Hoc quod ago non te gravet,
Sed me sanut et me lavet,
Inquinatum et ægrotum,
Sanguis fluens hic per totum,
    Ut non supersit macula.

IX.

In hac cruce te cruentem,
Te contemptum et distentum,
Ut requiram me impelle,
Et hoc imple meum velle,
    Facturus quod desidero.

X.

Ut te quæram menti pura,
Sit hæc mea prima cura,

It is no labor, Lord ; love sets me free ;
Then heal me, cleanse me, let me rest on Thee.
For love is life, and life is love—in Thee.

PART III.

TO THE HANDS.

I.

HAIL, holy Shepherd ! Lord, I worship Thee,
   Fatigued with combat, steeped in misery ;
Whose sacred Hands, outstretched in agony,
All pierced and dislocated on the Tree,
Are fastened to the wood of infamy.

II.

Dear holy Hands, I humbly worship ye,
With roses filled, fresh blossoms of that Tree ;
The cruel iron enters into ye,
While open gashes yield unceasingly
The precious stream down-dropping from the Tree.

III.

Behold, Thy Blood, O Jesus, flows on me—
The price of my salvation falls on me ;
O ruddy as the rose, it drops on me.
Sweet Precious Blood, it wells abundantly
From both Thy sacred Hands to set me free.

IV.

My heart leaps up, O Jesus, unto Thee ;
Drawn by those nail-pierced Hands it flies to Thee ;
Drawn by those Blood-stained Hands stretched out
      for me,
My soul breaks out with sighing unto Thee,
And longs to slake its thirst, O Love, in Thee.

Non est labor, nec gravabor,
Sed sanabor et mundabor,
    Cum te complexus fuero.

———————

PARS III.

AD MANUS.

I.

SALVE, Jesu, Pastor bone,
  Fatigatus in agone,
Qui per lignum es distractus,
Et ad lignum es compactus,
    Expansis sanctis manibus.

II.

Manus sanctæ, vos avete,
Rosis novis adimpletæ,
Hos ad ramos dure junctæ,
Et crudeli ferro punctæ,
    Tot guttis decurrentibus.

III.

Ecce fluit circumquaque,
Manu tua de utraque,
Sanguis tuus copiose,
Rubicundus instar rosæ,
    Magnæ salutis pretium.

IV.

Manus clavis perforatas,
Et cruore purpuratas,
Corde pimo præ amore,
Sitibundo bibens ore,
    Cruoris stillicidium.

V

My God, what great stupendous charity—
Both good and bad are welcomed here by Thee!
The slothful heart Thou drawest graciously,
The loving one Thou callest tenderly,
And unto all a pardon grantest free.

VI.

Behold, I now present myself to Thee,
Who dost present thy bleeding Hands to me;
The sick Thou healest when they come to Thee;
Thou canst not, therefore, turn away from me,
Whose love Thou knowest, Lord, is all for Thee.

VII.

O my Beloved, fastened to the Tree,
Draw, by Thy love, my senses unto Thee;
My will, my intellect, my memory,
And all I am, make subject unto Thee,
In whose dear arms alone is liberty.

VIII.

O draw me for Thy Cross's sake to Thee;
O draw me for Thy so wide charity;
Sweet Jesus, draw my heart in truth to Thee,
O put an end to all my misery,
And crown me with Thy Cross and victory!

IX.

O Jesus, place Thy sacred Hands on me,
With transport let me kiss them tenderly,
With groans and tears embrace them fervently;
And, O for these deep wounds I worship Thee;
And for the blessed drops that fall on me!

X.

O dearest Jesus, I commend to Thee
Myself, and all I am, most perfectly;

V.

O quam large te exponis,
Promptus malis atque bonis,
Trahis pigros, pios vocas,
Et in tuis ulnis locas
　　Paratis gratis omnibus.

VI.

Ecce tibi me præsento,
Vulnerato et cruento,
Semper ægris misereris,
De me ergo ne graveris,
　　Qui præsto es amantibus.

VII.

In hac cruce sic intensus,
In te meos trahe sensus,
Meum posse, velle, scire,
Cruci tuæ fac servire,
　　Me tuis apta brachiis.

VIII.

In tam lata charitate,
Trahe me in veritate,
Propter crucem tuam almam,
Trahe me ad crucis palmam,
　　Dans finem meis vitiis.

IX.

Manus sanctæ vos amplector,
Et gemendo condelector,
Grates ago plangis tantis
Clavis duris, guttis sanctis,
　　Dans lacrymas cum osculis.

X.

In cruore tuo lotum,
Me commendo tibi lotum,

Bathed in Thy Blood, behold, I live for Thee;
O, may Thy blessed Hands encompass me,
And in extremity deliver me!

PART IV.

TO THE SIDE.

I.

O JESUS, highest Good, I yearn for Thee;
O Jesus, merciful, I hope in Thee,
Whose sacred Body hangs upon the Tree,
Whose limbs, all dislocated painfully,
Are stretched in torture, all for love of me!

II.

Hail, sacred Side of Jesus! verily
The hidden spring of mercy lies in Thee,
The source of honeyed sweetness dwells in Thee,
The fountain of redemption flows from Thee,
The secret well of love that cleanses me.

III.

Behold, O King of Love, I draw to Thee;
If I am wrong, O Jesus, pardon me;
Thy love, Beloved, calls me lovingly,
As I with blushing cheek gaze willingly
Upon the living wound that bleeds for me.

IV.

O gentle opening, I worship Thee;
O open door and deep, I look in Thee;
O most pure stream, I gaze and gaze on Thee:
More ruddy than the rose, I draw to Thee;
More healing than all health, I fly to Thee.

V.

More sweet than wine Thine odor is for me;

Tuæ sanctæ manus istæ
Me defendant, Jesu Christe,
   Extremis in periculis.

PARS IV.

AD LATUS.

I.

SALVE, Jesu, summe bonus,
  Ad parcendum nimis pronus,
Membra tua macilenta
Quam acerbe sunt disenta,
   In ramo crucis torrida.

II.

Salve, latus Salvatoris,
In quo latet mel dulcoris,
In quo patet vis amoris,
Ex quo scatet fons cruoris,
   Qui corda lavat sordida.

III.

Ecce tibi appropinquo,
Parce Jesu si delinquo,
Verecunda quidem fronte,
Ad te tamen veni sponte,
   Scrutari tua vulnera.

IV.

Salve, mitis apertura,
De qua manat vena pura,
Porta patens et profunda,
Super rosam rubicunda,
   Medela salutifera.

V.

Odor tuus super vinum,

The poisoned breath of sin it drives from me ;
Thou art the draught of life poured out for me.
O ye who thirst, come, drink thereof with me;
And Thou, sweet wound, O open unto me.

VI.

O red wound open, let me draw to Thee,
And let my throbbing heart be filled from Thee!
Ah, see! my heart, Beloved, faints for Thee.
O my Beloved, open unto me,
That I may pass and lose myself in Thee.

VII.

Lord, with my mouth I touch and worship Thee,
With all the strength I have I cling to Thee,
With all my love I plunge my heart in Thee,
My very life-blood would I draw from Thee,—
O Jesus, Jesus! draw me into Thee!

VIII.

How Sweet Thy savor is!   Who tastes of Thee,
O Jesus Christ, can relish naught but Thee ;
Who tastes Thy living sweetness lives by Thee ;
All else is void—the soul must die for Thee ;
So faints my heart,—so would I die for Thee ;

IX.

I languish, Lord! O let me hide in Thee!
In Thy sweet Side, my Love, O bury me!
And may the fire divine consuming Thee
Burn in my heart where it lies hid in Thee,
Without a fear reposing peacefully!

X.

When in the hour of death Thou callest me,
O Love of loves, may my soul enter Thee ;
May my last breath, O Jesus fly to Thee ;
So no fierce beast may drive my heart from Thee,
But in Thy Side may it remain with Thee !

Virus pellens serpentinum,
Potus tuus potus vitæ,
Qui sititis huc venite,
    Tu dulce vulnus aperi.

VI.

Plaga rubens aperire,
Fac cor meum te sentire, ·
Sine me in te transire,
Vellem totus introire,
    Pulsanti pande pauperi.

VII.

Ore meo te contingo,
Et ardenter ad me stringo,
In te meum cor contingo,
Et ferventi corde lingo,
    Me totum in te trajice.

VIII.

O quam dulcis sapor iste!
Qui te gustat Jesu Christe,
Tuo victus a dulcore
Mori possit præ amore,
    Te unum amans unice.

IX.

In hac fossa me reconde,
Infer meum cor profunde,
Ubi latens incalescat,
Et in pace conquiescat,
    Nec prorsus quemquam timeat.

X.

Hora mortis meus flatus,
Intret Jesu, tuum latus,
Hinc expirans in te vadat,
Ne hunc leo trux invadat,
    Sed apud te permaneat.

PART V.

TO THE BREAST.

I.

O GOD of my salvation, hail to Thee !
O Jesus, sweetest Love, all hail to Thee!
O venerable Breast, I worship Thee ;
O dwelling-place of love, I fly to Thee,
With trembling touch adore and worship Thee.

II.

Hail, throne of the Most Holy Trinity !
Hail, ark immense of tender charity !
Thou stay of weakness and infirmity,
Sweet rest of weary souls who rest on Thee,
Dear couch of loving ones who lean on Thee !

III.

With reverence, O Love, I kneel to Thee,
O worthy to be ever sought by me ;
Behold me, Jesus, looking unto Thee.
O, set my heart on fire, dear Love, from Thee,
And burn it in the flame that burns in Thee.

IV.

O make my breast a precious home for thee,
A furnace of sweet love and purity,
A well of holy grief and piety ;
Deny my will, conform it unto Thee,
That grace abundant may be mine in Thee.

V

Sweet Jesus, loving Shepherd, come to me ;
Dear Son of God and Mary, come to me ;
Kind Father come, let Thy Heart pity me,

PARS V.

AD PECTUS.

I.

SALVE, salus mea Deus,
Jesu dulcis amor meus ;
Salve, pectus, reverendum,
Cum tremore contingendum,
    Amoris domicilium,

II

Ave, thronus Trinitatis,
Arca latæ charitatis,
Firmamentum infirmatis,
Pax et pausa fatigatis,
    Humilium triclinium.

III.

Salve, Jesu reverende,
Digne semper inquirende,
Me præsentem hic attende,
Accedentem me succende,
    Præcordiali gratia,

IV.

Pectus mihi confer mundum,
Ardens, pium, gemebundum,
Voluntatem abnegatam,
Tibi semper conformatam,
    Juncta virtutum copia.

V.

Jesu dulcis, Pastor pie,
Fili Dei et Mariæ,
Largo fonte tui cordis,

And cleanse the fountain of my misery
In that great fountain of Thy clemency.

VI.

Hail, fruitful splendor of the Deity!
Hail, fruitful figure of Divinity!
From the full treasure of Thy charity,
O pour some gift in Thy benignity
Upon the desolate who cry to Thee!

VII.

Dear Breast of most sweet Jesus, mine would be
All Thine in its entire conformity;
Absolve it from all sin, and set it free,
That it may burn with ardent charity,
And never, never cease to think on Thee.

VIII.

Abyss of wisdom from eternity,
The harmonies of angels worship Thee;
Entrancing sweetness flows, O Breast, from thee;
John tasted it as he lay rapt on Thee;
O grant me thus that I may dwell in Thee!

IX.

Hail, fountain deep of God's benignity!
The fulness of the immense Divinity
Hath found at last a creature home in Thee.
Ah, may the counsel that I learn from Thee
All imperfection purify in me!

X.

True temple of the Godhead, hail to Thee!
O draw me in Thy gracious charity,
Thou ark of goodness, full of grace for me.
Great God of all, have mercy upon me,
And on Thy right hand keep a place for me.

Fæditatem meæ sordis
    Benigne Pater dilue.

VI.

Ave, splendor et figura,
Summi Dei genitura,
De thesauris tuis plenis,
Desolatis et egenis,
    Manus clementer perflue.

VII.

Dulcis Jesu Christi pectus,
Tuo fiam dono rectus,
Absolutus a peccatis,
Ardens igne charitatis,
    Ut semper te recogitem.

VIII.

Tu abyssus es sophiæ,
Angelorum harmoniæ
Te collaudant, ex te fluxit
Quod Joannes cubans suxit,
    In te fac ut inhabitem.

IX.

Ave, fons benignitatis,
Plenitudo Deitatis
Corporalis in te manet,
Vanitatem in me sanet,
    Quod tu confers consilium.

X.

Ave, verum templum Dei,
Precor miserere mei,
Tu totius arca boni,
Fac electis me apponi,
    Vas dives, Deus omnium.

PART VI.

TO THE FACE.

I.

HAIL, bleeding Head of Jesus, hail to Thee!
Thou thorn-crowned Head, I humbly worship
  Thee!
O wounded Head, I lift my hands to Thee;
O lovely Face besmeared, I gaze on Thee;
O bruised and livid Face, look down on me!

II.

Hail, beauteous Face of Jesus, bent on me,
Whom angel choirs adore exultantly!
Hail, sweetest Face of Jesus, bruised for me—
Hail, Holy One, whose glorious Face for me
Is shorn of beauty on that fatal Tree!

III.

All strength, all freshness, is gone forth from Thee:
What wonder! hath not God afflicted Thee,
And is not death himself approaching Thee?
O Love! but death hath laid his touch on Thee,
And faint and broken features turn to me.

IV.

O have they thus maltreated Thee, my own?
O have they Thy sweet Face despised, my own!
And all for my unworthy sake, my own!
O in Thy beauty turn to me, my own;
O turn one look of love on me, my own!

V.

In this Thy Passion, Lord, remember me;
In this Thy pain, O Love, acknowledge me;
The honey of whose lips was shed on me,
The milk of whose delights hath strengthened me
Whose sweetness is beyond delight for me!

VI.

Despise me not, O Love; I long for Thee;
Contemn me not, unworthy though I be;

PARS VI.

AD FACIEM.

I.

SALVE, caput cruentatum,
Totum spinis coronatum,
Conquassatum, vulneratum,
Arundine verberatum,
Facie sputis illita.

II.

Salve, cujus dulcis vultus,
Immutatus et incultus,
Immutavit suum florem,
Totus versus in pallorem,
Quem laudat cœli curia.

III.

Omnis vigor atque viror
Hinc recessit, non admiror,
Mors apparet in aspectu,
Totus pendens in defectu,
Attritus ægra macie.

IV.

Sic affectus, sic despectus,
Propter me sic interfectus,
Peccatori tam indigno,
Cum amoris intersigno,
Appare clara facie.

V.

In hac tua passione
Me agnosce, Pastor bone,
Cujus sumpsi mel exore,
Haustum lactis cum dulcore,
Præ omnibus deliciis.

VI.

Non me reum asperneris,
Nec indignum dedigneris,

But now that death is fast approaching Thee,
Incline Thy Head, my Love, my Love, to me,
To these poor arms, and let it rest on me!

VII.

Thy holy Passion I would share with Thee,
And in Thy dying love rejoice with Thee;
Content if by this Cross I die with Thee;
Content, Thou knowest, Lord, how willingly
Where I have lived to die for love of Thee.

VIII.

For this Thy bitter death all thanks to Thee,
Dear Jesus, and Thy wondrous love for me!
O gracious God, so merciful to me,
Do as Thy guilty one entreateth Thee,
And at the end let me be found with Thee!

IX.

When from this life, O Love, Thou callest me,
Then, Jesus, be not wanting unto me,
But in the dreadful hour of agony,
O hasten, Lord, and be Thou nigh to me,
Defend, protect, and O deliver me.

X.

When Thou, O God, shalt bid my soul be free,
Then, dearest Jesus, show Thyself to me!
O condescend to show Thyself to me,—
Upon Thy saving Cross, dear Lord, to me,-
And let me die, my Love, embracing Thee!

PART VII.

TO THE SACRED HEART.

I.

HAIL, sacred Heart of God's great Majesty!
Hail, sweetest Heart, my heart saluteth Thee!
With great desire, O Heart, I seek for Thee,
And faint for joy, O Heart, embracing Thee;
Then give me leave, O Love, to speak to Thee,

Morte tibi jam vicina,
Tuum caput hic inclina,
   In meis pausa brachiis.

VII.

Tuæ sanctæ passioni
Me gauderem interponi,
In hac cruce tecum mori,
Præsta crucis amatori
   Sub cruce tua moriar

VIII.

Morte tuæ tam amaræ
Grates ago, Jesu chare,
Qui es clemens, pie Deus,
Fac quod petit tuus reus,
   Ut absque to non finiar.

IX.

Dum me mori est necesse,
Noli mihi tunc deesse,
In tremenda mortis hora,
Veni Jesu, absque mora,
   Tuere me et libera.

X.

Cum me jubes emigrare,
Jesu chare, tunc appare.
O amotor amplectende,
Temet ipsum tunc ostende,
   In cruce salutifera.

PARS VII.

AD COR.

I.

SUMMI Regis cor aveto,
  Te saluto corde læto,
Te complecti me delectat,
Et hoc meum cor affectat,
   Ut ad te loquar animes.

With what sweet love Thou languishedst for me!
What pain and torment was that love to Thee!
How didst Thou all Thyself exhaust for me!
How hast Thou wholly given Thyself to me,
That death no longer might have hold of me!

III.

O bitter death and cruel! can it be
Thou darest so to enter greedily
Into that cell divine?　O can it be
The Life of life, that lives there gloriously,
Should feel thy bite, O death, and yield to thee?

IV.

For Thy death's sake which Thou didst bear for me,
When Thou, O sweetest Heart, didst faint for me,
O Heart most precious in its agony,
See how I yearn, and longing turn to Thee!
Yield to my love, and draw me unto Thee!

V.

O sacred Heart, beloved most tenderly,
Cleanse Thou my own; more worthy let it be,
All hardened as it is with vanity;
O make it tender, loving, fearing Thee,
And all its icy coldness drive from me.

VI.

O sinner as I am, I come to Thee;
My very vitals throb and call for Thee;
O Love, sweet love, draw hither unto me!
O Heart of Love, my heart would ravished be,
And sicken with the wound of love for Thee!

VII.

Dilate and open, Heart of love, for me,
And like a rose of wond'rous fragrance be,
Sweet Heart of love, united unto me;
Anoint and pierce my heart, O Love, with Thee,
How can he suffer, Lord, who loveth Thee?

II.

Quo amore vincebaris,
Quo dolore torquebaris,
Cum te totum exhaurires,
Ut te nobis impartires,
    Et nos a morte tolleres?

III.

O mors illa! quam amara,
Quam immitis, quam avara,
Quæ per cellam introivit,
In qua mundi vita vivit,
    Te mordens cor dulcissimum.

IV.

Propter mortem quem tulisti,
Quando pro me defecisti,
Cordis mei Cor dilectum,
In te meum fer affectum,
    Hoc est quod opto plurimum.

V.

O Cor dulce prædilectum,
Munda cor menm illectum,
Et in vanis induratum,
Pium fac et timoratum,
    Repulso tetro frigori.

VI.

Per medullam cordis mei,
Peccatoris atque rei,
Tuus amor transferatur,
Quo cor totum rapiatur,
    Languens amoris vulnere.

VII.

Dilatare, aperire,
Tanquam rosa fragrans mire,
Cordi meo te conjunge,
Unge illud et compunge,
    Qui amat te quid patitur?

VIII.

O Heart of Love, who vanquished is by Thee
Knows nothing, but beside himself must be;
No bounds are set to that sweet liberty,
No moderation,—he must fly to Thee,
Or die he must of many deaths for Thee.

IX.

My living heart, O Love, cries out for Thee;
With all its strength, O Love, my soul loves Thee;
O Heart of Love, incline Thou unto me,
That I with burning love may turn to Thee,
And with devoted breast recline on Thee!

X.

In that sweet furnace let me live for Thee,
Nor let the sleep of sloth encumber me;
O let me sing to Thee and weep to Thee,
Adore, and magnify, and honor Thee,
And always take my full delight in Thee.

XI.

Thou Rose of wondrous fragrance, open wide,
And bring my heart into Thy wounded Side,
O sweet Heart, open! draw Thy loving bride,
All panting with desires intensified,
And satisfy her love unsatisfied.

XII.

Unite my heart, O Jesus, unto Thine,
And let Thy wounded love be found in mine.
Ah, if my heart, dear love, be made like Thine
O will it not be pierced with darts divine,
The sweet reproach of love that thrills through Thine?

XIII.

O Jesus, draw my heart within Thy Breast,
That it may be by Thee alone possessed.
O Love, in that sweet pain it would find rest,
In that entrancing sorrow would be blest,
And lose itself in joy upon Thy Breast.

XIV.

Behold, O Jesus, how it draws to Thee!
O call it, that it may remain in Thee!
See with what large desire it thirsts for Thee!
Reprove it not, O Love; it loves but Thee:
Then bid it live—by one sweet taste of Thee!

VIII.

Quidnam agat nescit **vere,**
Nec se valet cohibere ;
Nullum **modum** dat amori,
Multa morte vellet mori,
    Amore quisquis vincit**ur.**

IX.

Viva cordis voce clamo,
Dulce cor, te namque amo;
Ad cor meum inclinare,
Ut se possit applicare,
    Devoto tibi **pectore.**

X.

Tuo **vivat in** amore,
Nec dormitet in torpore ;
Ad te **oret, ad te** ploret,
Te adoret, te honoret,
    Et fruens omne tempo**re.**

XI.

Rosa **cordis** aperire,
Cujus odor fragrat mir**e,**
Te dignare dilitare,
Fac cor meum anhelare**,**
    Flamma desiderii.

XII.

Da cor cordi **sociari,**
Tecum, Jesu, **vulnerari ;**
Nam cor cordi similatur,
Si **cor** meum perforatur,
    Sagittis improperii.

XIII.

Infer tuum **intra sinum**
Cor, **ut tibi sit vicinum,**
In dolore gaudioso,
Cum deformi specioso,
    Quod **vix** seipsum **capiat.**

XIV.

Hîc repauset, hîc moretur,
Ecce jam post te movetur,
Te ardenter vult sitire,
Jesu, noli contraire,
    Ut bene de **te sentiat.**

www.ingramcontent.com/pod-product-compliance
Lightning Source LLC
Chambersburg PA
CBHW051509100726
47898CB00005B/1384